Mary Balogh grew up in Wales and now lives with her husband Robert in Saskatchewan, Canada. She has written more than 100 historical novels and novellas, more than 30 of which have been *New York Times* bestsellers. They include the Slightly sestet (the Bedwyn saga), the Simply quartet, the Huxtable quintet, the Westcott series and the Survivors' Club series.

Visit Mary Balogh online:

www.marybalogh.com
www.facebook.com/AuthorMaryBalogh

Praise for Mary Balogh:

'One of the best!'
Julia Quinn

'Today's superstar heir to the marvellous legacy
of Georgette Heyer (except a lot steamier)'
Susan Elizabeth Phillips

'Ms Balogh is a veritable treasure, a matchless storyteller
who makes our hearts melt with delight'
Romantic Times

'Balogh is truly a find'
Publishers Weekly

'Balogh is the queen of spicy Regency-era romance, creating
memorable characters in unforgettable stories'
Booklist

Also by Mary Balogh

The Ravenswood Series
REMEMBER LOVE
REMEMBER ME
ALWAYS REMEMBER
REMEMBER WHEN

The Westcott Series
SOMEONE TO LOVE
SOMEONE TO HOLD
SOMEONE TO WED
SOMEONE TO CARE
SOMEONE TO TRUST
SOMEONE TO HONOR
SOMEONE TO REMEMBER
SOMEONE TO ROMANCE
SOMEONE TO CHERISH
SOMEONE PERFECT

The Huxtable Series
FIRST COMES MARRIAGE
THEN COMES SEDUCTION
AT LAST COMES LOVE
SEDUCING AN ANGEL
A SECRET AFFAIR

The Horsemen Trilogy
INDISCREET
UNFORGIVEN
IRRESISTIBLE

The Mistress Trilogy
MORE THAN A MISTRESS
NO MAN'S MISTRESS
THE SECRET MISTRESS

The Survivors' Club Series
THE PROPOSAL
THE ARRANGEMENT
THE ESCAPE
ONLY ENCHANTING
ONLY A PROMISE
ONLY A KISS
ONLY BELOVED

The Simply Series
SIMPLY UNFORGETTABLE
SIMPLY LOVE
SIMPLY MAGIC
SIMPLY PERFECT

The Bedwyn Series
SLIGHTLY MARRIED
SLIGHTLY WICKED
SLIGHTLY SCANDALOUS
SLIGHTLY TEMPTED
SLIGHTLY SINFUL
SLIGHTLY DANGEROUS

The Bedwyn Prequels
ONE NIGHT FOR LOVE
A SUMMER TO REMEMBER

The Web Series
THE GILDED WEB
WEB OF LOVE
THE DEVIL'S WEB

Classics
THE IDEAL WIFE
THE SECRET PEARL
A PRECIOUS JEWEL
A CHRISTMAS PROMISE
DARK ANGEL/
LORD CAREW'S BRIDE
A MATTER OF CLASS
THE TEMPORARY WIFE/
A PROMISE OF SPRING
THE FAMOUS HEROINE/
THE PLUMED BONNET
A CHRISTMAS BRIDE/
CHRISTMAS BEAU
A COUNTERFEIT BETROTHAL/
THE NOTORIOUS RAKE
UNDER THE MISTLETOE
BEYOND THE SUNRISE
LONGING
HEARTLESS
SILENT MELODY

REMEMBER THAT DAY

A RAVENSWOOD NOVEL

MARY BALOGH

PIATKUS

First published in the US in 2026 by Berkley,
An imprint of Penguin Random House LLC
Published in Great Britain in 2026 by Piatkus

1 3 5 7 9 10 8 6 4 2

Copyright © 2026 by Mary Balogh

The moral right of the author has been asserted.

All characters and events in this publication, other than those
clearly in the public domain, are fictitious and any resemblance
to real persons, living or dead, is purely coincidental.

All rights reserved.
Penguin Random House values and supports copyright. Copyright fuels creativity,
encourages diverse voices, promotes free speech, and creates a vibrant culture.
Thank you for buying an authorized edition of this book and for complying
with copyright laws by not reproducing, scanning, or distributing any part of
it in any form without permission. You are supporting writers and allowing
Penguin Random House to continue to publish books for every reader. Please
note that no part of this book may be used or reproduced in any manner for
the purpose of training artificial intelligence technologies or systems.

A CIP catalogue record for this book
is available from the British Library.

ISBN 978-0-349-44287-7

Printed and bound in Great Britain by Clays Ltd, Elcograf S.p.A.

Papers used by Piatkus are from well-managed forests
and other responsible sources.

Piatkus
An imprint of
Little, Brown Book Group
Carmelite House
50 Victoria Embankment
London EC4Y 0DZ

The authorised representative
in the EEA is
Hachette Ireland
8 Castlecourt Centre, Dublin
15, D15 XTP3, Ireland
(email: info@hbgi.ie)

An Hachette UK Company
www.hachette.co.uk

REMEMBER THAT DAY

AUTHOR'S NOTE

Dear Reader,

In this book I bring together two families and two series—the Wares of Ravenswood and the Westcotts. I had great fun doing it, but I did realize there might be a bit of a problem for the reader. There were ten Westcott books and this is the fifth Ravenswood book. The joy of both series is how many characters there are. But even those of you familiar with both series may find it difficult in places to remember all the personalities involved and their often complex relationships with one another. To help you out, I want to provide a quick and clear summary so that whenever your head is in a spin, you can refer back to it. The Wares are relatively easy to sort out, the Westcotts not so much.

THE WARES

- **Caleb Ware**, Earl of Stratton, and **Clarissa**, his wife, had five children of their own. Caleb's son from a liaison before his marriage grew up at Ravenswood too as one of the family.
- The eldest son is **Ben Ellis**, married to Lady Jennifer Arden. There are three children: Joy (from Ben's first marriage, during his time at war), Robert, and Belinda. Ben and Lady Jennifer's story is told in *Always Remember*.
- **Devlin** is the eldest son born to Caleb and Clarissa. He became the Earl of Stratton after his father died in the first book. He is married to Gwyneth Rhys, who grew up on the neighboring estate. Their story is told in *Remember Love*. They have three children: Gareth, Bethan, and Awen.
- **Nicholas** is the second legitimate son and the hero of this book.
- **Philippa** comes next, the elder daughter. She married Lucas Arden, Duke of Wilby (and brother of Ben's wife). Their story is told in *Remember Me*. They have three children, twins Emily and Christopher, and Pamela.
- **Owen** is next, the third legitimate son. He appears in all the Ravenswood books, including this one. He is (as yet) unmarried.
- **Stephanie** is the second daughter and youngest child of Caleb and Clarissa. She is also (as yet) unmarried.
- **Clarissa**, the widowed Dowager Countess of Stratton, married Matthew Taylor in *Remember When*. Her parents, the Greenfields, are still living, as is her brother, George. He is married to Clarissa's close friend Kitty.

THE WESTCOTTS

- Humphrey Westcott, the late Earl of Riverdale, married Alice Snow in a secret ceremony that he hid from his family. They had a daughter, Anastasia. Despite these facts, when Humphrey ran into financial difficulties, he married the wealthy **Viola Kingsley** in a bigamous marriage.

- Alice was dying of consumption. Humphrey took their daughter and placed her in an orphanage in Bath under the name **Anna Snow**. She grew up there and then taught school there, having no idea of her real identity. She discovered it after her father's death, when the truth came out and she found herself to be a very wealthy woman. She married **Avery Archer, Duke of Netherby**. They have five children—Josephine, Rebecca, Jonah, Beatrice, and John. Anna and Avery's story is told in *Someone to Love*.

- Humphrey and Viola had three children. They grew up as an aristocratic family, but were dispossessed after the bigamous nature of their parents' marriage was revealed.

- The elder daughter, **Camille**, married Joel Cunningham. They live outside Bath with their three biological children (Jacob, Alice, and Samuel) and six adopted children (Winifred, Sarah, Robbie, Andrew, Susan, and Emma). Camille and Joel's story is told in *Someone to Hold*.

- Camille and Joel's daughter, **Winifred Cunningham**, is the heroine of this book.

- Humphrey and Viola's son, **Harry**, married Lydia Tavernor. Their story is told in *Someone to Cherish*.

- Humphrey and Viola's second daughter, **Abigail**, married Gilbert Pennington. Their story is told in *Someone to Honor*. There are three children: Katy (from a previous marriage of Gil's), Seth, and Ben.
- After learning that her marriage of twenty-three years had been bigamous, **Viola** resumed her maiden name. She married Marcel Lamarr, Marquess of Dorchester. Their story is told in *Someone to Cherish*.
- Marcel had two children from a previous marriage, twins Bertrand and Estelle Lamarr.
- **Estelle** married Justin Wiley, Earl of Brandon. Their story is told in *Someone Perfect*.
- **Bertrand** remains unmarried. But he appears in several Ravenswood novels because he and Owen Ware are close friends. Bertrand has stayed at Ravenswood a number of times.

But that's not all . . .

There is also the older generation of Westcotts, Humphrey's siblings, who refused to let go of Viola and her children after the truth of their brother's bigamous marriage came to light.

- **Matilda** is the eldest. She married Charles Sawyer, Viscount Dirkson. He had children from a previous marriage, one of whom is **Adrian Sawyer**. Matilda's story is told in *Someone to Remember*.
- **Louise** married John Archer, Duke of Netherby. His son from a previous marriage is **Avery**, who has been Duke of

AUTHOR'S NOTE

Netherby since his father's death and is married to **Anna**. So Louise is both Anna's aunt and her stepmother.

- **Mildred**, the youngest sister, is married to Thomas Wayne, Baron Molenor.

Complicated, right? But I hope these notes will help you understand who is who as you read.

And I do hope you will enjoy the book. I know many of you have been waiting for Winifred's story and hoping I would write it. Well, it is done, and I believe I have found her a good hero in Colonel Nicholas Ware.

Happy reading!
Mary Balogh

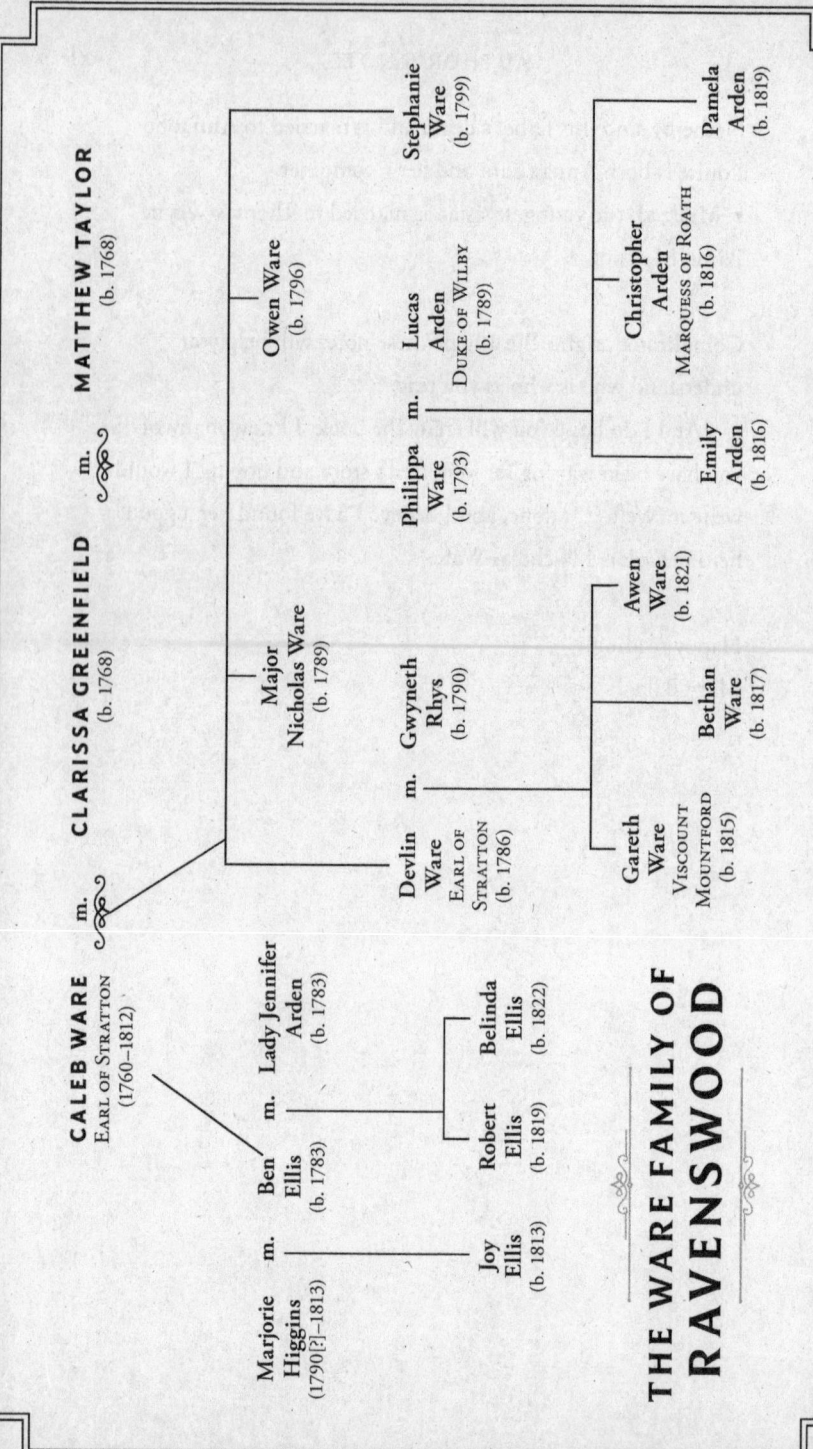

THE WESTCOTT FAMILY

GEORGE WESTCOTT m. **EUGENIA MADSON** (b. 1742)
Earl of Riverdale
(1724–1790)

- Charles Sawyer, Viscount Dirkson (b. 1761) m. Matilda Westcott (b. 1761)
- Marcel Lamarr, Marquess of Dorchester (b. 1773) m. Viola Kingsley (b. 1772)
  - Humphrey Westcott, Earl of Riverdale (1762–1812) m. Alice Snow (1768–1789)
    - Anastasia Westcott (Anna Snow) (b. 1787) m. Avery Archer, Duke of Netherby (b. 1781)
- Mildred Westcott (b. 1773) m. Thomas Wayne, Baron Molenor (b. 1769)
- Louise Westcott (b. 1770) m. John Archer, Duke of Netherby (1755–1809)

Children of Humphrey & Viola:
- Camille Westcott (b. 1790) m. Joel Cunningham (b. 1785)
  - Winifred Cunningham (adopted) (b. 1803)
  - Robbie Cunningham (adopted) (b. 1810)
  - Sarah Cunningham (adopted) (b. 1812)
- Harry Westcott (b. 1792) m. Lydia Tavernor (b. 1793)
- Abigail Westcott (b. 1794) m. Gil Bennington (b. 1783)

Camille & Joel's other children (adopted):
- Andrew Cunningham (adopted) (b. 1812)
- Jacob Cunningham (b. 1813)
- Alice Cunningham (b. 1815)
- Samuel Cunningham (b. 1817)
- Emma Cunningham (adopted) (b. 1820)
- Susan Cunningham (adopted) (b. 1820)

CHAPTER ONE

The streets of London were arrayed in full glory. Flags fluttered from every building, and multicolored ribbons streamed from every railing, pillar, and post, and even human hands. The pavements were crowded with people jostling one another for the best possible view of the parade that would march past, though that would not happen for a while yet. No one showed any noticeable impatience at the long wait ahead of them, however. The June sun beamed down from a clear blue sky, erasing all the anxieties of the past few days, when the gloom-and-doomers among them had predicted clouds, wind, rain, and even, in a few extreme cases, snow. The air was warm without being oppressively so.

Who could have asked for a better day?

When King George IV ascended the throne, his love of pomp and circumstance had prompted him to revive the public celebration of his official birthday in June with the ceremony of Trooping the Colour. Various British regiments, both infantry and cavalry, gorgeously clad in full dress uniform, would parade their colors before the king at Horse Guards Parade on Whitehall before processing along a predetermined route to the lively music of their bands and the delight of the cheering London populace that awaited them.

A privileged few had been invited to watch the full ceremony from the grandstands that had been erected for the occasion around the inner perimeter of Horse Guards Parade itself. Incredibly—she still could not quite believe it was so—Winifred Cunningham was among them. She—who had begun life as a nameless orphan, abandoned on the doorstep of an orphanage in Bath and finally adopted at the age of nine by parents who were themselves either orphaned or born illegitimate—was now seated with the elite of British society, waiting to behold the king and the full visual splendor of Trooping the Colour.

To be strictly accurate, she was not exactly *seated*. She was standing beside one section of the grandstands, having complained that the man who had come to sit in front of her was wearing a hat at least a mile high and the ladies on either side of him had gone out of their way to outdo each other and every other lady present with the size of their bonnet brims, the lavish display of flowers and bows that adorned them, and the plumes that waved above them. She had never seen anything more ridiculous in her life. Or anything more frustrating, under present circumstances.

She would not be able to see a *thing*, she had complained to the companions on either side of her, laughter in her voice. That was not strictly accurate if she was willing to duck and stretch and bob and weave to find a gap through which she could peer. If they would only keep still!

So they were going to watch from ground level, Winifred and

her two companions, unless some official came along to shoo them back up to their seats in the stands. She had one hand drawn through the reassuringly steady arm of Bertrand Lamarr, Viscount Watley, her stepuncle, and the other through that of the Honorable Owen Ware, youngest brother of the Earl of Stratton and a friend of Bertrand's from their university days. Winifred's adoptive mother was the daughter of the Marchioness of Dorchester, who had married the marquess, Bertrand's father, a few years ago. Bertrand and Estelle, his twin sister, were therefore her mother's stepsiblings and *her stepuncle and stepaunt.* Yet they were only seven years older than Winifred.

Yes, it was tricky. Unfortunately, it was not the only complicated thing about the Westcotts, Winifred's mother's family and therefore her own.

Bertrand was also gorgeous—tall, dark, and handsome, that age-old stereotype of the perfect man. It would be hard to find any fault with his appearance. He was charming and modest too, seemingly unaware of just how very attractive he was or of how many females of all ages sighed over him and daydreamed about him and set their caps at him. Fortunately, Winifred was not one of them. She was a very practical and sensible young lady and had always been aware that Bertrand was far outside her orbit in every imaginable way. She liked him immensely, however. She felt comfortable in his company. But she was not attracted to him.

The same could not be said of her feelings for Owen Ware, who was tall and fair-haired and good-looking without being startlingly handsome. He was invariably cheerful and amiable. He claimed to be rootless. He was approaching the end of his twenties without any clear idea of what he was going to do with the rest of his life. As a boy and the third son of a noble father—the third legitimate son, anyway—he had been designated for the church and had been duly packed off to university when he turned eighteen. He had done well there, though he had had lots of fun too. He was still toying with the idea of taking holy orders, but—to use his own words—he was somewhat put off by the religious stuff he would have to involve himself in when all he really wanted to do was serve people who needed a helping hand to get through hard times. It was no unrealistic dream. He spent much of his time performing all sorts of volunteer work, most of it grueling and quite unglamorous and unsung.

Winifred, listening to some of his accounts, found herself wanting to experience them with him. Her motive was not piety or a silly image of herself as a ministering angel to the poor and infirm and underprivileged. She knew all the frustrations of trying to help people who rejected help, often with fierce hostility. She had had practice. Her parents had adopted Sarah and her when they married, but they were only the first adoptees. Her parents had adopted several more children after that, most of them with problems no one else was able or willing to take on. They included a deaf boy, another with behavior problems that made him antisocial and often vicious to anyone who tried to be kind to him, and twin girls who suffered from massive insecurities resulting from having been separated for several months to live with couples who did not wish to take both, or perhaps were unable to for some reason. Winifred had a special love for those siblings, though she had no illusions about the ease of solving their problems.

She fancied working with Owen and perhaps . . . *marrying* him, presumptuous as such a private dream might be. He was, after all, the son of an earl. He definitely liked her, though to be fair, he tended to like everyone. They had talked endlessly, the two of them, since meeting a few weeks ago. Winifred loved serious, meaningful conversation between equals. Empty chitchat designed specifically for the delicate sensibilities of a lady soon irritated her or outright bored her. Owen treated her like a *person*. Whether he was also attracted to her was another matter, of course.

"Better?" he asked her now.

"Standing down here instead of sitting up there?" she asked. "Yes, indeed. Thank you. Though just to be in this place at all on such an occasion, even stuck behind an enormous black hat, is . . . indescribable. I want to pinch myself."

"It sounds painful," Bertrand said. "Best not to do it, Winnie."

"I will take your advice." She twinkled up at him before turning back to Owen. "You must be so looking forward to seeing your brother in the parade."

His elder brother was a cavalry colonel and would be leading one group of cavalry—what was the official word? *Battalion? Regiment? Troop?* Anyway, he would be leading them onto the parade ground. Winifred had never met him, but she was looking forward to seeing him today.

"Nick?" Owen said. "Yes. I wonder if I will even recognize him, though, all spruced up in his dress uniform as he will be, everything spotless and gleaming. He usually favors an old uniform, which looks rather as though he has been living in it for the past five years or so. As he probably has, though I hasten to add that his batman keeps it in pristine condition, and I am forever in envy of the shine on the boots he usually wears, old and worn though the leather is."

Colonel the Honorable Nicholas Ware was a career officer. He had spent many years fighting in the thick of combat, most notably in the Battle of Waterloo eight years ago. But more recently he had worked at the Horse Guards in a largely administrative capacity.

"How fortunate it is that you happen to be in London today of all days," Owen said.

"I would prefer to be in Bath," she said. "Or, rather, in our home in the hills above Bath, where I can make myself useful with the children or with any classes or workshops or retreats that are happening there. I generally find London too . . . *big*. And too bewildering." Not to mention dirty.

Her papa had inherited a large old mansion from the greatuncle he had discovered only very shortly before the latter's death, having grown up in the orphanage where Winifred too had lived until the age of nine. Papa, annoyed that the old man had chosen to keep his identity secret all those years, had not wanted to accept his inheritance, but at the time he was a struggling artist who also volunteered his services at the orphanage school, where Mama had recently taken employment. Mama had persuaded him that the house would be perfect for his studio and for all sorts of events associated with the arts, and even for school concerts and dramas. They had ended up marrying, and Mama had asked Winifred if she would like to go with them as their adopted daughter. What a glorious day that had been. The best day ever!

The house was always bustling with life and activity. Even when there was no event in progress, there was the family, a mingling of Mama and Papa's own children and the ones they had adopted—nine of them altogether, not counting Mama and Papa.

"I do too, Winnie," Bertrand said in response to her remark about London. "I am always tempted to become a hermit and shut myself up in Elm Court. I usually force myself to spend a few weeks of the Season in London, however. It keeps Estelle quiet if nothing else. And I must confess to being glad I am here today."

Elm Court was Bertrand's home in Sussex.

Estelle Wiley, Countess of Brandon, lived at Everleigh Park in Hertfordshire with her husband. Their first child was on the way, an impending event that had kept them at home this year. Estelle was eager to see her brother as happily married as she.

The stands had filled up, Winifred could see as she gazed around in awe. The only empty seats must be the three she and her two companions had vacated. Everyone, man and woman alike, it seemed to her, had donned their very best finery for the occasion. She must look like someone's country cousin in contrast, though Papa had offered to send her shopping for something new and fashionable. She had assured him she did not need anything new. And the trouble with fashion was that it became *un*fashionable in the blink of an eye. One would need a vast fortune just to keep up. But why do it at all?

"Bertrand tells me that the Duchess of Netherby's ball at Archer House next week is to be in your honor, Winifred," Owen said. "You did not tell me that, you modest creature. It is sure to be a grand squeeze. Those Netherby balls are rare events even when they are not celebrating the come-out of a new debutante."

Winifred grimaced. "It was Aunt Anna's idea," she said. "But when I assured her I would really rather the ball not be specifically for me, Uncle Avery fixed me with one of those bored expressions he is so good at and told me not to be tiresome."

Owen grinned and Bertrand chuckled. "That would do it," he said.

The Duchess of Netherby really was Winifred's aunt—in the

complicated way that characterized their family. She was Mama's half sister, though they had been unaware of each other's existence until they were both adults. Aunt Anna had also grown up at the orphanage in Bath and then remained there to teach until she was called away to London one bleak day—bleak for Winifred, that was—to be informed of her real identity as Lady Anastasia Westcott, only legitimate child of the late Earl of Riverdale and inheritor of all he had possessed except his title and principal seat. Though that last asset had been no treasure at the time, the late earl having allowed it to sink into shabby disrepair. The woman Winifred had always known simply as Miss Anna Snow had not greeted the startling announcement gladly. She had wanted to give up everything and return to her familiar life in Bath. But the Duke of Netherby had had other ideas. He had promptly married her and thus persuaded her to change her mind. He had probably given her one of his looks to persuade her. Winifred did not know how else he had done it. Meanwhile, Mama and her brother and sister as well as Grandmama had been abruptly disinherited of what they had always considered their own. Mama had ended up reacting with what Winifred thought of as her great defiance and taking Aunt Anna's place as teacher at the orphanage.

Now Papa had come to London to paint Lady Jewell's portrait and had been invited to stay at Archer House on Hanover Square with his old friend Anna, now also his sister-in-law, and the Duke of Netherby. Mama and Papa could rarely travel anywhere together. There were too many children and pets to be organized and too many events booked at the arts center that was their house. On this occasion Winifred had been persuaded to accompany Papa. Not that much persuasion had been needed. She liked to spend time alone with him, talking about his art, watching how he worked.

And she loved her aunt Anna, once her beloved teacher, and her five cousins. She even loved her uncle Avery, formidable as he was and intimidating as he could be. For all his air of ennui, he could not hide from *her* the fact that he adored Aunt Anna and all his children too. She would forgive him any number of eccentricities just for those facts.

"You will be going to the ball?" she asked Owen.

"Absolutely," he said. "I hope your dance card is not quite full yet."

"What a silly idea," she said, and was aware of the two men grinning at each other over her head. She had no illusions about her attractions, though. She was not pretty, she did not have any alluring curves, she had no feminine wiles, nor did she want any, and she had no birth or fortune to entice even the most desperate of suitors. She could only hope to eventually attract someone who looked for depth of character, someone who was searching more for a companion and helpmeet than an adornment for his home. Someone like Owen himself, perhaps, though it was altogether possible he would be beguiled one of these days by a pretty face.

She would not be brokenhearted if it never happened for her. If she did not find anyone, well . . . Then she would remain at home, where she was always happy and always useful. There were worse things to be than a spinster in a happy home.

"Indulge my silliness," Owen said. "The duchess is bound to have arranged for some highly respectable partner to lead you into the first set. Reserve the second for me."

"You are too kind," she said.

"You will be kinder if you say yes," he told her. "Imagine the humiliation of having Bertrand witness your rejecting me."

"I would never let you forget it," Bertrand said.

"Well, of course I will reserve it for you," Winifred said. "If I am not upstairs in my room hiding under the bed, that is. And thank you. But is it possible something is happening here?"

There was a noticeable swell in the volume of animated chatter from the packed stands, and all heads were turned in one direction, feathers waving and fluttering from hundreds of bonnets.

"Barely three minutes late," Bertrand said, consulting a pocket watch. "Impressive. It makes one proud to be British."

Large doors across the parade ground from them had opened. There were shouts of command from inside, and lines of foot soldiers, led by an officer on horseback, began a procession out onto the parade ground, all moving as one, their booted feet pounding the pavement like the single beat of a bass drum, their scarlet uniforms bright in the sunshine, their tall black beaver hats low on their heads and hiding most of their faces, it seemed, except noses and mouths and chins. How did they *see*? Their boots and their weapons gleamed in the sunshine. Arms and legs moved in perfect rhythm.

Winifred, clinging to the arms of her companions, was quite sure she had never seen anything more breathtaking in her life.

The soldiers marched past them to the lively music of their regimental band, turned at the end of the parade ground in a complicated maneuver, never losing a beat or the perfect unison that made them one unit rather than a collection of individual men, and marched back and into place. There they came to a stamping halt at the shouted command of the officer on horseback and stood perfectly still and at attention.

But that was not the end of it. More came, first infantry and then cavalry, until the parade ground was filled and there seemed to be no room for more. But there were more to come.

"Ah, here he is," Owen said, his voice bursting with pride. And another troop entered the grounds, led by an officer on horseback, like all his men.

The officer, Winifred concluded, must be Colonel the Honorable Nicholas Ware, Owen's brother. She watched his approach with interest, but it was impossible to detect any familial resemblance, if there was any. There was not enough of his face visible. His horse was enormous, its black coat sleek and gleaming. The man matched it. He looked massive to Winifred, with powerful thighs and a broad chest, his beaver low over his brow, the sunshine twinkling off the gold of his epaulets and the buttons on his coat and cuffs. He held a colorful pennant aloft in one hand.

He looked more than a bit menacing, she thought, his jaw set, his mouth in a thin, uncompromising line. And for the first time it occurred to Winifred that all these men, who were putting on such a magnificent display, were actually killers, that killing was what they were trained to do and what all of them had probably done multiple times. Colonel Ware had fought in Spain and Portugal during the wars against Napoleon Bonaparte, and at Waterloo.

She shivered, and Bertrand looked down at her and smiled.

"Formidable, are they not?" he said.

He—the colonel, that was—rode past them without turning his head or nodding acknowledgment of his brother's presence, without any indication that he saw him, in fact. It was not surprising, of course. One could hardly expect these men to wave their hats to their relatives in the stands. The very thought brought a smile to Winifred's face.

"A handsome devil, isn't he?" Owen said.

"I will take your word for it," she said. "I could see hardly anything of his face." Not his eyes, not his hair. "But he looks very impressive."

"Indeed," he said.

"He certainly has an impressive set of lungs," Bertrand said as the colonel bellowed out orders to his men. The company turned and made its way back along the parade ground to take up the remaining space at the center. He commanded them to halt, and halt they did, the horses as still as the men.

How did the men train them to *do* that? In her experience horses invariably tossed their manes and their tails and wiggled their hind quarters even when called to a halt.

The regimental bands fell silent. The regimental flags, also apparently known as the colors, held aloft by the officers who led the men, fluttered gaily in the breeze, the only movement on the parade ground. The cheering and chatter among the spectators in the grandstands had died away, replaced by an almost expectant hush.

Everyone awaited the main event of the morning, the parading of the colors past King George IV. Only one thing was missing.

"Trust the king to be late," Owen murmured out of the side of his mouth.

"Did anyone expect him *not* to be?" Bertrand asked, his voice also lowered.

Winifred smiled. She was in no hurry. She was enjoying herself enormously.

Trust the king to be late, Colonel the Honorable Nicholas Ware thought, resisting the dire need to scratch an itch at the side of his nose and wondering idly how many similar itches were being ignored all about him.

He was pleased that Owen had come, since he was the only member of the family currently in London. He had, of course, seen his brother as he rode past. There was not much he missed when he was leading his men, despite the obstruction his beaver could present to his line of vision. It was always important to see ahead and to either side without having to turn his head or tip it back or even swivel his eyes for a clearer look. Sometimes his very life and those of his men depended on it.

He had also procured a ticket for the young lady Owen wanted to bring with him. He had been very nonchalant with his explanation. "She is up from the country for a spell and believes she despises London," he had said. "I thought it would be good for her to see it at its most splendidly festive. Besides, she is a niece or cousin or stepsister or some such thing to Bert—Lamarr, that is. Viscount Watley. I daresay his father will see to it that he comes too. Actually, his father would probably have seen to it that Miss Cunningham came as well. He is married to her grandmother."

Presumably he referred to the marquis. But the young lady must certainly be Watley's stepniece, Nicholas had thought. Also, she appeared to be someone of interest to Owen.

Nicholas had had a good look at her too as he rode past the three of them a short while ago—Owen, Watley, and a young woman, presumably Miss Cunningham, standing in a row between two of the grandstands, her hands drawn through the arms of the two men.

She was not a beauty. She had nothing much for a figure, and her face was unremarkable. She had a wide brow, her hair pushed unbecomingly beneath her bonnet. She was neatly though not elaborately dressed. He guessed her clothes had been purchased or even handmade in the country, where she lived. Bath, he seemed to recall Owen saying. She had steady eyes, which had looked unwaveringly upon him without discernible expression.

Had she been assessing him as a future brother-in-law?

He liked the fact that she had not gazed at him with open admiration. Nicholas had been blessed with good looks all his life. It was not conceited of him to admit it. Women had adored him when he was a child and growing boy. They had continued doing so after he grew up, though the sixteen years since he had joined the military at eighteen had hardened him and weathered his face.

He had also always been told that he had a natural charm women found irresistible. It was not a conscious thing with him. He did not set out to conquer and seduce. Indeed, he had always been guarded in his manner toward the women to whom he found himself attracted. He had never wanted to give the wrong impression or, worse, find himself trapped in a marriage that was not of his choosing.

But he was now thirty-four years old. He had always planned to marry at some time. He wanted the companionship and, yes, the regular sex. He also wanted a family before he was too old to enjoy it.

He was aware that he could have almost any woman he chose. Apart from his looks and apparent charm, he was the son of the late Earl of Stratton, younger brother of the present earl, and in addition to his salary as a cavalry colonel, he had the generous portion his father had left him. He could more or less have his pick of potential brides.

It was not necessarily a blessing.

He was constantly assaulted by the lures of all the most beautiful young women in search of husbands, and pursued by fathers who approved his suit and mothers who were as susceptible to his charms as their daughters. He would not have been human, perhaps, if he had not looked with interest upon all that loveliness on offer. But being a bit perverse, he sometimes longed for an ordinary woman—whatever he might mean by the word *ordinary*. Someone . . . *real*. Someone who would see him as a person, not just a bundle of looks and charm and eligibility.

Was the infernal king *never* going to come? It was hard to keep his mind off his itching nose. The sounds of conversation were resuming in the crowded stands that surrounded the parade ground, in marked contrast with the silent stillness of the gathered regiments.

His thoughts wandered to Grace, to whom he was not betrothed, though he was perilously close. She was the only daughter of General Haviland, Nicholas's superior officer at the Horse Guards. She was twenty-nine years old and still unmarried, having suffered the loss of two fiancés during the wars, when she was still very young. Now it seemed that Nicholas had been chosen to put an end to the long period of her mourning, if that was what the last eight or nine years had been. The general and Mrs. Haviland had singled him out for more than usual attention in the past few months, and Miss Haviland herself seemed accepting of their choice, though perhaps she genuinely fancied him even without their prompting. It was hard to tell since her manners were always impeccable, perfectly refined and correct, and she was ever amiable. She was also incredibly beautiful, with very dark hair and eyes and a figure no man could resist admiring.

Nicholas had become something of an expert over the years at avoiding entrapment. This time, however, he had made less of an effort. It was time he married. Why not Miss Haviland? She had all the beauty and refinement he could ask for, she was familiar with military life, and he had to marry *someone*. He had been beginning to wonder if he would ever find that special someone he would instinctively recognize as the woman with whom he could happily live out the rest of his life. Miss Haviland was also the right age. He had no wish to pursue a young miss fresh out of the schoolroom, all giggles and surface charm.

Soon he was going to have to force himself to take the plunge and make his declaration. It was a somewhat alarming prospect, but once he had done it, he would be able to relax. There would be no going back from a formal betrothal.

Suddenly the band struck up a lively tune, and a great cheer went up from the grandstands.

The king, it seemed, had arrived.

CHAPTER TWO

Winifred stood in the middle of her dressing room at Archer House, staring glumly at her image in the pier glass. It was time to go downstairs, but she wished she were anywhere else on earth. Preferably at home in Bath, making herself useful. At the very least she wished she could simply snap her fingers and find that it was tomorrow, and this most dreaded of all nights was over and done with.

She would have been happy enough simply to be a guest at the Duke and Duchess of Netherby's ball. She was not immune to splendor and lavish festivities or even dancing, after all. Aunt Anna had predicted—just as Owen had at the Trooping the Colour last week—that this would be a grand squeeze of an event, since everyone to whom she had sent an invitation had replied in the affirmative. It would no doubt be an exciting spectacle and something that under normal circumstances would provide Winifred with great enjoyment and endless anecdotes to recount in a letter home to Mama and her brothers and sisters.

She could even have hoped to dance—with Papa, with Bertrand, with Owen, and even perhaps with Uncle Avery. Mostly, though, she would have been content to stand in a quiet corner, drinking in the sights and sounds around her, unnoticed and unselfconscious.

It was not going to be that way, alas. For she was not just any guest, an obscure niece of the duchess's who just happened to be staying at Archer House on the day of the ball.

She was the *reason* for it.

It was being given in her honor, a sort of come-out ball at the advanced age of twenty-one. Aunt Anna had insisted upon it, and Uncle Avery had quelled Winifred's protest with that bored look of his she always found terrifying. Papa had thought it a grand idea, and Mama, when appealed to for intervention in a hastily written letter, replied that she only wished she could be there with her daughter. Alas, it was not possible, she had lamented, but Aunt Anna would be a wonderful substitute mother for the occasion. Mama trusted her utterly.

Winifred remembered the time when Mama had hated Aunt Anna, blaming her quite unfairly—she even admitted it herself now—for her own loss of status and title and the ending of a betrothal when it was discovered that her father had still been married to an unsuspected first wife when he married Grandmama, making Grandmama a bigamous wife and her children, Mama, Uncle Harry, and Aunt Abby, illegitimate. Aunt Anna, meanwhile, having languished for most of her life in the orphanage in Bath, had found that she was the only legitimate daughter of a father she could not remember and the sole inheritor of his vast fortune, amassed, incidentally, with the help of a large dowry Grandmama had brought to the bigamous marriage.

That feud of the half siblings was a thing of the past. Sometimes—like now, for example—Winifred almost wished it were not. How awful of her.

They would be waiting for her in the ballroom, the duke and duchess, where she was to stand with them in the receiving line. She simply could not do it. Her stomach felt distinctly queasy. But she had no choice.

If she knotted together all the sheets from her bed and dangled them from the window, would they reach within jumping distance of the street below?

Her reflected image smiled briefly and bleakly back at her from the glass.

At least Aunt Anna had not insisted upon a white ballgown, all frills and flounces, the standard uniform of debutantes. She had agreed with Winifred that an ivory silk gown of slim lines and simple design, not a frill in sight, suited her far better. She had, though, persuaded Winifred to choose elbow-length gloves of dull gold and dancing slippers to match. Papa had presented her this morning with a double chain necklace of fine gold—*Nothing too elaborate, Winnie. I know you*—and with small gold earbobs.

Her hair had been a bit of a bone of contention. The maid who had been sent to style it for her, following definite instructions from Her Grace, had been rather tight-lipped when Winifred insisted upon a different style. Aunt Anna, when she came to inspect the results a short while ago, had tipped her head to one side and suggested that perhaps a few tendrils of hair curled over her ears and about her temples and over her brow would become her without looking too fussy. Winifred had insisted upon leaving it as it was, rather severely drawn back from her face and over the crown of her head and dressed in some sort of twist at the back. It was her normal look, except perhaps for the twist, which had involved a few braids rather than the simple knot she favored when doing her own hair. She had conceded that issue. She did not want her aunt or even the maid to think of her as *difficult* or stubborn, though the maid obviously did anyway.

But she stuck with her choice. She did not *want* to be a debutante, open to the critical gaze of half the *ton*—at *least* half of it— and found wanting. All the frills and flounces and curled tendrils in the world would not make a beauty of her. She did not *want* to be beautiful, not in any artificial way, at least. She just wanted to be Winifred Cunningham. Why did people always want you to be what you were not?

There was a tap on the outer door, and it opened a crack to admit Papa's head. He smiled at her and pushed the door wide.

"Perfection," he said, looking her over with approval. "You look beautiful, Winnie, as you always do."

He sounded as if he meant it. Papa was a portrait painter, much in demand by potential sitters. Yet he never flattered his subjects when he painted them. Rather, he spent time with them before he even set brush to canvas, searching out the person behind the appearance. The resulting portraits, which were always true to life, warts and all, nevertheless suggested the unique character and beauty of that person. It was quite extraordinary. Winifred admired him enormously.

He saw her, in all her plainness, as beautiful. Though he was, of course, biased, even discounting his artist's vision.

"We had better go down," he said, "before Netherby comes up and turns his quizzing glass on you. You would not enjoy that."

"Indeed I would not," she said, laughing. "But I wish I could simply erase the coming few hours, Papa."

"But just think of how disappointed Mama would be," he said.

"You win." She sighed and crossed the room to take his arm.

Nicholas declined an invitation to dine with General Haviland and his wife and daughter before the Netherby ball. He was close to being resigned to making a match with Grace Haviland, it was true, but the caution of years warned him against arriving at the ball with the lady on his arm while her parents came along behind, smiling their approval. He used as an excuse a promise already given to dine with his brother.

"You have invited me to dine with you," he told Owen on the morning of the ball.

"I have, have I?" Owen said. "It sounds like a ruse to me, Nick. We will go to White's, then? My man might be a bit put out if I inform him with so little notice that I will be dining at home—with a distinguished guest."

They arrived at Archer House in the middle of the evening after waiting almost fifteen minutes outside at the back of a long line of carriages. When they ascended the red carpeted steps to the front doors and went inside, it was to the sight of the curving staircase up to the ballroom crowded with chattering guests awaiting their turn to pass along the receiving line.

"You fancy the Cunningham girl, do you, Owen?" Nicholas asked.

His brother shrugged. "I am not sure I would use the word *fancy*," he said. "But I like her. I find her interesting. She does not go on and on, rapturizing over bonnets and such. She does not simper. Or giggle."

A lover's words indeed.

He had been right in his brief assessment of her at Trooping the Colour, Nicholas thought when they arrived in the doorway of the ballroom and waited to be announced. Miss Cunningham was standing between the Netherbys in a mercifully short receiving line. She was not beautiful. She was slender, with a figure that was neat but in no way alluring. She was at least sensible enough not to try prettying herself up with a frivolous gown. Her hair was dressed more severely than one expected of the guest of honor at a *ton* ball, and it was an undistinguished midbrown in color. Her face was plain. Not ugly. But not pretty either. She had perhaps been clever. All the frills and flounces and curls and ringlets in the world would not make a beauty of her. She had not tried. Rather, she had dressed for neatness and comfort, at a guess. Consequently, she stood out from the crowd. He approved of what he saw.

She was the daughter of Joel Cunningham and the former Lady Camille Westcott. Owen had told the latter's story over dinner. Miss Cunningham was an *adopted* daughter, apparently. She was certainly not going to attract an army of suitors tonight with that pedigree, especially when she had neither the looks nor the glamor to persuade any man to ignore the lack. She probably had no fortune to speak of either. Her father made his living as a portrait painter and manager of some sort of arts center in Bath, according to Owen.

She might be just what his brother needed, though. A sensible woman.

She was greeting everyone with quiet dignity. She was not doing a great deal of smiling and absolutely no simpering. Not, that was, until they had been announced and Owen appeared before her and offered his hand. She smiled with bright and open pleasure then, something her peers would doubtless consider a social blunder of major proportions if she wished to indicate an interest in him. A look of haughty indifference was the more accepted tactic to bring a man to heel.

Owen was smiling back as she placed her hand in his and he raised it to his lips.

"You have reserved the second set for me, I hope?" he said.

"You have not had a great deal of competition," she said. "I will be dancing the opening set with Bertrand."

No competition. The opening set with a relative. What other woman would admit the former or seem pleased about the latter? Though Watley was a handsome fellow, it was true.

Then it was Nicholas's turn to bow over the lady's hand. Her cheeks had flushed slightly and her eyes had brightened during her encounter with Owen. She looked at Nicholas with candid curiosity.

"You do not look so massive out of the saddle and without the scarlet uniform and the beaver helmet," she said, surprising him. "Your face, now that I can see it all, does not look so formidable or so—" She stopped abruptly.

He raised his eyebrows and waited for her to complete the thought.

"So *cruel*," she said. "I beg your pardon. That is too stark a word."

Cruel. No woman to his knowledge had ever used that word to describe him before now, even those he had disappointed by deflecting their advances. He prided himself on his good manners.

"May I hope that you still have the supper dance free?" he asked. He had not intended to dance with her at all unless, as was unlikely, she showed signs of becoming a wallflower during the evening. But that particular dance would give him a chance to sit and converse with her over supper, and . . . And *what?* Decide if she could possibly be the sort of bride to make Owen happy? As though his opinion mattered.

Cruel. He did not know whether to laugh or be offended.

"I do," she said, frowning slightly. "Shall I reserve it for you?"

"If you would be so good," he said, and moved on to shake hands with Netherby.

"Just look at this," Owen said as they moved on into the ballroom. "The place is bursting at the seams, and the dancing has not even started yet."

"Your Miss Cunningham must be pleased," Nicholas said.

Owen frowned. "She is not *my* Miss Cunningham, Nick," he said. "Mrs. Haviland is over there, trying to attract your attention. You had better go and pay your respects to *your* Miss Haviland."

"Touché," Nicholas said.

"She is devilish pretty," Owen said.

"Yes, she is," Nicholas agreed before he made his way across the ballroom floor, smiling as he went, to where the general's wife stood with her daughter. Though *pretty* was perhaps too tame a word to describe Grace. She was downright beautiful.

And apparently willing to accept his suit.

The part of the evening Winifred had dreaded most was over. A trickle of guests had still been making its way along the receiving line, but Aunt Anna had decided it was past time for the dancing to begin. In her opinion, anyone who arrived this late deserved to go without a personal welcome. She presented Winifred formally to Bertrand, who took her hand, bowed over it before placing it on his sleeve, and led her onto the floor, which had emptied of milling guests to make way for the dancing. He smiled at her and winked.

"Will you look less terrified if I promise not to tread on your feet or allow you to trip over mine?" he asked her. "Come, Winnie. You have danced at balls before. I have seen you—enjoying yourself quite exuberantly, I might add."

"But they were small family affairs and really not at all intimidating," she said. "I have never before been alone in the middle of a fashionable ballroom, with the gathered *ton* gazing at me and waiting for me to put one foot wrong."

"What?" he said. "*Alone?* I am nobody, then, am I? Besides, other couples are following our lead."

It was true. The floor was filling with dancers, forming long lines in anticipation of the first set. The orchestra had finished tuning their instruments. And those who *were* looking their way were more likely to be gazing at Bertrand, who had achieved the seemingly impossible to appear even more handsome than usual in crisp black and white evening dress. They must be pitying him, obliged as he was to lead off the ball with *her*.

But she was *not* going to start belittling herself just because there were dozens of young women more beautiful than she and certainly more elaborately dressed. She was Winifred Cunningham, and she was pleased with herself. Even her appearance. She did not want to be like other women. She wanted to be herself.

"You are certainly not *nobody*, Bertrand. I daresay every other woman in the room is gazing with envy at me." She grinned at him suddenly. "Those who are not gazing at *you* in envy, that is, because you have me for a partner."

"That's the spirit, Winnie," he said, chuckling.

But there was no more time for talk. A sort of hush had

descended upon the ballroom as Avery welcomed everyone from the orchestra dais and announced the opening set of country dances. The musicians struck a decisive chord, and the ball began.

Despite herself, Winifred felt a shiver of excitement along her spine.

There was a certain family resemblance between Owen Ware and Colonel Ware, she thought, though nothing particularly obvious. They were about the same height, though the colonel looked taller, with his very upright military bearing and his broad shoulders and what must be powerful muscles in his arms and chest and thighs. Both were fair-haired, but the colonel's hair was a mix of light brown and blond and waved over his head to give him a slightly tousled look. His face was more weathered than his brother's and somewhat more rugged. And there were his jaw and his mouth, firm, perhaps stubborn. They were what last week had left her with the impression of cruelty. One would certainly not wish to be one of his men, caught neglecting a duty. Or an enemy facing his sword.

Goodness, had she really called him *cruel* to his face? She felt her cheeks grow hot at the memory and looked at Bertrand, who smiled reassuringly back at her.

He was devastatingly good-looking—Colonel Ware, that was. And attractive. If there was a difference between the two. Not in the way Owen was handsome and attractive, though. He did not have Owen's lean grace or . . . *sparkle*. He was noticeably older—probably in his thirties? Owen, she knew, must be twenty-eight or thereabouts, the same age as Bertrand. They had been at university together.

She was twirling down the set suddenly, Bertrand's hand firm against her back to prevent her from spinning away out of control.

The other dancers in the lines, ladies on one side, gentlemen on the other, clapped in time to the music as they watched. Winifred laughed with exuberance. She did not expect to dance all night, but she did like dancing and must enjoy every chance she had—the next set with Owen, who had joined the other line with his partner for this set, and a dance later in the evening with Colonel Ware.

That was not a happy prospect, however. Somehow she found him a bit frightening—no, *intimidating* was a better word. And it was the supper dance. She knew what that meant. They would sit together for the meal, and unless she could maneuver matters otherwise, they would engage each other in almost exclusive conversation for at least half an hour.

Did he sense a possible romance between her and his younger brother? Did he intend to grill her to discover if she was worthy to be admitted to the ranks of his hallowed family? Had he already made up his mind? Did he intend to warn her off?

She had no intention of being intimidated. Correction: Since that was already happening, she had no intention of giving in to it. She was not at all sure Owen was interested in her in *that* way anyway. She was not sure she was interested in *him*. But she did know that she liked him enormously and that he was just the sort of man with whom she might settle happily.

He limped very slightly, Winifred thought, her mind returning to Colonel Ware. It was the only physical imperfection she had detected, though really it was very minor. An old battle wound, perhaps? She must ask Owen. No, she must not. It would really be an unpardonably indelicate thing for a woman to ask about a stranger.

The set was over far too soon, perhaps because she had not given it her whole attention. Gentlemen were leading their partners off the floor, clearing it for the next set.

"Thank you, Winnie," Bertrand said as he led her back to Aunt Anna's side. "You are an excellent dancer. Enjoy the rest of the evening."

"Thank you," she said. "I will."

"Yet suddenly you look again as if you are facing your own execution," he said. "Dare I predict you will dance every single set of the evening until the last guest totters homeward?"

Winifred laughed, though it occurred to her for the first time that he might be right. The Duchess of Netherby was hosting this ball and it was in *her* honor. Aunt Anna was always a perfect hostess. It would be a matter of great pride and importance to her to see that her niece was not without a partner all evening.

So much for that quiet corner.

Nicholas danced every set though he knew his leg would ache more than usual tomorrow. He had learned to ignore such inconveniences. He always enjoyed mingling with other people at the social events he attended. He enjoyed choosing his partners at balls. He liked conversing with them, as far as the figures of the dance allowed. He savored the opening set with Grace. She looked strikingly handsome in an emerald green gown. She lived up to her name in the way she danced. She smiled and gave him her attention. He felt that she genuinely liked him, as he liked her. But love? Did it matter if she loved him? Or if he loved her? They were both past such romantic nonsense, surely. Liking would give place to affection if they married and eventually to a sort of love, which might not be passionate but would be lasting. He would be able to trust her, he firmly believed, as she could trust him. Once he was married, his wife would have all his loyalty. All his fidelity. He had never been much of a philanderer anyway.

She would be a good mother—as he hoped he would be a good father. Different from his own. But he shook off that thought as soon as he became aware of it. His father had been who he was, just as he, Nicholas, was who *he* was. Why should he fear becoming his father all over again just because he looked like him and shared a basic gregarious nature with him? It was disturbing when other people still told him, as though they thought it was a compliment, that he was just like his father. One person had told him that just tonight. He had forced himself to smile.

His father had been enormously popular, both at home at Ravenswood and here in London, where he had spent the spring months, supposedly attending to his parliamentary duties while Mama and his children remained at home in the country. It was only when Nicholas was eighteen and about to leave home that he passed the age of innocence with an abrupt jolt when he discovered who, or rather *what*, his father really was.

He simply must make Grace an offer soon. There was no point in delaying. Her parents expected it. So, no doubt, did she. And he was not going to find anyone more suitable. He did need to ascertain first, however, that it was what she truly wished. He did not want to discover after their marriage that she had accepted him only because it was expected of her. Not that he would discover it even then, he supposed. Her vows made, she was unlikely ever to admit such an unsavory truth to him.

"Would it be too much to ask that you reserve another set for me later this evening, perhaps directly after supper?" he asked her as he led her back to her mother's side.

It was unexceptionable, he knew, to dance twice in an evening with the same partner, though he rarely did it himself.

"Thank you," she said. "I will."

Which left him wondering why he had not, even before tonight, reserved the supper dance with her. Having the meal together would have given them the chance for a private tête-à-tête, perhaps to be followed by a stroll in the garden. Instead, he had asked Miss Cunningham, in whom he could have no possible interest beyond the connection with Owen. He rather liked her despite, or perhaps because of, her outspokenness in the receiving line. But as a sister-in-law? As a lifetime partner for his fun-loving brother?

Owen's business was not his, of course. Even Devlin, their elder brother and head of the family as the Earl of Stratton, did not interfere in any of their relationships.

It finally came time to claim his partner for the supper dance. He had observed that she was a good dancer. She had danced all evening so far, which was not surprising. The duchess would have seen to that. If Owen did not come up to scratch, Her Grace would probably also procure some respectable marriage offer for her niece. He guessed that Miss Cunningham was in her twenties already.

They did not talk as they danced. They would do that later. Instead, they moved with the twirling crowds of their fellow dancers, and it struck Nicholas that her obvious exuberance was as unfashionable as her appearance. Most of the other ladies either smiled politely as they danced or looked fashionably bored. It would seem that most considered it undignified to show open enthusiasm. Even Grace . . .

But no, he was not going to pursue that thought.

"Allow me to escort you into the supper room," he said, bowing over Miss Cunningham's hand as the set drew to an end. "Shall we see if we can find a quiet table somewhere?"

She looked consideringly at him. "So you may interrogate me?" she asked.

Her blunt observations never ceased to take him by surprise. He smiled at her. "I promise not to use the thumb screws," he said.

"That is vastly reassuring, Colonel Ware," she said, setting her hand on his offered arm.

He led her in the direction of the supper room and was fortunate enough to find a small side table still unoccupied. He settled her on one side of it and seated himself on the other.

All around them there was a swell of sound as other guests found spaces and friends and settled into animated conversation, each person trying to raise his or her voice above the multitude. Fortunately, Nicholas had never found it difficult to make himself heard, even without resorting to the use of his parade ground voice.

"Now, why would you expect an interrogation?" he asked, regarding his companion with amusement.

CHAPTER THREE

Winifred was somewhat dismayed that Colonel Ware had found a small table not yet occupied by anyone else and promptly seated her at it. She would far prefer to be sitting at the long dining table, preferably close to Papa or Bertrand or Owen. Conversation was already lively there, as well as laughter.

She was not at all sure she liked Colonel Ware. Indeed, she was almost sure she did not. He made her uncomfortable. She felt at every moment that he was looking at her from his superior age and life experience, not to mention personal attractions, and finding her wanting. It did not help that he had a commanding presence and a magnetic personality. She had seen both in the occasional glances she had cast his way during the ball so far. All attention somehow focused upon him whenever he joined a group. He had danced with the most beautiful women, all of whom had looked slightly dazzled, as though he were paying them an extraordinary compliment simply by choosing them. Though that harsh judgment on her part was perhaps a bit unfair to him. He did not seem conceited.

She felt stifled anyway. He was not *her* commanding officer, yet she had followed him meekly when she might have expressed a preference for sitting with a group at the main table. Why had he even asked her to dance anyway? Because she was the guest of honor and he felt it was expected of him? Because he really had set himself the task of interrogating her over her relationship with his younger brother? Was he afraid it was more than a friendship? What Owen did with his life was surely none of his business. He was not even the eldest of the Ware brothers. He was not the Earl of Stratton. She wished it were Owen sitting across from her. She felt thoroughly comfortable with him. She never had to think about what she would say next. Conversation flowed naturally between them. She cast her eyes yearningly to where he sat with a group of young people on the far side of the long table.

"Because I am a friend of your brother's perhaps?" she said in answer to Colonel Ware's question when his silence told her that it had not been rhetorical.

"Ah," he said after allowing a servant to fill his wineglass and she had set a hand over the top of hers and shaken her head. "And I am playing the part of heavy-handed elder brother, am I, checking your credentials?"

"*Are* you?" she asked.

He smiled at her, and she saw that there was more to him than the hard-jawed, taciturn military officer whom she had described to herself—*and to him*—as cruel. Now she could see firsthand the charm that made him quite irresistibly attractive to women. He was a practiced slayer of hearts, she guessed. Though not of hers.

"Tell me about yourself, Miss Cunningham," he said. "Are you really the Duchess of Netherby's niece?"

"I am," she said. "My mother is her half sister. I grew to the age of nine at the orphanage in Bath where Aunt Anna grew up—and my papa. He was a volunteer art teacher in the school there when I was a child and Aunt Anna taught there. So did my mother after Aunt Anna was discovered to be Lady Anastasia Westcott, only legitimate daughter of the late Earl of Riverdale, who was an unbelievably wicked man. He hid her away at the orphanage so he could marry my grandmother before his lawful wife died and thus solve his financial woes with her fortune. My grandmother and Mama lost their titles and everything else, as did my uncle and aunt. It is complicated," she added weakly before she could launch into a full explanation. "Mama and Papa ended up marrying, and they asked me to go with them as their adopted daughter."

He looked steadily across the table at her while they both leaned back to give room to a couple of servants who bore platters of sweet and savory foods to set between them, and another who came to pour their tea.

"A very tangled web," he said then. "Do you know who your real parents were or are?"

"No," she said. "And I never will. I was left in a basket on the doorstep of the orphanage."

His eyebrows rose. "Does that fact bother you?" he asked.

"No," she said firmly. "Mama and Papa are my parents. My family is the children they had together and the others they adopted. I love them all very dearly."

It was true. She did not need or even want to know where she came from or what, if anything, she had been named before she became Winifred Hamlin after being dropped off at the orphanage. She had endured nine years of anxiety after she had been found and taken in, though she had not realized it at the time. She had tried ceaselessly to establish an identity, to be liked and even loved. She had made a constant effort to be good in the hope of winning the approval of the adults who could decide her future. She had tried to be pious for the same reason. Her efforts had often had the opposite effect of what she had hoped to achieve, however. She had never felt truly liked by the staff or her fellow orphans.

Until, that was, Mama adopted her and made it clear she did so purely out of love. Papa had added his assurances to hers. Winifred had never doubted them in all the years since.

Oh yes, they were her true parents.

"And what do you do in Bath?" Colonel Ware asked as she selected a few items of food and set them on her plate and he followed suit. "I thought that these days it was overrun by septuagenarians taking the waters in the hope of finding a cure for all their ills."

"We live in a large house in the hills above Bath," she said. "It is used for workshops and retreats and conferences for writers and artists and musicians. The children of the orphanage use it for concerts and dramas and sometimes simply for picnics or indoor parties. It is always busy. I am always busy—when I am not dancing at *ton* balls in London, that is."

"Your tone of voice tells me you would rather be there," he said.

"I feel useful there," she said. "But I was designated to come here as support for Papa, who has been engaged to paint Lady Jewell's portrait. And to enjoy myself."

She grimaced and he laughed.

"Mother's orders?" he said. "And *are* you enjoying yourself?"

She thought about it. "Yes," she said. "I will never forget that I have seen the king—is he not *enormous*?—and watched all the splendor of Trooping the Colour."

"You were dazzled by a display of Britain's military might, then, were you?" he asked her.

"I was dazzled by all the color of the uniforms and flags and by the music and the precision with which the regiments marched," she said. "I was *not* impressed by the display of military might. Quite the contrary. I am a firm believer in peace."

It was not entirely true. She knew life was not so simple. But his assumption was inaccurate enough to be an insult to her sensibilities—and her good sense.

He raised his eyebrows.

"It occurred to me during the parade that every one of those men was a killer," she said after waiting for a particularly gusty burst of laughter from the table right beside them to subside. "It occurred to me that every one of them had been trained to kill. That killing was their job. It was an appalling realization."

And this was an appalling conversation to be holding under the circumstances. Goodness, but the sounds of merriment all around them were growing louder, if that was possible. She doubted anyone else in the room had entertained a serious thought since coming in here. He must consider her very odd indeed.

But he smiled at her. Was he *laughing* at her? At her naïveté? She raised her chin and took a bite of a lobster patty, her very favorite savory delicacy.

"There are other responsibilities of the job apart from killing," he said. "Protecting civilian populations in war-torn countries against marauding hordes, for example. We are fortunate here in Britain never to have suffered an invading army—not for several centuries anyway. I suppose the Vikings were the last. Unfortunately, killing becomes necessary when a polite request that invaders remove themselves from someone else's country is ignored."

"But violence merely breeds violence," she said. "If the answer to a country's problems is simply to kill and overwhelm, then nothing will ever change. It is not the answer to individual problems either for that matter. All too often people who have been provoked by the silliest things raise their fists or wield a knife or a gun."

"When they should sit down and discuss their differences like civilized beings?" he said. His eyes were twinkling. He *was* laughing at her.

"They could at least try," she said. "Or simply turn their backs on the provocation."

"And when during the parade did this realization come to you?" he asked her. "When you noticed the cruelty of my face?"

It was precisely at that moment, in fact.

"I could not even see your face," she said. "Except for your mouth."

"A cruel mouth," he said. "Alas, to be judged on one's mouth."

"And your jaw and chin," she said. Oh, how had she got trapped in this ridiculousness? "But is this not an inappropriate occasion to be discussing such a subject?"

He laughed outright. "It is even more inappropriate for me to be discussing it with a lady," he said. "Owen told me you are an interesting person to talk to."

They had talked about her, then?

"But he did not tell me you sometimes talk in platitudes," he said.

She finished chewing the second half of the patty. That was a setdown if ever she had heard one. *Platitudes?*

"You are proud of being a killer, then?" she said. "You consider it a worthy way of using your life?"

"I am not ashamed of it," he said. "But strangely, I have found very few people to kill at the Horse Guards. Precisely none, in fact.

I have been out of practice as a killer for a number of years. When I took up my commission at the age of eighteen, however, as a lowly lieutenant in a cavalry regiment, Napoleon Bonaparte was already making a nuisance of himself. If he had not been stopped, he or his acolytes would still be ruling every country in Europe, and no doubt Britain too. I found that idea objectionable. I fought to stop him, and stop him we did. I do not regret those actions, Miss Cunningham, though it was regrettable that there had to be so much killing. Pacifism would not have accomplished anything. We must agree to differ on that. Unless, that is, you would rather put up your fists and fight it out with me."

She glanced at his hands. He could crush every bone in one of hers without even trying very hard.

"But I believe in peace at all costs," she said. "Besides, it would be an unfair match."

He laughed and looked about the crowded dining room. "All this is in your honor," he said in an obvious attempt to change the subject. "Does it make you happy?"

"I believe your assumption is wrong," she said. "It is a rare invitation from the Duke and Duchess of Netherby to attend a ball at Archer House that has brought out the *ton* in such large numbers. Not me."

"Do you always find it difficult to accept a compliment?" he asked.

Did she? Yes, she supposed she did. Far from feeling like the guest of honor here, she felt like an impostor. She had nothing to recommend her apart from her relationship with the duchess. She picked out her father from the crowd, and Bertrand and Owen. Owen caught her eye and smiled cheerfully.

"No answer," Colonel Ware said.

She looked back at him. "Compliments are unnecessary," she said. "I know my own worth." Too late she realized how pompous her words sounded. "But yes, I am happy to be here. Mama and my brothers and sisters will want a full written report. I will be able to inform them that until after supper at least I danced every set."

"And you did not expect to, I suppose," he said.

"Well, I might have known Aunt Anna would not allow me to be a wallflower," she said. "It would reflect upon her as a hostess."

"And so she has coerced a number of gentlemen into dancing with you," he said.

"I would hope no real coercion was necessary," she said. "*Encouraged* might be a better word."

"Yet I needed neither coercion nor encouragement," he said. "Nor, I would wager, did Owen."

"Ah," she said. "But you had a motive, Colonel Ware. You wished to interrogate me. And you were treated to the story of my origins in a basket in return and my total lack of personal identity. I might have been born to a chimney sweep's daughter or to a scullery maid."

"Or to a duchess," he said.

"It does not matter," she said.

"Oh, I believe it does," he said.

But if he had intended to elaborate upon that theme, he was foiled by the appearance beside their table of a large, fierce-looking gentleman, whom she remembered from the receiving line as General Somebody. He held out a hand toward her. Behind him Winifred could see that other guests were beginning to rise from the table. The dancing must be about to resume.

"General Haviland," he said, giving her hand a hearty, bone-crushing shake. "You probably don't remember me from earlier. The receiving line went on forever, did it not? Gratifying for you, I would think."

"It was," Winifred said.

"You must come and dance with me," he said. "If you do not have another partner waiting for you, that is. Colonel, Grace seems to believe she has promised this next set to you. I will relieve you of the necessity of escorting this young lady back to the ballroom, if I may make so bold."

"Thank you," Winifred said as both she and her supper companion got to their feet. The general was sending a clear message. Colonel Ware had spent quite enough time with her. She remembered that General Haviland had passed along the receiving line with his wife and a young lady she assumed was their daughter— the extraordinarily beautiful dark-haired lady who had danced the opening set with Colonel Ware.

It amused her that she was being seen as some sort of rival.

The general placed her hand on his arm and led her off in the direction of the ballroom.

So she had made her first known appearance in the world in a basket on the doorstep of an orphanage in Bath. Not many people could make such an extraordinary claim, and certainly not any people who ended up being guest of honor at a duchess's ball in a mansion on Hanover Square.

Had she told the story to shock him? Had she succeeded? She had no idea who her real parents were. Rather, she had embraced her adoptive parents and the family they had produced over the years, both products of their marriage and adopted. She claimed to love them all dearly, not even to want to know anything of what had preceded her appearance in the basket.

Nicholas did not believe her for a moment on that last point. There had been a certain lift to her chin as she made her claim. He suspected that it mattered a great deal to her that she would never know exactly who she was and where she had come from. Unlike her aunt, who had discovered after growing up at the same orphanage and even teaching there for a while that she was in fact a very wealthy titled lady of firmly legitimate lineage.

He wondered why, when he had asked her to tell him about herself, she had chosen to begin her story at the beginning as she knew it instead of starting with her adoption at the age of nine. To challenge him, perhaps, with her total ineligibility to marry the Honorable Owen Ware, son of an earl? To discover how he would react? Did she expect him now to try putting obstacles in the way of his brother's making a match with her?

Owen would, if anything, be charmed by her story.

But he was really not interested in whom his brother would end up marrying, if anyone. He was more concerned about whom *he* would marry. His choices had fast been narrowed to one. He knew General Haviland well enough to understand that his superior officer was severely annoyed with him for sitting with Miss Cunningham at supper instead of with his own daughter. It was time Colonel Ware resumed his real duty, the general's manner had implied when he came to lead Miss Cunningham back to the ballroom.

Nicholas went to claim his second dance with Grace. There was something a little arctic about Mrs. Haviland's smile, he thought. Grace smiled as graciously and sweetly as ever at him. The partner with whom she had sat for supper had disappeared. Nicholas bowed and smiled.

"My dance, I believe, Miss Haviland," he said. "The only waltz of the evening, I have been told."

She set her hand lightly upon his sleeve.

A fanatical *peace lover*, he thought with a private smile of amusement. She had no idea what she was talking about. Peace at all costs sounded like a worthy ideal. Any sensible person who had experienced anything of life would have to agree with her that violence never solved any problem but was in fact self-perpetuating. However, trying to solve an altercation with words or with *love* rarely worked except in the realm of dreams as one floated upon white clouds, which were *not*, incidentally, puffy pillows but rather clusters of chilly dampness ready to rain upon the world of reality below.

But enough of Miss Winifred Cunningham. He owed Grace his full attention.

CHAPTER FOUR

Winifred spent the morning following the ball writing a long letter home to her family in Bath. She filled it with as much detail as she could remember and boasted about dancing every set of the evening, including the waltz after supper, her favorite dance in the whole world. Unfortunately, since it was the only waltz of the evening, she had been obliged to dance it with the rather plodding General Haviland, who had come to her supper table breathing fire and brimstone to snatch her from the clutches of Colonel Nicholas Ware, who had promised to dance it with the general's daughter.

"As though I offered the lady some sort of competition," she wrote. "You should just have seen Miss Haviland. She was easily the most beautiful lady present, while I was—well, not that at least. Though I did feel very splendid indeed in my new ivory gown, and Papa, ever loyal, said I looked beautiful. Even Uncle Avery raised his quizzing glass almost all the way to his eye and told me I looked very smart. I would have had you all gasping with admiration."

She told them about dancing the opening set with Bertrand

and feeling quite convinced for the first few minutes—until he coaxed her into relaxing, kind man that he was—that her right foot had turned into a second left foot. She told them about the second set with Owen Ware, whom she had mentioned before when he and Bertrand escorted her to the Trooping the Colour ceremony. She had danced another set with Adrian Sawyer, son of Viscount Dirkson, who was married to Great-Aunt Matilda, Grandmama's sister-in-law while she had been supposedly married to the Earl of Riverdale.

She expected a long, lazy day ahead since Papa, having decided to take the day off work, had gone somewhere with Uncle Avery, and everyone else would surely be tired after such a late night. It would give her the chance to do some quiet reading and to spend time in the nursery with the five children. She always enjoyed playing with them.

She was not given the opportunity to pursue either activity, however. Just as she was sealing her letter and wondering if Uncle Avery would object to being asked to frank such a fat bundle—it included a double page of sketches for the benefit of her brother Andrew, who had been born deaf and thus could neither speak nor read and write—a footman came to ask Miss Cunningham to join Her Grace in the drawing room at her earliest convenience.

Winifred handed the man her letter before shaking out her skirt and running her hands over her head to make sure no long strands had worked their way free of her bun. She went upstairs to join Aunt Anna and Great-Aunt Louise, the dowager duchess, in the drawing room.

"Oh my!" She stopped abruptly in the doorway, gazing in amazement at the vases of flowers adorning every available surface.

"You have admirers," Aunt Anna said as Winifred advanced a

few steps farther into the room and the butler closed the door quietly behind her.

"I do?" Winifred said, looking incredulously at her aunt. "You mean these are all *mine*? But what nonsense."

"Your modesty does you credit, Winifred," the dowager said—she was another of Grandmama's former sisters-in-law. "However, calling nonsense the floral offerings chosen and sent by some of the most eligible gentlemen of the crème de la crème of society is perhaps a bit insulting."

"But I daresay they did it only because it was expected of them," Winifred said. "It is the custom, is it, Aunt Anna? I did not know."

The duchess exchanged an amused glance with her mother-in-law. "It is quite as we predicted, is it not?" she said. "It is a customary courtesy but not an obligation, Winifred. Why do you not look at the cards to see who has sent them all? I expect coffee to be brought here at any moment. In the meanwhile, you may wish to take note of which gentleman sent you which bouquet so you can thank them accordingly the next time you see them."

Winifred was embarrassed by the lavish displays, suggesting as they did that she had been enormously successful last evening and could now expect an army of suitors. Could society really be this . . . *silly*? The first card she looked at, which was attached to the largest, most ostentatious bouquet, was from General Haviland. She laughed.

"A most inappropriate response," Great-Aunt Louise said dryly. "The poor man, whoever he is."

"General Haviland," Winifred said. "Do you suppose he harbors a secret passion for me?"

"Well, he *did* waltz with you," Aunt Anna said. "Though I must confess he probably offered because he was afraid your supper companion might forget his obligation to dance it with his daughter and waltz with you instead."

"Which was utterly absurd of him if it is true," Winifred said, nevertheless entertaining a brief vision of herself waltzing with the colonel and dancing upon air.

"Only because Colonel Ware has meticulously good manners and would not have forgotten the obligation," the dowager said. "You looked far more striking last evening, Winifred, than you seem to realize. You have always favored simplicity over fussiness, for which I commend you. And do *not* look at me that way. I will not be told that my words are nonsense."

Winifred smiled at her and read the cards on her other bouquets. Some names she recognized—Bertrand's, Adrian's, Owen's among them. A few surprised her, most notably that from Colonel Ware, though he had just been described to her as having meticulously good manners, and obviously sending flowers to a lady the morning after she had made her official come-out into society was the correct thing to do. Some surprised her even more since she could not even remember the gentlemen from whom they came.

How . . . Well, absurd. Yet she was pleased by what Great-Aunt Louise had just said—*You looked far more striking last evening, Winifred, than you seem to realize.* The dowager was not given to flattery.

One more bouquet, arranged as the others were in a crystal vase, was delivered while they were drinking their coffee. She smiled when she saw it was from Papa.

After that Winifred expected the quiet day she had anticipated. It was not to be, however. Early in the afternoon her father was in the middle of telling them about his morning touring the houses of Parliament with Uncle Avery, when he was summoned to the library downstairs.

"To be continued later," he said before he left.

He returned to the drawing room after half an hour and looked curiously at Winifred. "Go down to the library if you will, Winnie," he said. "Uncle Avery is there."

So was a tall, thin, serious-looking young man with a beaky nose and eyeglasses, who made her a stiff bow. Winifred did not recognize him.

"The Reverend Bowles wishes a word with you, Winifred," her uncle said with what sounded like a weary sigh. "He has your father's permission."

Permission? Permission for *what*?

She was to find out as soon as Uncle Avery had strolled from the room and shut the door behind him.

The Reverend Bowles, who had apparently been at the ball last evening, though he had been unsuccessful in procuring her hand for a set of dances, had come to offer marriage.

He was a younger son of a gentleman of property and modest fortune, he explained, and was vicar of a church in a Shropshire village, where he was comfortably settled in a substantial vicarage. He enjoyed the services of a competent housekeeper, who undertook all the menial tasks of the household, including the cooking, but his bishop had pointed out his need of a wife to be his helpmeet in all the numerous duties that attended his position. Most of them were social duties—heading various ladies' committees, for example, and organizing the volunteers who supplied the floral arrangements that always adorned the church, visiting the local gentry, delivering baskets to the poor and sick, and occupying the front pew of the church during divine services as an example to the parishioners of both the devout worshiper and the perfect wife. In time it was to be hoped there would be children, who would be raised with the modesty and decency and piety expected of the family of a godly minister.

Winifred listened, appalled. She could not remember this man from last evening. She found his manner stiff and somewhat pompous, though no doubt he was nervous. His hands, which might have given him away, were clasped at his back.

"I wish to make *you* my wife, Miss Cunningham," he said in conclusion, bowing to her again. Neither of them had sat down, she realized suddenly. "I could not help but notice with approval last evening the modesty of your appearance and manner."

So much, she thought, for her great-aunt's pronouncement that she had looked striking. She had struck this man as plain and sober enough of demeaner to be a clergyman's bride—a clergyman she had never met before today.

"I thank you for your kind offer, Reverend Bowles," she said. "But I really must decline."

She was about to add some sort of explanation but decided against it. She did not owe him any. Had he really believed her to be so desperate that she would accept the offer of a total stranger? She supposed he must have convinced Papa that his offer was at least a respectable one.

"I have your father's nod of approval," he said, sounding surprised.

She doubted it. Papa, she guessed, would have given only his permission for the Reverend Bowles to address his daughter.

"My father allows me the freedom to think and make decisions for myself," she said. "He would not stand in the way of any reasonable offer of marriage I chose to accept, just as he would not urge me to accept an offer that was ab—that was not to my liking." She had been about to say *abhorrent*, but that would be cruel. "I am not looking for any offer of marriage."

"Yet what else can a young lady expect of life?" he asked her. "I assure you I am well able to support you, Miss Cunningham."

"I find my life quite fulfilling as it is," she said. "Good day to you, sir. A servant will show you out."

She turned and left the room without further ado. Well, at least, she thought as she climbed the stairs back to the drawing room, she would not have to go through life without ever receiving a single marriage offer. Success indeed. Something of which to boast in her spinsterish old age. She wished she had not already sent her letter on its way to Bath. She would have to write another tomorrow entitled *The Sequel*.

She shook her head. What an extraordinary thing to happen. Had he really expected . . . ?

Clearly he had.

Winifred never did find time either to read or to play with the children in the nursery. No sooner had she finished giving her account of what had happened in the library to Papa and Aunt Anna and Uncle Avery and Great-Aunt Louise than a steady stream of visitors began to be shown into the drawing room, most of them male. They came to pay their respects to the duchess and the dowager duchess and to compliment Miss Cunningham on her success the evening before. Several of them brought invitations from their mothers or sisters to attend other events of the Season—an evening at the theater, a garden party, a literary soiree, another ball.

She was launched upon society, Winifred thought as Adrian

Sawyer, who had escorted Great-Aunt Matilda here, grinned and winked at her from across the room. She had known him since she was a girl and thought of him as a cousin, which in a sense he was.

She did not want to be involved in the whole dizzying round of social entertainments with which the *ton* amused itself during the spring months in London. It was not why she had come here. Papa was ready to start painting Lady Jewell's portrait, and she would be needed to greet people who came to the small gallery he always rented to display some of his uncommissioned portraits while he was here, though the opportunity to work on those had lessened as his fame grew. Winifred was also needed to take new commissions for him, or at least to write down the names of those who wished to secure Papa's services. He always decided for himself which to accept.

It was at the gallery that she had met Owen Ware when he had come there with Bertrand one morning and she had explained to him how her father worked.

"Fascinating," he had said, and he had seemed to mean it. He had stayed when Bertrand was forced to leave to keep a prior appointment, and he had asked question after question and listened attentively to her answers. "I can see that Mr. Cunningham does not flatter his subjects. Yet he does." He had frowned at the contradictory nature of his own words as he gazed at the portrait of Mrs. Brown, widowed proprietor of a popular bakery in Bath, whose nose was broad and flat and redder than the rest of her face, and whose mouth was unnaturally small. Her cheeks, round as apples, had begun to droop from advancing age. No one could call her lovely, yet there was a look of kindness in her eyes that Papa had captured—Winifred never understood how he *did* that—and comfort in her overall expression that gave her individuality and a sort of beauty.

"Papa painted it from memory after visiting the bakery numerous times when he lived in Bath as a young man," she had explained. "But Mrs. Brown laughed when he showed the picture to her and declined to have it hanging in either the bakery or the rooms above it, where she lived. She told him he was going to have to make his subjects look stunningly beautiful and at least ten years younger than their real age if he hoped to make a successful career as a portrait painter. She did not understand his art at all. I am delighted that you do."

They had sat together on a bench facing the paintings and talked and talked until finally they were interrupted by the arrival of a couple of potential customers and Winifred had got to her feet to answer their questions.

They had talked, she and Owen, about every subject upon earth, it seemed, without ever having to force the conversation. She assured him she had no talent as an artist—or as anything else in fact. She explained to him about her family and what they did and how she helped and felt she made herself useful. She told him about Robbie, the brother who had had terrible behavior problems when he joined their family and the patience with which Mama and Papa had dealt with him, trying to find a way past his fierce hostility and temper tantrums to the frightened child they were sure lurked within. She told them about their eventual discovery that a dog helped enormously—the first of their menagerie of dogs and cats. She told him about Andrew and the frustration of not being able to communicate with him. She told him of the sign language she had devised to help them speak to him and he to them. She told him of her efforts to teach the signs, limited though they were, to her family.

Owen had been enormously interested.

"It is what I have been trying to do with my life ever since finishing my university studies and balking at the prospect of taking holy orders and so tying myself to the tedious and often frivolous demands of a country parish," he said. "All I really want to do is help people with troubled or difficult lives, especially *young* people, to find a solution so they may live independent, happy, and productive lives. Without in any way condescending to them, that is, or forcing on them my ideas of what those solutions must be. It is not easy, as I have discovered several times in the past seven or eight years. I have such a strong tendency, because I have always lived in wealth and comfort, I suppose, to assume I know the solution to problems of young people who have never known any such things. It is not easy sometimes to be humble, not to feel *superior* just because one wears decent clothes and speaks correct English and has never been either hungry or homeless."

They had talked on and on until the interruption of the new arrivals and again when he had called a few more times at the gallery alone, deliberately seeking out her company. They had grown comfortable with each other. Winifred had tried to persuade herself that it was a mere friendship they shared, but she had begun to dream of a closer connection. She had never been in love and never expected to be. Yet she had known for a few years that she could not marry without at least some deep mutual affection being involved. The security of being a married lady with a home and perhaps children of her own would not be enough.

Yet she did yearn to be married.

Perhaps Owen . . .

He had come calling this afternoon with Bertrand, who brought the news that his twin sister had been delivered of a son a few weeks earlier than expected. Owen took a chair close to Winifred's while her great-aunts exclaimed with delight and tried to soothe Bertrand's anxieties as he told them he would be leaving the following day to see his new nephew. Though he did turn to Owen to assure him that he still intended to attend the summer fete at Ravenswood, Owen's home, to which he had been invited.

"I am hoping," Owen said to Winifred, "that you will take advantage of the fine weather we are having today by driving in Hyde Park with me after all your visitors have left. I will return at five with my curricle if you will. You have not lived, you know, if you have never made an appearance there at the fashionable hour. Everyone who is anyone drives or rides or walks there daily to see and be seen." His eyes twinkled at her.

"Oh dear," she said. "I distrust that word *fashionable*. I doubt I have anything to wear that will be remotely suitable."

She had heard of the fashionable hour, when all the latest fashions, both male and female, were on full display and gentlemen ogled the ladies from horseback while the ladies flirted back from their open carriages by twirling their parasols and pretending not to notice or care.

Oh, but she absolutely *must* experience it for herself at least once in her life.

"Anything you wear seems to suit you," Owen said gallantly.

Plain and ordinary, in other words, she thought.

"I was about to ask you myself, Winnie," Adrian said as he came to stand in front of them, a cup and saucer in his hand, a shortbread biscuit balanced on the latter. "That will teach me to delay until it is almost time to take my leave."

Winifred laughed. "Perhaps the two of you should fight a duel over me," she said. "Or perhaps I will settle the matter without violence and accept your offer, Owen, since it was the first to be made. Thank you. I will look forward to it."

Her sprigged muslin dress would do, she thought, and her straw bonnet, which was sadly lacking in all adornment except for the blue silk ribbon that circled the brim and tied in a bow to one side of her chin. At least it was no more than one year old. She doubted she would be banished as a social impostor from that particular area of Hyde Park. Most people would remember her from last evening. Besides, she would be with the Honorable Owen Ware.

"Enjoy yourselves," Adrian said before strolling away to see if Great-Aunt Matilda would be ready to leave soon.

An hour later Winifred had changed her dress and settled her bonnet over her freshly brushed hair and tied the ribbons just so. Owen was already waiting in the hallway when she came downstairs. He nodded his approval.

"You will do very nicely, Winifred," he said. "Shall we go?"

Her father and Aunt Anna had come down behind her to see her on her way, but it was Owen who handed her up to the high seat of his curricle and made sure her skirt was arranged about her ankles and in no danger of catching on the carriage wheels. She waved to the two on the pavement as he gave the horses the signal to start, and the vehicle moved smoothly away from Archer House and on out of the square.

"I had a letter from my eldest brother—the Earl of Stratton, that is—this morning," he said. "He was interested to learn that you are the daughter of the famous Joel Cunningham, portrait artist. He is considering asking your father to paint a new portrait of our mother. Do you believe it is something he will be willing to do?

At Ravenswood, probably, rather than here. My mother has an aversion to London and comes here only when she absolutely must. It could be a project for the summer—if your father is free and agreeable, of course. I know he is a very busy man and chooses the subjects for his portraits with great care. He was telling me about it last evening at the ball. It seemed a bit of a coincidence that Devlin's letter came today."

"I cannot answer for Papa," Winifred said. "Though I will ask him if you wish."

"I am quite sure Devlin and Gwyneth would be happy for you to accompany him too," he said. "Ravenswood is lovely in the summer. At any time, in fact. They would probably welcome your mother too."

"And all my brothers and sisters?" Winifred asked him, laughing. "I am sure the earl and countess will be aghast when they learn of the broad invitation you are throwing out. I will not hold you to it, but I will talk to Papa."

He fell silent then while he maneuvered the curricle through the gates into the park and along a broad carriageway, which was crowded at this time of day. Denser throngs of people, horses, and carriages up ahead indicated the hallowed circuit, where the fashionable crowd paraded. The sounds of raised voices and laughter filled the air.

A few weeks of the summer at Ravenswood Hall in Hampshire, Winifred thought. It was a seductive prospect, especially if Owen intended to be there too. Not that Papa's accepting the commission was a foregone conclusion, of course. He was looking forward to being back home in Bath for the summer. And she was not at all sure Owen's brother and sister-in-law would be agreeable to the idea of having nine other people, apart from her and Papa, staying at their home, palatial as it was reputed to be. Or that Mama would be agreeable, or that leaving home would be possible for her.

"Tell me about your family," she said. She knew very little of the Wares except that his eldest brother was an earl and another brother was a cavalry colonel. "Tell me about your *mother*."

It was not a question he was able to answer in any detail, for his curricle soon joined the crowd at the circuit and began the slow progress around it. The object, of course, was not to get anywhere, except about an elliptical route, but rather to hail friends and acquaintances and, more often than not, stop for a chat with them while those vehicles behind were brought to a temporary halt. Winifred wished she had brought a parasol, as so many ladies around her had. They gave their owners something to do with their hands. She did not know what to do with hers.

They did their share of greeting and waving and holding short conversations. Owen appeared to be well known, and Winifred recognized a number of people who had been at the ball last evening. It was not so surprising, she supposed. The cream of society had been there and were here now. The same people probably went everywhere during the weeks of the Season. One wondered what they found to talk about every time—though gossip was probably endlessly new.

She was beginning to relax and even enjoy herself when her eyes alit upon a smart curricle that had just arrived on the scene. Colonel Ware was driving it, looking handsome in his uniform, though it was not the spectacular dress uniform he had worn at Trooping the Colour. He looked just as gorgeous. Perhaps more so, as one could see his face today beneath the brim of his shako. At his side sat Miss Haviland, who looked every bit as beautiful as she had last evening, clad in deep rose pink, an elaborately trimmed bonnet covering most of her very dark hair, which nonetheless looked sleek and shining as well as elegant.

They were a stunningly handsome couple.

The two brothers stopped to exchange pleasantries, while the two ladies nodded politely to each other. It seemed doubly absurd to Winifred that General Haviland had treated her last evening as though she were his daughter's rival for Colonel Ware's affections. Or perhaps he had simply been offended that the colonel had chosen to sit with anyone other than Miss Haviland.

"Miss Cunningham," Colonel Ware said, inclining his head to her.

"Colonel Ware," she said. "I must thank you for the bouquet you sent me today. It is lovely."

It struck her that it was perhaps not a tactful thing to say in the hearing of Miss Haviland, but the woman must understand that it had been merely a courtesy on his part.

"I am delighted you like it," he said.

"I do," she said, and a few moments later, they parted company.

"Miss Haviland is very lovely," she said as they drove back toward the park gates.

"She is indeed," Owen agreed. "She was twice betrothed as a younger woman, each time to a high-ranking military officer. But in each case the man was killed in battle, one in Spain, one at Waterloo."

"Oh," Winifred said. "How tragic for her."

"After a number of years, she seems ready to try again," he said.

"Or perhaps the general and his wife have talked her into it. She is at least my age, possibly older. They are probably afraid she will not marry at all."

"And Colonel Ware is the chosen one?" she said. "Another military man? Have they not learned their lesson?"

"Not everyone dies in battle, thank goodness," he said. "Though Nick came very close on one occasion. It was a good thing Devlin and Ben—our older half brother—were there in the Peninsula at the time with another regiment. Ben stayed with Nick for a long while to look after him. He refused to let him die. Nick says he often cursed Ben for it at the time. He had a long, painful recovery. And I do beg your pardon. I am not supposed to talk to ladies on such matters. I sometimes forget that I should treat you as I treat all other ladies. You are always so willing to talk about the harder, often seamier realities of life. You are very different. In the best possible way, of course."

She thought he meant it.

"Besides," he said, returning to the original subject, "there are no wars in Europe at the moment. Nick is not on active duty. And yes, the Havilands are pretty obvious about their matchmaking intentions. But Nick will marry Miss Haviland only if he chooses to do so. So far he has steered clear of any commitment. However, I do believe he may be ready to settle down at last."

He concentrated upon the traffic outside the park while he drove her back to Hanover Square.

How could Colonel Ware not be ready to settle down? He was not a very young man, after all. Miss Haviland had no noticeable flaws in either looks or manners. She knew the military life and the hardships it sometimes brought women. They were clearly being encouraged by her parents. Neither of them had looked reluctant either last evening or this afternoon.

But what about Owen?

So far, he has steered clear of any commitment.

Had he been describing himself as well as his elder brother?

You are always so willing to talk about the harder, often seamier realities of life. You are very different. In the best possible way, of course.

One friend to another.

Not the slightest hint of any romantic intent.

CHAPTER FIVE

Nicholas had still not decided quite when he would ask for a formal interview with General Haviland and where, after that, he would pay his addresses to Grace herself, assuming the general granted his suit, which he would surely do. Nicholas was increasingly aware of his procrastination. If only he could be *sure*. Did other men have this problem?

His mother helped him make up his mind. There was a letter from her on the breakfast table in his rooms a week or so after the ball. He settled to read it after helping himself to food and leaning to one side as his man poured his coffee. She had heard from Kitty, her longtime friend, now also her sister-in-law, married to Uncle George Greenfield. The two of them were in London for part of the Season and had attended the Duchess of Netherby's ball. Nicholas had seen them there and talked briefly with them. Nicholas, Aunt Kitty had written to Mama, had paid marked attention there to Miss Haviland, daughter of his superior officer at the Horse Guards. He had danced twice with her.

"Kitty describes her as a paragon," his mother had written. "Beautiful, elegant, and accomplished, with polished manners and impeccable lineage. You had better be careful if you do not wish to have your name linked inextricably with the lady's. Kitty is, of course, a bit of a gossip, but one can be sure that what she has noticed, other people have noticed too. On the other hand, if you have fallen in love at last and are ready to declare yourself but are ever hesitant about the time and place—I know you so well, you see— perhaps you should suggest bringing the young lady and her parents to Ravenswood for a few weeks of the summer. How delightful that would be, and Gwyneth agreed with me when I suggested it to her. We could have a betrothal celebration involving both families. Simply say the word and Gwyneth will send an official invitation. Owen will be here too and Stephanie. Ben too for the week of the summer fete. Perhaps even Pippa."

Gwyneth was the Countess of Stratton, Devlin's wife. Stephanie was Nicholas's younger sister. Ben was his oldest brother—half brother, to be exact. He was the natural son their father had had with a mistress before his marriage. Pippa—Philippa Arden, Duchess of Wilby—was the elder of his two sisters.

Nicholas lowered the letter to the cloth and shook his head in exasperation as he tackled some of the food on his plate before it got cold. Trust Aunt Kitty! In his opinion, she was more than *a bit of a gossip*. Now the whole of his own family as well as General and Mrs. Haviland were in imminent expectation of a betrothal. Though perhaps having his hand forced was not such a bad thing. Maybe it was just what he needed. If he asked Gwyneth to send the invitation, then he would indeed have no choice but to move ahead with his marriage proposal—provided the invitation was accepted, that was. Nicholas could think of no reason why it would not be.

He had *not* fallen in love. But his mother saw everything in terms of love and romance these days. She had remarried a few years ago and had been blissfully happy ever since with her second husband, who was the village carpenter of all things, though he was also a gentleman in his own right and her childhood friend. They lived what appeared to be an idyllic life in the picturesque cottage they had had built in a secluded spot on the banks of the river that divided Ravenswood property from the village of Boscombe.

Now Mama longed to see her remaining unmarried children—himself, Owen, and Stephanie—happily settled in love matches, though to be fair, she rarely pushed the issue. She was generally content to let her children live their lives their own way while she lived hers.

He nodded to the offer of a second cup of coffee and picked up the letter again. He would write to Devlin and Gwyneth, he decided, and suggest the invitation himself. The request would be better coming directly from him. He had no doubt they would do as he asked. They always enjoyed having houseguests, especially during the summer. Once the invitation was sent and accepted, a few bridges would have been burned, for no one would be able to doubt his intentions.

He read the rest of the letter, in which his mother informed him they were also possibly expecting the presence at Ravenswood of Mr. Joel Cunningham, the renowned portrait artist, for a few weeks. Devlin was trying to engage the man to paint *her* portrait. Succeeding would be quite a coup, apparently, since the artist's services were much in demand and his time was at a premium.

"He takes a few weeks to produce one portrait," she explained. "For a week or so he simply observes and talks to the subject and gets to know her as a person. Only then does he paint and reveal that person from the inside out, so to speak. It sounds quite alarming. I am not sure I would enjoy having my soul laid bare by a stranger intent upon depicting me just as I am for the world to see. However, Matthew feels I should do it, and so I will if the artist agrees to come. It is all very well for Matthew, of course. *He* is not the one facing the ordeal of being painted. Apparently, Mr. Cunningham does not paint couples or families but only individuals."

Joel Cunningham was Miss Winifred Cunningham's father, Nicholas remembered. A young woman of curious appeal. She was not pretty or well endowed with feminine attributes. She dressed simply and wore her hair scraped severely back from her broad forehead to make herself look even plainer than she might otherwise be. She made no attempt to be charming or alluring. She was opinionated and wrongheaded. She was opposed to all warfare, for the love of God, and considered him cruel because he was a military man. She was unfeminine in every imaginable way—or ought to be. The curious thing was that she was not. Owen seemed taken with her. Was it possible he was considering marrying her? Perhaps it was Owen who had suggested the portrait to Devlin. Perhaps he expected that she would accompany her father if he did indeed accept the commission.

The image of the baby abandoned on the steps of an orphanage in a basket had somehow seared itself on Nicholas's memory. Life had done well enough for her since then, it was true. But how could one recover completely from such an inauspicious start? It had been total abandonment. Not even a stranger turning over a bundle of baby to someone inside the orphanage, with perhaps a pathetic explanation and tears. She claimed quite adamantly that the mystery of her origins did not bother her, that she considered Cunningham and his wife to be her real parents and all their children to be her siblings.

Nicholas did not believe her.

He roused himself to finish reading his mother's letter. Apparently, Cunningham was not sure of his answer. He usually spent the summer at home with his family and was unwilling now to be away from them after a bit of a lengthy stay in London. He had written to his wife for her opinion.

"Gwyneth has written to her too," his mother wrote. "She explained that she understood completely and would respect the need of the family to be together at home during the summer months if that was what they wished. However, if Mrs. Cunningham would come with him to Ravenswood, and all their children too, she and Devlin would be delighted to have them, especially as there is to be the village fete during the summer and the children would be sure to enjoy it. And other guests are expected too. It would all be very jolly. So this is where matters now stand, Nicholas. I remember the large gatherings I used to host at the hall during the summers and long to see a return of the merriment, especially as someone else would be organizing it all this time and I could retreat here to the cottage whenever I wanted some peace. Apparently, the Cunningham family is rather large. But you have met the eldest daughter. Kitty mentioned that the Netherby ball was in her honor and that both you and Owen danced with her."

Nicholas wrote to his elder brother before going off to the Horse Guards for the day. He dared not delay to ponder the wisdom of making such a decisive move. The time for procrastination was over.

Joel Cunningham had indeed been inclined to refuse the invitation to Ravenswood to paint the dowager Countess of Stratton's portrait. The commission would take a few weeks of the summer at just the time he always tried to be at home and did not schedule any events there. He and Camille sometimes took the children to visit other family members—usually Camille's brother Harry and his wife and children, or her mother, the Marchioness of Dorchester, both of whom had homes large enough to accommodate them all. At other times they stayed at home to enjoy picnics and day excursions and generally relax in the slower pace of life before all the usual activities began again.

This invitation was intriguing, however, not to mention startling, since it had eventually included his whole family. Ravenswood was reputed to be a vast mansion with a correspondingly large park surrounding it. The children, even those who were old enough to protest that designation, would enjoy themselves enormously, he suspected. So would Camille. And there would be the added carrot of a summer fete to dangle before them.

Even so, he would possibly have refused without even consulting Camille if he had not had a sudden thought. Owen Ware made frequent visits to the small gallery—which also served as Joel's studio while he was in London—and sat, sometimes for hours, on the hard, backless bench facing the few paintings on display, talking with Winnie. He had taken her with him to watch Trooping the Colour from privileged seats. They had danced at the duchess's ball. He had taken her driving in his curricle the following day, the same day she refused a marriage offer from that thin, seemingly humorless young clergyman, who nevertheless had a secure, useful future to offer her. She and Owen Ware had visited a few larger galleries together and a few charitable projects favored by young Ware, who seemed to have a strong social conscience, just as Winnie did.

Had he been blind? Had a romance been blossoming between the two young people under his very nose without his realizing it?

Camille would cluck her tongue and toss her glance toward the ceiling if she knew he could be so stupid. She frequently accused him of living half his life with his head in the clouds and the other half seeing nothing but the canvas before him. Perhaps she had a point.

Young Ware was a handsome young man, of course, and ever cheerful and gregarious. He was attractive to the ladies, as had been evident at the ball. He was a younger brother of the Earl of Stratton but must have independent means since he kept bachelor rooms in London and showed no signs of poverty or debt or the need to find gainful employment. Joel estimated his age to be in the late twenties, a few years younger than his military brother. Would it be surprising if Winnie was dazzled by his attentions?

Was Ware able to see past the deliberate severity of her appearance and the forthright honesty of her conversation? Was he considering making a match with her? Was it possible she would accept if he offered marriage? Was it possible the young man had devised a scheme for luring her to Ravenswood, where he could pursue his acquaintance with her at his leisure and decide if he wished to move the friendship to a different level? Was that why he, Joel, had been invited to paint the dowager countess's portrait and why his family had been invited to go with him to Ravenswood when it had seemed he would not accept for himself alone?

He was desperately fond of his eldest daughter and would have given her the moon and the stars if they had been available to him. He felt that way about all his children. Did he have a right now to refuse the commission without consulting Camille so he could discover her thoughts on the matter? He missed her dreadfully when they were forced apart, usually by his work. He always thought of her as the other half of himself. The better half, to use the old cliché. By far the more sensible half.

He wrote to her, only to discover that the Countess of Stratton had already sent a very warm and genuine invitation to the whole family to be their guests at Ravenswood. Camille thought they ought to accept. It would be such a wonderful change for the children to see new places and meet new people. Apparently, there were to be other guests there too.

Winnie seemed pleased when he told her. There was even an unusual blush of color in her cheeks and a brightness in her eye.

"It will be good for the children," she said, unconsciously echoing her mother. "The park there is huge, according to Owen's description. There is a large lake. And boats. It will be good for Mama too."

"And for you?" he said.

She hesitated. "Yes," she said. "For me as well."

So they were going. Bag and baggage. Utter madness. Eleven of them. All for one portrait.

Or *was* that all?

One month later, Winifred was less sure the visit to Ravenswood Park was a good idea. Mama had always said that when the family went anywhere all together, they were like a traveling circus. Today Winifred had to agree with her. They were squashed into two carriages, all eleven of them, with another trundling along behind, laden with all their baggage and Nelson, Robbie's large dog, who was not at all happy about being separated from his master and promptly threw up his breakfast all over the floor after a scant two miles. The only good thing about it was that he was not packed into one of the other carriages. Robbie looked a bit green after cleaning up.

Actually, it was ten of them who occupied the carriages. Papa had chosen to ride up on the box with the coachman, to a clamor of protest from Robbie and Jacob and Alice, who each thought *they* should go up there too. Mama had vetoed that idea in a hurry even though Robbie had recently turned fifteen and considered himself a man.

They were on their way to Ravenswood Park, Papa to paint a portrait of the Dowager Countess of Stratton, the rest of them to give him company and enjoy the hospitality of the earl and countess, who did not know what was facing them. If they were expecting rows of perfectly groomed and perfectly behaved children, who spoke only when spoken to, they were going to be shockingly disappointed.

And if *she* had been looking forward to seeing Owen again—in the hope of his being largely responsible for bringing Papa here and thus the whole of her family, meaning that he wished to pursue a relationship with *her*—then she was rapidly changing her mind. She had hoped, when she left London with Papa, that Owen felt for her as she felt for him—a definite romantic attraction, that was, as well as a friendship. She had hoped he might make her a marriage offer while she was at Ravenswood, and they could celebrate their betrothal there, both families together, and proceed to live happily ever after.

It seemed an absurd hope after she had returned home.

She had always told herself, of course, that she really did not mind remaining single all her life, that it would be infinitely better than making a loveless marriage with someone worthy but tedious. And she had meant it. But there had always been the dream too of meeting someone she *could* love as well as find endlessly interesting. She had just never expected it to be more than a dream. Who would want her, after all? She had nothing to recommend her. Only the Reverend Bowleses of this world would even think of offering for purely practical purposes—to bear and raise his perfect, pious family, to head the ladies' church committees, to hand out charity baskets to the deserving poor, and to gaze adoringly up at him from a front pew as he delivered his sermons at divine services, while everyone else in the congregation fell asleep.

During the weeks she had spent in Bath, reality had set in. Owen Ware was the brother of an *earl*. He would demand—and his family would expect—something far more in a bride than Winifred could offer. She had mistaken friendship for something more romantic. Foolish of her! It was really quite embarrassing.

And now, when they were finally on their way to Ravenswood, it struck her that they might all be seen as vulgar, even though Mama was herself the daughter of an earl and had been *Lady* Camille Westcott until the great catastrophe had stripped her of everything, including her lifelong devotion to behaving with pride and dignity and strict observance of all that was correct for a lady of her rank and standing. She had been a detestable snob, she admitted cheerfully now.

Winifred sometimes wished she could see her mother as she had been then. She was totally different now. She almost always looked slightly disheveled, with hair that refused to remain confined by pins, no matter how many she used, and clothes that were sometimes slightly rumpled and even grubby from the hands of children clinging to her skirts or climbing into her arms to nestle on her shoulder. She often went barefoot in the house, sometimes even outdoors. And she was happy and relaxed, rarely allowing her temper to be ruffled despite crying children or quarreling children or children who liked to shriek with excitement as they dashed about, playing. There was a nursery in the house, but it was one of the most perpetually empty rooms there.

Owen would take one look at them and flee. He would find some friend to visit for a few weeks until they had all gone back home. But had she not heard that Bertrand was going to Ravenswood for the fete? Owen would have to stay to entertain him.

Goodness only knew how the earl and countess would react to their arrival. Poor things. They would find themselves hoping Papa could complete this particular portrait in record time.

But she would soon find out. The carriages had just turned off the main highway to drive through the pretty village of Boscombe. They skirted the edge of a large village green, the church and an inn and a smithy as well as a shop on the far side of it to their left, while to their right flowed a wide river, and across the water a very picturesque thatched cottage with a bright red door set in an exquisitely colorful garden.

Winifred knew they were close. She guessed the cottage belonged to Owen's mother. He had described how she had had it built just before she remarried even though the mansion at Ravenswood was vast.

Winifred heard the echo of that thought—*the mansion at Ravenswood was vast*—just as it came into sight on a slight rise farther back from the river. She swallowed awkwardly and ignored all the exclamations of awe and excitement from her siblings. *Vast* was not an extreme enough word. Not even *mansion* was. It was *palatial*, a gray stone structure three stories high, with large windows and a central arch and tall turrets at either corner. One of them was topped with what looked like a large glass onion. From her vantage point as the carriage rumbled across a stone bridge and proceeded to climb the slope between two flowering meadows occupied by sheep, which had stopped their grazing to watch them pass, she could see that the side of the house was as long as the front. It must be square. Was there a central courtyard through that arch?

"Oh," she said, her voice drowned by those around her. It was not really an exclamation of wonder, however. It was more a moan of despair. *This* was where he had been born and raised? And she had had the effrontery to hope he would marry *her*?

Her hopes, which had been fading anyway during the past month, plummeted into oblivion.

The very first person she saw was Colonel Nicholas Ware, who was coming on foot out of a side lane to their right, an older lady on his arm. His mother? Winifred felt instant dismay and tried to lean back out of sight. A man accustomed to rigid military discipline would be horrified by the lack of discipline in the Cunningham family. He would be disgusted. It had not even occurred to her that perhaps he would be here too. Did military officers get leave occasionally, then?

He was not in uniform, nor was he wearing a hat. His nearblond hair was ruffled by the breeze. He was sprucely dressed, though, in clothes more suited to the country than to town as he frowned up at the carriages and raised a hand in greeting. Winifred was not sure if he had seen her or not. He was probably acknowledging Papa.

She scarcely noticed the lady with him, though she was, presumably, the reason they were all here. She must be the Dowager Countess of Stratton. They must be coming from her cottage.

"Who is *that man*?" Sarah asked. She had been just a baby when Mama and Papa adopted her from the orphanage at the same time as they had adopted Winifred. She was blond and exquisitely lovely and growing up fast. Her voice was filled with awe and admiration. "He is *gorgeous*."

And probably twenty years or more older than Sarah. Winifred had to agree, though—with the greatest reluctance. He did indeed look gorgeous. No man had the right to look like that. Or to ruffle her feelings when they were already threatening to overwhelm her.

"Colonel Nicholas Ware," she said. "Younger brother of the Earl of Stratton. And the lady is probably his mother. She lives at the cottage we saw from the village."

But there was more to worry about than just Colonel Ware and his unexpected appearance here. Why did she always feel so self-conscious in his presence anyway? As though he was constantly looking at her and passing unfavorable judgment upon her. As he no doubt was when he thought about her, which was probably not often. She had called him *cruel* to his face. She had also made an idiot of herself by telling him she was opposed to warfare when it was not exactly true. Why should she care what he thought of her, though? She did not. It was Owen in whom she was interested. Though only as a friend, she told herself firmly.

And now she was about to meet the earl and countess, whom she could see descending the steps from the front doors of the main house. At least she assumed it was them. A young lady was coming behind them—as well as Owen, looking his usual genial self and beaming at her when he spotted her in the second carriage.

Mama was in the first carriage with the younger children. The earl waited for a footman to open the door and set down the steps and then offered his hand to help Mama descend. He greeted her with a bow while the countess smiled and said something to her before turning her attention to the children, who were spilling out behind Mama and gathering about her like frightened chicks to grab a fistful of her skirts lest they be torn away.

Owen bowed to Mama and smiled at the children while the young lady—Lady Stephanie Ware?—said something to them and coaxed Samuel and Alice to take a few steps away from their mother.

Then Papa was down from the box of her own carriage and shaking Owen's hand while the earl came to help Winifred out of the carriage and her siblings came tumbling after her. They fairly filled the courtyard.

"Miss Winifred Cunningham, I assume?" the earl said after introducing himself. "Welcome to Ravenswood."

He included Andrew in his greeting. Her brother was clinging to her arm, making incoherent sounds of distress.

"These people are friends," she told him in the sign language she had devised over the years. "We will be staying here." She indicated the whole family and the house before them.

"I am so glad you were all able to come," the countess said while her husband greeted Papa. "The summers are for family and friends. We always enjoy sharing our home during these months. There is enough space for an army, as you can see. Our housekeeper will see you to your rooms, where you can settle in before coming to the drawing room for tea."

"*All* of us?" Mama asked.

"Why not?" the countess said. "Our own children will be coming down too. They have been awaiting your arrival with barely leashed impatience. Ah, here comes Mother. You will want to meet your reason for being here, Mr. Cunningham. We feel very honored to have secured your services. Not many people are so fortunate, we have heard."

Owen strode up to Winifred at last, smiling warmly. He took her hand in his and squeezed it.

"I am delighted you were able to come," he said. "You will enjoy Ravenswood, I am sure."

She expected him to continue with an assurance that he would enjoy showing it to her, but instead he turned to smile at Andrew and shake his hand. And Winifred was aware every moment of the approach along the terrace of Colonel Ware with the dowager countess.

She felt stifled and was considerably annoyed by the feeling. What *was* it about him?

Chapter Six

Nicholas led his mother into the thick of the fray. All was noise and bustle as children of all ages, newly released from two of the carriages, quickly found their voices and their legs and dashed about, calling to one another and pointing—at the sheep in the meadow below the house, at the archway into the courtyard, at the glass sunroom on top of the west wing, at the lake just visible in the distance.

His mother was undaunted. She even seemed enchanted by all the chaos and smiled warmly at the children as she went to shake Mrs. Cunningham by the hand and express the hope she had not found the journey from Bath too exhausting.

"Not at all," that lady assured her. "I only wish I had more than one lap. All the children wanted to cuddle on it, but only the twins succeeded, one on each knee. The others complained and yawned and fidgeted and asked a hundred times if we were *there* yet until they finally dozed off out of sheer boredom."

"And you?" Mama asked, laughing.

"Not a wink," Mrs. Cunningham said cheerfully.

She took Nicholas by surprise. She was really very young—and rather lovely. She could not be much older than he was, perhaps no older at all. But of course, Winifred Cunningham was her *adopted* daughter. It was possible there were no more than thirteen or fourteen years between them in age. The thought was a bit jolting. Even Joel Cunningham, to whom he had been introduced at the Netherby ball, was probably no older than forty.

Nicholas looked about at the family after bowing over Mrs. Cunningham's hand and shaking her husband's. They looked like a happy group of youngsters. He hated to see children so rigidly disciplined that they would not move a muscle or open their mouths when outside the nursery.

He liked children generally. It really was high time he had some of his own. He hoped Grace was not of the school of thought that decreed children belonged in the nursery and should speak only when spoken to when they were out of it.

Devlin was introducing Mama to Mr. Cunningham. Nicholas had assured her she would like the man. He had seemed a decent sort during the brief conversation they had had at the ball.

A large dog of shaggy appearance and no obvious breed had just been released from the baggage coach. It shook itself furiously and galloped toward the oldest boy before throwing itself against his legs in an ecstasy of joy at their reunion. The boy rubbed its head with both hands and pulled its ears, and it panted happily up at him before trotting about the gathered masses, identifying friends and sniffing at strangers. It paused before Nicholas and tried to sniff his crotch.

"Nelson!" the boy and Miss Winifred Cunningham said in

unison, the former with stern authority, the latter in an agony of embarrassment.

"Sit!" Nicholas commanded and was a bit surprised when the dog obeyed. "He is a family pet, is he?"

"He is mine," the boy said, a certain degree of hostility in his voice. "And he does not do that for anyone but me."

"I am delighted he made one exception for me today, then," Nicholas said. "How do you do, Miss Cunningham?" He shook her hand. "I trust you had a comfortable journey?"

The dog trotted to the edge of the terrace to gaze longingly across the lawn to the sheep in the meadow. Another word of command from the boy convinced him to abandon any idea of galloping off to terrorize them.

"Yes, thank you, Colonel Ware," Miss Cunningham said.

She stood very still, her hands clasped before her, looking anything but comfortable now. She was expecting him to bark them all into military order, perhaps? She really did not like him, did she? Perhaps because he had ridiculed her claim to be opposed to all warfare.

"Before everyone disappears inside," he said, "perhaps you would be so good as to identify them all."

"Certainly," she said. "Though you will not remember them afterward. You have already met Mama and Papa. Emma and Susan are clinging to Mama's skirts, one on each side. They are twins, identical twins, as no doubt you can see."

"And which is which?" he asked. They were remarkably alike. They even wore identical clothing.

"Susan is on Mama's left and Emma on her right," she said. "It is scarcely necessary to be able to tell them apart, however. They are inseparable and tend to be known collectively as Emnsue. And lest you think Mama is not sensible enough at least to dress them differently, I must explain that dressing them the same was not her choice. They have always insisted upon it, even down to the color and width of the bows in their hair."

They were maybe three or four years old.

"Samuel is the one climbing into Papa's arms," she said, "though he has been told repeatedly that he is getting too old to keep on doing that. He is six."

"But why grow up before one must?" he said.

"Alice, the one with the curls, is holding Sarah's hand and looking toward the meadow," she said. "She is eight. Sarah was adopted with me when Mama and Papa married. She was just a baby at the time."

The older girl, Sarah, was perhaps twelve or thirteen years old and showed all the promise of great beauty.

"Andrew is the one standing apart and gazing at the stonework on the house," she said. "Mama and Papa adopted him when no one else would. He was born deaf and thus is unable to speak or read and write or communicate with others. He is very special."

Very special to *her* maybe, Nicholas thought, while others might find it more comfortable to avoid a boy who could neither hear nor speak—nor read or write. Miss Cunningham's look softened on her brother, however, and he half smiled back at her as he turned away from the house. Perhaps that old cliché about love needing no language had some truth to it. Owen had been attracted to her because she cared, as he did, for people who might need a helping hand. But how could one help such a child?

"And the one with the dog is Robbie," she said. "He came to us because the orphanage could not do anything with him. He was . . .

difficult. No one wanted to keep him. Two families who took him brought him back within a week. Mama and Papa adopted him without a trial period. He had to belong *somewhere*, Mama explained to us. Why not with us? Why not, indeed? We all adore him."

The boy was about fourteen or fifteen, a dark-haired lad with a dour, morose look about him. He was the sort of boy who often ended up as a recruit in a foot regiment, being whipped into shape by a sergeant, sometimes literally. Such boys often ended up as sullen, ruthless killers.

Miss Cunningham would disapprove.

So, incidentally, did he, though often it was a preferable fate to ending up in one of Britain's jails or kicking away their lives at the end of a rope.

And that was the family. As well as Winifred Cunningham herself, of course, the eldest. Disciplined, as neatly and plainly dressed as she had always been in London, without any obvious attempts at feminine appeal. Except that he had thought of her numerous times in the past month, especially after he had learned that she would be coming here for a few weeks of the summer with her father and the rest of the family.

He had already committed himself by then to coming too. He had given Gwyneth and Devlin the nod, and they had invited General Haviland and his wife and daughter to Ravenswood. He was still plagued by doubt about the expectations he must have aroused, but soon it would be too late to change his mind. It was already too late, in fact. They were due to arrive tomorrow, and they would hardly be coming if Grace intended to say no.

Devlin and Gwyneth were making a move to lead everyone inside. Devlin offered his arm to Mrs. Cunningham while Gwyneth took Cunningham's. Owen gave his arm to Mama.

Which left him with an obvious role to play, Nicholas thought. But before he could offer to escort Miss Cunningham inside, Stephanie came hurrying up to her and shook her hand and kissed her cheek.

"You are Winifred," she said. "I have been so looking forward to meeting you. Owen has told me much about you. I do hope we will be friends. I am Stephanie, by the way, Owen's younger sister and the only one he could try to bully when he was a boy. With sad results, I might add—for him, that is. Let me take you up to your room. You are in the east wing, on the top floor. I believe you will love the view from your window."

She linked an arm through Miss Cunningham's and led her toward the house.

Nicholas made sure all the children were following their parents inside. Not that he was called upon to herd them along. They went scampering up the steps in pursuit as though the only alternative was eternal abandonment. The twins held each other's hands as though their very lives depended upon it.

They were an interesting lot, Nicholas decided.

Colonel Ware had stood scowling on the terrace while Winifred identified the children. Or so it had seemed to her. Perhaps she was being unjust. He had greeted Mama and Papa kindly enough, and he had asked her to identify the children for him when he might have ignored them as beneath his notice. Winifred stood in front of the window in her bedchamber, absently brushing her hair. Perhaps he had been merely squinting in the sunlight, not frowning at all. He very probably would not remember a single name for the rest of their time here, however. She had probably wasted her breath.

Except, perhaps, Nelson's name. That wretched dog. What an embarrassment *that* had been. Also, very surprising. Nelson had never been known to obey any command that did not come from Robbie. Yet he had obeyed Colonel Ware instantly. Robbie had not liked it.

She had been disappointed when Owen chose to escort his mother inside rather than her. She had also been alarmed at the possibility that Colonel Ware would then feel obliged to do the honors himself. Thank heaven for Lady Stephanie, who had taken over her care and brought her up here along with Sarah and said again she hoped they would be friends. Oh, Winifred so hoped they would. Lady Stephanie, she estimated, was a few years older than she. Yet she was still unmarried. It would be interesting to discover the reason since her mother and the earl and countess had surely given her all the exposure to high society she could possibly need. She was the daughter of an earl. She probably had a large dowry and was much sought after. She had a round, pretty face, which was animated and glowing with good health. She was warm and friendly.

Winifred was always interested in young women who remained single, apparently by choice more than by lack of opportunity. She wanted to know the reason why. She suspected that many such women were of strong, decisive character—such a rarity—and would not settle for less than perfection. Perfection as *they* saw it, that was, not as society dictated.

The room that had been allotted Winifred was not in the nursery wing with the younger children, she had been pleased to discover, or to be shared with any of her siblings. Sarah, *very* pleased not to be classified as one of the children, was in the room next to hers on one side while Mama and Papa were on the other side. Robbie was up here too, next to Sarah.

This was a lovely, spacious room, bright and cheerfully furnished and decorated in varying shades of yellow and spring green. It had a view over rolling parkland to the east of the house and what looked like a walking alley in the middle distance with a straight line of trees on either side of it and possibly a summerhouse at the north end—she could not see the structure fully from here. In the far distance was a line of hills.

She longed to get outside to explore. She had hoped Owen would offer to show her around later, both inside and out. There must be so much to see. She hated to admit it, but she had been a little disappointed when he had not done so but instead had given his attention equally to her whole family, as his siblings were doing.

The Earl and Countess of Stratton had welcomed them warmly. So had the dowager countess. Winifred believed Papa would thoroughly enjoy painting the dowager, though he sometimes actually preferred to tackle subjects who were not obviously beautiful. The Dowager Countess of Stratton was, though she was an older lady, probably in her fifties. She was also dignified and elegant and gracious in manner. She had not frowned at the somewhat unruly behavior of the children out on the terrace. Papa would no doubt see it as his job to bring out that graciousness—no, *kindliness*—in his portrait while not downplaying the beauty and dignity. Winifred knew so well how his artist's mind worked. She had spent years listening to him and wishing she had some of his talent. Even one ounce. Alas, she had none.

She washed her hands and face in the small dressing room

attached to her bedchamber and set her hair in its usual knot at the back of her head. She was pleased to note that her bag had already been unpacked and everything neatly put away or, in the case of the toiletries, displayed on the washstand.

Was Owen pleased to see her? Her as an individual, that was, not just as a member of her father's family. He had told Stephanie about her. She still dreamed of working with him, for they shared a vision of the life they both wanted to live. She had thought herself in love with him by the time she went home from London with Papa. But that had been absurd and not at all typical of her. At home, after all, she met all kinds of men at their various events. With a few she had enjoyed a friendship. But love? What exactly *was* love anyway? Romantic love, that was. Unfortunately, it was impossible to define. And how could one trust to only feelings anyway? During the past month she had felt a yearning for Owen Ware. But had it been any stronger than her yearning when she was in London to settle back into her old, familiar life at home with Mama and Papa and the family and the busy schedule of the arts center?

How could she yearn for both? Were they not mutually exclusive?

She was very glad of the tap on her door that interrupted her tumbling thoughts. Lady Stephanie had come to take her and Sarah down to the drawing room for tea. Apparently, Robbie was already down there, though not in the drawing room. He was walking Nelson outside.

"For the first few days you may feel as if you need a ball of string to help you find your way back to familiar territory," Stephanie said as Winifred stepped out into the corridor to join her. "But you will soon grow accustomed to the house—four distinct wings and a courtyard in the middle."

Winifred had guessed correctly about the courtyard, then.

Sarah was coming out of her room too. "What a gorgeous house this is," she said. "Though I was afraid to venture out of my room lest I get lost and never be found. Thank you so much for coming to fetch us, Lady Stephanie."

Winifred realized how parched and hungry she was. But were they really to be treated as honored guests in the drawing room rather than as a motley group somewhat in the nature of resident servants in a lesser room? She had not been sure before they came here.

Lady Stephanie laughed and offered an arm to Sarah. "Then hang on," she said. "I promise to try not to get lost myself. If I do, at least we will have company."

Sarah beamed happily.

After tea, a merry affair during which there was much talking, even from the younger children, and a great deal of eating, Nicholas escorted his mother back to the cottage. She was expecting Matthew to be home soon after his day's work was finished, if indeed he was not already there. She protested her son's accompanying her since the cottage was within the confines of the park and it was still full daylight, but Nicholas insisted.

"They are a delightful family, are they not?" she said when they were on their way. "Noisy and what some might call unruly, but cheerful and polite too and respectful of one another. They are being well brought up. I really like Mrs. Cunningham. Mr. Cunningham too. He seems to be an easy-mannered, amiable man. It is such a relief. I was terrified he was going to be a flamboyant, temperamental artist, who would regard me as though I were a mere object to be examined from the inside out and then painted."

Nicholas laughed and she joined in.

"Life is certainly not going to be dull here for the next few weeks," he said. "Gareth and Bethan and Awen are ecstatic to have so many new friends."

The three children belonged to the Earl and Countess of Stratton.

"I *do* like the eldest daughter," his mother said as they turned onto the path to her cottage. "Winifred. She is different from what I expected. There is no glamor there, is there? But she seems a very sensible young lady and endlessly patient with all those children. Is Owen *really* interested in her, Nicholas? In *that* way, I mean. Kitty seems to think so. Does he mean to marry her? Although my acquaintance with her has been very brief so far, it seems to me she might be just the sort of woman he needs."

"I am not privy to his plans, Mama," Nicholas said. "But they certainly became close friends in a very short time in London, and he seems pleased that she is here."

"Then I will hope for a happy outcome, whatever it is," she said. "And Miss Haviland will be here tomorrow with General and Mrs. Haviland. A renowned beauty, from all I have heard. You must be longing to see her again. Will she suit you, Nicholas? I desperately want to see all my children settled happily, even while I try to keep myself and my hopes and opinions to myself. Without much success, I am afraid. Matthew laughs at me. Please ignore my questions."

"It would really be too bad if I were to decide at this late date that she would *not* suit me," Nicholas said. "I asked Devlin and Gwyneth to invite the Havilands here, and it must be clear to them—as well as to everyone else—that I could have only one possible motive for doing so. Ah, I see Matthew has arrived home before you."

He was standing by the hollyhocks beside the red front door, smiling at their approach.

"The guests have arrived, then?" he said.

"In a great burst of numbers and energy," the dowager countess said. "I am exhausted, Matthew. You will like them. Have you had a tiring day?"

They were beaming at each other, engrossed just like a pair of young lovers. Nicholas said a quick goodbye and strode back toward the house.

Yes, Miss Cunningham would suit Owen, he decided, though his brother showed little sign of being either smitten or ready yet to settle down. He seemed to be enjoying life too much, both the unpaid work part of it and the social part.

Was *she* smitten with *him*? Nicholas rather hoped not. He did not want to see her hurt if she had pinned her expectations upon his brother's coming up to scratch during the next couple of weeks.

He *liked* her.

CHAPTER SEVEN

All was noise and merriment out on the wide lawn before the house the following afternoon when Nicholas stood at the drawing room window, watching and waiting for the arrival of General Haviland's carriage.

Owen, his shirtsleeves rolled to the elbow, his coat abandoned on the grass, was kicking a ball around with some of the younger Cunningham children as well as Devlin's three. All the youngsters seemed to be shrieking. Miss Cunningham was in their midst too, flushed and laughing, her hair less sleek than usual, as she helped the twins and three-year-old Awen connect with the ball instead of kicking into the wind as it sailed on by. Robbie was playing with his dog, which was trying to join in the game and bowl over the smaller children in its excitement.

Mama and Mrs. Cunningham stood talking at the edge of the terrace, though even as he watched, Mrs. Cunningham stopped the ball with her foot as it rolled her way and returned it with a vigorous swing of her leg. Sarah and her father cheered encouragement to every child who needed it. He had one arm loosely about Andrew's shoulders to include him with the group. The boy otherwise tended to stand alone with just his silent world for company, though interestingly enough, he never looked actively unhappy.

Nicholas could hear the noise of the children through the open windows of the drawing room and only wished he could go down and join in the fun. However, he owed it to the guests Gwyneth and Dev had invited at his request to appear to them as if their arrival was important to him—as indeed it was. It would not be at all the thing to greet them while panting and sweating in his shirtsleeves, his hair wild.

A watched pot, it was said, never boiled, and a watched-for carriage never arrived. It was impossible, of course, to predict the exact time a carriage coming all the way from London would arrive. But at last he saw it approaching, and he checked the folds of his neckcloth and brushed his hands down the sleeves of his coat.

"They are here," he said.

Stephanie came to join him at the window. "I can hardly wait to meet Miss Haviland," she said. "I hope we will be friends. Do you love her very dearly, Nick?"

His younger sister, still unmarried at the age of twenty-five, nevertheless was a hopeless romantic.

"I am looking forward to seeing her again," he said.

She chuckled at the evasiveness of his answer. "It was a rhetorical question anyway," she said. "You must love her or you would not have had her invited here." She turned as Devlin and Gwyneth got to their feet to go downstairs to greet the new arrivals. Nicholas offered Stephanie his arm and followed them.

"Is she as beautiful as Aunt Kitty assured Mama she is?" she asked as they descended the stairs.

"You may judge for yourself in a moment," he said.

"Aunt Kitty said you make a particularly handsome couple," she said.

"Well." He looked sidelong at her. "You have your answer, then. Is Aunt Kitty ever wrong?"

"Miss Haviland would have to be very beautiful indeed if she has attracted you, though," Stephanie said. "You could have any woman you want, Nick—with the famous exception of Gwyneth, who preferred Dev." She smiled impishly at him.

"Minx," he said. "And of course I have been bravely nursing a broken heart ever since."

They were on their way down the steps to the terrace. The general's carriage was just drawing to a halt, and a groom was hurrying forward to open the door and set down the steps. The children were still at play, though Owen had rolled down his shirtsleeves and was shaking the grass off his coat before pulling it on and striding briskly up to the terrace. Mama had crossed it to wait at the bottom of the steps.

Houseguests were always given a warm welcome to Ravenswood by as many of the family as were in residence.

Devlin handed Mrs. Haviland down and bade her welcome. Nicholas helped Grace descend. Not a crease marred the folds of her forest green carriage dress. Beneath the small brim of her matching bonnet, not a hair was out of place. There was no sign of weariness on her face despite the length of the journey.

"Welcome to Ravenswood," he said. "I hope your stay here will be a happy one."

"Thank you." She smiled at him and turned to meet Gwyneth and then Devlin, who bowed over her gloved hand and raised it to his lips. She acknowledged Mama and Stephanie with a smile. Ever the cool, gracious lady.

And she was indeed beautiful. The word *perfect* leaped to mind, but surely no one was perfect.

"Mr. Ware," she said, offering her hand to Owen. "We met in London."

Nicholas recovered his manners and shook the general's hand and asked Mrs. Haviland if she had had a comfortable journey.

"I did, Colonel," she assured him. "Goodness, what a noisy crowd of children. I see Mr. Cunningham is watching them. I assume they are his family?"

Mrs. Cunningham and her eldest daughter had approached to greet the new arrivals. Winifred, looking slightly flushed, was introducing her mother to Mrs. Haviland and then Grace, who smiled at them as she had smiled at everyone else. Were there never any variations in that smile? He had not particularly noticed that about her before.

"Three of them are Devlin and Gwyneth's," he said in answer to Mrs. Haviland's question of a few moments before. "There is no happier sound, I think, than children at play."

"There is a time and a place," she murmured. She smiled as she said it, but he guessed she was less than enamored of the noise of playing children.

"There is one set of twins among them?" Grace asked.

"Emily and Susan," Nicholas said while Miss Cunningham turned her head to look sharply at him.

"They are extraordinarily alike," Grace said. "How does anyone ever tell them apart?"

"Susan has a tendency to tip her head slightly to the right," he said. "Something I have not noticed in her sister. I believe it is because when they are together, they usually hold hands and Emily stands to the right of her twin."

"How clever of you, Colonel Ware," Mrs. Cunningham said. "I had not even noticed that myself. Had you, Winnie? I have never been able to explain how exactly we distinguish between them, though we have never found it at all difficult."

"I had not noticed either," Winifred said. "But I believe you are right, Colonel."

"Alice is the giggler," he said. "But so is Samuel." He was showing off now for Miss Cunningham. She had not believed yesterday that he would remember the children's names. He had acquired something of a reputation when he was on active service in the Peninsula for knowing each man under his direct command by name, down to the lowliest recruit. Miss Cunningham was looking at him with raised eyebrows.

"Allow me to escort you inside, ma'am," Devlin said, offering his arm to Mrs. Haviland while Gwyneth slipped a hand through the general's arm.

Nicholas turned to a smiling Grace, and they followed the others inside.

"What a magnificent house this is," she said. "I look forward to seeing more of it in the coming days and more of the park."

"It will be my pleasure to show them to you," he said.

The following morning brought a note from Cartref, the neighboring estate to the east of Ravenswood, on the other side of the hills, inviting the Havilands and the Cunninghams and their eldest daughter to join Sir Ifor and Lady Rhys for morning coffee. Gwyneth laughed when she read it aloud at the breakfast table.

"They cannot wait to meet you all," she said. "Shall I accept? I had promised to give everyone the grand tour of the house this morning, but I suppose it can wait. I will go with you, of course. They are my parents."

"It is a gracious invitation," Mrs. Haviland said. "We will be delighted to go."

"I made arrangements with the dowager countess last evening to call upon her and her husband at their cottage this morning," Mr. Cunningham said. "It is time I got to work."

"It is very kind of your parents to invite us, Lady Stratton," Mrs. Cunningham said. "I would be delighted to go, but Joel and I cannot both abandon the children."

"I will stay with them, Mama," Winifred said.

She was a bit disappointed by the invitation, flattering though it was, especially for Mama and Papa. She had been looking forward to the tour of the house this morning. Owen had been going to come too. He had even promised to show Winifred his favorite parts. She had been hoping for some time just with him. However, as the countess had pointed out, the tour would wait. And Mama must not feel obliged to be tied to the children every moment of her stay here.

"There is a nurse perfectly competent to care for and amuse a whole army of children," the earl said. "Our own children adore her. She gives them what Gwyneth calls firm love. And there are a few maids who are only too happy to be called upon to assist her when there are more children in the nursery than just our own. You must feel free to enjoy your stay here, ma'am. You too, Miss Cunningham. Did I hear Owen tell you last evening that he would give you a bit of a personal tour this morning?" He looked at his brother with raised eyebrows.

"I would be delighted still to do so," Owen said, beaming at Winifred. "I am always happy to show off the family home to a new and appreciative audience."

"Thank you," Winifred said. "That would be lovely."

She did, however, end up going to Cartref. She went directly after breakfast at the invitation of Stephanie to fetch Siân Rhys, young daughter of Idris Rhys and his wife, to play with her cousins at the Hall.

"What difference will one more child make to the minders, after all?" Stephanie said cheerfully as she drove the gig. "And I daresay I will be one of the minders."

Winifred was touched by the warm welcome with which she was greeted at Cartref and enchanted by the lilting Welsh accents of Sir Ifor and his wife and Idris Rhys and his wife. She really had not known what to expect from the stay at Ravenswood. But it seemed they really were to be treated as honored guests, just as General Haviland and his family were.

Lady Rhys pressed coffee and cake upon her and Stephanie even though they had come directly from the breakfast table. And they urged Winifred to come back when *that young scamp* Owen had not decided to lay claim to her time.

"Oh, we have stories we could tell you about that lad that would raise the hairs on the back of your neck, Miss Cunningham," Sir Ifor said. "Stephanie will bear us out."

"He is hardly a lad any longer, Dad," Idris said. "He is close to thirty."

"You are showing your age, Ifor," his wife said. "He is a very responsible young man now, I have heard."

Sir Ifor laughed.

But the little girl made sure they did not settle in for a longer visit. She jumped up and down in front of Lady Stephanie's chair.

"Can we go now, Aunty Steph?" she begged.

Meanwhile, her baby brother was lying in his mother's arms, his plump cheeks still rosy from a recent sleep, and chuckling helplessly as she pretended to eat the fist he held up to her mouth.

"Give Aunty Steph and Miss Cunningham a moment to sit and finish their cake, Siân," Eluned Rhys said. "Go and kiss Dad and Grandma and Grandpa before you go."

"Sir Ifor is the most glorious organist," Stephanie told Winifred on the way back to Ravenswood while the little girl bounced with excess energy on the seat between them in the gig. "You will hear him at church on Sunday. And he conducts all the choirs—boys, girls, mixed, and adult. I swear he could make stones sing. He occasionally takes us to competitions in Wales, and almost always we win. He looks so disappointed if we do not that we promise faithfully to practice our heads off so it will not happen again."

They both laughed. But really, Winifred thought, how lovely it would be to have such neighbors. And to have a friend like Stephanie, who seemed good-natured and genuinely pleased with her company.

. . . that young scamp. She smiled inwardly. Yes, she could imagine it.

Nicholas did not go to Cartref with the Havilands. He had been planning to accompany Gwyneth as she showed them about the house this morning. He had hoped he could steer Grace away from the group at some point for more private conversation.

Perhaps he would take her out to the courtyard and sit in the rose garden with her. She would surely like that. It had occurred to him that she was perhaps uncertain of him, not sure that he really wanted to marry her. Perhaps her reserve, the fact that her smiles for him were no warmer than were those she bestowed upon everyone else, reflected her uncertainty. He wanted to change that.

She had preferred, however, to accompany her parents and Gwyneth to Cartref this morning. It was the polite thing to do, she had explained to him, rather pointedly, he had thought, in the hearing of Winifred Cunningham, who had made the opposite decision. But Miss Cunningham was more spontaneous than Grace, more likely to do what she wished to do rather than what others might think she ought to do.

Directly after waving the carriage on its way to Cartref, Mr. Cunningham, sketchbook in hand, set out for the cottage by the river for his first preportrait interview with Mama. He wanted to see her in the setting of her home, he had explained, where she was doubtless most comfortable. He was right about that. Mama spent most of her time there with her husband when he was not working at his carpentry business. They often wandered outside, hand in hand, among the flower beds they had planted with such care after the house was finished. Sometimes they sat in the small rose arbor on the east side of the cottage with books they rarely opened because there was too much distraction in the river and all the scenery, both natural and cultivated, around them. And in each other.

Nicholas hoped Cunningham would be able to capture his mother's deep contentment with her life. It was more obvious to him, he supposed, than it would be to anyone who had not known her as she used to be. It had never occurred to Nicholas, or to any of his brothers and sisters, he would guess, that she might be unhappy while they were growing up. She had always been perfectly poised and elegant. She had always given freely of her time to friends and neighbors—and to her own family. She had organized dinners and musical picnics by the lake and parties and—most taxing of all—the annual summer fete.

After what Nicholas always thought of as the great catastrophe of his father's infidelities being found out in the worst possible way at a village fete, his children had lost faith in a father they had admired and adored. Their mother had lost far more, however, though her marriage limped on for several years before their father's sudden death of a heart seizure one night while he was in the taproom at the inn.

Now she was both happy and contented. There was no mistaking the changes her second marriage had wrought in her life. Nicholas hoped Cunningham would somehow see that, though he doubted she would tell him about the ordeal of her first marriage. For while she had shielded them from knowledge of their father's infidelities during the spring months he spent in London without them, she must have known. She had chosen, as so many ladies in her situation did, to keep a dignified silence on the matter.

Nicholas found himself unexpectedly at loose ends this morning. Stephanie had undertaken the task of helping the nurse entertain all the children, including Siân Rhys. Perhaps he should help? However, when he peeped in at the nursery, he saw that Devlin was there too. He raised a hand in greeting and closed the door on the chaos of what seemed to be preparations to go outside. They would manage without him, though it was not going to be an easy task. The Cunninghams were a rambunctious lot and varied widely in age and temperament. His own nephew and nieces were high-spirited.

Owen was giving Winifred Cunningham a private tour of the

house, something upon which Nicholas would not dream of intruding—as he would not have appreciated being intruded upon if Grace had remained here. However, he soon discovered that young Sarah and Andrew Cunningham had felt no such compunction to be tactful and allow romance to take its course—if it was indeed a romance between those two. Sarah no doubt felt she was too old to be lumped in with the children. Andrew was probably bewildered by his silent, unfamiliar surroundings and considered his eldest sister the safest harbor in the absence of both his parents.

If Owen was disappointed, he was too good-natured to show it.

"Come along, then," he was saying cheerfully to his group as Nicholas came down to the hall, having decided to go for a ride. "The more the merrier."

And if Miss Cunningham was disappointed, she did not show it either. She made no attempt to dismiss her siblings. Nevertheless, it would be a kindness to join them too, Nicholas decided. At least he could keep the younger two distracted while the prospective lovers had some chance to be just with each other.

How *did* one distract a boy who could neither hear nor speak, though? How did one entertain him? He did it largely by chance when he beckoned the boy over to the French windows on the west side of the ballroom, where they began the tour. The boy's sisters had been exclaiming in awe over the size and splendor of the room, and now young Sarah was twirling in the center of the floor, her arms out to the sides while Winifred laughed and clapped her hands and Owen gazed indulgently at them both.

Nicholas pointed to the hill a short distance from the house and the temple folly perched on top, from which there was a panoramic view over the park and river and the village and countryside beyond. He slid open one of the doors and filled his lungs with fresh air. Devlin and Steph and the nurse had taken the children out there. Some of them roared around, intent upon a game difficult to identify, while others climbed the grassy slope on the south side of the hill—there were trees down the north side—and swung around the pillars of the temple. Two of them were running back down, shrieking as they tried to keep their feet beneath them. A few of the smaller children tried rolling down, screeching with fright. But Dev and Steph caught them before they came to grief, and the nurse gathered them about her to pet them and brush grass from their clothes and examine various bumps and bruises. There was no sign of blood, as far as Nicholas could see. The twins clung to the nurse's skirts, one on each side of her, until they gathered the courage to run up the hill again, hand in hand.

Andrew gazed out at all the activity and at the rolling parkland beyond it and the lake in the distance. He waved a hand when Robbie waved to him and then beckoned him. He looked inquiringly at Nicholas.

"Go," Nicholas said, indicating with a shooing gesture of his hands that Andrew had his permission to join his family if he wished.

The boy dashed outside and across the grass to his brother. He caught up Robbie's dog in a tight hug, and Nelson panted and licked his face.

"I share Nelson with Andrew," Robbie said when Nicholas strolled out after him. He looked wary and hostile, as though he thought Nicholas was planning to haul his brother back inside. "I look after him. He does not need you."

"I am happy to hear that," Nicholas said, ignoring the boy's rudeness. He squeezed young Andrew's shoulder and indicated, when the boy looked up, that he intended to go back into the ballroom. "Do you prefer to stay here?" He accompanied the words with raised eyebrows and a pointed finger that indicated the ground upon which they stood.

"He wants to stay," Robbie said. "With me. And Nelson. You can go."

Nicholas could see that he was still a difficult boy, always on the defensive, always expecting the worst of strangers. What had happened in his long-ago past to give him that general attitude of hostility? Or perhaps nothing had happened. Perhaps the boy had been born that way, just as some people—Sarah, for example—had been born with a sunny nature.

"I'll do that," Nicholas said, smiling at Stephanie and raising a hand to Devlin, who had Awen perched on his shoulder and Siân beside him, talking.

The tour continued with the family portrait gallery on the floor above the ballroom. It often served during the winter or inclement weather as a playground for the children, Owen explained, and as a place for adults to stroll.

He moved slowly along the room, describing each portrait, when it had been painted, whom it depicted, any special story attached to it. He was doing it for Winifred's sake, Nicholas saw. He had her attention riveted, and she examined each portrait closely and asked intelligent questions. She exclaimed with delight over some family resemblances she detected in long-ago ancestors.

Meanwhile, Sarah was becoming restless. Nicholas took her to look out the window at the southern end of the gallery. It was one way of amusing her and giving his brother a little more privacy. Sarah gazed out at the view.

"We have a lovely view from our home," she said. "How fortunate we are to live in the hills with all of Bath spread below us."

"There is a glass viewing room right above here," he told her. "It has prospects in all directions."

"Oh," she said. "The onion room?"

He chuckled. "Some people call it a glass tear," he said. "Though it is not the sort of room much associated with sadness. We used to go up there particularly often during wet or cold weather. It is always warm there. And cozy. Children love it most for the dozens of cushions they can use for napping or pillow fights. Do you want to go there?"

"I am not a child," she said, on her dignity.

"I spoke of children of all ages," he said. "No, you are not. You are very nearly grown up." She was at that betwixt and between age, when a growing child was never taken seriously as the adult she felt herself to be. He could remember the frustration.

She sighed. "I do envy Winnie," she said. "She is twenty-one. An undisputed grown-up. She even has a beau." She flushed suddenly and bit her bottom lip, perhaps realizing to whom she spoke. "At least, I think Mr. Owen Ware may be her beau. Though she has never said that. She believes she is far too plain to attract any suitor."

"You would like to see the onion room?" he asked.

"Oh yes, please," she said eagerly, and he called to Owen to let him know where they would be.

CHAPTER EIGHT

Fifteen minutes passed before Owen came up to tell them it was time for coffee, which was going to be served in the courtyard. Winifred exclaimed with pleasure when they reached there and she saw the fountain surrounded by a rose arbor in the center, the covered stone cloisters all the way around the perimeter, and the immaculately manicured lawn that filled the empty spaces.

"Ah. The *smell*," she said, inhaling deeply of the scent of the roses as Owen indicated a wrought iron seat among them. "Is it not glorious, Sarah?"

It was a fragrance soon rivaled by that of the coffee a servant carried out on a tray with buttered scones after they had seated themselves. They busied themselves spreading strawberry jam on the scones and heaping generous spoonfuls of clotted cream on top.

The sisters entertained them as they ate with a description of some of the activities that went on in their home in the hills above Bath. Sarah liked the musical events best—orchestra and choir workshops and performances as well as individual instruction for singers and instrumentalists. Winifred preferred the literary events—writing workshops and poetry readings and drama presentations. She also loved the art classes but insisted she could not participate because the amount of talent she had would not fill even a thimble. They both looked forward to the school performances there by the children from the orphanage where they had both spent some time before being adopted, though Sarah had no conscious memory of it. They enjoyed organizing picnics and parties for the children.

"Who would like to see the stable block in the north wing?" Owen asked when they had finished their coffee.

"I would," Sarah said, jumping to her feet. "I love horses, though there has been very little chance to ride at home. Papa keeps only carriage horses there."

"Then we must correct that omission while you are here," Owen said. "You can ride safely at Ravenswood without ever leaving the park."

Nicholas got to his feet.

"Will anyone mind if I remain here until you come back?" Winifred asked. "It is so lovely. Who would willingly exchange the scent of roses for the smell of horses?"

"And you must admit you are afraid of horses, Winnie," Sarah said, and laughed.

Owen laughed too. "By all means stay here, then," he said. "We will not be very long."

Nicholas hesitated, but good manners prevailed. "I will remain with Miss Cunningham," he said. "I spend a great deal of my life with horses. How often do I have the chance to commune with roses?"

Owen chuckled as he offered his arm to Sarah. "Thank you, Nick," he said.

But what had he done, Nicholas wondered. Miss Cunningham did not look any happier about his decision than he felt. Perhaps she had been looking forward to some quiet time, savoring the sight and smell of the roses and watching the rainbow of colored light dancing in the waters of the fountain. There seemed to be precious little alone time in her life. Actually, if he had been thinking clearly, he would have offered to take young Sarah to the stables while Owen stayed with her sister. But muddleheaded gallantry had won the day. In his world, it was not done for two men to wander off with one lady while another was left to her own devices.

He sat down.

He just wished she was not so dashed uncomfortable with him. She made him uncomfortable in his turn, a feeling that was totally foreign to his nature. With other people, including other *women*, he never had to search his mind for something to talk about.

This was what she got for sulking, Winifred thought. But really ... First her hope of spending a whole morning exploring the house with only Owen as a guide and companion had been thwarted. Then, just when it seemed it was going to happen anyway, a whole cavalcade of other people had joined them without so much as a by-your-leave. Well, three other people. Not that she had minded dreadfully about two of them. Sarah did not want to be classified with the children. That was understandable. And Andrew was feeling insecure. He did not like what was unfamiliar. But Colonel Ware? Really? Was he sulking because Miss Haviland had gone off with her parents to visit Sir Ifor and Lady Rhys when he had expected to spend the morning with her? But must he spoil *her* morning as a result?

And now, when Owen had suggested going to see the horses

and had asked if anyone else wanted to go, Sarah had shown not one ounce of sensitivity or tact but had jumped to her feet, all eagerness to join him. Winifred had ignored for the moment the fact that she really did not like horses. Or rather that she was afraid of them except when they were safely harnessed to a carriage. She had actually preferred to remain behind to nurse her grievances.

Served her right.

She frantically searched her mind for a topic of conversation. It would be tedious to rhapsodize again over the beauty of the courtyard or the splendor of the ballroom and portrait gallery. It was just what a lady guest could be expected to do—fill the silence with empty noise, that was. She refused to do it. She could try explaining to him that though she was against warfare in theory, she understood that that attitude did not solve all problems. But then he would look at her with that same condescending amusement with which he had regarded her at the ball. She could ask him about the village or about his mother's husband, whom she had not yet met. But that topic would suggest a gossip's intrusive curiosity. She could ask him about the summer fete, which was to take place while she was still here with her family. Or she could ask about . . .

Why did she never have this problem with Owen? With him, she just opened her mouth and started talking. And they always had interesting, intelligent discussions on a vast array of topics.

She did not have the problem with anyone else either, for that matter. Just him.

"I make you uncomfortable," Colonel Nicholas Ware said. "Is it because I am a military man?"

No, it is because you are gorgeous.

The very thought that she might have said the words aloud made her clench her hands together in her lap.

And impossibly attractive.

"I am not uncomfortable," she said. "How long have you been a military man?"

"Since I was eighteen," he said. "I am thirty-four now."

Thirteen years older than she. She had no business finding him attractive. But . . . did one always feel intensely self-conscious in the company of an unusually attractive man? She did not feel this way with Owen, though, and he was both good-looking and charming—and only seven years her senior, assuming he was the same age as Bertrand. For that matter, she did not feel this way about Bertrand himself, though no one could be more handsome and personable than he.

"I was the son brought up to be a cavalry officer," he said. "Just as Devlin was raised to be the earl and Owen to be a clergyman. Our father had very conventional ideas about the roles his sons would play in the world, according to the order of their birth. My sisters, of course, were raised for matrimony and motherhood."

"Of course," Winifred said. She was not sure she had kept the sarcasm out of her voice. Clearly she had not. He laughed.

"However," he said, "they were free to choose their own husbands. Steph, at the age of twenty-five, has still not chosen. She sees herself as ugly and unmarriageable with any but the most desperate men—widowers with six young children, for example. It has happened. She does not see *fat* as also beautiful. And she does use that word of herself."

Winifred would not even think of describing her as *fat*. What a merciless word that was.

"I received one marriage offer the day after Aunt Anna's ball," she said. "It came from a young man who had attended the ball, though I did not dance with him or even remember him passing along the receiving line. Perhaps he arrived after the dancing had begun. He is a clergyman in a village parish, whose bishop advised him to acquire a helpmeet in the form of a bride to take on all the duties associated more with a woman than a man—heading ladies' committees, for example, visiting the local gentry, and delivering baskets of food to the poor and infirm. Oh, and gazing up at him with devotion from the front pew of the church as he delivers his Sunday sermon from the pulpit. I was to raise the perfect family for him—a *pious* family, that is. He seemed surprised and somewhat offended when I declined his offer."

"That was poor sportsmanship on your part," he said. "I assume he proceeded with perfect correctness and spoke with your father first."

"Well, he did," she said. "But I do not blame Papa for allowing him to make his offer directly to me. He respects all his daughters well enough to allow us to make our own decisions."

"I applaud you for deciding as you did," he said, grinning at her suddenly while she felt her stomach turn over inside her.

"It was not difficult," she told him. "Are you going to marry Miss Haviland?"

She could have bitten out her tongue.

"She is very beautiful," she added, digging a deeper hole for herself and hoping her cheeks did not look as hot as they felt.

"She is," he said. "Do you think I ought to marry her?"

"Oh," she said. "I have no business giving an opinion on the matter. I do beg your pardon for raising it."

"Besides," he said, "she may not say yes, you know, even if I do ask. She has given no indication that she will."

Except to come here with her parents.

As she had come here with hers.

And he was so gorgeous it was difficult to imagine that any woman could possibly refuse him.

Owen was gorgeous too.

"Some of the events of the fete at the end of next week will happen in here," he said, indicating the courtyard with a sweep of his arm. "The baking and needlework contests almost certainly. Possibly the fortune-teller's booth. Other events will happen outside on the terrace or out in the poplar alley. You may have seen it from your room in the east wing. It is where the archery contest is always set up, though there is never any competition over first place. Matthew Taylor always wins that. Everyone else competes for the honor of coming second or third behind him."

"Your mother's husband?" she said.

"I have no idea how he does it," he said. "He almost never misses the very center of the target. And he shoots his arrows in such quick succession that one can hardly see his arm move from the bow to the quiver over his shoulder and back again."

"I will enjoy seeing that," she said.

"All the other events take place in the village," he said. "There will be booths set up around the perimeter of the green, and children's races and maypole dancing on the green. Among other things. And the culminating event, a grand ball, will be here in the evening. My mother used to organize the whole thing when we were growing up, and everything happened here. Those duties have now been taken over by a committee, which often boasts and sometimes complains of all the work involved."

"You must have had an idyllic childhood," she said. "Owen has told me a bit about his. According to Lady Stephanie he spent much of his time tormenting her, the only sibling who was younger than he."

"He rarely succeeded," the colonel said, grinning again. "Steph always gave as good as she got. If she felt a large spider crawling over her face while she was asleep in her bed, it was soon in *Owen's* bed and waking him with a roar of fright."

"He has admitted that he never got the better of her," she said, laughing.

"Has he told you about our eldest brother?" he asked her. "Ben?"

"He has mentioned him," she said. "He was your father's son from a connection before his marriage, but he lived here with you through most of his growing years, after his mother died."

"A by-blow," he said. "It meant he could not inherit when my father died even though he was older than Devlin. But he was and is a much-loved member of our family. He lives with his wife and children on the coast not far from here, overlooking the sea. They will be coming next week for the fete."

"I was almost certainly a by-blow myself," she said. "As was almost every other child at the orphanage. We did not have the security of a loving family. Or even an identifiable family at all in most cases."

She frowned. She had not meant to sound defensive or self-pitying.

"I have had security in abundance since I was nine, however," she said. "Though I must admit to having felt some envy while I was looking at your family portraits earlier. It must be wonderful to know your family history reaching back centuries and generations and to see the family likeness in some of the portraits, even the ones from two or three hundred years ago."

"I suppose it is," he said. "I have taken it very much for granted, that feeling of having family roots that run deep. I am sorry you do not know the feeling."

"I have all the love and security I could possibly want," she said. "I could not ask for better parents or brothers and sisters."

She hesitated.

"I will have to plant my own roots," she said. "Assuming I marry and have children, that is. It is by no means assured. I have refused the only proposal of marriage I may ever receive. But I am quite happy as I am."

He sat back in his seat, a slight smile on his lips while his eyes roamed over her face.

But oh, it was not true. There was an endless ache of emptiness where her past and her real family ought to be. And constant denial. And guilt that she should show such ingratitude to the fates, which had cared for her far more tenderly than she could possibly have deserved. First Aunt Anna had left Bath and married the Duke of Netherby. Then Mama—known to her as Miss Westcott at the time—had announced she was leaving to marry the art teacher. Winifred had almost not dared to attach her affections to anyone. Nothing lasted. No one *belonged* to her. Yet the more she tried to be good and pious so she would have friends and people who loved her, the more she seemed to repel them. She could understand it now, but at the time she could not.

"I am sorry," he said softly.

"For what?" she asked sharply. "For being happy as I am? Not *all* women crave marriage above all else, you know."

"That was not my meaning," he said. "But I would not wish to intrude more deeply into your pain. My guess is that you keep it strictly to yourself, and we all need secrets."

She gazed at him, dismayed. And could not prevent herself from lashing back.

"And do *you* harbor secrets, Colonel Ware?" she asked.

"Very much so," he said, surprising her. "One always hopes they will go away if one presses them deep enough."

She stared at him. Regrets over some of the atrocities of war, perhaps? She would not ask. His next words seemed to confirm her suspicions, though.

"You believe I must have had an idyllic life here," he said. "You are right about that. Until I was eighteen, that is."

He had left home to take up his commission at that age.

She waited, wide-eyed, for him to continue, but he did not do so. Sarah had come dashing into the courtyard from the north wing, flushed and disheveled, several steps ahead of Owen.

"Winnie," she cried as she came. "You ought to have come too. We went *riding*, even though I am not suitably dressed. Owen said it did not matter. He put a sidesaddle on one of the horses—the sweetest mare I have ever seen. I did not feel at all unsafe on her back. Of course, Owen did hold on to a leading string so I need not fear having the horse gallop away with me. We rode partway along the carriage path to the lake, and the children spotted us from the hill and came dashing down to watch. They were ever so envious."

"I fear I might be spending much of my time here for the next week or so giving riding lessons and leading rides," Owen said, though it did not sound as if *fear* was the appropriate word. He was smiling indulgently at Sarah, who was looking her age now that she was not concentrating upon being a grown-up lady.

And so any hope she had of spending time alone with Owen took another hit, Winifred thought. He was going to be busy entertaining the children. And serve her right again for wanting him all to herself.

There were times over the following week when Nicholas fervently wished Devlin and Gwyneth had not invited Joel Cunningham and his family to come at this particular time. Or that he himself had not suggested these two weeks for the visit of the Havilands. It could have waited until later in the summer, though everything at Ravenswood did tend to revolve around the summer fete.

He could not stop himself from making comparisons.

There *was* no comparison between the two relationships. Owen's with Winnifred Cunningham was a close friendship, perhaps a romance too, perhaps not. His with Grace Haviland was more of a formal courtship, with the prescribed end more or less written in stone.

He made the comparisons anyway.

Owen and Miss Cunningham were having a marvelous time of it, playing vigorous, noisy games with the children. Stephanie was usually with them too. The children, like those everywhere, never seemed to run out of energy. Neither did the adults who chose to play with them. Mrs. Cunningham often joined in, as did her husband when he was not working. Gwyneth and Devlin as well.

But not Grace. Nicholas was strolling on the terrace with her and her mother one afternoon when the older children were involved in a vigorous game of ball with Owen and Winifred. Stephanie had drawn Awen and Susan and Emma and Samuel apart to one side of the lawn to play a game that involved holding hands and chanting while they moved around in a circle until, at the end, they all fell down with a collective shriek. Owen called for Nicholas to come and join his team, which seemed to consist of a minority of one as everyone else was firing the ball at him. Stephanie invited Grace to join the circle game.

Nicholas grinned. "Rescue is at hand, Owen," he called, and stepped onto the grass. "Brothers united." He turned to smile at Grace.

But she had not moved. "Not today, Lady Stephanie," she said. "I am wearing the wrong dress, and my shoes are unsuitable."

"We will go inside away from all the noise," Mrs. Haviland said quietly, probably intending to be heard only by her daughter. But Nicholas heard too.

He hesitated for a moment but then stripped off his coat and strode onto the battleground to cheers from some of the children even though he was about to be their adversary. He proceeded to have a grand time.

On another day most of the children dashed off into the wooded area that bordered the river west of the meadow for a game of hide-and-seek. Owen and Winifred and Stephanie went with them. Gwyneth and Mrs. Cunningham would have gone too, but they were expecting Lady Rhys.

"Come too, Nick and Miss Haviland?" Owen called.

"Delighted," Nicholas said. "Grace?"

"It would be impolite of me not to be here for Lady Rhys's visit," she said.

So Nicholas went without her.

He invited her one morning to join a ride with two of the children who had proved they were safe on quiet mounts without his having to walk alongside making sure they did not slide off. He knew that Grace was an excellent horsewoman and thought she might enjoy the exercise, though it would not move at a pace to which she was accustomed. She said no. She had promised to accompany her mama and Lady Stratton to the shop in the village.

Nicholas went riding without her.

It was very hard to find time alone with her, even in the presence of others. While Owen and Winifred often sat in the drawing room after dinner, deep in conversation with each other, their heads almost touching, Grace always made sure she was part of a group. It might include Nicholas, but she gave him no more attention than she gave anyone else. It was perfect drawing room etiquette, of course. But this was not a London drawing room filled with fashionable guests. This was a relaxed family setting at Ravenswood. It was a *courtship* setting, as everyone understood.

When she did talk exclusively to him, as might happen if he was seated next to her at the dining table or in the drawing room, she always gave him her full attention and the full force of her charm and her smile. Her conversation was polished—and impersonal. Sometimes he got drawn in by her sheer beauty and believed that they were close after all, that she was merely being cautious because most of the people surrounding her were little more than strangers.

But he was frustrated and a bit worried.

He wondered about her avoidance of the children. Was it because of a basic shyness and unfamiliarity with them? She had no siblings, after all, and therefore no nieces or nephews. Or was it because of a definite aversion to children? Would she be different with her own? Or would she be the sort of mother who would visit them in the nursery at an appointed hour each day and leave their upbringing and education to nurses and governesses? That very real possibility filled him with misgiving.

And by God, he thought before the first week was out, he really did not know much about the woman he was now obliged to marry, did he? Except that she was perfect—in ways that had seemed to matter before he considered reality as opposed to the ideal. Who *was* Grace Haviland? It frankly terrified him that he did not know the answer. Why had he not realized it before getting Devlin to invite her here and thus committing himself?

He knew why, though. He had given up seeking out the one woman who could make him happy and whom he could make happy. He had given up on love and intuition and the heart and chosen instead to go with the head. A head that had not been functioning as it ought. A head that had considered beauty and dignity and perfect good manners to be enough. He needed to discover if there was more to Grace than met the eye, however. Surely there was. Though what could he do if there was not? There was nothing. He was committed.

The children brought his own childhood back to him with an ache of nostalgia. He and his siblings had had the same sort of freedom as the Cunninghams had. He had often used his to walk over to Cartref, where he would play for hours on end with Gwyneth or, when they were no longer young children, they would climb trees and lie along the limbs while sharing their dreams of the future. But much of his time was spent at home. He and his older brothers—and Pippa—had constantly found scrapes to get into. The younger children had squabbled endlessly until Ben or Devlin would threaten to bash their heads together, a threat that was never put to the test. Both their parents had been remarkably indulgent. Mama had spent a great deal of time with them during the spring months while their father was in London, taking them on walks and picnics, rowing them all, a couple at a time, across the lake to the small island and playing imaginative games with them there. Or swimming with them.

Those had been good days. Unfortunately, the disastrous way they had ended had caused Nicholas to block out the memories as he concentrated upon making a success of his career. He could not have those days back, of course. They were irretrievable for all sorts of reasons. But he could visit his family more often, and he could produce a family of his own. He could hope that Grace's ideas of child-rearing would not clash too drastically with his.

He knew Winifred's did not. Her claim to adore her family was no empty boast. She even paid attention to the two who often held themselves apart. She was always available to Andrew, communicating with him with the rudimentary sign language she had devised. She was always patient with Robbie, who tended to glower suspiciously at the world from beneath heavy hair, which had been allowed to grow too long. She would stand beside him, an arm loosely about his shoulders when he looked as if he might be about to erupt into a temper tantrum. He never turned his ire upon her.

Owen had the same open appreciation of children. If it was indeed courtship between the two of them, it boded well for the future. They seemed perfect for each other.

Ah, he could not keep himself from making the comparisons. He could not stop feeling a faint envy of his brother.

But what of Grace herself? She would almost certainly accept his marriage proposal. But why? Because her parents were pressing it on her? Because she was close to thirty and had decided it was time to put an end to her spinsterhood and the long years spent mourning the deaths of two fiancés? Had she loved either or both of them?

Did she love him?

He tried to tell himself that the answer did not really matter. But then he would look at Devlin and Gwyneth and at his mother and Matthew Taylor, even at Mr. and Mrs. Cunningham, and know that it *did* matter. The sooner he proposed marriage to Grace, the better it would be for him since it was something he could not avoid now.

But by God, he *wished* the visits of the Havilands and the Cunninghams had not coincided as they had.

CHAPTER NINE

The countess had taken the Cunninghams and her own children to the lake for a picnic tea. Stephanie had gone with them. The earl was to join them later, after seeing to some estate business that could not wait. Owen had gone to visit Clarence Ware, a cousin and close friend from his childhood, who had come home with his wife to attend the fete next week. General and Mrs. Haviland and their daughter had been invited to take tea with a retired military man, Colonel Wexford; his daughter, Ariel; and his sister, Miss Prudence Wexford. Colonel Ware would presumably go with them.

Winifred had been on her way to the lake with the picnic party. She had been looking forward to it, having seen the lake only from a distance so far. She loved picnic teas. Food somehow tasted more appetizing when eaten outdoors. She liked both the countess and Stephanie. However, Andrew, as he sometimes did, chose not to keep up with the pace set by the others, all of whom were eager to be at the lake so they could swim or splash around in the water or ride in one of the boats. He chose, rather, to explore every meandering rise and dip that made the terrain of the parkland so varied and attractive. Mama had offered to remain behind with him for as long as he needed, but Winifred persuaded her to go on with the others. Mama was greatly enjoying this visit—perhaps, Winifred thought, because it reminded her of the time when, as Lady Camille Westcott, she had been invited to numerous house parties.

Andrew often seemed overwhelmed by large numbers of people and boisterous activities. Even though he did not hear sound, he was very aware of his surroundings. He preferred sometimes to ignore the group and gaze at the ever-changing skies, at views, at flowers, and even at grass. And they all understood—even the younger children—and treated him with great patience, though the delay he was causing today was a bit hard for them to bear.

"I will stay with him," Winifred said. "Go on, Mama. We will be along later."

She often wondered about Andrew's inner world. It would be too easy to look at him from the outside and pity the poverty of his existence. But how could a person with hearing and speech *know* and make that judgment? Perhaps his life was as rich as hers, though in a different way, incomprehensible to her. Yes, she had devised a sort of sign language to allow some communication between them, but it was severely limited and dealt only with facts, not feelings or thoughts or dreams.

After the others had disappeared, taking all their energy and exuberance with them, Winifred felt suddenly and unexpectedly sad. Papa had finished his initial interviews with the dowager countess and was ready to paint her portrait. He expected to be finished sometime next week, though he and Mama had agreed to stay at Ravenswood for the fete on Saturday since it would be fun for all of them, especially the children. More houseguests were expected, including more children. On the Monday after, though, they would return to Bath.

They would have been here a little longer than two weeks. Any dream Winifred had had that Owen would use this opportunity to court her and make her a marriage offer had faded, and she had told herself she was content with that. There was the day of the fete itself, of course, most notably the evening ball, which sounded very romantic. But she was not optimistic that the present state of affairs would change between them. He was as friendly as he had ever been with her, as interested in the children, and as curious as ever to find out more about them, particularly Robbie and the morose, unruly behavior he had demonstrated when Mama and Papa had brought him into their family from the orphanage.

Owen had long had ideas of working with troubled and delinquent children, though various stints at volunteering his help at homes in London had opened his eyes to the fact that it was not easy or even, in most cases, possible. Feeling compassion was not nearly enough. He dreamed of a different life for them, as he told Winifred during that first week, perhaps on a farm that would give them access to the countryside and wildlife and fresh, clean air as well as vigorous hard work to help run the place and fun time for games. He wanted to encourage them to talk about what troubled them and somehow help them learn to let it go. Oh, he understood it would be no easy thing to do, that there would be no magical solution. He knew that getting into the heads of such children to understand *why* they were as they were would often be impossible. He knew they would need medical, specialized help as well as the patient assistance of other adults who felt as he did. He knew there would be disappointments and outright failures along the way. Love and the mere eagerness to help were not nearly sufficient to change the world.

But he dreamed anyway.

Winifred was excited by his ideas, especially his hope of settling down in a country home of his own, which apparently he felt he could afford. How she would love to work alongside him there, though she knew all about how difficult and frustrating such work would be. Of course, she would be unable to live on a country estate with him just as a friend.

So far, he had not hinted that he would even like her help. And, if she was honest with herself, there had never been any suggestion of romance in their friendship, either in London or here. A few evenings ago, the Earl of Stratton had suggested after dinner that Owen show her the poplar alley since she had seen it so far only from the window of her bedchamber. They could stroll along it and perhaps sit for a while in the summerhouse at the end of it, he had said. It might be a good idea, the countess had added, if they took a lantern with them in case darkness fell while they were still out there.

It was an obvious ruse on their part to give the two of them time alone together in a secluded, potentially romantic setting. Mama had smiled and nodded her encouragement. Owen had been totally oblivious. That was quite obvious to Winifred.

"A splendid idea," he had said, beaming at her. "Winifred?"

"I would love to see it," she had said. "It must be particularly lovely in the early evening and at sunset."

"Would you care to join us, Miss Haviland? Nick?" he had asked.

So they had gone off together, the four of them. At first, they had divided into their respective couples, some distance between them, but while they were strolling along the grassy alley between the two straight rows of poplars, they merged into a foursome and remained that way until they reached the summerhouse. There they sat and conversed until Miss Haviland suggested that perhaps they should return to the house before darkness fell. The alley had been quiet and secluded and all lushly green. The summerhouse was cozily furnished and gave views back down the alley and about the park. The alley and summerhouse must be among the most romantic spots in the whole park. And the early sunset had shown promise of being truly breathtaking. They had walked back in a group of four, talking cheerfully as though the word *romance* had never been invented.

But she would not think about that disappointing evening, Winifred decided now. It had merely confirmed what she had already known anyway. Thinking about it would only send her spirits plummeting even further.

She joined Andrew in one of his favorite activities when the terrain was suitable. The parkland was neither uniformly grassy nor perfectly flat. Rather, it undulated, slight rises making for energetic climbs and unexpected views, corresponding dips leading down to secluded hollows, some of them exquisitely cultivated as quiet nooks, with wrought iron seats, colorful flower beds, and the occasional lily pond or fishpond.

It was not the nooks that interested Andrew, however. It was the downward slopes. He stopped and pointed at one particularly long one and looked eagerly at Winifred, his arms flapping. She nodded and ran down with him, the two of them flying like birds and shrieking at the speed and laughing helplessly. She always loved the strange sounds he made when he laughed. They did it several more times until Winifred plopped down close to the top and indicated that she could not do it even once more.

Andrew continued alone while she sat watching, her arms wrapped about her raised knees—and felt the sadness wash over her again. She could not stop thinking of the portrait gallery above the ballroom in the west wing of the house and the long line of the Ware ancestors, stretching back several generations. She felt again the stabbing of raw longing they had caused her as she realized there was not a single portrait of any of her ancestors. Or at least, none that she knew of.

She had spent most of her life determinedly counting her blessings while suppressing all thought of her missing life before she became conscious of her existence at an orphanage in Bath. It was a very *good* orphanage, it was true, but nevertheless it was home to a large number of other children like her, with no knowledge of just who they were or where they had come from. The remaining children, fewer in number, were perhaps even worse off. They knew, but they had been abandoned anyway. Unwanted. Unloved.

She hated the times when she could not suppress such thoughts and the self-pity that came with them. They plunged her into deep gloom, from which it was almost impossible to find instant consolation in all her many blessings. She watched Andrew and felt a welling of love for him. It did not help lift her spirits, however, for she feared for him too. What did the future hold for him? Mama and Papa, surely the kindest people on earth, would not live forever even though they were still young now. And there was Robbie. And the twins, who were more than usually needy and clung to each other almost constantly. They had been separated for several months before Mama and Papa heard of their plight, each of them inconsolably pining for the other and miserable even though they were still only babies at the time. Mama and Papa took the children into their own home—together. The girls had wept a great deal for the first weeks, unwilling to let each other go even for a moment. They had never quite recovered from that forced separation, though they could have no conscious memory of it. But what did their future hold in store?

Andrew came to stand beside her to catch his breath and make sure she was watching. Then he went hurtling down again, laughing and flapping his arms like wings.

"What bird *is* he?" a voice asked from the top of the slope behind her. Colonel Nicholas Ware's voice.

She did *not* want further company. Not now. And certainly not him.

Please go away.

"I have no idea," she said. "Something big and powerful. I do not believe it matters just what it is, however, provided it is one that loves to fly free."

The fishpond at the center of the nook had caught Andrew's attention at last, and he knelt on the edge for a closer look at the fish.

"You look as though you wish you could do that too," he said.

"I did a number of times," she said, hoping he would go away if she did not turn her head to look at him. "But Andrew can sometimes run forever before he tires out."

"I meant you look as though you wish you could fly free," he said.

She shrugged. "I am not a bird."

"What is it that ties you to the earth?" he asked her.

A strange question. He spoke softly, and for a few unguarded moments she allowed tears to trickle down her cheeks while she hugged her legs more tightly.

"I have no wings," she said.

An even stranger answer. Factually it was true, yes. But even she could hear the longing in her voice.

Please, please go away.

He came down the slope then and sat on the grass beside her. He held out a clean white handkerchief and she took it wordlessly and dried her cheeks, feeling all the humiliation of crying over nothing at all. She rarely cried, even when there was a definite cause.

He took the handkerchief from her when she did not know what to do with it, and it disappeared into one of his pockets.

"Do you want to talk about it?" he asked.

And she realized something she had been steadfastly ignoring since conceiving her unfavorable opinion of him on the day of Trooping the Colour as a killer by trade and cruel by nature—never really a fair, considered judgment. She knew why she had done it, of course. It was because it would be ridiculous to develop an attachment to a man who was so gorgeous and charming and liked by everyone. Especially when she was falling in love with his brother and hoped to marry him and live the life she had always dreamed of.

The charm was real and neither forced nor insincere. Colonel Ware genuinely liked people of all ages. He liked her brothers and sisters. He liked his nephew and nieces. He even seemed sometimes to like her, despite things she had said to him that might have elicited disgust toward her.

He was *kind*.

That alone could prove her undoing if she did not guard against it.

He was going to marry Miss Haviland. At least, that was the general assumption. Why, after all, would he have allowed her to be invited here to Ravenswood with her parents if he did not have serious intentions toward her?

Miss Haviland was perfect in every way. Except, perhaps, that she lacked something in warmth. It was because she was shy, Winifred had concluded, and because she had been raised always to be dignified and behave as a perfect lady was expected to behave. She would be the perfect wife for Colonel Ware.

Except that . . .

Oh, he deserved someone who matched him in warmth, someone who *loved* him. And not just him but everyone. Her brothers and sisters did not like Miss Haviland, though only Sarah had actually said so.

But he had just asked her something—*Do you want to talk about it?*

She did not. Oh, she did not. She wished he would go away. She *never* spoke of her pain. Not to anyone, even Mama or Papa.

"I do not know where I came from," she said. "I do not know who I am."

It sounded so foolishly abject. He would think she had taken leave of her senses. He did not say anything. He did far worse. He reached out and took her hand in his and rested their joined hands on the grass between them.

"You were born and grew to consciousness of your existence with a mother and father and two brothers and a sense of identity and belonging," she said. "You learned of the parts of your life you could not remember. Baby stories. And you met other relatives and learned of your family history. You grew up with all the security of knowing exactly who you were."

Still he said nothing.

"My life began abruptly in a basket on the doorstep of an orphanage," she said. "But it had an actual beginning before that. No one has ever been sure how long before. It was estimated that I was about one month old. My birthday was set accordingly. No one knew if I had been given a name during that month of my preexistence. I suppose my mother and my father both had surnames. I do not know either. I was randomly named Winifred. Winifred Hamlin. It has never felt quite like my name, which is probably a stupid thing to say. Do you *feel* like a Nicholas? Nicholas Ware?"

"Yes," he said when she waited for his answer. "Were you treated kindly at the orphanage?"

"Oh, I was," she said. "One hears horror stories about some orphanages. None of them applied to the one in which I grew up until I was nine. I was always fed well and clothed adequately and treated kindly. I was played with and educated well at the school on the premises. Papa was my art teacher. My first teacher of everything else was Aunt Anna, whom I knew at the time as Miss Snow. I loved her dearly. And eventually, after a brief spell with an unkind teacher, Mama was my teacher."

He did not speak. Nor did he break away, get to his feet, announce his intention of going to the lake or back to the house. He waited.

Why had she even begun this?

"I was always anxious," she said. "I was always afraid of being turned out. And I *knew* I would have to leave when I was fifteen, though I would be helped to find employment. I would have nowhere, however, where I belonged. I tried very hard always to be good, always to be better than the other children, in the hope, perhaps, that I would not have to leave when the time came but space would be found for me on the staff. I became pious. I became detestable. And the more I tried to be liked, even loved, the more the other children and even the staff were repulsed by me. For I liked nothing better than to instruct the other children in what they were doing wrong and reporting them to the housemothers and the teacher when they failed to change. For their own good, of course, and to highlight the contrast with me."

Why was she doing this? She had never spoken thus to anyone.

"I was very unhappy," she said. "And very self-pitying. I had been abandoned because I was unlovable. But I could not make the strangers among whom I lived love me."

"And this is why you are sad now?" he asked her. "Even though all that has changed?"

"Usually I count my many, many blessings," she said. "But these moods come upon me occasionally. I do not invite them. I fight them and refuse to sink deeper into depression. It would be so . . . *ungrateful*."

"I think you have all the reason in the world to throw a massive tantrum," he said.

She turned her head toward him, startled. She laughed.

"I never talk about these things with *anyone*," she said. "There is nothing less attractive than a person who is constantly low-spirited and attempting to drag someone else down with her for company by whining. I beg your pardon for speaking of them to you."

"Tell me," he said. "In all the experiences you have had of life in the past twenty-one years minus a month or so, what was your happiest day?"

"I do not even have to think about it," she said. "It was the day Mama—Miss Westcott at the time—announced in school that she would be leaving as our teacher in order to marry Mr. Cunningham. I felt at first as though the bottom had fallen out of my world—again. I tried so hard to be happy for her and to tell her so. And then she sent for me for a private talk. She asked me if I would like to go with them as their adopted daughter. They wanted it, she explained, for no other reason than that they loved me. I had to offer nothing in return. They would not expect gratitude or endless piety and good behavior. They would always love me no matter what. *That* was by far the happiest day of my life, Colonel Ware."

He was holding her hand tightly, almost to the point of pain.

"I want you to promise me something," he said. "I cannot console you for your basic sadness. I cannot offer you any knowledge of your past, what preceded that basket. But I want you always to remember that day, the happiest of your life, when you are feeling overwhelmed by depression. Not a vague feeling of gratitude for all the blessings your life has given you but just that one day. Promise me."

She continued to gaze at him despite the fact that her vision had blurred.

"Remember that day?" she said. "I could never forget it if I tried. But I know what you are saying. Focus upon that to recover my happiness. I promise."

"Thank you," he said, and handed her the handkerchief again as he got to his feet and strode down the slope toward Andrew.

CHAPTER TEN

Nicholas shook his head slightly as he strode down the slope. Since when had he been a doctor for souls that had been bruised perhaps beyond repair? What good was that advice when he had no idea how to help her?

Remember that day and all your woes will be solved . . .

He could not even imagine what it must feel like to be so rootless. He had always had family in abundance.

But dash it all, he *liked* her.

The best thing he could do now was give her some privacy. She had never shared her inner self with anyone else, she had told him. He had no idea why he was the privileged one. She did not even like him or feel comfortable with him. But he believed her. She was neither a whiner nor a complainer. She had a fierce attachment to her parents and her family, especially, he had noticed, this deaf brother and the troubled one—Robbie—with the dog. And the young twins, who would undoubtedly have nasty scars of their own to carry into the future.

At least his wounds—both the physical ones acquired during the wars and the terrible blow of discovering what a blackguard his beloved father was—had come when he was old enough to deal with them. He wondered sometimes about Owen and Stephanie, who had been children at the time.

Andrew, he discovered, was no longer gazing into the fishpond, though he was still squatted down on the ground beside it. His eyes were on a pile of stones of various sizes and shapes that had been artfully arranged to one side of it in a sort of cairn. He was touching them and smoothing a finger, sometimes his whole hand, over a few of them.

Nicholas squatted beside him. The boy turned his head and frowned at him for the first moment, though he did not seem to resent his presence. He would not have heard him come, of course. The boy pointed to one large, roundish stone at the bottom of the pile. It looked as if it might be holding up the whole structure. He patted it and looked with eager inquiry at Nicholas.

"Pretty," Nicholas said. It was a stupid thing to say, not least because the boy was deaf.

Andrew touched the stone with both hands then and made a pulling gesture. There might be an avalanche if he tried pulling it out. Nicholas touched his hand and pointed to a similar stone almost at the top. But the boy shook his head vigorously and patted the stone at the bottom.

What the devil?

He wanted it, a stone that had no apparent merit except to be a weight bearer—and virtually inaccessible. But Andrew's pulling gestures were becoming more insistent. He looked intently at Nicholas and made an incoherent sound in his throat.

How *did* one communicate with someone who was totally deaf?

What on earth did he want with a large stone and a specific one at that? A dashed *inconvenient* stone. Obviously no other was going to do, however. And he was probably going to pull the whole heap down upon himself if Nicholas simply shook his head or walked away.

He sighed.

Someone was going to be displeased about this. The gardener who discovered the vandalism would complain to the head gardener, who would complain to Devlin's steward, who would complain to Devlin himself. The whole episode would become an *incident*. Assuming, that was, Andrew had not been half buried in tumbling stones and the fish stunned at the bottom of the pond.

Nicholas could see that it was going to be impossible to remove that specific stone while leaving the rest of the cairn intact. There was only one way to do it. He was going to have to dismantle the whole thing from the top down and try to piece it back together afterward, one stone short. It would not be easy. The cairn must have been there for some time. There were blades of grass and even a few wildflowers growing out from the spaces between stones, all to very picturesque effect.

He was not going to be popular with his brother.

It took a good ten minutes, perhaps longer, and that was just removing the stones one at a time. And let no one say that individual stones, even the smallest, were light in weight or easy to grip. A few of the larger ones weighed a ton—an exaggeration, of course, but they *felt* that heavy. And who would have guessed there were so many of them?

He had grown soft during the last few years from spending too many hours at an office desk, Nicholas decided. That was not a good thing. He batted the boy's hands away when he tried to help.

He did not want to have to deal with squashed fingers as well as a vandalized cairn. But Andrew grew visibly excited as his stone was gradually exposed and he could touch more of it, both hands spread over it.

Oh, for some communication tool, Nicholas thought. What went on inside the head of someone who had no way of sharing or explaining himself to others? A whole, rich world? An empty void? Nicholas suspected the former. Winifred had devised some system of sign language to convey basic information. Which was admirable of her, but it could not possibly be satisfactory. Yet the boy always seemed happy enough, even if he preferred to be alone most of the time. That last was understandable, of course. How could he be a sociable person even if he wanted to be?

Nicholas allowed the boy to help him lift the stone clear of its berth at the bottom of the pile. This one weighed a ton and a half. He hoped Andrew had no plan of carrying it all the way back to the house. But what did he want it for? It would not make the prettiest of ornaments.

Perhaps Winifred would understand, but he did not want to intrude upon her just yet. She was still sitting at the top of the slope, her arms wrapped about her updrawn legs, as they had been when he first came upon her. Her forehead was resting on her knees.

She had not told her story, including the most important missing part of it, to Owen, then? Yet Owen was the one ready and willing to help suffering humanity—as she was herself. It was not difficult to understand the connection between those two, but just how close was it as a personal relationship if she was suppressing part of herself? Was a full and lasting relationship possible without complete openness?

Was Grace suppressing a part of herself? But he did not want to revive those doubts and worries today. He did not know Grace Haviland. He had already admitted that to himself.

Andrew kneeled on the grass beside his stone while Nicholas rebuilt the pile to the best of his ability. He did not have an artistic soul, he decided at last, or an engineer's eye. The new structure seemed sturdy, but would it stand the test of time? It did not look nearly as picturesque as the old. It looked now merely like a pile of stones. But it would have to do.

Andrew was smoothing his hands over his stone, his head bent over it, his eyes closed. Nicholas would have given a great deal to know his thoughts.

He stood when he was finished, and flexed his back. Andrew looked up at him and smiled. It was an unexpectedly sweet smile. He scrambled to his feet and stooped to lift his stone. He did indeed intend to take it with him, then? Nicholas made a staying gesture with one hand. This was something he was going to have to do himself, with the boy's help. But Winifred was coming down the slope, his neatly folded handkerchief clasped in one hand. All traces of her tears were gone.

"Thank you," she said, holding the handkerchief out to him. "Has Andrew found a stone?"

"A large, not particularly pretty one," he said. "It was at the bottom of the pile. Do you have any idea why he wants it and seems determined to carry it back to the house?"

"Oh dear, it *is* large," she said. "It must be very heavy. He has seen something in it, though. It happens occasionally, and he will not rest until he has it."

"Something?" He frowned at her, mystified.

"Oh." She laughed. "That would make no sense to you, would it? Andrew is amazingly talented as a stone sculptor. My father tried very hard to teach him to paint as a way to pass the time and release his emotions. He was terrible at it and seemed quite uninterested. Then Papa discovered Andrew one day chipping away at a stone with a sharp knife. He was terrified he would cut himself and took the knife away from him—Andrew was still very young at the time. Somehow over the next few days, however, he found a knife to replace the confiscated one, and then another. It was Mama who said Andrew should be allowed to continue what he was doing, under supervision. She promised to watch him and make sure he did not hurt himself. And he produced the most exquisite mouse, all curled up and fast asleep. It was rudimentary compared with what he has done since then, but his talent was obvious from the start. Mama says he can see things in certain stones that he must release, as he cannot always release what is walled up inside himself."

She gazed fondly at her brother as she spoke and squeezed his shoulder when he looked up and pointed at the stone. She smiled and nodded.

"You and I," she said, though not aloud. She pointed first at him and then at herself, then gestured with both hands in the direction of the house and did not need to speak aloud. "We will take it back to the house together," her gestures said.

"While I stroll along behind like a benevolent uncle, my hands clasped at my back?" Nicholas said.

She flashed him a grin. "We could manage," she said. "But did I just hear an offer to carry it yourself—with my help?"

"With *your brother's* help," he said. "He ought to know every step involved in pursuing his passion. He is big enough. You may stroll along behind like a benevolent aunt and describe to me some of the things he has sculpted since that mouse. I once saw Michelangelo's *Pietà* in Rome. It was breathtaking. Matthew Taylor, my mother's husband, saw it once too and it inspired him to take his wood carving to the next level of skill. If you have not seen any of his carvings, you should ask to do so. They are in the rooms above the smithy in the village. I am sure Owen would be happy to take you there."

He was lifting the stone with Andrew's help as he spoke. He wondered what the boy had seen in this one. He hoped it was more than an ant or a ladybird.

"You are going to have to do all the talking," he said as they made their way back to the house. "Andrew and I have more important things to do—like breathing, for example."

She laughed.

She seemed to have recovered her spirits. He guessed he had come across her earlier in one of her rare moments of open vulnerability. She had never struck him as a moody person. She spoke warmly now of the figures, mostly animals, her brother had released from a seeming eternity of captivity inside stone. And yes, they were always bursting with animation as though at any moment they might breathe and move. Only his first effort, the mouse, had been sleeping.

"While I," she said as they approached the stables at the back of the house, "have no artistic talent whatsoever despite all the benefits sound and sight bring me and the proximity of a marvelously talented father and a mother who encourages all her children to try their wings even if they sometimes crash. It is very provoking." She sighed, but there was laughter in the sound.

"Believe me," he said. "You have talents in great abundance." He felt embarrassed then, hearing the fervent intensity in his voice. But it was hard to believe this was the goody-goody, overpious schoolgirl who had been detested through much of her needy childhood, if she was to be believed. And the change had come entirely because she had been offered love, total and unconditional, on the happiest day of her life.

She seemed to spend her days now giving back that love in superabundance.

She was directing them to set the stone down in a clear space just inside the stable doors and squeezing the boy's shoulder again.

"We will know exactly where to find Andrew for the next week or so," she said. "Papa brought his tools. We do not go anywhere far from home without them. He is usually the most patient boy in the world, but when he has found a new stone, he will not rest until he has it and all the tools to work on it."

She was really quite delightful when she forgot herself. Owen was going to be a fortunate man—if he ever got to the point, that was. He did not seem to be in any hurry, though the two of them were undoubtedly the best of friends. Why on earth had he not taken that opportunity for the romantic encounter Gwyneth and Devlin had offered on a platter by suggesting a walk in the alley at sunset? He would have said a firm no to Owen's suggestion that he and Grace join them if Grace had not first accepted it.

But what made him an expert on relationships?

Winifred was talking to Andrew without the medium of sound, enticing him back to the house for tea, assuring him that the stone would be safe where it was, that no one was going to run off with it. She signed something else Nicholas could not decipher until Andrew turned and offered his right hand and bobbed his head in an obvious gesture of thanks.

Nicholas shook it and winked and smiled at him.

The boy smiled back.

They must have been on their way to the lake to share in

Gwyneth's picnic, as he had been too, he thought. But they had been ambushed by a large ugly stone.

Winifred drew Andrew's arm through hers and led him out of the north wing, through to the courtyard, and on into the house for tea. Nicholas fell into step behind them.

Who would have guessed that such a seemingly plain, almost drab creature was so filled to the brim with life and warmth?

Winifred took Colonel Ware's suggestion and asked Owen at the breakfast table the following morning if he could arrange for her to see Mr. Taylor's wood carvings sometime. She had heard he kept several in the building that housed the smithy in the village. She had also heard they were well worth seeing.

"But of course," he said, beaming at her. "We will go this afternoon if he is not busy. He will be delighted that you are interested. He is sure to have something entered in the wood-carving contest at the fete next Saturday, of course, but there will be many more to see. He will almost surely take first prize at the fete, but when he offered to refrain from entering anything one year so other people would have a chance, there was a storm of protest, even from some of his most fierce competitors. He is very popular, you know. I think it is because he is so unassuming. He mingles with everyone, high and low alike. He lived a quiet, humble life in those rooms for years before he married my mother. I tell you what we will do, Winifred. We will call on Mama at the cottage first. Have you been there yet?"

"No," she said. "Though I have seen it from the village."

He chuckled. "We all thought she had taken leave of her senses when she begged Devlin for permission to have it built on Ravenswood land," he said. "I do not believe she even had it in mind to marry Matthew at the time. She intended to live there alone. There was the whole of this vast house for her to kick around in, and she had a very spacious and luxurious apartment here for times when she wished to be private. I always thought it was a sort of house within a house. But she was adamant. She was turning fifty, she was going through some sort of crisis, and she wanted a place of her own. We were all dashed upset about it and worried about her. But she assured us that none of us had done anything to offend her—except try to smother her in loving care, I suspect. We so wanted to make her life comfortable, as she had made ours when we were children. We were always afraid she would be lonely while we rushed about on our own selfish business. It's funny how sometimes we can love someone too much, isn't it?"

"I suppose most of us want to be free as well as loved," she said. "I suppose mothers want some freedom to be themselves again after all their children are grown. But will your mother mind if I arrive at her cottage unannounced?"

"I very much doubt it," he said. "She loves to entertain close family and friends. I'll dash off a note to her, though, if it will make you feel easier in your mind. You will enjoy yourself there, and I will enjoy seeing you enjoy yourself."

It was one of those moments when she felt that there was something about her after all that made her special to him—just as there was something about *him*.

They set out an hour or so after luncheon, alone together miraculously. No one else had attached themselves and decided to come too. Everyone had something else to do.

Papa was in the gallery, working on his portrait. Mama had gone too, taking the twins and Awen Ware with her. Their real destination, though, was the glass sunroom above the gallery, where there was a basket of children's books as well as masses of cushions to be jumped on or fought with or napped upon. Robbie and Nelson were out in the north wing, keeping guard with fierce intensity at the entrance to the stables to make sure Andrew was not disturbed as he carved his stone. The other children had gone with Stephanie and the earl and countess to play at Cartref with Mr. and Mrs. Rhys's children. Sarah went too to play with their baby.

Colonel Ware had taken Miss Haviland for a drive out to the hills that bordered Ravenswood to the east. He had explained to her that there was a narrow but quite safe road along the top with views across Ravenswood on the one side and Cartref on the other. Inevitably General and Mrs. Haviland had gone with them—at the invitation of Miss Haviland herself, though that had not been the colonel's intention, Winifred realized with one glance at his face before he masked his annoyance and smiled politely. What was *wrong* with that woman?

The dowager countess was strolling in her flower garden when Winifred and Owen arrived at the cottage. She smiled warmly at their approach.

"I am delighted Owen has brought you to take tea with us, Miss Cunningham," she said, reaching out a hand for Winifred's. "I am happy too that it is a perfect day so you can see the cottage and garden at their best. I am quite sure nerves are fraying for miles around here, with everyone fearing that the weather will break any day now and we will be rained upon for the fete. By some miracle it has never happened before, but the naysayers will warn that there has to be a first time for everything."

She had been leading the way inside the house as she talked and was seating them in the cozy living room as Mr. Taylor came downstairs to join them, his hair damp from a washing.

"Good to see you, Owen," he said, shaking him by the hand. "We were delighted that you were bringing Miss Cunningham for tea. I will be more than happy to take the two of you into the village afterward to see my wood carvings. It is always flattering to be asked. Though you must promise to heap praises upon them, Miss Cunningham. I am very sensitive about such matters." He shook her hand, smiling with a distinct twinkle in his eye. "I finished work early today and even did a quick tidy-up of the workshop for your benefit."

"You always do before leaving there, Matthew," the dowager said. "You hate bringing even one speck of sawdust into the cottage."

"I live in fear that you will banish me back to live where I came from if I did, Clarissa," he said.

The dowager explained to Winifred that he had lived in the small rooms next to his workshop above the smithy for years before marrying her, earning his living as a carpenter. Yet he had been born and raised a gentleman on the estate adjoining that of her own parents, ten miles or so from here. They had been very close friends during their growing years, until she married the Earl of Stratton and came to live and raise a family at Ravenswood. Mr. Taylor, meanwhile, disappeared off the face of the earth for several years, only to reappear to settle in those rooms in Boscombe. A few years ago they had rekindled their friendship.

And rather more than just friendship, Winifred thought. They were clearly very deeply in love.

Their housekeeper carried in a laden tea tray and set it down on the table between the fireplace and the sofa upon which the dowager countess sat with her husband.

How cozy this room must be in the winter, Winifred thought as their hostess poured the tea and her husband offered them dainty sandwiches and cakes. Even now the room was warm and welcoming.

Mr. Taylor was a gentleman who had chosen to give up the trappings of gentility to live and work quietly and humbly in a country village. Yet he still owned some property where he had grown up, Owen had told Winifred. He had lived in their village for twenty years or so before marrying his old friend. There must be a whole story attached to those brief details, Winifred thought, intrigued. She would love to know it in its entirety. But she had to remember that genteel people did not blurt out impulsive and intrusive questions just because they wanted to *know*.

"I am so glad your story ended happily," she said.

"Not *ended*, I hope, Miss Cunningham," Mr. Taylor said.

"I beg your pardon," Winifred said. "It was a poor choice of word."

"Mr. Cunningham is hard at work on your portrait, Mama," Owen said. "He thought at the start that it would be a difficult project because it did not offer enough challenge. You are too lovely for his artist's taste."

"Oh dear," his mother said while Mr. Taylor patted the back of her hand.

"But he changed his mind during the days he spent talking with you," Owen said. "He says you have multiple complexities of character."

"That sounds more promising," she said. "Your family runs a sort of artists' colony close to Bath, Miss Cunningham?"

"Artists of all kinds," she said. "Painters, sculptors, musicians, writers. And plays are performed there and concerts for both full orchestras and individual musicians. Lady Stephanie has told me about the choir in which she sings, with Sir Ifor Rhys as conductor.

I am quite sure they would draw an audience at home. I must suggest to Mama and Papa that they be invited."

"Splendid," the dowager countess said. "They occasionally go to Wales to compete in an *eisteddfod*. I hope I have pronounced that correctly. Bath would be almost on their route."

Mr. Taylor laughed. "Perhaps," he said, "you should have that discussion with your parents, Miss Cunningham, before Clarissa spreads the word and it is all organized."

"Oh, but they will be delighted," Winifred assured him. "And we all have a say in what happens there. We have a close connection with an orphanage in Bath. It is where I grew up until the age of nine, when Mama and Papa married and adopted me. They were both teachers there at the time."

She went on to give some details while they had their tea, hoping she was not shocking them. But they *seemed* interested and asked questions that kept her going.

Mr. Taylor got to his feet at last. "I will take you to see some of my wood carvings, Miss Cunningham," he said, "since you specifically requested it. Are you coming too, Owen? Clarissa?"

"But of course," Owen said, reaching out a hand for Winifred's and squeezing it as he helped her to her feet. "It is why we came."

"I believe I *will* come, Matthew," the dowager said. "Though I told you earlier I would not."

They set off along the path to the drive, where they turned left onto the bridge and so across the river to the village green. The smithy was on the far side of it, on the same side as the church and the inn and village shop. They ascended steep outside stairs to the rooms above the smithy, once the home of the blacksmith and his family, now a carpenter's workshop. How lovely it must be, Winifred thought, to live in or close to a picturesque rural village, where everyone knew and watched out for everyone else. Though there would also be the reverse side of that coin too, she supposed. Everyone probably knew everyone else and all their business too.

She was enchanted when they stepped inside the rooms, not least by the sounds and smells coming from the smithy below and the smell of wood up here. The rooms of the old living quarters, still kept intact and largely dust-free, were small but cozy. The window in the living room offered a picturesque view over the street and across the green and the river to Ravenswood land, though the hall itself was invisible from here.

But they had come to see the carvings, which Mr. Taylor kept on a high shelf in the large inner workroom. He had moved most of them down onto the worktable, though, for ease of viewing today. She was touched that he had prepared for her visit, as though she were someone important.

She feasted her eyes on the carvings. Some were small and exquisitely detailed. A few were larger and bolder: a field worker leaning on his hoe, squinting into the middle distance, a battered straw hat pushed to the back of his head, presumably because of the perspiration one could almost see on his brow; an elderly lady sleeping in her rocking chair, eyeglasses slipped down her nose, her mouth half open; a couple of children, their heads almost touching, intent upon the open book they held between them on their crossed legs; a baby curled into a plump ball and quite clearly rocking with laughter as it tried to suck a big toe. And more.

But it was a small pug-nosed puppy, standing firmly on all four feet, looking alive and ready to take on the world, that she stroked with one light finger while she smiled at it in delight. *Yes, little dog, confront the world. Never cower from it.*

"You are an artist after my father's own heart," she told Mr.

Taylor. "Your work pulses with life and feeling. I do look forward to seeing your contest entry at the fete."

"Thank you," he said while Owen squeezed her hand again.

"I'll buy that puppy for Winifred," he told Mr. Taylor. "So she will remember today."

"You do not need to *buy* it, Owen," Mr. Taylor said. "I was about to give it to her as a gift."

But Winifred, eyes wide with surprise and wonder, noticed the look he exchanged with his wife, and her almost imperceptible shake of the head as she glanced sideways at Winifred.

"However," Mr. Taylor said, "I will not deprive you of the pleasure of purchasing the gift and giving it yourself, Owen."

"Oh," Winifred said. "I will always treasure it."

Both men smiled at her while the dowager countess nodded. And Winifred realized something with a bit of a shock. Owen's mother thought there was a *romance* developing between her son and Winifred. And she was giving it her tacit blessing.

Was there? A romance developing, that was. And did she really want there to be? It was so hard to read Owen's mind. Or to understand her own.

But as they walked back to the hall later, having left the older couple in the workshop, Winifred felt that it was a long time since she had spent such a happy day. How lovely it must be to belong to this place and this family.

Perhaps . . .

Oh, perhaps *nothing*.

"They like you, Winifred," Owen said, covering her hand on his arm with his own. "But how could they not?"

"Thank you so very much for my gift," she said, clutching the puppy, which had been carefully wrapped, in her free hand. "I was thinking of purchasing it myself, you know, partly as a thank-you to Mr. Taylor for taking me there and partly because I really wanted her."

"Her?" Owen said, sounding amused. "The puppy is female, is it?"

"Certainly," she said. "Female and proud of it."

He laughed.

Nicholas meanwhile had arrived back from the drive over the hills he had intended to take in his curricle. But with four people, he had been forced to take the barouche instead. A narrow roadway ran along the crest of the hills, connecting the southern path through the park with the northern. It had been a perfect day, the sky blue above them and nothing to obstruct the stunning views in all directions. General and Mrs. Haviland had been fully appreciative of every vista that opened up before them and to either side. The general had even stepped down from the barouche with Nicholas for a few minutes to walk to the edge of the rise and peer over the steep sides, almost sheer in a few places. Grace had assured her mother that she was neither afraid of the heights nor made queasy by the ups and downs of the road. She had smiled at Nicholas when they arrived back at the house and thanked him for giving them such a pleasant afternoon.

Nicholas had dismissed the coachman and returned the barouche to the carriage house himself. He had unhitched the horses and brushed them down and fed and watered them while dealing with his frustrations until he could let them go. It was perfectly unexceptionable for a man who was conducting a serious courtship under the indulgent eyes of his own family and hers to take her off once in a while for a private drive in an open vehicle on his family's land. Why, in the name of all that was sacred, did she constantly avoid letting it happen? Did she not want to be alone with him? Get to know him better? Perhaps indulge in a chaste kiss with him?

He stopped beside Robbie Cunningham on his way out of the stable block. The boy and his dog were standing guard over an oblivious Andrew, who was chipping happily away at that hideous rock. The dog—Nelson—thumped its tail on the floor and panted a sort of welcome. The boy glowered.

"He is quite safe," he said as though Nicholas had declared otherwise. "I am watching him."

Andrew looked up, distracted for a moment, and smiled his sweet smile when he saw Nicholas.

"Good lad," Nicholas said, addressing Robbie. "It is what brothers do, is it not? They look out for one another. I have brothers of my own. It is what we do. They are very precious to me. *Family* is very precious."

Robbie looked suspiciously at him as though waiting for some harsher judgment. But Nicholas patted him on the shoulder and continued on his way. He tried not to imagine how Winifred Cunningham might have reacted to that drive over the hills. He had the feeling that it would have been she demanding to be let down from the carriage for a closer look at the slopes of the hill to either side of the narrow roadway. Her face would have been flushed with animation, with no thought to guarding her complexion from the sun. Grace had held a parasol over her bonneted head most of the time. But he would *not* keep making comparisons, he told himself firmly. Or keep imagining himself doing things with Miss Cunningham that he knew would make her happy.

Owen had taken her to the cottage this afternoon for tea with their mother. Nicholas suspected that his mother would be looking upon her as a potential daughter-in-law. He rather thought she would approve, unsuitable as Miss Cunningham might appear to be to other people of their class.

He, meanwhile, was all but betrothed. He was not free to dream of standing close to the edge of a precipice, holding the hand of another woman while she laughed and pretended to feel no fear at all.

CHAPTER ELEVEN

During the following week, all attention turned toward the upcoming fete as preparations proceeded in earnest. The Countess of Stratton was no longer expected to organize the whole thing, but Ravenswood was very involved nevertheless, for a significant number of the events were to take place there—the woodcarving, baking, and needlework contests, for example, and the archery and log-hewing contests. The ball too, of course, the grand culminating event of the day, but it was the organizing committee that looked after that. The ballroom at Ravenswood was the venue only because it was larger than the assembly rooms above the inn, and the ball was always very well attended, not just by adults but by children too, at least until suppertime, when they would all pile up to the nursery and schoolroom for a feast of their own and some quiet games for the older children while the younger ones were put to bed until their parents were ready to take them home.

Gwyneth went to Cartref one afternoon for a final meeting of the organizing committee, of which Eluned Rhys, her sister-in-law, was head this year. Mrs. Haviland and Grace went too to take tea with Lady Rhys and Lady Hardington, whose daughter Barbara was also a member of the committee.

Devlin was out in the stable block in the north wing, hauling out all the archery equipment, which was carefully stored between fetes, though a number of the contestants brought their own. He was checking that none of the bows or arrows had become warped since they were last used and that there was a sufficient supply of fresh string for the bows. He was also looking over the targets, which were always newly purchased for the event. No one, after all, wished to shoot into surfaces already pockmarked from the arrows of previous years.

Nicholas was out there too, examining the logs that had been hauled in, great monsters that would have to be hacked in two during the log-hewing contest, always one of the most popular events of the fete. He selected the logs that were most nearly identical in both height and girth. It was not a task to be undertaken carelessly, for there was inevitably the odd complainer among the spectators, the one who swore to having noticed small differences that had affected the outcome of a certain bout—always to the detriment of a relative or friend who had just lost. The contestants themselves had always been good sports. Nicholas examined the axes too, though they would not be given their final edge until the morning of the fete. Those also had to be as identical as they could possibly be.

Cam Holland, the old blacksmith's son, now the blacksmith himself, was almost always the winner in Nicholas's day. But that was a long time ago. Cam was still as strong as an ox, but he had retired from competition almost ten years ago. Nicholas shook his head. How time flew by. And what sort of cliché was *that*? He had lived every day of the intervening years to the full and was satisfied with what he had done with his life so far. Only one thing remained to be done to complete his contentment. He must marry, set up his nursery, and . . . And what? Proceed to live happily ever after?

But he had better not delve too deeply into that thought, which could only lead him to the uneasy feeling that he might have made a horrible mistake. The fact was that he had made his choice, based upon what had seemed to be sound reasoning. There was no going back now, and he could only make the best of the future. Being married to Grace Haviland was not going to be such a terrible fate anyway. She was everything a man of his station could desire in a wife. They were sure to grow closer once they were married. He would see to that, and he did not doubt she would too.

They were both honorable people, after all.

But why, devil take it, had he not realized until very recently that though they had been friends of a sort for a few years, he really did not know her at all, mainly because *she refused to be known*?

"Done?" Devlin asked.

"Eh? Oh, yes," Nicholas said. "Everything is ready to go."

"The archery equipment too," Devlin said. "I won't have the bows strung until the end of the week, though."

"Can anyone defeat Matthew Taylor this year?" Nicholas asked.

"Not even close," Devlin said. "I would love to know his secret. There is bound to be one. Owen is ever hopeful of actually hitting the target at least once during the contest. Do you like his chances?"

Nicholas grinned. "He is out there now with Clarence, practicing," he said. "General Haviland went with them. He told them he was something of an expert at archery when he was a young man.

That will only play more on Owen's nerves—as though he needs the provocation. One has to admire our brother's grit. His technique has always been wrong, so his chance of improving is dim. But who am I to judge? It is a skill I have never even tried to master."

Devlin slapped Nicholas on the shoulder. "I had better go and lure the general away with the offer of a glass of ale at the inn," he said. "I fancy one myself anyway. Will you join us?"

"I had better take Soldier out for an airing," Nicholas said, glancing along the stable block to the stall where his horse was snorting crossly and tossing his head. "I have been neglecting him a bit. He is not suitable as a mount for the children. If they were to inadvertently give the wrong signal, he might well go galloping off with them and not be seen again until a week from next Friday."

Devlin laughed and squeezed his shoulder. "I am off, then," he said. "I hope General Haviland is standing back from Owen's arrows by a hundred yards or so. Robbie went out there too with his dog, but I had better not invite him for a glass of ale. I might get in trouble with his parents. I rather like the boy, though. He looks like someone who has known some demons but has learned to control them. Owen has taken an interest in him."

Most of the children were out exploring the parkland near the distant hills with Stephanie and Mrs. Cunningham.

Andrew was still busy with his stone. He had spent every day working on it since discovering it, locked happily in his own silent world. At least, Nicholas thought he was happy. It would be totally presumptuous to pity him anyway. None of the Cunninghams seemed to do so. They were a remarkable family. Robbie had stood guard by his brother every day except today. His eldest sister had persuaded him to go and enjoy himself while she watched their brother. She sat now on a bale of hay someone had brought for her, her arms clasped about her knees, a far enough distance from Andrew that he would not feel intruded upon.

Nicholas had been aware of her since he came here with Devlin, though she had made no attempt to speak to either of them. Her patience was admirable. So was her love. Hours that no doubt flew by for Andrew must be long and tedious to his minder. She had brought a book out with her, but it had remained unopened on the bale beside her. She looked more informal than ever with her hair in two long braids, one over each shoulder, instead of the usual bun.

Devlin squeezed her shoulder and said something to her on his way out. She smiled up at him.

Nicholas led Soldier out of his stall and spent some time grooming him until his coat gleamed and every tangle had been brushed from his mane and his tail. He would be given a good gallop before he went back to his stall, perhaps to the lake and back. It would benefit both of them. Nicholas was feeling depressed and annoyed with himself. Life as he knew it was about to change, by *his choice*. It would be up to him to make sure it was a change for the better.

He thought of Winifred Cunningham's harrowing story, of the way her life had changed considerably for the better after that happiest day of her life when she was nine years old. And perhaps it was about to change for something even better. Her wedding to Owen, if it happened, would doubtless be the new happiest day of her life, and she would move from strength to strength with a man who suited her in every conceivable way.

Their mother approved. She had said so to Nicholas in a passing remark about the possibility of seeing *two* sons happily settled in the near future. She had been looking at Winifred at the time, weaving her way over the terrace and down over the lawn with a line of giggling children behind her as each held to the waist of the one in front.

"She is a treasure, is she not?" his mother had said. "So seemingly insignificant when one first sets eyes upon her but filled to the brim with love and a sense of fun. Owen is going to be a fortunate man."

Nicholas sighed. Envy did not help lift his spirits. It was also beneath him.

Now as he glanced her way, he saw that Winifred was watching him.

"Would you care for a ride?" he called impulsively, pausing in his task of saddling Soldier.

"I have not ridden much," she said. "There has not been the opportunity. Besides, I am wary of horses. I like to look at them, but from a distance. I am not dressed suitably anyway. And I have promised to stay with Andrew."

"Too many excuses." He grinned at her. "I believe you are a coward, Miss Cunningham."

"Well, that too," she said, and laughed.

"I can ask my own groom to keep an eye on Andrew," he said. "Though I am guessing your brother will not even notice you are gone. He has a remarkable ability to focus for long hours at a time."

"It is not so remarkable if you think about it," she said. "His whole life is spent inside himself, without the outlets for associating and sharing with others the rest of us have. He has been specially blessed since he has a talent that requires total concentration."

That was one way of looking at the boy's deafness, he thought. What most other people would consider one of the worst possible afflictions, she saw as a special blessing.

It was all a matter of perspective.

"Which is it to be?" he asked her. "Courage or cowardice?"

"You are being ruthlessly unfair," she said. "Who would choose cowardice?"

"I will put the sidesaddle on Flora," he said. "She is the mildest-mannered creature in the horse kingdom. You will enjoy yourself."

"Now *that* is a claim I protest," she said. "You cannot possibly know what will bring me enjoyment and what will bring me stark terror instead."

He chuckled, gave Soldier the order not to move a muscle, and went to fetch Flora, who nosed him amiably and came trotting out of her stall to be made ready for a ride.

Miss Cunningham, he could see, was rubbing Andrew on the back and indicating to him with clear hand gestures that she was going to go riding for a while but would be back before long. He looked up and nodded vaguely before returning to his emerging sculpture. He did not look the least like a boy about to disintegrate into panic.

Michael would take care of him.

But who would take care of *him*?

What had he let himself in for now? The fewer personal interactions he had with Miss Cunningham, the better, he suspected. He enjoyed her company too much. And, strange as it seemed, he was beginning to find her far too attractive for his own good. It was hard to understand. She certainly did nothing deliberately to attract him. She had actively disliked him until very recently, and perhaps still did.

Besides, she was Owen's love interest.

And besides again, Miss Cunningham was thirteen years younger than he. He had always thought a five-year age gap was the widest he would consider for himself. But that was when he had been planning matrimony with his head, without reference to his heart.

Idiot that he had been.

She was standing just behind him when he turned, eyeing poor Flora with obvious misgiving.

Seen close up, the horse was *huge*, and Winifred was terrified. It was not a good combination. But her courage had been challenged. She had allowed herself to be goaded into proving she was no coward. She glanced from this mount to his—the same horse he had ridden at Trooping the Colour. And her horse, the one he had saddled for her, *the mildest-mannered creature in the horse kingdom*, was almost as large. This just could not be done.

You will enjoy yourself, he had said.

Ha!

She had seen him give her brothers and sisters rides on this very horse, and they had always looked perfectly safe. *He* had looked perfectly dependable. She had never feared that they might fall off and kill themselves or, at the very least, break a limb. They had always come back from their short rides excited and begging for more. And safe.

A part of her had been envious. There was no point in denying it. How wonderful it must feel to do something so daring. To conquer her fear. To enjoy having his full attention. But she must not explore that last thought too closely.

She had been feeling a bit cross that Owen had not invited her out to the alley to watch him practice shooting arrows. He was supposedly no good at it—according to him and everyone else. Perhaps he had not asked because he was embarrassed by the thought of her watching. But he *had* invited Robbie. Of course, she had not needed to be asked. She could have just gone. Would he have been annoyed if she had? Or secretly pleased, perhaps? But did it matter either way? Was she becoming dependent upon one man's approval?

So instead of going out to the alley, she was about to act independently by doing something daring and terrifying and just a little bit exciting. With Colonel Ware of all people.

"Right," he said, turning back to her. "Let us get you up into the saddle."

It was only then that she wondered just how it was to be done. It was not as though she could prop a ladder against the horse's side, after all.

It was done very smoothly, as it turned out. He must have had a great deal of practice at this. Well, of course he had. He cupped his hands for her foot while she reached up to grasp the pommel of the saddle. She sprang upward when instructed to do so and turned to sit in the saddle. She hooked her right leg over the higher of the two horns peculiar to a sidesaddle, set her left foot in the stirrup as he adjusted it and her left knee close to the curved horn, sat upright and grasped the reins he handed her, and felt very proud of herself. And surprisingly secure. She had always thought sidesaddles must be a death trap. How did one stay on them without tipping forward—or backward—right off the horse? But this one was molded in such a way as to hold her firm and well balanced.

"You can let out your breath now," he said, grinning up at her.

She let it out on a whoosh of air. "I feel so high up," she said foolishly.

He mounted his own horse and looked immediately as if he might have been born in the saddle. He was perfectly dressed for riding, even down to the whip and the tall hat pulled firmly onto his head, and the boots, sturdy and gleaming from a recent polishing, though the leather was old. She, on the other hand, could not be more inappropriately clad if she had tried. Her dress was of a soft cotton; her bonnet was in her room at the house, as were her shawl and her gloves; her shoes were sturdy enough for the stables but not, perhaps, for riding.

But this had not been her idea, had it? Begging for a ride had been the very last thing she had intended when she came to the stables. In fact, it had not made the list at all, even in the bottom position.

And heavens, she remembered suddenly, she was wearing her hair in schoolgirl braids, as she sometimes did when she expected not to be seen by anyone outside her own family. She had only been planning to sit quietly in the corner of the stables with her book, after all.

Colonel Ware rode slowly out into the stable yard, giving Flora the order to follow him, which she did with no protest at all.

Oh. Winifred heard the firm clopping of hooves, felt the motion of the animal beneath her, and saw the ground moving a few miles below. When she had told him a short while ago that she had not done much riding in her life, what she had really meant was that she had done none at all. There had been chances—when they had stayed with Uncle Harry, for example, or with her grandparents. Various people had offered to teach her, to lead her out, to show her how easy it was and how much fun. But she had never been convinced. Riding in a gig was the closest she had got, and that was quite close enough for her.

He looked across at her. "Well?" he asked. "Good?"

"Oh, marvelous," she said. "Is that the end of our ride?"

He chuckled, but she had been only half joking.

"We will ride around to the carriage path below the front of the house and along it a little way," he said. "You must tell me if you wish to return sooner than that. I was intending to ride to the lake to give Soldier a proper airing, but we need not go so far."

She would try to make it down to the path and along it until they were past the west wing of the house, she decided, and the hill with the temple folly was in sight to their right. She gritted her teeth and followed his lead. At least, Flora did. All Winifred had to do was sit there, wishing the reins did not feel quite so flimsy, and absorb the feeling of riding while she enjoyed her surroundings and admired the proud set of his shoulders when he got a bit ahead of her. Colonel Ware's shoulders, that was.

She was *doing* this, and she was *enjoying* herself.

It was true. She laughed out loud, and he turned his head to look at her.

"I have the feeling," he said, "that this is your first ride ever, Miss Cunningham. Am I correct?"

"Well," she said. "Yes."

"Then I am honored that you have entrusted your first ride to me," he said, pulling his horse back level with her own.

"Always," she said, and then felt excruciatingly embarrassed. "I saw you on parade, remember? And I have seen you with the children."

The hill was already on their right. They had cleared the house. She was enormously proud of herself.

"Shall we go a little farther?" he suggested.

"Yes, please," she said. "But am I holding you back? This pace probably does not feel very fast to you."

"I believe we could give a tortoise a good contest," he said, and grinned again.

"You are making fun of me," she said.

"Never," he said. "I applaud your courage. And even at this pace we will get to the lake eventually. Shall we give it a try?"

"I have never yet been there," she said, and he looked at her in some surprise. "I have always been otherwise occupied. Last week, when I was finally on my way with a few pauses to run down hills with Andrew and pretend to be a bird, my intentions were thwarted by a certain stone, which then had to be carried back to the house."

"Then you will see the lake today," he said. "It was always our favorite playground when we were children. It was the scene of many a picnic, sometimes with just our mother, often with relatives and friends from the village and the surrounding countryside. Once a year, sometimes twice, our mother would organize a grand evening picnic there, with the glory of a sunset to watch, and hundreds of candles to be lit about the base of the trees and hung in colored lanterns from their branches to turn the darkness to magic when it descended, and an orchestra playing from the pavilion out on the island. And a special dispensation for the children to stay up late. That was always our favorite part. No, that is not strictly true. Every part was our favorite. Some of the adults would even dance on the grass."

"How could you bear to go away?" she asked him.

"I was the second son," he said. "It would be Devlin's home after our father's time. He would never have turned any of us out, of course. But it would not have felt like a permanent home any longer. I took the path that had been allotted me since my birth."

"And has it made you happy?" she asked.

"It made a killer out of me, Miss Cunningham," he said crisply.

She winced. "I am *not* a fanatical peace lover, Colonel Ware," she said. "Not entirely, anyway. I recognize the necessity of fighting the wars against Napoleon Bonaparte. Unfortunately, doing so involved the slaughter of thousands of men, most of them conscripted against their will. I beg your pardon for what I said at Aunt Anna's ball."

He smiled at her. "It has been the right career for me," he said. "I have felt—and feel—useful."

"Did you acquire your limp on the battlefield?" she said, and then wished she had not asked something so personal. Her wretched tongue.

"I did," he said. "And I have Ben—my oldest brother—to thank for the fact that I still have a leg at all. He threatened to bang a few heads together if any physician tried to take it off. Out in the Peninsula, physicians were regularly known as sawbones, a name they came by honestly. And I beg your pardon for adding that unnecessary detail. I sometimes forget you are a lady." He grimaced. "I did *not* mean that the way it probably sounded. I meant that I tend to think of you as a regular person."

"And ladies are not regular people?" she asked.

"I think I had better change the subject," he said, "before I dig this hole even deeper. Have you realized we are almost at the lake? Well done."

She had realized it, and the knowledge thrilled her.

"I am marvelously clever," she said, and laughed.

"Marvelously courageous," he said. "I am proud of you."

"Did we beat the tortoise?" she asked.

"By a head," he said.

Her right leg was beginning to ache from its unaccustomed positioning. The stirrup was digging into her left foot, and she understood why riders normally wore heavy boots. She was going to be stiff all over by the time they got back to the stables.

"You were right," she said, gazing at the sunlight sparkling on the waters of the lake. "This has been so much *fun*. Thank you for your patience."

"It has been fun for me too," he said, and there was something in his voice that made her turn her head to look at him. "You are good company. Would you like to get down and rest awhile before we return? Perhaps allow me to row you across to the island?"

It was very close. It looked picturesque and inviting with its small pavilion designed to look like a miniature replica of the temple perched on top of the hill close to the house. There were numerous trees to offer shade and mystery.

"I may never get back up on the horse," she said.

"You will," he said. "Trust me."

"Very well, then," she said, and he dismounted and came to lift her down after she had unhooked her right leg.

This had perhaps been a mistake, she thought with a shudder of awareness a moment later as her hands, which were braced on his shoulders, failed to keep her clear of the rest of him. She slid down his hard man's body all the way to the ground, and his hands remained on either side of her waist longer than was strictly necessary and even tightened a little as he looked down into her upturned face.

Oh dear.

She had been about to make an utter idiot of herself.

"Will you tether the horses?" she asked.

"It is not necessary," he said, releasing her and stepping back. "Not if I tell them to stay." He murmured something to Soldier and patted Flora on the rump.

Looking up, Winifred was inordinately proud of herself. She had ridden up there all the way from the house. She flexed her right leg a few times to loosen the muscles while his face was turned away.

She *had* enjoyed herself enormously. Even so, she ought not to have come. She was finding it harder and harder to ignore the foolish attraction she felt for Colonel Ware. She had masked it as discomfort and dislike for too long to keep convincing herself.

He sometimes forgot she was a lady. He thought of her as a regular person. It was some sort of compliment and ought to please her. It did. But Miss Haviland was unmistakably a lady, a very proper lady. *She* would not be caught out alone with him like this, talking about battle wounds and physicians known as sawbones. Miss Haviland was the one he would marry—because she was a lady. And very beautiful, of course.

Why had Owen not asked her to come and watch him practice archery? Someone else would have watched Andrew, as someone else was doing now—Colonel Ware's own groom, who had been standing a few feet behind her brother when she left the stable, looking quite good-humored about having to do something so potentially tedious.

But why had she not walked out to the poplar alley anyway?

"I'll fetch one of the boats from the boathouse," Colonel Ware said, and strode away.

CHAPTER TWELVE

He was enjoying himself far too much, Nicholas thought uneasily as he gave her a hand to help her step out of the boat and onto the island. He wondered if he would be having nearly as much enjoyment if this were Grace instead of Winifred Cunningham, but the stabbing of guilt he felt at the thought was pointless. It never would be Grace, not, at least, until after they were officially betrothed. That had become perfectly clear to him. She seemed not to feel any necessity to get to know him better. But even after they were betrothed or even married, would she ever be as openly happy as Winifred seemed to be now?

That was surprising, if he thought about it. Winifred had always avoided him and felt intensely uncomfortable with him when she was forced into his company. There had been signs of it today too—when he lifted her from Flora's back, when he grasped her hand tightly to help her into the boat and then out of it a few minutes later. She had withdrawn her hand as soon as she was able. But what if the discomfort had a different cause than what he had always assumed?

What if, even as far back as the Netherby ball, it had been an uncomfortable . . . awareness of him? It almost certainly had been that today when he lifted her down from the horse's back. And by God, he had felt it too. It had been unpardonably careless of him and certainly not deliberate to allow her to half fall against him and slide all the way down his body to the ground until she had her feet under her. Even then . . .

Well, even then he had found it difficult to let her go. He had come very close to kissing her. The very thought that he might have done so turned him clammy. Would she have resisted? Slapped his face? But he suspected she had felt it too for a moment.

It was a dashed good thing they had both resisted. Giving in would have hopelessly complicated both their lives.

Good God!

"I can fetch a couple of chairs if you like so we can sit awhile in the pavilion," he said. "Or I can give you the grand tour first. Which would you prefer?"

"Oh, the grand tour by all means," she said, turning to look back over the stretch of water they had just crossed to the bank and the park beyond it, with the house in the rather distant background. The horses were grazing contentedly on the grass close to the carriage path.

"I used to believe there was no lovelier place on earth than Ravenswood," he said. "I had nothing with which to compare it, of course. I did not believe I needed anything else. Though I did spend a great deal of my time over at Cartref, playing with Gwyneth, talking with her, dreaming with her. Devlin often came with me, but he spent his time with Idris and stayed away from us."

"I love to stand in the garden at home," she said, "and look at the view—hills all around and Bath spread below, the buildings all appearing pure white, especially when the sun is shining. I always think it must be the loveliest place on earth to live. I suppose there are thousands, even millions, of such places, but for many of us there is *one* that is lovelier than all others because we feel it with the heart as well as experiencing it with our senses."

And the thing was, when she said such things they were said with conviction, not, he was sure, out of any desire to impress.

"I can understand why this is one such place for you," she said.

"Come," he said, and without realizing what he was about to do until he did it, he grasped her hand in his again. Then it would have been even more conspicuous if he had dropped it. She did not snatch her hand away either. After the first moment her fingers curled about his. "I will show you the beach first."

It was at the opposite side of the island.

"A *beach*?" she said.

He laughed. "It is a pretentious name for a stretch of land that does not boast even a single grain of sand," he said. "It is actually a grassy bank that slopes into the water and keeps on sloping very gradually for some distance out, so that by the time the water reaches to the level of one's chest, one almost needs a telescope to see back to the island."

She laughed as they came up to it—it was really a very small island. "You do like to exaggerate, do you not?" she said. "I do not need a telescope to see all the way over to the far bank."

"Our mother used to bring us here when we were very young," he said. "We could all pile into the water here and splash around with very little danger of getting out of our depth and drowning, and none while her eye was upon us, as it always was. She taught us all to swim. One needs to row a boat with care when passing here. More than once as a boy I got hung up on the shallow bottom and cursed and swore when I had to jump in to heave it off."

"Are not cursing and swearing the same thing?" she asked.

"If there is a difference," he said, "then I did both."

They both laughed.

"You had a happy childhood," she said. It was not a question.

"Until I was eighteen," he said.

"You have said that before," she said. "Until you went away to join your regiment, then? Did that put an end to your happiness?"

"No," he said, annoyed with himself for answering as he had. "That was not what I meant. Shall we explore the forest?"

But she did not immediately respond to the suggestion. "Yet your tone when you said it implied that something *did* happen," she said. "Something painful. Something more than just a reluctance to leave your home behind and launch into a new chapter of your life. Oh, I do beg your pardon. Sometimes I let curiosity get the better of me. It is none of my business what happened, if anything did. None whatsoever."

He never spoke of it, even to his own family, who knew all the facts. He did not *want* to speak of it. It was a pain he would always carry with him, he supposed, pushed deep, where it belonged. He almost never even thought of it. What was the point? The past could not be changed. He guessed that they all still suffered too, in their own ways—Devlin, Pippa, Owen, Steph. Ben. *His mother*— though somehow she seemed to have dealt with it. She had all her family back, though it had scattered at the time amid great bitterness. Several years after their father's passing she had married Matthew Taylor, who, Nicholas guessed, had been her girlhood sweetheart. She was undoubtedly happy now.

"My world came to an end," he said lightly, and turned to her with what he hoped was a grin. "What more melodrama could you possibly ask for?"

"I do not ask for melodrama," she said. "Or for any other explanation, Colonel Ware. But you did somehow induce me to share my pain last week, and your answer then has given me great comfort."

He winced. "About remembering the happiest day of your life when you are feeling down about your basic lack of identity?" he said.

"Yes, that," she said. She smiled brightly. "I would indeed like to explore the forest. Is it a magic place?"

He sighed. "Let us sit here awhile," he said. He shrugged out of his coat and spread it on the grass for her to sit on. She sat in what was becoming a familiar pose, knees raised, arms wrapped about her legs, and gazed out over the lake. He sat beside her a short distance away. He could not believe he was about to do this, but apparently he was.

"I was always very like my father," he said. "More so than any of my brothers and sisters. And it was not just in looks. I had his nature too—outgoing, fond of talking with other people, sunny natured. I was what people called charming. I was aware from a very young age that I was well liked, that I never had to try hard to be noticed in a roomful of people or to draw smiles my way. People used to call me a young replica of my father, and I basked in the comparison. He was loved wherever he went and adored by people of all stations in life. He was the proverbial life and soul of every gathering he was in, small or large, but he did not seem self-centered. He liked other people and was willing to talk with anyone. He was good-looking, warm, and vital. There was no falseness in it at all, no insincerity. And it all came naturally. He was specially gifted.

"His family all adored him too, me most of all. I loved to believe that I was just like him, that I always would be. He could do no wrong in my eyes. I thought I was the most fortunate boy in the world, and the happiest, to be his son and just like him."

He stopped talking to draw a few deep breaths. She neither said anything nor looked his way. Hardly realizing that he was talking aloud, he recalled that last day of their happiness, the day of the fete, when everything had proceeded perfectly all day long, and the family gathered in the ballroom in the early evening prior to the final ball. Most of the expected guests who had been at Ravenswood all day had gone home to change their clothes and snatch a brief rest, but they would return soon, for the ball was everyone's favorite part of the day. His father, strikingly handsome in his evening clothes, had beamed on all his family with great love and pride, and they had all beamed back. There was always something a bit poignant about the ball. It was a happy occasion, yes, but it was also a bit sad because it was the end, and they would have to wait a whole year for the next. That year in particular there had been a hint of melancholy for Nicholas, who had arrived at his eighteenth birthday and was to leave for his new life in September. Who knew if he would be able to return for next year's festivities, or the following year's for that matter? Or ever? The wars against the aggression of Napoleon Bonaparte had been heating up, after all. He had tried consciously to enjoy every moment of what had remained of this fete, his last for perhaps a long while.

Little had he known just how much of an ending it would prove to be.

She listened without interrupting.

"He spent the spring months in London each year to attend the parliamentary session," he said. "He took great pride in observing his obligations as a member of the House of Lords. We all remained in the country with our mother, almost counting the days until his return. He was always so happy to be home again. He always shed a few tears and set us off too, until we were all laughing and hugging him and gasping in wonder over the gifts he brought with him.

"But that particular year, while we were all as busy as ever, our mother most of all, preparing for the fete, a stranger appeared in the village and settled there in an empty cottage. She was a young and pretty widow, come to find some peace in the countryside while she mourned her dead husband and recovered her spirits. She knew no one, but she was treated kindly and invited almost everywhere. She had an elderly relative living with her for respectability."

Winifred hugged her knees more tightly, almost as if she sensed what was coming. She would not have guessed all, however.

"How innocent we all were," he said. "She was our father's mistress, or one of them, whom he had invited to join him close enough to Ravenswood that they could continue their liaison. It became clear later, of course, that he had always lived a double life, but he had been marvelously discreet about it. Not a whisper of it had reached us. He had never tried to mix the two lives—until then. Perhaps his life had become too predictable and therefore dull. Perhaps he had a special fondness for this particular woman. Perhaps he had always had mistresses and whores reaching all the way back to Ben's mother, before his marriage to our mother. We had all been assured that Ben's mother was our father's exclusive partner at that time and that he had lived a life of monogamous virtue since his marriage. It was what Ben himself believed.

"The new resident was invited to the fete and to the ball and came to both. During the ball our father took her out to the hill for some air and to see the view from the top in the moonlight. Devlin and Gwyneth, who had finally acknowledged their love for each other that day, discovered them inside the temple folly. They were *not* focused upon the view or the moonlight, however. They were focused upon each other.

"Devlin must have been shocked to the core. He exploded. He would not allow the two of them to return quietly to the ballroom and postpone a confrontation until the morning. He followed them and publicly denounced them to the whole gathering—family and neighbors alike. It was really quite catastrophic. My uncle, my mother's brother, marched the woman away from there and back to the village. She was gone by the next morning, never to be heard from again. My maternal grandfather tried to restore some control over the situation by announcing that the ball was over and ordering Devlin to go to his room to calm himself before meeting the whole family in the library after everyone had left. But it was too little too late. Our world was at an end. It shattered about us."

Winifred Cunningham had lowered her head to rest her forehead on her knees. "I am so sorry," she said. Her hair was parted with great precision down the back of her head. A braid hung over each shoulder and hugged her ears.

"I had no business telling you all this," he said. "It is I who beg *your* pardon."

"I did ask," she said. "And sometimes it is a relief to unburden oneself to a virtual stranger."

Was that what she was? He supposed it was. She was merely the daughter of a portrait painter staying at Ravenswood with his family for a couple of weeks while he painted the dowager countess. She was more than a stranger, though. She might be his sister-in-law soon, a fact that ought to make more of a stranger of him, not less.

He had had no business bringing her here. Or of enjoying her company so much. And he *did* enjoy it. There was something fresh and new and spontaneous about her. She was intelligent and liked to speak her mind and talk on topics that would give many ladies the vapors—or else bore them silly.

"I went away a few months later," he said. "I began the career I have had ever since, and I do not regret it. But during my leave-taking, I would neither shake hands with my father nor allow him to hug me. I would not even look at him. My mother had turned to marble since that night. Devlin was gone—banished by our mother on that very night. Ben had unexpectedly gone with him. Only Pippa and Owen and Stephanie remained at home with our mother. Two of them were still children. Pippa was at a very delicate age. She had been expecting all the excitement of a come-out Season in London the following spring. It was no longer to happen, by her choice. She had turned to marble too. Our father died four years later of a sudden heart seizure. He had been as jovial as ever in the meanwhile, I have been told, though there must have been a hollowness to it. I did not return home in all that time.

"And that is my sad story, Miss Cunningham. For years after I left, I hated the man who had been my rock and my inspiration all my life. I despised him. And I was terrified that I was no different from him and would become a replica of him. What had been my fondest dream since early childhood became my worst nightmare. I was a good military officer, I believe. I concentrated upon being just that, since my father had never been in the military and so it was a clean slate for me. But in all else I was crippled. I would suddenly see him in what I did and hear him in what I said. I was afraid to smile at other people, to talk with them, to relax with them. I had a horror of being called charming, though it happened all too frequently anyway. I steered clear of women except in the most superficial way. In a word, I was a mess."

She had lifted her head and turned her face toward him. "Past tense?" she said.

"I am thirty-four years old," he said. "I know I am *not* my father. I even know he was not an evil man. He could not have deceived us so totally for so long if he had been. His affections were genuine, as was his pride in us all, even our mother. He was just a—*flawed* man. A complex man. I do not make excuses for him. He did a great deal of harm, most of it to the very people he professed to love the most. But he was as he was. And I am as I am. People still tell me how much I am like him, and it is always said as a compliment. But I am *not* him in all the ways that matter."

Except that he was here on the island with an unchaperoned woman, who should be watching Owen shoot arrows in the poplar alley. Damn Owen! He was neglecting her. Perhaps because he was taking her affections for granted? Or because he liked her as a friend but really did not want to encourage her to believe there was more to their relationship? And why was *he* not at Cartref with Grace and Mrs. Haviland? It was true he had not been invited, and it had sounded like a gathering just for ladies, but he could have gone anyway, especially since it must be common knowledge that he was courting Grace. He had chosen to remain behind to help Devlin.

"It will always be there, the sadness," he said. "I never saw him again after that farewell, when I rejected his overtures of love. I never forgave him. He died before I had a chance to relent. But life continues. After a few difficult years, to say the least, we are a close family again, even a happy one. I suppose we all have scars, but we deal with them privately and carry on. I am especially pleased to see my mother so happy—happier than she ever was, I believe. For of course she must have *known*. It would have been virtually impossible for her *not* to know. But she protected the innocence of her children and did a superb job of it."

"Always remember," Winifred said, "that almost everyone who knows you now did not also know your father. They see you as yourself, as they ought. Just as most people who know Mama now did not know her when she was Lady Camille Westcott, cold and proud and intent upon being the perfect lady and aristocrat and not a very nice person at all, if she is to be believed. Mama is dearly loved now, and rightly so. She is everything she used not to be, yet strangely she must still be the same person. You are you as you are now, Colonel Ware, and the person you will become through the rest of your life. Yet you are still that boy who charmed all who knew you. That boy was *you*, not your father. And listen to me turned preacher."

He laughed and she joined him.

"Do you still want to explore the magic forest?" he asked.

"It must be *very* magical," she said. "I do not even see a forest, only some clumps of trees."

He winced. "You must not spoil my illusions with cold reality," he said.

"But yes," she said, scrambling to her feet without his assistance and brushing the creases out of her skirt. "I want to see it."

The undergrowth on the one side of the island had always been thick and impenetrable to children, especially as it included some prickly plants. They had never been cleared out. The other side was different. There *was* undergrowth and some boggy ground, but it had been paradise when they were little. And their mother had never discouraged them despite the muddy shoes and occasional torn trousers and shirts and skirts they took home with them, as well as tangled hair and sweaty bodies, though they had often cleaned those at least with a vigorous swim in the lake.

Nicholas shook the grass from his coat and pulled it back on before absently grasping her hand.

"There are wild animals and monsters of all types in here," he said, leading her into the forest. "Even a dragon or two lurking in the inlets of the lake. And there are birds of prey in the trees. The type that love nothing better than to carry off a child to their nests. And when one climbs to the higher limbs of the trees, one occasionally spots a pirate ship creeping silently between the island and the mainland, the pirates all lining the deck, waiting for their chance to jump off, their cutlasses jammed between their teeth."

"And almost every one of them with either a black eye patch or one wooden leg, I suppose," she said.

"Ah, you know the ship, do you?" he said.

"And the wild animals and monsters," she said. "There are children in my family, remember. When the children from the orphanage come for a picnic, they often join in a hunt for the monsters. They encounter pirates and highwaymen too. Sometimes there is so much screaming that Papa warns that the powers that be down in Bath are probably considering sending a rescue mission and a constable to arrest him and take him to their jail in chains. But Mama always says there is plenty of food for the would-be rescuers if they come."

He laughed and squeezed her hand. How lovely it was once in a while to become a silly child again, or at least to have fond memories of such times. She even looked the part, with her braids bobbing against her bosom with every movement.

"Oh, watch!" he said suddenly, and she teetered at the edge of a boggy patch of ground, one foot raised, her body already in motion to move forward. He released her hand in order to wrap his arm tightly about her waist and pull her back to safety. She would have ended up with a muddy foot and perhaps a shoe hopelessly lost. "I beg your pardon. I was not watching where we were stepping, something that is always essential here."

But he became aware of her pressed to his side, of the lithe slenderness of her body that he found curiously attractive. He looked into her face as awareness came into it too. Despite the braids, her hair was brushed back over her head with no attempt to disguise the broadness of her forehead. Her face was quite unremarkable, though all her features were in the right place. He tried to remember that she was plain and largely shapeless, but it was too late for that. He saw nothing but beauty and that elusive *real* woman for whom he had searched, though he had never known how he would recognize her when he saw her.

He recognized her now.

Too late, he thought, even as she licked her lips in an unconsciously provocative gesture, and he closed the gap between their mouths and kissed her.

She kissed him back, as he might have expected of her if he had been thinking at all. There was nothing missish or coquettish about Winifred Cunningham.

But even as he turned her in his arms to draw her against the full length of his body, they came to their senses. Simultaneously. He took a step back, careful that she did not do the same and land in the bog after all. But they did not stop gazing at each other.

"Win," he said, and swallowed. "That was not intended. Please believe me. And it will not be repeated."

"No," she said. "It was part of the magic."

"Which am I?" he asked. "A wild beast, a bird of prey, or a pirate?"

"Oh," she said. "You are Nicholas."

And with that, he fell in love with her.

A thought to be severely curbed as soon as they got out of this so-called forest. It could not be true, and if it was, it *would* not be true. There were too many insurmountable obstacles to make his loving Winifred Cunningham a possibility, not least the age gap between them. Good God, he was possibly no more than a year or two younger than her *mother*.

"It was merely part of the magic, part of the make-believe," she said. "We will put it behind us. I would like to return to the house now, please. I have left Andrew alone for too long."

Ever practical. No sign of hysteria or helpless weeping. Or recriminations. Or embarrassment. He guessed all those would be kept strictly to herself.

He led the way back to the boat without touching her.

CHAPTER THIRTEEN

There was a burst of general conversation at the start of dinner that evening as they all shared accounts of their varied activities. Winifred hoped she would be able to go unnoticed provided she ate her food and looked interested in what others were saying. It was *not* easy, though, and that was the understatement of the decade.

And it was the very evening when Owen had come to sit beside her, beaming and happy to see her again and have the chance to talk with her. Clarence Ware, his cousin, had gone home.

"Did you have a successful archery practice, Owen?" Mama asked him.

He grimaced. "It depends on what you mean by *successful*," he said. "I was never any good at it, you know, but if we only ever did things we are good at, we would live pretty unadventurous lives, would we not? I always fancied myself as an archer. Archery, unfortunately, does not fancy me."

There was general laughter, in which he joined.

He must still like her if he had sat with her, Winifred thought. And oh, she still liked him. Very much, in fact. Perhaps even more than that. Suddenly, she desperately wanted to love him beyond all doubt. He might never fall in love with her, of course, but she needed to cling to the faded hope that there was something more between them than just casual friendship. She wanted her mind taken off Colonel Nicholas Ware, who was seated on the other side of the table, though mercifully not directly across from her. He had Miss Haviland on one side of him, Mama on the other. He looked perfectly relaxed.

Eventually the general sharing of news died down and everyone turned to the more usual conversations with their immediate neighbors. Winifred had been very thankful for the general chatter, however. It had helped her calm her thoughts and steady the painful beating of her heart. She must not, not, *not* think about this afternoon. She felt horribly, hideously guilty. She had recognized before today, of course, that she found Colonel Ware attractive. How could any woman *not*? So it was hardly surprising that she had given in to temptation when it had offered itself in the form of that marshy ground she had almost stepped in and his strong arm to pull her back from the brink.

What had she been *thinking*?

What had *he* been thinking?

The trouble was, she had not been thinking at all, and he could not have been either—or why on earth would he have done it? He could not possibly find her attractive.

She had had her hair in *braids*. Heavens! It was *mortifying*, to say the least. She could hardly recall how he had got her into the boat afterward and out of it and up onto her horse and down from it in the stables. He had had to touch her on all four occasions.

Somehow he had made it impersonal, and *she* had made it impersonal, though the journey back to the stables had seemed to take forever as they made a few dismally failed attempts at conversation. She could not now recall a single thing either of them had said.

The only thing that had kept ringing in her head was his calling her *Win* just after kissing her. No one had ever called her that. She had always been Winifred or Winnie, or, as the eldest daughter of the house, Miss Cunningham. *Win* had sent shivers up her spine. It had sounded like a caress. How was it possible to make a caress of the name Winifred? She had always wished that at the orphanage they had named her almost anything else on earth. It made her sound like a cross horse. Perhaps that was why she had always had an aversion to horses.

"Perhaps you are a better bowman than you think," she said to Owen. "I have heard that Mr. Taylor is an extraordinarily skilled archer. Perhaps you have always compared yourself to him. And perhaps that has been a mistake."

"When it was my turn to shoot during the last contest," he said, "I observed a noticeable reaction in the crowd of spectators even before I began. They always stand well back for their own safety, of course. But for me, they shuffled back another quarter of a mile."

"Oh, what a tall story," Winifred said, laughing.

"I say, Winifred," he said. "I have been itching to see you and tell you about your brother. Robbie, I mean."

"I hope he did not get in your way in the poplar alley," she said. "But he had spent a great deal of time watching Andrew in the stables, without once complaining, and I knew he wanted to watch you practice. Andrew is no great company for anyone, especially when he is engrossed in one of his carvings."

"He did not get in our way at all," Owen said. "I kept talking to him while I was shooting—or, rather, while Clarence was shooting. I talked from some distance away, though. I did not move close enough to make him feel threatened. After a while he talked back and asked a few questions. He came to stand behind us to watch, and he allowed me to pet his dog when it was not my turn to shoot. He wanted to know how to shoot an arrow. Talk about coming to the wrong person, and Clarence is not much better than I am. In fact, he will probably take the second from bottom place in the contest on Saturday. But I do know *how* it is done."

"You taught Robbie?" Winifred asked.

"How to hold the bow, yes," he said. "How to fit an arrow and aim it. How to release the arrow. He took to it like a duck to water. After a few tries he was already better than I am. I told him so too, and he actually laughed. Does he do that often?"

"No." Winifred was enthralled. "And he has never held a bow and arrow in his life. Not to my knowledge, anyway."

"Well, he can wield one now," Owen said. "He did not want to give it up. He kept shooting until he finally actually hit the outer edge of the target. He only frowned at that, though, because it was not the center. I think you have a perfectionist on your hands, Winifred. He would have kept going, but Clarence needed to head on home to Charity before she divorced him or sent out a search party. I couldn't wait to see you and tell you about it. I thought you would be pleased to hear that your brother has found something that fascinates him and something he can be good at with some practice. Perhaps *very* good. I wonder if I ought to ask Matthew—Matthew Taylor, that is—to have a look at him, perhaps give him a few pointers or even an actual lesson. I guessed you would understand my excitement and share it."

"I *do* understand," she said. "I believe you must have felt as

Mama and Papa felt several years ago when they discovered that a dog could help with Robbie's moods and tantrums. They went immediately and got one for him, though he chose it himself. Nelson made a huge difference to Robbie's life—and ours."

Owen beamed at her, and she felt a welling of renewed affection for him.

"I wonder," he said. "If I ever do start that farm for troubled youngsters, would Robbie be interested in coming to work for me? Do you think it would be a good idea to employ one of their own, so to speak, to help them? People like me can have all the goodwill in the world as well as the resources and the compassion and the longing to help and make a difference, but it is pointless unless one can somehow enter into the experience of a person who for some reason is angry with the world and everyone in it, who trusts no one and nothing, who has not a spark of hope that life will ever offer something of worth, something to live for. Robbie has been one of the fortunate ones. He was adopted by your parents, who steadfastly refused *not* to love him, and acquired siblings who followed their lead. And he has discovered someone—Andrew—who needs him, and his dog, and now archery. Is that the key, do you think, Winifred? Finding something about which a person can be both skilled and passionate, whether it be shooting an arrow or carving stone or stacking sheaves of wheat or riding bareback? Not that I would expect there to be a single key. Life is not nearly as neat as that. But might it be *a* key?"

"*A* key, yes, Owen," she said. "And if you can make it all happen, it will be interesting to see how Robbie would greet the opportunity to work for you and with you." She beamed back at him and at the same moment, quite by accident, caught the eye of Colonel Ware across the table. He was half smiling at them. She felt a bit sick. If only she could go back and say a firm no when he had offered to take her riding. She had promised to stay with Andrew, after all.

"I say," Owen said. "Shall we go walking after dinner? Maybe down by the river? There is a path, though not as well trodden as the one to my mother's cottage. It is on the opposite side of the drive. It always seems to be especially lovely in the evening. I wonder why that is. Something to do with the light, I daresay."

"I would like it very much," Winifred said, though part of her wanted to go to her room, shut the door to all comers, and brood over the day's tumultuous events. It would be very out of character to do that, however, and someone would be sure to come to ask if there was something the matter with her. If it was Mama, she was afraid she might burst into tears. The very thought was horrifying.

When dinner was over, she waited for Owen to invite someone else to join them and held her breath in the hope that it would not be Colonel Ware and Miss Haviland. Please, please not them. But he did not ask anyone. He merely told the earl and countess where they were going for a breath of air. No one suggested joining them.

Was this *it*? Winifred wondered. Was it to be what she had hoped for when she came here? More recently, though, she had lost hope and convinced herself she did not want any closer relationship with him than friendship. Was he going to ask her to join him in bringing his plans to life? Was he going to ask her to marry him?

Were all her dreams about to be restored?

She could not imagine a happier outcome.

If she blocked the memory of this afternoon, that was.

Oh, she was so mixed up, so very unsure of *what* she wanted. Probably what she *needed* to do was to go home to Bath next Monday as planned and get back to her familiar life there. She could be happy at home, as she had always been with Mama and Papa and her brothers and sisters and all the people who came to their house to pursue their own dreams. It was a happiness that had held true since she was nine years old.

But she was twenty-one now. Things had changed, though she did not know quite what she meant by *things*.

Anyway, perhaps Owen intended nothing more than a walk and a continuation of their conversation. She hoped that was all. For now, anyway. Perhaps after she had had time to think in the familiarity of her home surroundings and got her head straight on her shoulders again . . .

Well, who knew what would happen *after*? One could be sure only of the present.

It was an enormous relief to Nicholas to watch Owen and Miss Cunningham at dinner—seated side by side and talking almost exclusively to each other. That was not normally acceptable in polite circles. One was expected to converse equally with one's dinner companions on both sides. However, this was more a family gathering than a formal occasion, and he was glad to see them wrapped up in each other, talking with bright animation, laughing together, their heads almost touching. Neither of them ate a great deal. They were more interested in talking. More interested in each other, by the look of it. And then, at the end of dinner, Owen told Devlin that they were going to walk along the riverbank—in the opposite direction from the cottage, Nicholas imagined. And though he held his breath in the hope that Owen would not ruin his sense of relief by inviting someone else to join them, it did not happen.

It was his sincere hope that all was well between those two, that he had not done irreparable harm this afternoon by making a full outing of his ride with Miss Cunningham and holding her hand and actually kissing her on the island. He still felt hot under the collar when he remembered that.

In the meantime, he was taking care of business on his own account, though *business* was probably an unfortunate word to choose. He sat beside Grace at dinner and addressed most of his conversation to her. It did him good to be reminded of how quietly dignified, even charming, she was. When he did not try to look deeper, that was. She seemed to have very much enjoyed her visit to Cartref this morning. She told him that Lady Rhys had talked at tea about her former home in Wales and all the family she still had there. She and Sir Ifor spent several weeks of each summer with them, and it was always good to discover that they still had not forgotten how to speak Welsh, even though their relatives insisted that they had very English accents.

"I believe that part of Wales would be a lovely place to visit," Grace said to Nicholas. "It is by the sea and close to long golden beaches."

Nicholas found himself almost promising to take her there for their honeymoon. He caught himself in time. There needed to be a proposal and a wedding before there could be any honeymoon.

"They are a people full of music and warm, spontaneous emotion," he said.

He thought that for a moment she looked almost wistful.

"Would you allow me to order a tea tray sent up to the glass room on the west tower?" he asked her. "It is a lovely place to spend an evening like this and watch the sunset."

She hesitated. "Will you invite Mama and Papa too?" she asked him.

"No," he said firmly. "But I will certainly inform them that we are going up there. It is in many ways a very public place, you know. One can see for miles in all directions through the glass, but one can also be seen by anyone who cares to look up. Have you been up there?"

"No," she said. "I have been to the portrait gallery, but we did not go up to the turret room. Mama was too weary."

"Will you come now?" he asked.

"Yes," she said. "Thank you."

General and Mrs. Haviland, when applied to for permission, looked only too happy to give their consent.

Grace did not immediately sit down when they got to the tower. She turned slowly all about, gazing at the views. Nicholas could see Miss Cunningham and Owen on the road down to the bridge, about to turn right onto the river path, which would take them past the bottom of the meadow and under the overhanging trees beyond. They would have some privacy there. They were obviously talking, their faces turned toward each other, though she did not have her arm through his. She was holding a shawl in place about her shoulders, and Owen had his hands clasped behind his back.

Nicholas wondered if Owen had made up his mind. Did he intend it to be a romantic tryst?

But this was not the time to be thinking of his brother. Or, more important, of Winifred Cunningham.

"It is lovely here," Grace said. "How wonderful it must have been to grow up here at Ravenswood."

"Indeed it was," he said. "And it is lovely to be able to come back here whenever I wish. Devlin and Gwyneth are very sociable. They are never happier than when they have guests here, whether family or friends. Even family and friends with children. And dogs."

It struck him that she had had a very different upbringing from his. General Haviland as a man of means owned a large home on one of the fashionable squares in London. Mrs. Haviland and her daughter would always have remained there in spacious luxury when he had distant postings. When they were not so distant, they would have joined him and seen a bit of the world. But there was no home in the country.

"They have been very kind," she said.

A servant arrived carrying a tray with tea for two and a plate of fruitcake sliced thin. He poured the tea for them and withdrew quietly. Grace sat down on one of the sofas, and Nicholas sat beside her. He was relieved to discover that he felt a wave of affection for her.

"You have been avoiding me," he said.

Her face visibly paled as she stared back at him, her eyes wide. "That is quite untrue," she said. "It is unfair of you to say such a thing, Colonel Ware. I—"

"Yes, it is," he said, instantly contrite. "You have been unfailingly courteous to everyone, including me. What I meant was that you have avoided being alone with me. On the day we went driving over the crest of the hills, for example."

"Just as I have avoided being alone with any gentleman here," she said. "Even those who are married. I have been raised always to behave with strict propriety even while remaining courteous to all."

"And you do it superbly well," he said. "However, we both know why you have been invited here."

The color had not returned to her cheeks. "Papa is your commanding officer," she said. "You have become friends. Lord Stratton has been kind enough to invite him here for a few weeks of the summer with his family."

Her cheeks flooded with color then and she turned her face away and looked out toward the lake.

"I do beg your pardon," he said. "We have enjoyed an easy friendship for some time, Grace, you and I. I have been a frequent guest in your home. I have been invited to join a number of your family outings—to the theater, to Kew, to private soirees and concerts. You have driven in Hyde Park with me. You have been unfailingly charming and amiable. But it has occurred to me since you came here how little I know you."

"What more do you need or want to know?" she asked. She picked up her cup with a steady hand and drank from it.

"Tell me about your betrothals," he said. "Or is the subject too personal? Still painful, perhaps? Did you love them both? You were very young at the time, I understand. Do you still grieve?"

He really ought not to have asked. The questions were indeed too personal and intrusive. But he needed to know. He needed to know *her*. Had those betrothals been the result of duty, pressed upon her by her parents at the appropriate time, when she was still in her late teens and very early twenties? Or had they been personal choices? Had the deaths of the two men been merely painful? Or had they been heartbreakers, sending her to hide deep inside herself behind the facade of the perfect lady? He needed to know.

She opened her mouth as though to speak and then closed it again. She sat and thought for a while. He had offended her, he thought. Then she drew a deep, not quite steady breath.

"Oh, I was a foolish girl," she blurted. "Giddy. I believed in happily-ever-after even while the men with whom I mingled lived the most unsafe existences possible. They were all military men at a time of warfare. I fell deeply in love with both of them, Colonel Ware. Separately, of course. I fell in love with the second two years after losing the first. Each time my heart was broken irrevocably—or so I thought."

She stopped speaking and swallowed awkwardly. "I believe I was in love with the idea of being in love," she said. She sounded unusually bitter, and he knew the admission had cost her dearly.

"But eventually you recovered from your grief?" he asked after a few silent moments.

"I moved onward with my life," she said.

Which was not necessarily the same thing. He watched as she almost visibly dragged her usual dignity about herself again. She finished her tea and set her cup down quietly on the saucer. He drank his own, though by now it was merely tepid, the way he most hated drinking tea.

"I am no longer that girl," she said. "I learned my lesson and am far happier for it."

He felt chilled. She was telling him, or so it seemed to Nicholas, that she was no longer foolish enough to believe in romantic love or any display of feeling—passion anyway. And it struck him that she was not happy. How could she be when she had amputated that part of herself that could bring joy and all the other array of emotions to her own life and to the lives of those around her? Loss, heartbreak. She had insulated herself against them all.

"You are ready again for marriage?" he asked.

She turned her face sharply away again. For a while she did not say anything. "Mama and Papa will not live forever," she said. She did not elaborate. He did not know if General Haviland would leave everything to her or if there was a male relative somewhere who would take precedence over her. He had not yet had that conversation with her father. But clearly she felt the insecurity of a future in which she might be alone.

It was an understandable reason for choosing to marry.

But did he want such a bride?

He had no choice now, though. Could he make her feel again? Trust love again?

"But do you *wish* to marry?" he asked her. An unfair question. How could she answer it honestly when he was the man who had been chosen for her, the man she had tacitly accepted when she came here? Winifred Cunningham would answer such a question honestly, but the two women were as different from each other as night and day.

"Wishes are such pointless things," she said. "Magic wands, fairy godmothers—they are for children, Colonel Ware. I am not a child. I am close to thirty years old."

She had neatly sidestepped the question. He had not used the word *wish* in the sense she described. But he would not press the issue. She had effectively answered him by refusing to answer.

She was not in love with him, or anyone else for that matter.

She did not wish to marry him. But she would do so because it was the practical, sensible thing to do. She would not do it cynically, however. He knew that much about her. She would be a good wife, even a perfect wife. And she would be a good mother, though he guessed she would not raise her children to be free and spontaneous as the Cunninghams did. Or as Devlin and Gwyneth did.

She poured them a second cup of tea before sitting back on the sofa and looking out calmly over the lawn and meadow and across the river and village to the patchwork of open fields beyond.

"I hope this lovely weather will hold for Saturday and the fete," she said. "There will be many disappointed people if it rains."

"Strange as it may seem, given the unpredictability of the British climate," he said, "it never seems to rain on the day of the fete.

I daresay there will be many indignant people if this year should prove to be the exception. There are always alternative plans, of course, but one always hopes they will not have to be implemented."

Their discussion was at an end, it seemed. She wanted no more of it.

The daylight was gradually turning to dusk. There were the beginnings of sunset in the west, with pale pinks and lemons lighting the sky. The colors would multiply and become more intense and fiery within the next half hour or so, and the sky a darker blue and star-studded. The hour for romance.

Nicholas found himself wondering if Owen and Winifred Cunningham were finding romance at the sight of the sunset both on the horizon and reflected in the water of the river.

For one unguarded moment he felt the ache of envy.

CHAPTER FOURTEEN

The river path bordered the meadow until it reached the line of trees and then was shaded by their overhanging branches. Winifred and Owen strolled side by side along it, deep in conversation about Owen's dream. It was not a one-sided conversation, however. It never was with Owen. Winifred talked just as much as he, and he listened and commented and argued and commended just as she listened to him. They were always in perfect accord when they talked. He was always absorbed when the subject was dear to him, but he was never *self*-absorbed.

Winifred loved that about him.

When they were eventually under the shade of the trees, sheltered from the view of anyone at the house or in the park, open countryside across from them, the village of Boscombe behind them to the left, they sat on the riverbank and Winifred gazed at the water. It turned glassy in appearance as the sun sank toward the horizon and the pale colors of early sunset promised more glory to come.

If she had tried to imagine the most romantic of all settings, she could not have done any better than this. At first, she felt a pang of longing, knowing that Owen was not feeling it at all. She guessed he was quite oblivious to their surroundings as he talked on. And she loved his focus. But she knew in that moment, without any shadow of doubt, that he would never have romantic feelings toward her. She waited for heartache to strike, but she felt only a pang of regret. It had been such a beautiful dream, she and Owen as partners in every imaginable way. As Mama and Papa were in what they had set out to do when they married and began adopting children who needed their love and opened their home to artists of various kinds in search of a gathering place. Mama and Papa were able to give it in such abundance because they loved each other. Deeply and—Winifred guessed—passionately.

She would never know that sort of love herself. Her mind flashed unwillingly to riding with Colonel Ware this afternoon and crossing to the island on the lake in a small boat and enjoying his memories of his childhood there and listening with deep sympathy to the story of his loss of innocence, when the true nature of the father he had worshiped and emulated all through his boyhood had been so cruelly revealed. And walking in the forest with him, her hand in his, being silly and laughing with him. Being kissed.

It was strange how the mind could be occupied with two quite distinct threads of thought without losing the ability to concentrate upon both. She continued the conversation with Owen, listening to him, talking in her turn, even while she was aware of her personal pain. For the memories of this afternoon must be put aside. They must be forgotten, though she knew how difficult, perhaps impossible, it was to forget what ought not to be remembered.

She would go home next Monday—she could hardly wait

now—and immerse herself in her busy, *happy* life, and all this would soon be like a dream, just as being in London had already become like a dream before she came here. If time was not a healer, at least it was a soother.

"I say," Owen said. "That is quite the sunset, is it not?"

"Sunset twice over," she said. "In the sky, and reflected on the river. A double blessing."

He took her hand in his and squeezed it. "Sometimes," he said, "I wonder why I live in London at all when there is all this beyond its borders." He made a wide sweeping gesture with his free arm. "I am glad for you that you do not live actually in Bath but in the hills above it."

"It is beautiful there," she said.

"I believe it," he said. "I would like to see it one day."

They gazed at the scene around them in silence for a while, and she knew that one thing remained intact anyway. She had a deep affection for Owen Ware, and she knew he returned it.

"Perhaps you will come and visit sometime," she said. "Perhaps meet the children from the orphanage. We usually have at least one picnic for them during the summer. They are there all day, playing and feasting. Sometimes they plan a concert for us."

He turned his head to gaze at her. "I am going to have to stop dreaming, am I not?" he said. "I am going to have to start *doing*. What are dreams without action, after all? I need to purchase some land in the country—a farm. I have some ideas on that. And then I am going to have to start employing suitable candidates, both male and female, to run it. Do you think?"

"There will be an enormous amount of work involved," she said. "But yes, I think you are ready, Owen."

She saw his bright, happy expression in the gathering dusk.

"Perhaps you will be part of it," he said. "Though it is not the life one ought to offer a lady, is it? Will you? Will you marry me so it will all be proper? I believe you are fond of me, as I am of you. I believe we would deal splendidly together."

Oh no, Winifred thought. *Not now.*

She did not know quite what to say. Should she allow herself to get caught up in his enthusiasm? Or say an out-and-out no? Maybe ask for time to consider? He was very obviously sincere. They *were* fond of each other, and they shared a dream, but she had learned during her acquaintance with him that sometimes he could be carried onward by an impulsive enthusiasm. The sunset had tipped his affections her way.

He seemed to be having the same thought.

"Oh, I say," he said. "I am doing this all wrong. Blurting out a proposal as though the idea had only now popped into my head. I have always known you are special. But I ought to have prepared the way. I ought at the very least to have talked with your father before asking you. And I ought to have led up to the actual offer with some sort of ardent speech."

Despite herself, Winifred laughed.

"But it is your spontaneity that I have always loved most about you, Owen," she said. "I want to ask you something, though. And I want you to think carefully before you answer. I want it to be an honest one. We have always been honest and open with each other. Do you love me? I mean, are you *in love* with me?"

He transferred his gaze to the river and said nothing for a while.

"They are words," he said. "I know they mean something special to many people, but quite honestly I do not know exactly what they do mean. Love, yes. But being *in love*? You know I love you, Winifred. Surely you know that."

"Yes," she said softly.

"But more than that I cannot say in all honesty," he said. "I am sorry. Perhaps I ought to fake it because maybe I am in love with you and have just never quite understood that phrase. Or—"

"No," she said. "Thank you for not pretending, Owen. And the thing is, you see, that I feel exactly as you do. I love you dearly. You are the best friend I have ever had. But I do not believe I am *in love* with you. And it is not a mere trick of words, you know. My mother and father are in love with each other. I believe your mother and Mr. Taylor are too, and other couples I could name. It is unmistakable when you see it."

"Yes," he said. "It is. I am sorry, Winifred. Sorry I have embarrassed you, that is. I—"

"You have not embarrassed me," she said. "You have helped clarify something in my mind. And your marriage proposal is a feather in my cap, you know. I have now had *two* offers of marriage since the ball at Archer House. It will be something to boast of during my old age."

She laughed and Owen smiled at her.

"To your grandchildren," he said.

"Perhaps," she said. "So, is it true that Bertrand is coming here in time for the fete?"

"It is," he said. "Devlin and Gwyneth love to fill the house for the fete, and this week all the family will be here. You will enjoy yourself, Winifred."

"I know I will," she said, smiling fondly at him.

Well, this had been a night to remember, she thought as he helped her to her feet, offered his arm, and led her back in the direction of the drive and the house above it. It was deep dusk, almost dark, but it would not be a black night. The sky was already studded with moon and stars. This might well have been one of the happiest evenings of her life, she thought. Instead, it had brought a certain melancholy, but also a sense of rightness. There had never been any aura of romance about her relationship with Owen Ware, only kinship of mind and a genuine *liking*.

She was happy that the matter had been cleared up once and for all.

Perhaps—oh, perhaps—she would fall in love one day with a man who would fall in love with her. And if not, well, she would make happiness out of what she had. And she would always remember that day, the happiest of her life, when Mama had offered her the possibility of a permanent home and security and unconditional love.

She thought of Colonel Ware advising her always to remember that day when she slid into one of her rare moods of depression.

And she thought of him kissing her this afternoon and calling her *Win*, a low, caressing tone in his voice. She would always remember it without allowing her heart to break. He and Miss Haviland were obviously made for each other, and she would be happy for them when they were betrothed, perhaps this week.

She really would.

Winifred found it strangely freeing to wake up the following morning to the realization that what she had hoped for with varying degrees of intensity, and denial, for the past few months—in London, at home in Bath, and here—was just not going to happen. *By her own choice*. Owen had offered and she had refused. She could have lain in bed and let her mood spiral downward into depression. It was finally over, that dream. Instead, she bounded out of bed, threw back the curtains at the window, drew a deep breath of the fresh morning air through the open window, and felt herself fill with excitement for the coming days. The Earl and Countess of Stratton's new guests would be arriving, starting this afternoon with the earl's elder half brother—the late earl's *by-blow*, whom Colonel Ware credited with saving his life in the Peninsula, or at least his leg.

But her excitement extended beyond the arrival of new guests and the fete on Saturday. Her mind was exhilarated too about the future in general. She could do whatever she wished with it. What an unbelievable gift the future was.

First on the agenda was to be a walk into the village after breakfast. Last night she had agreed to accompany Stephanie to a choir practice at the church. She had liked Sir Ifor Rhys the first time she met him at Cartref. She had been enthralled by the music he produced from the great pipe organ when she attended church on Sunday. Now she looked forward to hearing what he could do with a choir. According to Stephanie, he could make stones sing if he wished. This morning Winifred would hear two of his choirs—the children's, which would sing at the ceremony that would open the fete, and the adults', which would sing at a midday organ and choral recital on the same day.

Listening turned out to be pure pleasure. Winifred thought of how much both choirs would be appreciated if they performed a concert at home in Bath. Stephanie had a solo part with the adult choir. She had a pure soprano voice. Winifred would have loved to hear more of it.

"You are an enormously talented singer," she said as they walked home together later.

"Thank you." Stephanie blushed. "But I take no particular credit."

"Sir Ifor is clearly a talented musician himself, and he recognizes talent in others," Winifred said. "He would not have singled you out to sing solo before a crowd of people at the fete if he did not see talent in you. No doubt he has helped nurture you. But even if he were not here, you know, you would still have the voice. And you would surely have chosen to use it and share it, even if only among family and friends. But I will not embarrass you further. It seems to be a role sometimes thrust upon me at our arts center, though, that of chief encourager. That is the name one group gave me, anyway. I only hope it was meant as a compliment. I have noticed, though, that many people belittle their own talents and never develop them to the full simply because they lack belief in themselves or are afraid of appearing boastful. So they deny themselves the happiness of knowing who they really are. Oh dear. Sometimes I do run on and on. You may tell me to be quiet anytime you wish."

But Stephanie was laughing as she linked an arm through Winifred's.

"Very well," she said. "I believe you. I am the best soprano in the world, and Boscombe and its surrounds are privileged beyond belief that I will condescend to sing to them."

Winifred joined in her laughter.

"What a happy week this is going to be," she said. "It must be lovely for you to have all the rest of your family coming home for the occasion. Are you especially close to your sister?"

"I am now," Stephanie said. "It was not always so. Pippa is almost six years older than I. It was too wide an age gap to bring us close when we were growing up. But it is surprising how that gap seemed to narrow as we grew older. I sometimes spend time with her at Greystone Court when she cannot come here. I was there for several months while she was expecting Pamela. The twins were terribly energetic—at least, Emily was. Christopher has always been the more placid twin. Lucas—my brother-in-law—is fond of saying Christopher would not even fight for his rights when he was born. Emily is half an hour older than he. I was able to take some of their care off Pippa's hands while I was there, though they have always had an excellent nurse, and Lucas is a very attentive husband and father. He does not make an excuse of his busy duties as Duke of Wilby."

"Family is terribly important, is it not?" Winifred said, smiling. "I missed my own very much when I spent a few weeks in London with my father earlier this spring. It is lovely to have them all here. It was extraordinarily generous of the earl to invite us all."

"I am very glad he did," Stephanie said. "I love your mother. She is so full of fun and energy. And the children all seem to look out for one another. I cannot wait to see Mama's portrait your father has painted."

"And one more member of our family will be coming this week," Winifred said. "Did you know Bertrand Lamarr—we never think of him as Viscount Watley—is Mama's stepbrother? My grandmother married his father eleven years ago, and we all love him—and Estelle, his twin sister. Is he not the most amiable gentleman you have ever known? Not to mention *handsome*. I danced the opening set of a ball at Archer House with him this spring, and I could see I was the envy of every other woman present. I hope he finds the perfect bride one day so he can live happily ever after. Estelle wants it too, now that she is married herself. Mama always says the poor man has become the victim of the worst possible oppressors, well-meaning female relatives."

She turned her head to look at Stephanie, expecting to share laughter with her again. But her friend was grimacing. "I *wish* he was not coming," she said. "But I beg your pardon. He is your relative, and you are eager to see him again."

"Has he made himself . . . objectionable to you when he has been here before?" Winifred asked. But it was hard to imagine.

"No," Stephanie said. "He has only ever been all that is amiable. It is just that I really do not want to see him again. The first time he came here with Owen, I was seventeen and I was absolutely smitten. Not in a good way, I must add. I was mortally afraid that if I smiled at him or made conversation with him, he would think I was *flirting*. I thought he was perfection and I was just the opposite. Everyone kept telling me when I was a child that my baby fat was adorable but it would go away when I grew older. I waited and waited, but it never happened. It still has not, for that matter. And I had this great shiny moon face and still looked like a child of twelve. I went to extraordinary lengths to hide from him, and when that was impossible, I blushed from my toes to the crown of my head and could never think of anything to say. It was downright humiliating."

They had come to a halt on the bridge over the river. The sun was sparkling on the water as it flowed beneath.

"Oh, dear," Winifred said. "But that was all some time ago. It is altogether possible he has forgotten—if he even noticed. And you are very far from being unattractive. You have a lovely, well-proportioned figure, even if it is a bit fuller than some would consider the feminine ideal. Sometimes I lament my very shapeless figure, but all the lamentations in the world will not change it. I know also that I am not pretty. I decided long ago that I am as I am and that actually I am quite happy about it. I would hate to be someone else."

Stephanie laughed. "I used to think it was so unfair that Pippa is flawlessly beautiful," she said. "But I would not want to *be* her. I want to be me. I doubt Viscount Watley has forgotten, though—unfortunately. I met him again when I was nineteen and Mama persuaded me to go to London for a come-out Season. It was disastrous. He was at the very first ball I attended, and he was so pleased to meet us again and introduce us to Lady Estelle Lamarr, his sister. She was his female counterpart—beautiful and poised and charming. And *slender*. But you know her, of course. I went all to pieces, Winifred. I tripped and stammered and blushed—and fled from London as soon as I could. Pippa and Lucas were in town, but Pippa was increasing at the time and longed to be back home. When Lucas took her there well before the Season ended, I went with them. I had never in my life been happier for an excuse."

"Oh, poor Stephanie," Winifred said.

"That was six years ago," Stephanie said. "I have grown up since then and am very happy with my life even though I am still single in my middle twenties. But enough about me. I am glad for your sake and your mother's that Viscount Watley is coming here tomorrow. I am glad too that you and your family are staying for the fete. It is my favorite event here, though it no longer happens every year, as it used to when I was a child. All we need now is for this perfect weather to last. It surely will not be unkind enough to rain upon us on that one special day, will it?"

"It would not dare," Winifred said as they walked on. "I do look forward to meeting your eldest brother this afternoon."

"Oh, me too," Stephanie said. "I adore Ben."

CHAPTER FIFTEEN

Nicholas allowed himself a few days in which to bask in the pleasure of being among his family again. Perhaps now, more than ever, when his life was about to change irrevocably, he valued what he had and realized just how much he had always taken it for granted. It was wonderful indeed to be a Ware of Ravenswood, to belong, to have a mother and siblings and their growing families and a larger family of grandparents, uncles, aunts, and cousins. And a neighborhood of friends and friendly acquaintances.

Winifred's stark story of her own origins had struck home. For he understood that having a loving family now did not make up for what had been missed during her first nine years of life.

A few of his siblings had their own lives far away and quite separate from life here, of course, as he did. He had never been sorry that he was the son intended for a military career. Even at his darkest moments—and there had been more than a few of them during the war years—he had never doubted that he was living the life he wanted to live.

But this week his family was to be all together. It was time to be cherished. And there was the summer fete to look forward to, to help with, to enjoy—but to face with a certain misgiving too, for it would mark the time after which his life would never be the same again. For no later than that day he was going to have to formalize the connection with Grace. And then he was going to make the best of it. He was, after all, a man of honor. But in the meanwhile, he gave himself permission to relax and enjoy each moment.

Ben and Jennifer were the first to arrive, with Miss Delmont, Ben's elderly aunt, his mother's sister, who lived with them, and their children, Joy, now ten—was it possible?—four-year-old Robert, and two-year-old Belinda. Ben was the brother to whom Nicholas owed the fact that he still had two legs instead of one. They hugged each other warmly after Devlin and Gwyneth had had their turn. In the meantime, Jennifer's wheeled chair had been taken down from a second carriage and Ben lifted her into it while Devlin helped Miss Delmont to alight. The three children came scrambling after her, Joy already talking, the little one bouncing with excitement, as Nicholas remembered her elder sister doing as soon as she learned to stand. And somehow Gareth and Bethan and Awen had escaped from the nursery to greet their cousins, bringing Alice and Samuel Cunningham with them. All was glorious noise and confusion and laughter.

And pure joy to Nicholas.

There were several arrivals the following day. His Grandmama and Grandpapa Greenfield were first in the late morning. They had come with Uncle George and Aunt Kitty, who had finally made the decision to live permanently with them since they were finding it increasingly difficult to live alone, even with the help of servants. Mama was delighted at the prospect of having her brother only ten miles away, especially as Uncle George happened to be married to one of her closest and oldest friends. These new arrivals had a quieter reception than Ben, with children excluded out of deference to the weariness the grandparents were bound to be feeling. Mama hugged her parents before Gwyneth and Devlin led them to their rooms, where they could rest for a while before luncheon.

Mama and Aunt Kitty meanwhile hugged and chattered to each other and even squealed a time or two, altogether like a couple of girls, while Matthew and Uncle George grinned at each other and shook hands.

Nicholas smiled happily at them all and set an arm loosely about Stephanie's shoulders. She was reveling in all this as much as he was.

She was nowhere to be seen, however, an hour or so later when Bertrand Lamarr, Viscount Watley, arrived. He had been Owen's friend since their university days. Although he lived a quiet life on his country estate for most of the year, alone since the marriage of his twin sister to the Earl of Brandon a year or so ago, he and Owen had kept up their friendship. He had come here now almost directly from his sister's home in Northamptonshire, where he had gone to see her new baby. He shook Gwyneth and Devlin firmly by the hand and turned to Owen and Nicholas just as Mrs. Cunningham came hurrying from the house and almost hurled herself into his arms. She was, of course, Watley's stepsister.

"Bertrand," she cried. "Looking as handsome as ever. And just returned from Northamptonshire. How is Estelle? I take it all is well despite the baby's early arrival. She is over the moon with delight over her first child, I expect. And Justin too. I want to hear all about them. The baby is David? What a lovely name."

He laughed as he hugged her back. "Will you allow me a few moments to catch my breath, Camille?" he said. "I will say, though, without any bias at all, that my nephew must be the handsomest baby ever born. You are looking very fine, I must say. Glowing, in fact. And here come Joel and Winnie. The country air must be agreeing with you all."

And then, in the late afternoon, Pippa arrived with Lucas, Duke of Wilby, her husband, and their three children, twins Emily and Christopher, now seven, and Pamela, four. Yesterday's merriment replayed itself, though Pamela hid behind her father, an arm wrapped about his leg, and refused to show her face.

"She is shy," Pippa said unnecessarily. "Just give her time."

They had brought a nurse with them to help with the care of the children, a real blessing as there were many children here.

Pippa was the next sibling in age to Nicholas and had always been exquisitely lovely, with her blond hair and delicately complexioned face. It looked as if Pamela would closely resemble her, though Pippa had always been an outgoing girl. She had had to be, with three older brothers. She was *so* happy to be home for a short while, she told them. And just *look* at Joy, all skinny and long limbed. And at Robert, who had been born only days after his cousin Pamela. And oh, yes, at Belinda, who at barely two years old still had not shed the adorable chubbiness of babyhood. She swept her niece up into her arms and kissed one plump cheek. Lucas meanwhile was hugging Jennifer, who had come outside to meet them, using her crutches instead of her wheeled chair. She was Lucas's sister. She had surprised the fashionable world when she, the granddaughter and sister of a duke, permanently lame as the result of a crippling childhood illness, married Ben, illegitimate son of the Earl of Stratton, and went to live with him in a modest manor on a smallish estate close to the sea thirty miles away. But the two appeared to have been happy ever since.

Nicholas hugged his sister and the twins and shook Lucas by the hand before the two children went dashing off with an assortment of Wares and Cunninghams and Ellises in the direction of the hill and the temple. They all seemed to find plenty to shriek about even before they rounded the corner of the west wing.

Lucas picked up his youngest child while the nurse supervised the unloading of the children's baggage from the carriage in which she had traveled with Pippa's maid and Lucas's valet.

And they were all present and accounted for. Matthew's relatives had arrived earlier, his brother and wife to stay at the cottage, his nephew and family to squeeze into the rooms above the smithy. There was room for them all at the cottage and certainly at Ravenswood Hall, but apparently they all considered a few days spent in those rooms a special treat.

Stephanie was coaxing Pamela out of her father's arms and distracted the child by taking her to the edge of the terrace and pointing at the sheep down in the meadow. Nicholas smiled down at Belinda Ellis, who was watching them, and she opened her arms to him, wanting to come up. And what a crowning joy it was in these dizzyingly busy days, Nicholas thought as he picked the child up and took her to join Stephanie, to hold a chubby child who was still little more than a baby, and to feel her hand about his neck while she bounced in his arms and pointed at the sheep.

"Shall we go a little closer?" Stephanie said, and stepped out onto the grass.

Why, oh why had he not married and had children of his own long before now? But it was not too late. Although he was about to marry a woman who was close to thirty and he was past that age, there was still plenty of time to have children. Plural. A family of his own. A family of *their* own.

Grace would want children too.

She had greeted his siblings and their spouses as well as his grandparents with her customary courtesy and charm. She seemed happy to see Uncle George and Aunt Kitty and Bertrand, with all of whom she already had an acquaintance. Mrs. Haviland was everything that was gracious, and General Haviland beamed about him with genial goodwill. He looked like a man who thoroughly approved of the family into which his daughter was about to marry.

Meanwhile, in the house and in the village, busy preparations were being made for the upcoming festivities on Saturday. Tables were being set up about the perimeter of the courtyard for the displays of needlework and baking, and a gaily striped tent was being erected in the northeast corner for the fortune-teller. More tables were ready on the terrace for the wood carvings—and one stone carving.

Andrew Cunningham had finished creating an exquisitely realistic sheep, solid and woolly and placidly maternal, with a spindly legged lamb at her side, leaning against her but looking outward with an eager, barely contained energy that would soon send it gamboling away from her to explore its new world. It was not just a skilled carving. It pulsed with life and had movement and joy, though all were illusions, of course. In reality, it was just a block of stone. Mr. Cunningham and Matthew had somehow persuaded Andrew—Winifred with her signed messages had helped a great deal—to enter it in the contest at the fete. The contest was, strictly speaking, for wood carvings, but that was only because no one had ever tried to enter a stone carving.

"And *that* came from the ugly old stone we lugged home from ten miles away?" Nicholas said to Winifred when they were both out in the stables to view the newly finished work of art with her parents and Robbie, Matthew and his brother, Bertrand and Owen. He had studiously avoided her since the afternoon of their ride, just as she had avoided him. But she was looking so happy for her brother that he could not continue to keep his distance from her. "Now I know what your mother means when she says Andrew sees something in stone, something full of energy that he absolutely must release. It is quite exquisite, though somehow that seems to be not quite praise enough. Language can be very limiting."

"I do indeed say that," Mrs. Cunningham said. "I always find it astonishing. I am so very proud of my son."

"I believe Matthew may have competition this year," Owen said. "Andrew may tip him off his throne."

"I would not stop sulking this side of Christmas," Matthew said.

"It was not ten miles," Winifred said to Nicholas. "You do like to exaggerate."

"What?" he said. "You mean it was *eleven*? It is no wonder my back has been protesting ever since."

She laughed.

Mr. Cunningham was hugging his deaf son, the suggestion of tears in his eyes.

The summer fetes had halted abruptly after the year of what most people in the neighborhood thought of as the great catastrophe. When it resumed a few years later, it had been on the initiative of an organizing committee of volunteers drawn from among the villagers and people of the surrounding countryside, who sorely missed the annual frolics. One of the first decisions of the new committee was to move a number of the events to the village itself—the vending booths, the maypole dancing, the children's races, to name a few.

Nicholas liked the changes, for the burden upon his mother had been enormous. However, it was because of those changes that he hesitated over his original plan to have Devlin announce his betrothal at the evening ball. It would be inappropriate to put the focus upon the Ware family when it was the community that had planned the whole thing—music, decorations, and refreshments. It would feel very like stealing their thunder to intrude upon their community ball.

He had decided instead that the traditional family dinner on the eve of the fete, when the house would be full of guests, both family and close friends, would be by far the more appropriate setting for the announcement. All of which meant that Friday was going to be a busy day for him.

It began after he asked General Haviland for a private word in the library after breakfast. The general put him through his paces, just as though he had not been working toward this very moment with Mrs. Haviland for the past year or more and just as though he knew nothing of Colonel Ware's circumstances and ability to give his daughter the sort of life she had been raised to expect. It ended as Nicholas expected, of course. Permission was granted, and all that remained for him to do was pay his addresses to Grace herself.

He had indeed cut off all possibility of retreat now, he thought as he left the library with a jovial General Haviland and escaped for a while to the stables, where Devlin and Ben, quite like old times, were making sure all was ready for the archery and log-hewing contests. Both welcomed him. Neither made any mention of the meeting in the library, though they must have been fully aware of it.

Everyone had plans for the afternoon, some to entertain the

children, others to help however they could with preparations for the events that would take place at Ravenswood. Aunt Kitty was helping Mama set up the needlework displays in the courtyard, though she did explain to Winifred, who went to help too, that they might as well stand back and admire and not interfere. Her sister-in-law was very fussy about what went where on that table. The baked items would not arrive until early on Saturday morning.

Mr. Cunningham, who had finished the portrait, was helping Gwyneth set up the wood-carving display on the terrace, though the word *wood* was going to have to be dropped this year. Young Andrew Cunningham's stone sheep stood prominently on the table with Matthew Taylor's pensive shepherd, Uncle George's cockerel greeting the morning and looking for all the world as though it were waking all sleepers within a wide radius, and numerous others. Bertrand had gone out to the poplar alley with Owen to supervise the setting up of the targets and the marking of the line from which each archer would shoot.

Nicholas found Grace in the drawing room with Mrs. Haviland, Miss Delmont, and his grandparents. He made general conversation for a few minutes, but he could tell instantly that all of them knew full well why he was there. Mrs. Haviland in particular was tense with waiting. Grace herself, dressed in a manner more suited to a London drawing room than an informal house party in the country, sat very upright on her chair, her hands clasped in her lap, her face looking rather as though it had been carved of marble.

"Grace," he said, getting to his feet and bowing to her. "With your mother's permission, may I take you for a stroll along the river path below the meadow? It is very picturesque. Much of it is shaded by trees and is cooler in the heat of the afternoon than the more open paths and carriageways in the rest of the park."

He was babbling a bit.

"Do go, Grace," Mrs. Haviland said. "I will stay and give Mr. and Mrs. Greenfield and Miss Delmont my company."

"Thank you, Colonel Ware," Grace said, getting to her feet. "Some fresh air will be welcome."

They walked arm in arm across the terrace, down the driveway toward the bridge, and then onto the river path—just as Owen and Winifred Cunningham had done a few evenings ago. Nicholas still did not know if anything significant had happened during that walk. But he was beginning to doubt that Owen could have asked her to marry him. She would almost certainly have said yes if he had, and he was bound to have said something to someone by now. Had he at least held her hand once they were out of sight, kissed her, moved one step closer to making a declaration? Perhaps he had. Perhaps he intended to have his own betrothal announced this weekend.

But Nicholas did not want to be thinking about his brother. Even less did he want to be thinking about Winifred. That perfect evening for romance was then; this perfect afternoon for a marriage proposal was now. Two different couples.

While they strolled below the meadow, in sight of anyone in an upper window of Ravenswood who was looking out or anyone in Boscombe who cared to glance this way, they were largely silent, just occasionally remarking on the beauty of their surroundings. He could feel her hand tense on his arm, though she gave the general impression of being perfectly at ease. She was *so* well trained to behave as she ought and push any personal feelings deep.

Then at last they were in the shade and privacy of the trees. The air was instantly cooler, the glare of the sun less intense. The river turned from sparkling silver to deep green. And instead of the bleating of sheep and the sound of the breeze in the long grass of the meadow, there was birdsong and the gentle rustling of leaves overhead. And the sweet smells of clover and water.

"Perfect," he murmured.

"It is," she said.

"Grace," he said. "You must know I think *you* are perfect too. You must know that I spoke to your father this morning. You have been expecting this. However, before I proceed to it, I must ask you one more time. Your happiness is important to me. I am ready to devote the rest of my life to cultivating that happiness to the best of my ability. But all the effort in the world will not suffice if you are not happy *now*, if you are doing only what is expected of you—by your parents, by your hosts and fellow guests here, by society. By me. Are you willing to give me an answer that comes from the deepest part of yourself, regardless of anyone else? Do you want me? Do you love me?"

He had tried to practice the speech. It came out all stilted and formal when he had wanted a relaxed atmosphere between them, in which she would perhaps share her real self and her real feelings with him.

It took her a while to answer.

"I hope I will always do what is expected of me," she said. "It is how I have been raised. Your appeals to emotion now and a few evenings ago up in the glass room are foreign to my nature, Colonel Ware. I can only say that I have a deep regard for you. And a firm trust in you."

It was hopeless. He could only rely upon the softening effects of intimacy after they were married. He knew she would never give him a moment's trouble. She was indeed perfect.

"Will you do me the great honor of marrying me, then?" he

asked her, stopping on the path and turning toward her. He had taken her hand in his and was gazing deeply into her eyes, but he had *not* gone down on one knee. He did not want anything theatrical about this moment. He wanted, God help him, *sincerity*.

She raised her eyes to his and opened her mouth to speak. And closed it again after a few moments. He squeezed her hand and raised it to his lips. And watched, appalled, as two tears spilled over from her eyes and trickled down her cheeks.

"I cannot do it to you," she said. "I care for you enough, Colonel Ware, to know that I would be doing you a terrible disservice by marrying you. You need someone who will love you according to your definition of the word. Any of that sort of emotion I ever knew dried up many years ago after I had loved passionately twice and lost both men. I have a great deal to give to a marriage now, but I could never be the sort of wife you deserve. Oh, what can I *do*? Everyone is expecting . . ."

No, Nicholas thought. All emotion had not dried up in her. It had only been suppressed for a long time, but it was bubbling to the surface now. He felt her distress. He held up a staying hand and she left her sentence unfinished.

"We will not worry about that," he said. "I will merely tell everyone that we had a good discussion here this afternoon and came to the mutual and amicable conclusion that we would not suit after all. We will not be lying. I hope we *have* reached an amicable decision and that we will remain friends. I really do like you exceedingly well, Grace. And I do consider you perfect. You are a thoroughly gracious lady."

She surprised him again then by laughing. But he could see that a great tension had left her and that for the moment, at least, she had let all her defenses slip in order to be herself.

"Thank you," she said. "But I will take the blame with Mama and Papa. I will not have them thinking that somehow you did not come up to snuff. You have to work daily with Papa at the Horse Guards, after all."

He wondered if she would have accepted his proposal if he had proceeded directly to it without any preamble. He believed she almost undoubtedly would. But he also believed it would have gone against her real wishes. So he could not feel guilty for probing her inner feelings both today and a few evenings ago.

He had probably done her a favor while virtually forcing her to look inward. If she could do it more often, think for herself, *feel* for herself, perhaps real happiness lay in wait for her somewhere. Though not with him. He very genuinely hoped for her happiness. She was dear to him.

"Shall we stroll a little farther?" he said. "I rarely walk here, but when I do, I wonder why I do not come more often. It is easily one of the most beautiful and certainly the most soothing parts of the park."

"It is lovely," she said. "But I think I would prefer to go back to the house, Colonel Ware. Mama and Papa will be waiting."

"Yes," he said. "Would you like me to face them with you? Or instead of you?"

"No," she said. "That will not be necessary."

She had already put herself back together, he saw as they turned back and walked a little more briskly along the path than when they had come. She took his arm when he offered it, but neither of them spoke.

There would be no announcement at dinner tonight, then, he realized suddenly. Or tomorrow. He was free. It was a bit of a dizzying thought. He had not felt free for months. For the first while he had persuaded himself that he was doing the right thing, that he had needed the nudge General and Mrs. Haviland had undoubtedly been giving him. Then he had felt trapped, though he had still convinced himself that all would change once he was married. More recently he had felt a sort of hopeless panic while still trying to persuade himself that he was doing the right thing, that he wanted and needed to be married and begin setting up a family of his own.

Now all those dreams had died again, or at least any hope of fulfilling them soon. He was going to have to start all over again without allowing himself to get trapped until he was quite sure he had made the right choice—right for him and right for the woman.

But for the moment he was free. And he did not know quite what it was going to mean to him over the coming days and weeks and months.

At the moment his predominant feelings were guilt—yes, it could not be totally dismissed—and distress for having upset Grace, who did not deserve unhappiness.

CHAPTER SIXTEEN

~

Winifred bounded out of bed on the morning of the fete and threw back the curtains, which had been designed to protect a light sleeper from the bright rays of the rising sun. As far as she could see to left and right and straight ahead, there was not a cloud in the sky. She opened her window wider and felt the cool morning air on her bare arms. Her ears were already being assailed by birdsong. She could see the Earl of Stratton and Mr. Ellis making their way out to the poplar alley, no doubt to check that all was ready for the archery contest this afternoon.

Owen had told her at dinner last evening that he had been seriously considering withdrawing from the contest since all the practice he had been doing had not improved his aim by one inch. But Mr. Clarence Ware, his cousin, had talked him into carrying on.

"It is because he did not want to place last in the contest himself," Owen had said while grinning at her.

Winifred had laughed. "I think he probably does not want you defeating yourself without even trying," she said.

"Do you mean that a miracle may happen overnight?" he asked her.

"One never knows," she said, and he had first grimaced and then laughed.

"Anyway," she said, "do you *enjoy* competing?"

"Well, I do," he had admitted. "I suppose that with every shot there is hope for that miracle. You do know that your brother is competing, I suppose? He is a novice, but he is already vastly better than I am."

"Robbie?" she said. "Yes. Mr. Taylor gave him a couple of lessons and told him he showed promise and would improve immeasurably with practice and lots of it. Years of it probably if he wants to be *really* good."

She wondered if Mr. Taylor realized how much those words had meant to Robbie, who would have reacted with surly cynicism to indiscriminate praise. *Years of practice* would have made sense to a boy who never seemed to look for or expect easy answers.

"The whole Cunningham family will be out there to cheer him on," she said. "And to cheer for you too, of course."

They had laughed together.

It had been a relief over the last few days to discover that Owen was as friendly as ever and that she felt as comfortable in his company as she had before the evening down by the river. She even felt happier with him because she no longer looked upon him as a possible suitor. Just as a friend. Friendship was as precious in its own way as courtship.

She dashed into the small dressing room attached to her bedchamber to wash in tepid water—someone must have brought it in earlier when it was hot. She pulled on the dress she had selected for the day and brushed her hair and twisted it into its usual knot at her neck. She was impatient to be downstairs to start the day. She did not want to miss a moment of it.

She did pause, though, as she remembered last night's dinner. It had been a splendid affair, the dining room crowded, everyone in high spirits. The climax had been the unveiling of Papa's portrait of the Dowager Countess of Stratton, which had stood on an easel, a canvas cover over it, throughout the meal. There had been a collective gasp when the cover was removed, and Winifred had been convinced, as she always was when she saw each new portrait, that it was her father's best. Papa had succeeded in making the dowager look both brightly intelligent and quietly dignified. He had made her look beautiful, but not falsely youthful. Perhaps best of all—and this was his signature skill—he had given the viewer an inside glimpse of her soul, if that was the right word. He had made her look like someone who cared deeply for everyone and everything in her world. A genuine kindness beamed from her eyes and somehow pervaded her whole face and form.

Yet nothing in the portrait was inaccurate or exaggerated or downplayed. There on full display in her portrait was Mrs. Taylor, the Dowager Countess of Stratton, just as she was. The picture made one understand—was it too fanciful?—just why she had needed to build that cottage by the river and why she was so happy there. Even why she had been content to marry the village carpenter.

All that just from looking at her portrait.

It had been a proud moment for Papa, though he had reacted to the spontaneous applause and the chorus of praise that had followed it with his customary modesty. Mama had beamed at him and looked young and beautiful herself. Sometimes Winifred forgot that Mama was barely fourteen years older than she was.

It had been a happy evening. But . . . There had been no

announcement of the betrothal of Colonel Ware to Miss Haviland, though Winifred had braced herself to expect it. Word had spread quickly enough during the morning that Colonel Ware had gone to the library with General Haviland and then in the afternoon that he had taken Miss Haviland to walk by the river. That same romantic path where *she* had walked a few evenings ago with Owen. But no announcement had been made at dinner. That meant another day of suspense while she waited for an announcement to be made at tonight's ball. She had so wanted something definite last evening. She had wanted to be fully and finally *free* to enjoy today.

She shook her head to rid it of such thoughts. She was going to enjoy it anyway.

Stephanie had gone into the village ahead of everyone else, having promised Sir Ifor that she would help organize the children's choir in time for the opening of the fete. Everyone else went together a short while later in a large, disorganized group. Children darted everywhere, making a great deal of noise. Only two of them rode—Belinda Ellis on her father's shoulder, one chubby arm wrapped around the back of his head, and her brother, Robert, astride Nicholas's shoulders, pretending his uncle was a horse and drumming his heels against Nicholas's chest.

Matthew Taylor was emerging from the path to the cottage with his brother, their wives just behind them, and joined the larger group while loud, cheerful greetings were exchanged. Almost at the same moment they all had to jump aside to give room to the open barouche, which was taking Mr. and Mrs. Greenfield Senior, Miss Delmont, and Jennifer Ellis into the village. Mrs. Greenfield waved to them with exaggerated gentility, as though she were royalty, amid general laughter. Belinda wanted to ride with her mother and had to be lifted from Ben's shoulder into the barouche.

Nicholas strode along in the middle of the pack, obliging Robert with the occasional neigh and bucking movements while he grasped the boy's ankles more firmly and Robert shrieked and laughed and gripped his hair.

General and Mrs. Haviland had behaved with perfect good breeding since yesterday afternoon. Whatever Grace had said to them must have convinced them that Nicholas had indeed proposed marriage to her and she had refused. He did not know what reason she had given. But since then, they had treated him as though nothing had happened to rock their world. And Grace had looked . . . happy? She was too well bred, of course, and too much the lady to show any feeling openly. But it had seemed to Nicholas at last night's grand dinner and now again this morning that there was a certain lightness to her step and brightness in her customary smiles. She was walking now with Gwyneth and Owen, beautiful and fashionably dressed as though for a stroll in Hyde Park. And . . . happy. Surely he was not mistaken. Even as his eyes rested upon her, she laughed at something Owen was saying and then smiled at Robbie Cunningham, minus his dog, who had come up on Owen's other side.

Winifred Cunningham had one arm drawn through Bertrand Lamarr's and the other through Andrew's. She smiled frequently at Andrew while chattering happily with Watley.

Nicholas had watched his younger brother closely during the past few days, but Owen had given no hint of what was going on with his romance—or *non*-romance. Nicholas had been half expecting an announcement at dinner last evening, but though Owen and Winifred had sat together, there had been nothing. Maybe tonight at the ball? Or maybe not at all?

Would she return home with her family on Monday and that would be that? End of story? Nicholas would be sorry about that. It was unlikely he would ever see her or hear of her again.

But he would always remember . . .

And he would always wonder what had happened to her.

But why? What was it about her? There had been that kiss, of course, and his conviction at the time that he was in love with her. But . . . Well. It had all been so unexpected and so *forbidden* that he had squashed both the memory and the feeling with the ruthless discipline he had always applied to his military life.

However . . .

Well, he was free now. But was she?

This was *not* the time to get engulfed in such thoughts. They had crossed the bridge and were almost immediately swallowed up by the crowds already gathering on the village green and in the streets surrounding it. Robert wanted to get down and went dashing off with some other children—new or old friends, it never seemed to matter which to children. All the children seemed headed toward the maypole, which had just been carried out from the inn and was being erected on one side of the green, its brightly colored ribbons fluttering in the breeze.

Children darted in and out among the vending booths that had been set up around two sides of the green, though there was little to be seen yet. They would remain covered until after the opening ceremony. The children were undeterred. Some of them dashed toward the duck pond in the center of the green, but the wise ducks had stayed away today. One little boy, who became instantly popular, had brought a boat, which he pulled along with a string. Other children clamored for a turn.

Ben was unloading Jennifer's wheeled chair from a wagon,

which had followed the barouche from the house, and then lifting her into it. The barouche drove around the green and over the bridge on its way back to the house. Belinda squeezed herself in beside her mother as Nicholas could remember Joy, Ben's child from an earlier marriage, doing even before Jennifer married Ben. Joy had chosen her for a new mother just as Ben had chosen her as a second wife. Joy was standing now by the maypole, all long legged and half grown up, arm in arm with Pippa's Emily and another girl, who might be one of the Coxes from a nearby farm.

Andrew had joined his father. Bertrand had gone inside the inn with Grace and Uncle George and Aunt Kitty, presumably to have some coffee or tea before the opening ceremonies.

Nicholas went to stand beside Winifred, who was looking about her with seeming satisfaction.

"I simply adore the atmosphere here," she said. "Totally festive, as though the world and all its problems do not even exist. And surely everyone from miles around has turned out, young and old. I do not see a single frown as I look about. How lovely that is. If only we could always be like this."

One of her unrealistic dreams, like her opposition to all violence. But he knew, as he had not known during that first ball, that she also dealt with harsh reality with a cheerful hope that she could do some good in the world.

"The penalty for anyone who does frown is a night spent in the village dungeons," he said. "They are reputed to be dark and damp. With spiders."

She tutted and then laughed. "You made that up on the spot," she said. "Oh look, the church doors are opening. Does that mean the fete is about to begin?"

"There will be rioting in Boscombe if it does not happen soon," he said. "Fortunately, we have a vicar who is always punctual and never long-winded. He will begin with a welcome to all and a prayer, and then the children's choir will sing a few songs."

"Were you ever a member?" she asked.

"For a while," he said. "I fancied myself as a singer when I was younger. Gwyneth and I used to sing duets to my pianoforte accompaniment during visits to various neighbors, when music was called for. We used to be very close friends. I believe I spent almost as much of my boyhood at Cartref as I did at home. Unfortunately, people got the wrong idea as we grew older. It was embarrassing to both of us. Some friendships between male and female are just that. Friendships."

"Yes, indeed," she said with such conviction that he wondered if perhaps she was thinking of her friendship with Owen.

"The person for whom Gwyneth had nursed a secret passion for years was Devlin," he said. "He had had a passion for her too but had not said anything because he did not want to tread upon my toes. Absurd, was it not? But all ended well. One only has to look at the two of them now to see that they belong together."

"You did not just pretend that you did not care because you did not want to hurt either of them?" she said.

"Absolutely not," he said. "I did not even know their feelings for each other until afterward. Neither gave any hint. I was actually vastly relieved when I did know it. I was a little worried that I had hurt Gwyneth and that *she* was pretending she did not feel that way about me."

"I wonder how many people get trapped in relationships only because they care about the other person's feelings and do not wish to hurt them," she said.

"A good many, I would imagine," he said. "Honesty is the better policy, do you not think?"

"I do." She sighed. "Though being open and truthful is not always as easy as it sounds."

He wondered if she had been hurt. By Owen. But if so, it was better for her to know now than to find out later, when the two of them were trapped in a marriage in which all was brave pretense on the one side and a dawning realization of the truth on the other.

But the children's choir was lining up on the pavement outside the church under Stephanie and Sir Ifor Rhys's direction, in two long rows. Some were inclined to chatter and fidget and dart out of line, while others appeared frozen with terror. A few looked about anxiously to locate parents and grandparents in the crowd. Finally, the Reverend Danver emerged from the church in full clerical vestments and raised his arms. Silence fell on his gathered parishioners and their visitors. Even the children miraculously stopped their dashing about and their shrieking.

And it was beginning, yet another summer fete. Nicholas intended to enjoy it to the full, to allow the day's activities to seep into his bones and nourish his soul. Extravagant words, perhaps, but true, nevertheless.

Winifred Cunningham beside him was gazing at the vicar and choir with glowing eyes and rosy cheeks, and it struck Nicholas that she was actually the most beautiful woman he had known. In her own unique way, that was.

She turned her head briefly his way and smiled at him.

It was magical. There was no other word.

The vicar said a short prayer, followed by a brief welcome to the large hushed crowd, and the children's choir sang three songs to enthusiastic applause. Mrs. Eluned Rhys, head of the organizing committee, added a word of welcome and explained briefly what would be available in the village for everyone's pleasure—vending booths, children's races, maypole dancing, morning refreshments and midday luncheon outside the inn, or inside for those who wished to withdraw from the sunshine for a short while.

And, inside the church, there would be a short organ recital by Sir Ifor Rhys, her father-in-law, at midday and a presentation by the adult choir. She told them what they could expect during the afternoon, mostly at Ravenswood—the log-hewing and archery contests, the displays and judging of the needlework and baking and carving contests.

"Please note," she added, "that I did not say *wood-carving* contest. This year we have one stone carving, and rumor has it that it is in the running for a prize."

"How I *wish* Andrew could hear," Winifred said.

"And a picnic tea on the lawn before the house," Mrs. Rhys said. "And, of course, dancing this evening in the ballroom. Now go and enjoy yourselves."

There was an enthusiastic burst of applause.

"But how could anyone *not*?" Winifred said. To her, all this was purely breathtaking. It was the most exciting thing she had ever experienced, even including Trooping the Colour. And while she always loved the concerts and picnics and parties that happened with some frequency at home, there had never been anything on this scale, everyone in the community and beyond gathered for the simple purpose of enjoying one another's company and the many and varied activities that had been prepared for their pleasure throughout the day.

"I do not believe it would be possible," Colonel Nicholas Ware said from beside her, and she realized that it was to him she had spoken, sounding like an overenthusiastic child. She chuckled anyway.

"I suppose," she said, "I ought to be waving a fan languidly before my face and looking about me as though I found the whole scene almost unbearably rustic and tedious."

"But then I would not like you half as well," he said.

"Oh." She felt the color deepening in her cheeks. "*Do* you like me, then?"

"Twice as much as I would if you were feigning ennui," he said.

They both laughed. But of course, she realized why everything had been feeling so very magical in addition to everything else. It was because he had remained standing beside her throughout the opening ceremony. And *he* had not shown any signs of ennui. He had applauded with everyone else. He had raised two fingers to his lips when the children finished singing and let out a piercing whistle of appreciation. Just like an exuberant boy.

She ought not to be enjoying herself just because he was her companion, however. Nor was she, if she was strictly honest with herself. She would be enjoying herself anyway, even if she were standing here alone or with someone else. But . . .

Well, she chose not to explore that *but*.

Where was Miss Haviland anyway? He had not walked down here with her. He had not sought her out when they got here. She was with Lady Rhys and Mr. Idris Rhys and Owen, Winifred saw when she took a quick glance around.

"Winnie." Alice was tugging her arm, while other little girls beamed up at her. "Come with us to *that* stall." She pointed. "They have the most darling purses and bags and handkerchiefs and all sorts of things."

"Will you come?" Olwen Cox said. She was Joy Ellis's friend, whom Winifred had met a few days ago.

"Uncle Nick." Bethan Ware was tugging his hand. "Come too?"

Joy and Julia Taylor, one of the children staying in the rooms above the smithy with her parents, gazed eagerly up at him.

"I suppose this is going to be an expensive morning for me," he said with a sigh.

"Not on my account," Joy said. "Papa has given me spending money."

"My papa did too," Alice said.

"And mine," Olwen said at the same moment.

"Grandpapa gave me some," Julia said.

Bethan sighed. "We all have money, Uncle Nick," she said. "We did not come to beg."

"It would, however," he said, his eyes twinkling down at them, "be a pity to spend all your money in one place almost before the day has begun. Come along, then."

Alice took Winifred by the hand and bore her off with them.

The small reticules and coin purses had been made by hand and brightly decorated with embroidery and sequins and beads. The reticules had bright plaited shoulder or wrist straps. The handkerchiefs had also been brightened with embroidered flowers of all colors. There were headbands too and woven plaited bracelets. The whole stall was exuberant with color and was a young girl's dream come true. Winifred found everything enchanting and engaged the two young ladies who had made the items in conversation. Needlework had never been her forte, but she admired those for whom it was. The girls each bought something—with their own money. Alice bought a bag with a shoulder strap for herself and a purse for Mama.

Colonel Ware stood back and watched the girls' enthusiasm indulgently, giving his opinion when it was called upon. But he did not suggest paying for anything, to Winifred's relief. It seemed important to the girls to spend some of the money they had been given.

"And look at the *jewelry*," Julia said, glancing at the next stall after she had made her purchase. "Do we have any money left?"

"Mama bought me a necklace and bracelets and rings there before," Joy said. "And she bought matching ones for herself. I do not really remember. I was very little then. But we both still have them, and sometimes we put them on and think we look very splendid. And Papa calls us his pretty ladies and we laugh."

Winifred smiled at her. Joy seemed to love her stepmother. Her father had met and married her mother in the Peninsula during the wars, Winifred had learned in the past few days, but she had died of a winter chill. Mr. Ellis had carried their infant daughter home after the last battle had been fought in Toulouse. Joy would not remember her mother, of course, but at least she would know *of* her. There were stories her father would have told.

But envy was not productive. It was totally inappropriate today, when all was happiness.

The girls had to bump elbows with others as they looked over all the jewelry—garish beads, gold and silver chains that looked *un*goldlike and *un*silverlike, necklaces, bracelets, bangles, rings, brooches, and earrings. But they were all particularly drawn to the chains, which glittered with fake splendor in the sunshine. For a few moments they stood in a huddle, counting the money they had left.

To a chorus of halfhearted protests, Colonel Ware paid for what they wanted and then had to endure hugs and kisses from his nieces and fervent thanks from the others. They dashed off to display their treasures to parents and siblings and grandparents.

Winifred was left with Colonel Ware—and at least a dozen other people jostling one another for a closer look at the jewelry. They stepped out of the way. She must make an excuse and leave him, Winifred thought, a bit flustered. She did not wish to give the impression that she was following him. How ghastly *that* would be. But before she could open her mouth, he asked if she would like a glass of lemonade at the inn.

"But will Miss Haviland mind?" she asked, and then *wished* her wretched tongue would not keep blurting out thoughts before she could filter them.

He raised his eyebrows. "Why should she?" he asked.

She could feel her cheeks grow hotter.

"I am sorry," he said. "That was an unfair question. I do not doubt it was common knowledge that I was courting the lady and actually took her off for a private tête-a-tête yesterday morning after speaking with her father. I did indeed make the offer, Miss Cunningham. It was rejected."

"Oh," she said, startled. "I am so sorry."

"You need not be," he said. "I was actually relieved. She is not the woman for me. And I am not the man for her. Fortunately, we came to a mutual agreement on that point. She is without any doubt as relieved today as I am to be free. I like her very much, I must add. I will always consider her a friend."

"I am sorry," she said again.

"Lemonade?" he asked.

"Yes." She walked across the green with him while parents organized the youngest children for a three-legged race, and the maypole dancers, all dressed attractively to coordinate with one another in pale pastel shades, straightened the ribbons, and the fiddlers who would play for them after the races had been run tuned their instruments.

"And you?" Colonel Ware asked after settling Winifred at a small table outside the inn. "Will Owen mind that you are here with me?"

Owen was with Stephanie now. They were helping organize the races.

"We are very good friends," she said. "In all truth, that is so. We have specifically agreed to it."

"And you are not . . . upset that there is nothing more?" he asked her after two large glasses of lemonade had been set before them.

"No," she said. "Sometimes two people were designed to be friends but nothing more. Like you and Lady Stratton when you were both very young."

"Have you ever watched maypole dancing?" he asked.

"A few times in Bath," she said, relieved that the subject had been changed, though she was still feeling a bit dizzy.

He was not going to marry Miss Haviland.

"It is a skilled exercise," he said, "and calls for a lot of trust. It needs only one of the dancers to go astray and the whole pattern falls into disarray. This is a good troop, though. Sidney Johnson has directed it for years. He farms not far from here. The dancers practice every week throughout the year in his large barn. Pippa was once a member, and I believe Stephanie has dabbled. The dancers are marvelous to watch."

They were both free, Winifred was thinking. But that did not mean . . . She gave herself a mental shake. This was a day that had begun magically. She was determined that it would continue that way. As soon as they had finished their lemonade, she would make an excuse to go somewhere he was not going—to watch the last few races, perhaps. She was not going to trap him into feeling he was stuck with her company.

And she was not going to be stuck with his, she thought with a slight smile.

But he was pulling back the folds of a clean white handkerchief he had taken from a pocket and setting a small silver brooch—very *un*silverlike—on the table between them. It was in the shape of a daisy.

"A priceless gift I thought must have been made just for you," he said, laughter in his eyes and in his voice. "A daisy. A humble, often overlooked, underrated flower that is nevertheless one of the prettiest and most enduring of all."

"For me?" she said, hand to chest.

"It was a huge extravagance, I know," he said, laughing. "Surely real silver, of course. But you ought to have something by which to remember a summer fete at Ravenswood and Boscombe."

"Oh," she said. "The day has barely started, but I know I will always remember it no matter what. Now I will be able to look at my daisy—my priceless daisy—whenever I do. Thank you, Colonel Ware."

He set it in her palm and closed her fingers about it.

A humble, often overlooked, underrated flower that is nevertheless one of the prettiest and most enduring of all.

Did he mean that *she* was like that too?

She got abruptly to her feet. "I am going to watch the races," she said. "I can see Mama and Papa over there. Some of the children must be participating."

He stood too. But he did not attempt to escort her or follow her when she left the table.

. . . one of the prettiest and most enduring of all.

He could not possibly mean . . .

She clutched her brooch lest she drop it and lose it. She would take time to pin it to her dress as soon as she was able. She would be brokenhearted if she lost it.

She would always treasure it.

CHAPTER SEVENTEEN

Nicholas wanted to go too. He would enjoy watching the children race. *With Winifred.* But her leaving so abruptly was clearly a dismissal. For whatever reason, she needed to be away from him for a while. At least, he hoped it was just for a while.

He sat back down and absorbed the sights and sounds all around him. He looked for people he knew, and found them everywhere—the Misses Miller, longtime owners of the village shop, a central hub for local gossip; Oscar Holland, the retired blacksmith, though rumor had it he still came to the smithy almost daily to tell his son all he was doing wrong, criticism Cam good-naturedly ignored; Alan Roberts, the schoolteacher, who was married to the former Sally Holland, the dressmaker's daughter; Prudence Wexford, Colonel Wexford's sister, and Ariel, his daughter, who had been a pretty girl and was now a handsome woman and betrothed to Dr. Isherwood; James Rutledge, son of Baron Hardington, a boyhood friend; Jim Berry, longtime landlord of the inn, who stood in the doorway of his establishment for a few minutes in his long white apron, taking a break from his busy day in the kitchen with Mrs. Berry. There were numerous others. The sight of them filled Nicholas with nostalgia.

A number of people stopped to greet and chat with him. James Rutledge sat with him and was joined by Owen and Bradley Danver, the vicar's son. The four of them reminisced about their boyhood and laughed over some of the memories.

Nicholas continued to look about even as he joined in the chatter. His grandparents were seated outside the church with a few other older folk, including Miss Delmont; Amy Holland, Oscar's wife; and Mrs. Barnes, who had once been their nurse at Ravenswood. Mrs. Haviland, arm in arm with Lady Rhys, was moving along in front of the stalls, examining the merchandise. General Haviland stood a short distance away from the inn with Colonel Wexford and Charles Ware, Nicholas's uncle, each of them with a tankard of ale in his hand. Grace was with Clarence and Charity Ware and Bertrand Lamarr, watching the preparations for the maypole dancing. Ben and Jennifer in her wheeled chair were about to join them. Grace turned to smile at Jennifer.

And Winifred was with her mother and young Sarah and a cluster of other adults, helping out with the children's races and cheering on the contenders, children from Ravenswood and strangers alike. She was smiling and animated and looking pretty. He saw her now, in fact, with quite different eyes than the ones through which he had looked when he first met her.

"Come and join us," Owen said, pulling another chair close to their table. He was addressing Robbie, who tended to hover close to him, Nicholas had noticed. "Have you all met Robbie Cunningham, a budding star at archery? I would wager he will be able to give Matthew Taylor a run for his money in a year or two if he keeps at it. Let me introduce you to Bradley Danver and James Rutledge, Robbie."

The boy sat down, his face a wary, glowering mask as Owen smiled cheerfully at him. "I will never be so good," he said. "Mr. Taylor is a genius."

"And who is to say you are not?" Owen said. "I bet at your age he had never even held a bow. In fact, I know he had not. He told us so one day."

"Pleased to meet you, lad," James said, clapping a hand on Robbie's shoulder. "You must be the painter's boy. I look forward to watching you shoot this afternoon. You are entered, are you?"

Robbie looked warily at him and nodded curtly. He clearly did not like to be the focus of attention.

"I do believe the Cunningham twins have just won the three-legged race," Nicholas said as the shrieks of excitement from the children rose to a crescendo. "It is hardly surprising, I suppose. They move as one even when their legs are not tied."

Mrs. Cunningham was sweeping Emma up into her arms while Winifred hugged Susan.

"They are special," Robbie said. "They are my sisters."

"Lucky girls," Bradley said. "But how do you tell them apart, Robbie?"

"When you love someone, you do not get them mixed up," Robbie said defensively, as though he thought someone was arguing the point.

"I think the maypole dancing is ready to start as soon as the races are over," Owen said.

Ah, the harsh lessons in life children had to learn, Nicholas thought as one very young child wailed inconsolably when he did not win his race. But there was no point in sheltering them, perhaps by persuading them not to compete. At some time or other all must learn that life when lived to the full was an inevitable mingling of triumph and disappointment and everything in between. It was as well if one could experience both extremes once in a while when one was young and learn that neither was lasting. It was never a good idea to encourage children to hide from life.

Was that what he had been doing all his adult life? It was a strange thought to be having at this of all times. *Was* it, though? The Ravenswood fetes had always had particular significance in his life, most of them dizzyingly happy, one at the very opposite extreme. Was it possible he had never got over the terrible discovery he had made about his father on that day? Had he guarded himself from future pain ever since by never feeling very deeply about anything—or anyone? Was that why he had neglected his home and family? Oh, he had not cut himself off entirely from them, it was true, and he had not stopped coming here. If someone had ever accused him of being neglectful, he would have denied the charge with some indignation.

But he was thirty-four years old and unmarried. That was not the way he had expected his life to unfold when he had looked ahead as an eighteen-year-old boy. He had expected to have a home and a wife and family to enrich his chosen life as a cavalry officer long before he reached the age of thirty. He had expected his wife to be someone he loved with all his heart, and his children to be a joy he would share with her.

It had certainly never occurred to him that he would eventually choose a bride with cool deliberation, as he had with Grace. He had been enormously fortunate to be released from that commitment at the last possible moment. And doubly fortunate to know that she had been equally relieved. She actually looked happy today, something that had seemed to be absent from her demeanor all the time he had known her. He hoped with all his heart that she would find love again, as she had as a very young woman, and trust it and discover the happiness that was surely hers by right.

He was free again to find love. There was no point in dwelling on the wasted years or upon his age. He was *only* thirty-four, and he had everything to give, and everything to expect in return.

The conversation flowed about him, unheeded for the moment.

He had fallen in love with Winifred Cunningham on the island that day of her first ever horseback ride. The most unlikely woman in the world. Yet perhaps she was perfect for him. Had he not longed to find someone who was *real* more than anything else— more than outwardly beautiful and accomplished and of impeccable lineage?

No one was more real than Winifred. Or more grounded in real life. Or more likable.

At the time, he had ruthlessly squashed his realization that he was in love with her, for neither of them had been free. They both were now. But he must be careful. He did not want to rush into anything he might regret. Or rush her into anything *she* might regret. He was not at all sure how she could fit into his life or how he could fit into hers. She saw all soldiers as killers. And she was not wrong. She did not like London, where he needed to be, at least for the foreseeable future. She loved her rural life in the hills above Bath.

She was twenty-one years old. He was thirty-four. It was a significant age gap. He had always thought five years either side of his age was the limit he was prepared to go. Grace was just four years younger than he. Winifred was thirteen.

"The races are all done," James said, getting to his feet. "I am headed for the maypole."

A crowd was already forming there. The maypole dancing by Sid Johnson's troupe had become increasingly popular over the years. There were several reasons. The dancing was a musical and visual spectacle, the men dancers all clad in shirts of varying pastel shades, their female partners in similarly shaded dresses. The ribbons were brightly multicolored. The fiddles were toe-tappingly good. But perhaps most popular of all were the brief lessons the troupe gave afterward to whoever was brave enough to step forward before a large audience, possibly to make spectacles of themselves. Young and old always took up the challenge, each to be partnered with one of the regular dancers while Sid called out clear instructions and the steps and patterns of the dance were kept simple.

Robert came running as the men approached and demanded a perch on Uncle Nick's shoulders again so he would be able to see. Most of the children wormed their way to the front. Stephanie was there with Winifred, their arms linked. Owen went to stand behind them and set a hand on a shoulder of each. Bertrand came along with Uncle George and one of Matthew Taylor's great-nephews.

The dancers were ready, each with a brightly colored ribbon in hand. A near hush fell on the crowd. The fiddles struck a decisive chord and launched into a lively tune. The dancers were off.

Nicholas marveled at their skill as they moved about the maypole, half going one way, half the other, performing intricate dance steps as they stretched over and ducked under one another's ribbons until to the spectator it seemed they must be impossibly tangled. But they never were. The dancers moved onward, and the ribbons untangled themselves as one set of the overall pattern was completed and a new one began. They were light-footed and graceful, smiling at one another and never making a false move. Just one would have hopelessly snarled the whole thing and ruined the dance.

There was a roar of enthusiastic applause when the first dance finished. Robert tightened his grip on Nicholas's chin and drummed his heels against Nicholas's chest as his uncle set two fingers to his lips and whistled his appreciation.

The troupe danced again, to a faster tune this time while their audience watched with awe and bated breath. The crowd was not willing to let them go when they were finished, and they obliged with two brief encores.

When the applause died away at last, Sid held up both arms for quiet. The usual lessons would be conducted a little differently this year, he announced, in order to accommodate all those who were courageous enough to try. They would be arranged in age groups, the over-fifties first. Who wanted to try?

Amid enthusiastic applause, Nicholas's mother stepped forward with Matthew Taylor and his brother. Aunt Kitty and Uncle George followed them and—great surprise—Mrs. Haviland. The other volunteers were villagers and people from the surrounding farming areas. Miss Jane Miller was among them.

Nicholas set Robert down so the child could wriggle his way forward to watch with other children.

The music was slow, the instructions simple and clear. The group did remarkably well, aided by the regular dancers who partnered each of them, having to stop only twice during the minute or so they danced so the ribbons could be unsnarled and everyone could return to their appointed stations.

The forty- to forty-nine-year-olds came next to undiminished enthusiasm from the crowd. Then it was the turn of the thirty- to thirty-nine-year-olds. Volunteers stepped forward to a great deal of merriment and teasing from the younger group. Nicholas was among them, as well as Pippa and Lucas and Mrs. Cunningham.

They did not do terribly well, thanks to the presence among them of one woman who persisted in dancing to her own tune and had no concept whatsoever of team play, and of one man who pranced about with frowning concentration and no sense of rhythm or timing. One wondered why he had volunteered.

Nicholas laughed as family and friends jeered good-naturedly at him. He caught Winifred's eye and winked. She laughed back and he knew he had not mistaken his feelings out on the island.

It was her turn then with others who were in their twenties. She and Stephanie dashed forward to volunteer. Owen and Bertrand and—yes, indeed—Grace followed them. Grace had shed her bonnet and her gloves and parasol somewhere along the way. They were far more successful as a group. Winifred, Nicholas saw as he watched, danced with sheer joy. Her younger brothers and sisters shrieked loudly in appreciation.

"She is *my sister*," Nicholas heard young Alice tell her companions.

"Well done, you sweet young twenty-or-so," Nicholas said to her as she left the maypole and brushed past him, flushed and happy.

She laughed at him as she walked on by. "You did not do too badly yourself, you old man," she said cheekily.

"Ha! You walked right into that one, Nick," Owen said from behind him with a roar of laughter.

Nicholas laughed too. And he noticed his little silver daisy pinned to the bodice of her dress as the sunlight caught it.

"I wonder if Mr. Johnson and his dancers would be willing to conduct a workshop at our home in Bath," he heard her say as some of the ten- to nineteen-year-olds pushed forward, including Robbie, surely to the surprise of all who knew him. A few of the neighborhood girls were eyeing him with interest, Nicholas noticed. "It would be enormously popular, I am sure."

Nicholas smiled. She was forever thinking of her home and her beloved arts center there and of ideas to expand their programs so they would not stagnate.

"I would wager Sid would be flattered by the offer," Owen said. "Whether he and his group would be able to accept is another matter, though. They are all working folk."

"Well, of course they are," she said. "But if we all gave up on certain dreams just because they are difficult to accomplish or because we do not have time for them, then dreams would be pointless, would they not? And life would be insufferably dull."

"Yes, Miss Cunningham, ma'am," Owen said.

"I asked for that," she said, laughing. "Sometimes I get very dogmatic in my opinions."

"If I were you, Winifred," Stephanie said, "I would talk to your parents and suggest that one of you ask Sid. The worst that could happen would be for him to say no. But I believe he and his dancers would be flattered."

"Amen," Nicholas said, turning toward them.

Winifred raised her eyes to his and flushed a deep crimson before looking back toward the maypole to watch the dancing lesson.

The morning was almost over. After weeks of preparations and eager anticipation, time was flying by. But there was still a luncheon snack to enjoy on the grass of the green or at the tables that had been set up outside the inn. The food, most notably the meat pasties for which Mrs. Berry was famous, had been lovingly and lavishly prepared in the kitchen of the inn. Lemonade and ale flowed freely. The coffee and tea urns were kept filled. It was going to be a day of feasting, with a picnic tea on the lawns and terrace of

Ravenswood during the afternoon and refreshments and supper to be served at the ball. In addition, there were the sweetmeats on sale at one of the booths, which had done a roaring trade all morning.

And there was the choir concert and organ recital to be enjoyed over the noon hour, after which most of the action would move up to the house for an afternoon packed with activities.

A largish number of people attended the concert. Many of them had a relative or neighbor or friend in the choir. And Sir Ifor was generally revered as a man of extraordinary talent. When he had inherited his title and property years ago as a young man and moved from Wales, barely able to speak English, he had been hugely disappointed that there was no organ in the church at Boscombe or indeed in any church within miles. He promptly bought a pipe organ at huge personal expense and installed both it and himself as organist in the Boscombe church. Then he discovered to his horror that there was no church choir and no congregational singing beyond a few low growls to the music pounded out on an ancient pianoforte. He soon set about putting that lack to rights. The vicar at the time had been astounded to discover his congregation growing every Sunday. He had set about paying more attention to the preparation of his sermons.

All the family and guests from Ravenswood attended. Stephanie was in the choir and had a solo part in one of their pieces. And it was the countess's father playing the organ. Even without that connection, though, Sir Ifor and Lady Rhys were openhearted neighbors and friends.

Nicholas sat at the back of the church so he could see everyone as well as savor the music. He felt a welling of love for all these people, most of whom were part of his roots and would always figure largely in his memories. He had deliberately opened up his memory today.

He had thought about that last fete before he left home. He had thought about his father, who had played such havoc with the lives of his wife and children and caused years of bitterness afterward. But Nicholas had let it go today. Holding grudges, retaining resentment, ultimately hurt the person doing it and put a certain blight on his life. He had come perilously close during the past week to making a loveless marriage because he had lost faith in love. It had been blind of him. He had only to look about at his own family and circle of friends to know that love was very much alive and life-giving.

The choir was in fine form. So was Steph, who looked, as she sang her solo part, almost ethereal in the dimness of the church, lit by the multicolored rays of the sun filtering through the stained glass windows. The bulk of the blond braids wound twice about her head looked like a halo. Her face shone with the joy of singing.

Sir Ifor filled the church with music by Bach, making it feel for the moment like a cathedral.

And all the time Nicholas was aware of Winifred, sitting in the midst of her family several pews in front of him, Emma on her lap, while Susan sat on Mrs. Cunningham's beside her. Andrew, sitting next to his father and unable to hear the music, gazed about at the architecture and the windows. Robbie was being watched and whispered over by a trio of young girls in the pew behind him. Sarah too had been attracting her share of admiration from the boys of the neighborhood.

She hated London. Winifred, that was. She far preferred the hills around Bath. She had a horror of the military with its ranks of killers, himself included. She was realistic about the shortcomings of out-and-out peace loving but was as close to being against all violence as she reasonably could be. She was a nameless orphan, who had been abandoned in a basket on the steps of an orphanage when she was about one month old. She was, from any objective standpoint, neither beautiful nor pretty. She had no figure to speak of. She was thirteen years his junior. *Thirteen*. She was Owen's friend. *Close friend*. She was very attached to her family and to the family enterprise in Bath, in which she was fully involved.

All of these facts, which had been churning in his head since yesterday, spelled just one word when added together. *Impossible*.

Not just unlikely or improbable.

Impossible.

Except that he was in love with her.

His daisy in a garden of elaborate, exotic blooms.

The recital was not a long one. It had been planned so in order not to cut into all the afternoon activities. The choir sang one encore when the audience demanded it of them, and that was it.

Stephanie accepted all the praises that were heaped upon her singing after the concert was over with her customary comment that it was the whole choir that had made the song so memorable. The last person to congratulate her was having nothing to do with such modesty, however.

"Rather, I would say it was you who made the choir memorable during that song, Stephanie," Bertrand Lamarr, Viscount Watley, said.

Stephanie smiled fleetingly as she thanked him and turned away. Fortunately, she had recovered from the terrible infatuation she had once felt for him and the feeling of inadequacy that had plagued her the last time he was here at Ravenswood, and in London during that horrid come-out Season. She had far more self-confidence these days, as she ought to at the age of twenty-five. She had not lied to Winifred a few days ago when she had said she was quite happy despite her single state. She rather enjoyed being single. And she did have prospects, amiable relationships with eligible gentlemen that might or might not blossom into definite courtship. She was certainly not desperate. However, she would be happier without the reminder of her former self in the form of Viscount Watley. She wished he would go away.

"May I walk back to Ravenswood with you?" he asked.

It was impossible to say no without being unpardonably rude. The choir had dispersed. Sir Ifor was leaving the church with Lady Rhys. She sighed inwardly.

"Thank you," she said.

He was smiling and looking thoroughly amiable. Did he ever *not* look amiable?

"Tell me about your sister's baby," she said as they walked. "David, I believe? This must be a very exciting time for her and her husband. And for you."

"Well," he said, "he is the most handsome baby in the world, of course." There was laughter in his voice.

"I am familiar with the conviction that there can be no more beautiful a baby than the one that has just been born," she said. "I was here when Devlin and Gwyneth's children were born, and I spent time with Pippa when Pamela was born. Oh, the wonder of it. I love being an aunt. Do you love being an uncle?"

"I do," he said as they crossed the bridge out of the village. "Will you reserve a set for me at tonight's ball, Stephanie? Preferably a waltz?"

Oh, she *adored* waltzing. But really? With Bertrand Lamarr, Viscount Watley? What had prompted him to ask her of all people? She had not been impolite to him since his arrival, but she had not encouraged him either.

And then, just as she was opening her mouth to say a polite yes, it happened—the overpowering urge to wipe the amiable expression from his face. Suddenly, it looked not amiable but . . . complacent.

"Thank you, but no," she said.

He looked at her with raised eyebrows. "Ah," he said. "You have promised the waltz to someone else, have you? Perhaps, then, some other—"

"No." She cut him off. "I do not wish to dance with you, Viscount Watley. I wish you would leave me alone. I wish you would not assume that you can have whatever you want whenever you want it. I do not wish to dance with you, this evening or ever."

She listened to herself, appalled. When had he ever shown any sign of arrogance or entitlement? When had she ever been rude to anyone? Courtesy at all costs had been drilled into her from childhood on.

"Besides," she said, "this is a country ball. No one has to reserve a set ahead of time."

His face was blank of all expression. But there was surely a bit of a flush in his cheeks.

"I beg your pardon." He made her a stiff bow. "I did not realize I had been pestering you and that my attentions, such as they have been, are unwelcome to you. It will not happen again."

He turned on his heel and left her standing in the middle of the bridge.

CHAPTER EIGHTEEN

Winifred spent some time with her mother and Sarah, looking at the display of items for the baking contest along the western side of the courtyard and the needlework items on the eastern side. The dowager countess had arranged everything there in what itself was a sort of work of art. Everything had been carefully placed so that one color and shade blended into that of its neighbor along the whole length of the tables. And the needlework itself was nothing short of exquisite.

There were many other people, mostly women, looking at the displays too, trying to guess which items would win prizes.

"There is certainly no shortage of talent in the neighborhood," Mama said.

"I do not envy the judges," Sarah said. "How will they choose a winner? I think they *all* deserve a prize."

"I would have to agree," Winifred said.

They looked at the woodwork entries—and the stonework one—displayed on a long table out on the terrace and were left with the same impression. All were deserving of a prize. Andrew was there too with Papa, running his fingers lightly over a few of the wood carvings, though onlookers were not supposed to touch. But touch seemed important to the artist in Andrew, and he was being treated with kindly indulgence by everyone who understood his affliction—if one chose to call his deafness that. Perhaps it was merely a special ability, which was what Papa always said. And everyone knew that he was the one with the stonework entry.

How lovely it would be if he won a prize. But the competition was stiff, and they must not expect him to be given special treatment in the judging.

Blankets had been spread on the grass for the convenience of families. There were chairs in clusters for the older people, though a salon indoors had also been opened for any who wished to escape from the noise and bustle and heat of the sun for a while. Jennifer Ellis was in there currently, with young Belinda fast asleep on her lap. Ben's aunt kept her company. There were tables on the terrace with jugs of lemonade and urns of tea as well as plates of freshly baked biscuits of all kinds.

Children were running about on the lawns, released from the formality of the races as they played games of their own devising. These involved a great deal of noise and shrieking. Winifred watched them for a while from the edge of the terrace, but she was eager to go out to the poplar alley, where the archery contest was due to begin soon. A number of other people were already on their way there. Winifred was eager to see Owen compete, and Mr. Taylor, whose shooting was apparently the stuff of legends in the neighborhood. Especially, though, she wanted to watch Robbie, though she felt horribly anxious for him. She hoped he would not do terribly and disappoint himself. She hoped he would not feel humiliated if that happened. Oh, *please* let him acquit himself at least respectably. She knew, though, that Owen would find some way of cheering him up. For some reason Robbie had become attached to Owen, a fact that perhaps boded well for Owen's most fervent dream of working with troubled young people and perhaps employing Robbie to help him.

Winifred turned away from the activity outside the house and hurried to the alley. She did not want to miss a single shot. She joined a group that included her parents, Andrew, Ben Ellis, and Lucas, Duke of Wilby. Colonel Ware joined them just before the contest began.

It was all very exciting, Winifred thought. There were twenty-five contestants, varying, she discovered during the course of the contest, between those who were both experienced and skilled and those who were new to the sport or quite lacking in the basic skills necessary to improve with practice. But all were entertaining to watch. Each was given four minutes in which to shoot six arrows. The Earl of Stratton was keeping the time. Several of the contestants began their set reasonably well, but as they became aware of their time speeding by, their aim became more erratic.

"However do they hit the target at all?" Winifred asked of no one in particular. It looked like an impossibility to her. The target seemed to be too far away from the line behind which each archer had to stand. But most contestants succeeded in sinking their arrows into it, though very few reached the inner rings, which carried the highest scores.

"With a good eye and a steady arm," Colonel Ware said.

"And lots of practice," Mr. Ellis added.

"It looks as though many of these archers practice for a day or two before the fete," the Duke of Wilby said, chuckling, "and do not give it a thought for the rest of the year. However, I admire the fact that they are willing to compete at all. It is a difficult sport."

Winifred held her breath when it was Owen's turn. *Please don't let him utterly disgrace himself,* she prayed to some unnamed deity. Was there a god of archery in any culture? She hardly dared watch. But moments after he shot his first arrow, there was a roar from the spectators. It had hit the very center of the target.

"There is a God," Colonel Ware said. "He has never come even close before."

Alas, two of his remaining arrows hit the outer rings of the target while the remaining three fell harmlessly to the grass, not even close.

He looked delighted with himself afterward as he grinned at his family and friends.

"A pure fluke," he said.

And then it was Robbie's turn. Mama was clutching Papa's arm, Winifred noticed, and Andrew was watching intently. She held her breath as the earl gave the signal to start and Robbie raised the bow into position. He shot all his arrows with a minute to spare and hit the target with all but one of them. None stuck within the inner rings, but he looked eagerly at Owen anyway when he had finished, and he smiled.

Oh, it was so rare to see Robbie smile.

Mama and Papa were both hugging him. So was Andrew. And so was Winifred.

"Oh, well done," she cried.

But an expectant hush had fallen all about them. Mr. Taylor had taken his place at the shooting line. He was the final contestant. He fixed his eyes on the target and half closed them. Winifred could see that his concentration was total. She guessed he was quite unaware of all the people waiting with bated breath for him to shoot his arrows. He did not even move when the Earl of Stratton gave him the signal to start. He stood quite still for at least half a minute longer and then raised his bow unhurriedly. His quiver of arrows was slung over one shoulder. And then he shot—six arrows, one after the other, with no discernible pause between.

The near silence of the crowd held for a few moments after the last arrow had left his bow. And then they roared as one as it became clear that every single arrow had found its way to the very heart of the target.

"Good God," Papa said irreverently. "Is it possible?"

"No," Colonel Ware said. "It is not. But we have all seen it done anyway. I wonder what his secret is."

Winifred turned toward him and smiled.

The dowager countess was hurrying toward her husband to be caught up in a tight hug.

Ah, what a wonderful time this was, Winifred thought. Robbie had placed fourteenth out of the field of twenty-five. How extraordinary when he had only just discovered the sport. Owen placed twenty-second, his best ever result. He boasted of it, laughing, as his brother and his cousin, who had placed two positions lower, slapped him on the back.

"Did you see that first arrow of mine, Winifred?" he asked.

"I did indeed," she said. "It was a magnificent shot."

"I am thinking of having that arrow cast in bronze," he said, "to mount on the wall of my bedchamber to remind me of my greatest moment."

The whole group laughed.

He was such a good sport, she thought. She walked back to the house between him and Colonel Ware.

"Are you going to watch the log hewing, Winifred?" Owen asked. "Lots of women do. It is coming up next."

"But of course," she said. "I do not want to miss a single thing."

"I wonder," Colonel Ware said, "if you would reserve the first waltz of the ball for me, Winifred. I thought I would get my word in before Owen."

"There is to be more than one waltz," Owen said. "There always is. Everyone loves the dance even though there are a few diehards who still consider it a bit scandalous. Anyway, Nick, you know very well that this is always an informal ball. One does not have to reserve sets in advance."

"Except when one wants to be certain of a particular partner for a particular dance," Colonel Ware said. "Win?"

She was having difficulty catching her breath, which was very silly of her. It was just a dance, after all.

"I will squeeze your name onto my very full dance card," she said.

He had danced with her at Aunt Anna's ball perhaps because he had felt obliged since it was her come-out ball, and perhaps because he had wanted to grill her over her eligibility to be courted by his brother. It had not been a waltz. It had not gone well, that dance and the supper that followed it. She had made an idiot of herself by saying she was a hater of all warfare and telling him her first impression had been that he was a cruel man. And he had firmly defended himself for being a killer, as all military men who had seen battle were.

That seemed like a million years ago.

She looked at him now, her teeth sinking into her lower lip. What was his motive this time?

"I am flattered," he said.

Why did time always seem to speed up when one was enjoying oneself? It was already well into the afternoon, and Nicholas was desperately trying to live every moment to the full and commit it all to memory. Home, family—how infinitely precious they were. It was *not* a very original thought, of course. And it was not as though he had not thought it before. He had not neglected either or taken either for granted. He had wanted his own home and his own family too. But while trying to force the issue during the past few months and choosing a woman he had thought would be the perfect wife, he had forgotten that there was something that bound together home and family and superseded them both. He had forgotten love.

He had quite deliberately stopped loving after being hurt so crushingly by his father. It *did* hurt to love. He simply would not do it any longer and so make himself forever invulnerable, he had decided. Oh, he had not done so consciously, but he had done it nevertheless. He had been unable to forgive his father for betraying them so selfishly. He had been unable to forgive his mother for hiding the truth from them all their lives. Or for sending Devlin away, as she had done the night it all happened. He had not been able to forgive his own naïveté.

But love had played a trick on him. For it would not die. It might be denied, pushed deep, replaced by practicality and common sense. It could not be killed, though, like an enemy in battle. It had been needling at him for a while now, especially during the past couple of weeks. Today, at the summer fete, the occasion that had started it all many years ago—sixteen, to be precise—it had finally burst free. He even saw with new eyes today. Everything seemed brighter, almost as though he had been looking through a veil of gauze and now saw a glorious dazzle of color.

Even before they reached the house on their way back from the poplar alley, he could hear the music. Bright, cheerful, toe-tapping music. The huge lawn before the house was crowded with people of all ages, as it always was at this stage of the fete—children and their parents, older people seated on comfortable chairs about the perimeter so they would not cut into the playing area. The fiddlers who had played for the maypole dancing in the village had come up to the house, bringing their violins with them. It looked as if most or all of the dancers had come too. They were out on the lawn now, surrounded by eager children, who were learning the steps of a simple country dance. The children were dancing with enthusiasm and varying degrees of skill. A few, especially the toddlers, were simply bouncing in place, clapping their hands.

It was something new. Nicholas could not remember it happening at any other fete. The adults were listening and watching, many of them clapping in time to the music. The sun beamed down from a cloudless deep blue sky.

And he felt almost like weeping. Could there possibly be a more perfect moment in an already perfect day?

There was no time to linger, however. The log-hewing contest was due to begin very soon. It was always a popular event. He went back to the stable yard with Devlin and Ben and Owen and Robbie, taking a shortcut through the courtyard and so out through the north wing. The courtyard was crowded with people, mostly women, looking at the displays of baking and needlecraft and guessing who the winners would be. There was a short line of people waiting outside the fortune-teller's tent in the far corner.

The stable yard was packed with spectators, mostly men but not entirely. Stephanie was there with Winifred and Sarah and Matthew Taylor's niece. And, Nicholas saw with some surprise, Grace was there as well, with James Rutledge and Bradley Danver and Bertrand Lamarr. She even appeared to be enjoying herself. Indeed, she had looked the same way all day, and very popular she had been too with the single men from miles around.

Had she also been released to love again and enjoy life again and look forward to the future with hope again when she had found the courage to refuse his marriage offer yesterday? And good God, had it really been just yesterday? Was he getting a glimpse today of Grace as she had been as a very young woman? He caught her eye across the yard and smiled at her. She smiled back.

The first bout of the contest was about to begin. Two brawny young men, neither of whom Nicholas knew, wearing only thin white shirts open at the neck with their breeches and boots, sleeves rolled to the elbow, took their places before the massive blocks of wood that awaited them and grasped their axes. Their bare arms and broad chests fairly rippled with hard muscles.

Devlin gave the signal to start.

The two blocks might have been made of butter for all the resistance they could offer the would-be champions. One was hacked through in under two minutes, the other mere seconds later. The winner pranced around the yard, flexing his muscles and celebrating with the cheering crowd. At this rate they would all be hoarse before the contest was over.

There were four elimination bouts before the winners went head-to-head with one another and the number was whittled down to two finalists. They were going to be exhausted afterward, Nicholas thought. There were going to be sore muscles and blistered palms tomorrow.

The eventual winner was a young laborer from David Cox's farm a mere two miles from Boscombe. The crowd applauded and cheered and whistled over his win, while the loser, in the true tradition of the sport, congratulated his opponent and raised his arm high in the air. He had lost by a mere whisker.

"Next year I'll get my revenge," he said with a broad grin. "My block was harder than yours this year, and my axe was blunter."

Nicholas could hear that the fiddles were still playing at the front of the house. The presentation of ribbons to the winners of the various contests would be made soon, and that would be followed by the picnic tea being prepared in the Ravenswood kitchens. The days when the refreshments and supper for the ball were prepared there too were long gone, however. The planning committee had taken charge of all that, and Jim Berry and his wife had taken it on, with the help of a small army of volunteers.

Ah, the ball. And the first waltz. Would it finally erase the leftover bitterness of that ball sixteen years ago? Winifred had been five at that time and living in an orphanage in Bath, without roots or family or the assurance of unconditional love and a lasting home.

And he had thought *he* had troubles!

But . . . Inadvertently he had reminded himself of that thirteen-year gap in their ages.

And she still felt an attachment to Owen. She was talking with him now as they made their way back to the front of the house. They looked as absorbed in each other's company as they ever had.

Nicholas thought back to the fete sixteen years ago, soon after he and Gwyneth had agreed to pull back on their friendship, which was being misunderstood by all who knew them. He remembered his surprise, not all of it welcome, at seeing the romance that blossomed between her and Devlin during that day. It had not been exactly jealousy he had felt. It had been more the feeling that he had been set back upon his heels, that he had thought he knew her through and through when he had missed that obvious fact about her. All the time she had been his close friend, she had been hiding an intense attraction to his brother. He had missed all the signs—just as he had missed all the signs that his father was not the paragon of virtue and devotion to family Nicholas had always believed him to be.

Was he just very bad at reading signs?

Would Winifred be laughing if she knew he had fallen in love with her? No, surely not that. She was not the type to ridicule others. There was no cruelty in her. Would she be horrified? That a military man, a killer, who lived and worked in London, expected her to give up the family and the life in Bath she clearly loved so dearly for him?

Not that he *expected* any such thing.

But it was unlike him to be so unsure of himself. He had always been confident in his dealings with women. He had always expected to be liked by men and women alike, and it seemed to him that most people did like him. Perhaps because he liked most people.

But he was as nervous as a schoolboy about his dance with Winifred this evening. His *waltz* with her.

Her younger siblings came dashing toward her across the grass when she reached the terrace and bore her off to join the other children in some unidentifiable game. The fiddlers were no longer playing for them. They were moving about the edge of the lawn instead, playing for the older people, who paused in their conversations to listen and tap their feet and smile.

But he must forget about the ball and enjoy the moment to the full, Nicholas decided as he went down on his haunches to talk to his grandparents and Miss Delmont and a few other elderly people sitting with them. He would enjoy every moment as he lived it and let the ball take care of itself.

He would remember this day, though, as some sort of turning point in his life. A turn surely for the better, even if . . . Well, *even if*. He was not going to close his heart to love again. Sixteen years was quite a long enough spell.

Remember that day. He heard the echo of the advice he had given Winifred when he came across her as she was watching her deaf brother run down a slope, pretending to be a bird, and Nicholas realized he had surprised her in a moment of uncharacteristic despondency.

He still thought it had been decent advice. He would apply it to himself. He would remember today.

Though tonight's ball was still an unknown.

For the moment he was content to leave it that way.

One moment at a time.

CHAPTER NINETEEN

As she dressed for the ball, Winifred tried to decide what had been her favorite part of the day so far. It was almost impossible. Every part had been her favorite.

A main contender, though, must be the moment when they had learned that Andrew had won the carving contest with his stone sheep and lamb. Mama had squealed as the card marked *First Place* had been set beside it and she jumped up and down like a girl. Papa, unable to hold back his tears, had hugged Andrew tightly while Winifred explained to her brother in sign language what had happened. Robbie, quite forgetting to look sullen, had smiled broadly as he thumped Andrew on the back, and the other children joined Mama in jumping up and down, cheering. Susan and Emma hugged Andrew's legs, almost tipping him over. He was laughing in his ungainly fashion.

Oh, yes, that had definitely been a highlight of the day. Perhaps *the* highlight. Winifred could feel tears well in her eyes just at the thought of that scene and Andrew's excitement as Papa led him forward a short while later to receive his winner's red ribbon from the Earl of Stratton.

Oh, but there had been other highlights too—browsing with the little girls at the stall with all the purses and bags; watching the maypole dancing and then actually participating herself; listening to Stephanie and the choir and the organ in the cool dimness of the church; watching the archery and the log-hewing contests; sitting on the grass during the picnic tea, listening to Mr. and Mrs. Greenfield and Miss Delmont reminisce about days long gone; and . . . Oh, and being asked to reserve a waltz for Colonel Ware at the ball tonight. Apparently, no one *ever* reserved dances ahead of time for that event. It was not a formal affair, after all. But Colonel Ware, who must have known that, had reserved the waltz with her anyway.

Winifred dared not ask herself what it meant beyond the fact that she was going to dance at least one waltz tonight—and not with General Haviland this time.

Suddenly, looking herself over in the pier glass in her small dressing room—she was wearing her longtime favorite muslin dress, which wafted about her when she moved and made her feel very feminine—she squeaked and made a dash for the bedchamber and the daisy brooch she had set down on the dressing table for safekeeping before taking off the dress she had worn all day. She had almost forgotten it. She took it back into the dressing room and pinned it carefully to the bosom of her dress. It was her only piece of jewelry. The gold Papa had given her for Aunt Anna's ball would not suit the muslin.

She smoothed her fingertips over the brooch and smiled at her image. Another definite highlight of the day. She knew it was cheap and not even close to being real silver, but to her it was priceless.

She turned her head from side to side. She liked what she had done with her hair. It was pretty much in its usual style, but she had managed to get the knot high on the back of her head without leaving behind long strands of hair to dangle untidily over her neck. Her neck somehow looked longer with her hair this way.

And since when had her appearance really mattered to her? She had decided long ago that she was not pretty and there was no point in lamenting the fact. Being neat and tidy was good enough. She only ever looked in a mirror for practical purposes. She very rarely looked *at* herself.

She looked now and was pleased with what she saw. She was a young woman, eager to proceed with her life—and all the rest of her life stretched before her, filled to the brim with possibility. She could do and be whatever she wished. She was neither pretty nor shapely, but she was not an antidote either. Tonight there was even color in her cheeks and a sparkle in her eyes. And her smile, she decided, trying it out, was . . . nice.

She did not know how much she would dance tonight. This was not her come-out ball, after all, with Aunt Anna to make sure she had a partner for each set. But she would not mind if no one else asked except Colonel Ware—though surely *someone* would. She was now acquainted with a largish number of people here, and she felt comfortable with them. She would dance a waltz at least. Oh, she wished she could slow time when it began and waltz forever.

She laughed at the silly thought.

There was a knock on the door of her bedchamber, and she poked her head out of the dressing room to call to whoever it was to enter. Sarah, dressed all in pale pink, looked impossibly pretty. She was fairly bursting with excitement.

"I cannot *believe*," she said, "that I am allowed to dance. Is this not the most exciting night *ever*, Winnie? Oh, you do look nice. I like your hair that way. You look . . . elegant. And pretty."

"And you look extremely pretty," Winifred said. "Shall we go down to the ballroom?"

"Oh yes," Sarah said. "Do you think any of the boys I met today will ask me to dance?"

"If they can find the courage," Winifred said, laughing. "But you know how self-conscious and unsure of themselves boys can be, especially with pretty girls."

Sarah had attracted a following of them during the day, blushing boys who had gazed worshipfully at her and bolder boys who had acted tough and shown off for her. They had tended to cluster in groups to give one another courage.

Ah, courage!

But she did not need to find it, Winifred told herself. She had already been asked for a waltz. Her heart was beating almost painfully in her chest anyway as she left the room with her sister and closed the door behind her.

She wondered if she would remember today as one of the happiest of her life, as she remembered that other day when she was nine years old.

Nicholas had been to other summer fetes since the one that had ended so disastrously sixteen years ago. He had always shut his mind to the memories and enjoyed himself anyway. All day this year he had been unable to forget. Tonight, memory pressed on him, and he no longer tried to block it.

The family had always gathered in the ballroom ahead of everyone else, just as they had now. In those days, of course, they had been the hosts. They had greeted all the guests with a handshake and words of welcome even though they had been mingling all day with those same people. The fete had been all about warm hospitality in those days. His father had thrived on such occasions, and his mother had always exuded the warm charm for which she was known. The rest of them had grinned and been happy.

They had met here on that particular evening, and his father had greeted them with a beaming countenance and effusive praise of each member of his family. His love for them all had brought him close to tears. After that night, Nicholas had looked back bitterly on the hypocrisy. For his father had been expecting the arrival of his mistress before much longer and was planning a private liaison with her outside in the temple folly.

Now Nicholas was not so sure it had been all hypocrisy. His father's love for his family, including his wife, had always seemed genuine. It was far more likely that his tearful sentimentality that evening had been caused by guilt. He must have realized that he was about to go one step too far, that he had hopelessly mingled his two lives, which he had kept strictly apart during the more than twenty years of his marriage.

It was difficult to forgive him anyway. His infidelities, made so public on that occasion, had wreaked terrible havoc with all their lives. Yet afterward, his father had continued as he always had been, the genial, gregarious family man and friend and neighbor, as though he felt no shame. But was that possible? Mama had been publicly humiliated. His two oldest sons had left home the very next day and ended up in the Peninsula, one of the most dangerous places on earth to be. His third son had left a couple of months later for the same destination and had said not a word of farewell to his father. Pippa, left behind with the younger two, had been pale and listless and withdrawn even before Nicholas left, while Owen and Stephanie were bewildered and desperately unhappy, the security of their childhood lives forever snatched away from them. And the bright and busy social life of Ravenswood, in which his father had so reveled, had come to an end.

His father could not have remained oblivious to it all, Nicholas realized. He must have suffered dreadful anguish, seeing what his thoughtless, selfish actions had done to his beloved family, knowing that it was impossible to put things right. For the last few years of his life, he had surely been weighted down by guilt and misery, his surface joviality just a front for what he had felt inside. It might all have contributed to his sudden, early death.

This understanding of how the catastrophe might have affected his father did not render his actions forgivable, of course. But often, even perhaps usually, *not* forgiving did far more harm than good to the one who refused forgiveness. It was a case of righteousness versus compassion. And whereas compassion often seemed weak, righteousness could make one brittle and bitter and essentially unhappy.

Stephanie came now and linked an arm through his. "I am very glad that Mama—and Gwyneth—have not had to do all the planning for tonight on top of everything else Mama used to do," she said. "However did she do it, Nick?"

"By scarcely sleeping or even sitting down for weeks on end before the fete," he said. "And then by appearing relaxed and happy on the day as though all the perfection had just happened."

"I am so glad she has Matthew now," she said. "She deserves a happily ever after, does she not?"

It was as close as she had ever come to referring to the past. He wondered how badly she had been affected. He could remember her crying inconsolably when Devlin and Ben left so abruptly, almost in the middle of the night, and then breaking down in tears again and clinging to him when *he* left less than two months later. Poor nine-year-old Steph.

She had adored their father. He had been her idol, and she had been his special pet.

"I am certainly happy that other people are doing all this," he said, indicating the floral arrangements that had turned the ballroom into an indoor garden and the long tables lining the wall and covering one set of the French windows on the other side, with their crisp white cloths ready to be loaded with refreshments. An inner room was bustling with activity and the sound of voices, most notably that of Jim Berry, landlord of the inn, who had been in charge of all the food today, a gigantic task he had undertaken for years past with great enthusiasm and delicious results. Mrs. Berry did much of the cooking, with the help of volunteers, but he worked just as hard as she. They were a good team.

"And yes, I am happy for Mama," he said, looking across at her. She was talking with Pippa and Lucas. She exuded happiness, and Matthew Taylor, watching her as she talked, her arm drawn through his, was beaming with pride.

"The ball is always both a happy and a sad occasion, is it not?" Devlin said, strolling up to them. "Happy because it is the culmination of the day's festivities and sad because the fete is almost over for another year. Ah. I believe people are beginning to arrive."

They were no longer the official hosts, but the ballroom *was* part of Ravenswood, and they would hover close to the doorway to shake hands with guests as they arrived and make them feel welcome.

Nicholas's leg had been aching earlier from all the walking and standing he had done today. But he had forgotten it now. He would dance all evening and suffer any consequences tomorrow. The ball never continued late into the night anyway, as *ton* balls in London tended to do. Many of the folk here had chores to get up for. Cattle and other farm animals would not wait to be fed or milked or exercised just because the farmer had danced the night away. And babies would show no mercy to their mothers when they were hungry in the early morning.

Nicholas shook a number of hands before he saw the person he most wanted to see. She came with her parents and her siblings—except for the very young ones, who would have remained in the nursery, to be joined by other infants from the neighborhood. They would enjoy a party of their own under the supervision of nurses and a few volunteers from the village and be put to bed when they were ready.

Winifred was not dressed formally, as indeed none of the family were, but she looked pretty in her light-colored floral muslin dress with her hair high on her head in a style that made her look youthful and flattered her neck. She wore no jewelry—though even as he thought it, Nicholas noticed the daisy brooch pinned to the bodice of her dress.

Owen was the first to greet the Cunninghams and stand chatting with them for a few moments before turning his attention to other new arrivals. Pippa came to greet them too and kissed Winifred and Sarah on the cheek. Nicholas shook hands with a young couple, tenant farmers from a few miles away, before greeting the Cunninghams himself.

"Thank you for painting such a lovely portrait of my mother," he said, shaking Joel Cunningham by the hand. "And thank *you*, ma'am, for taking on the gargantuan task of bringing all your family here. You have all been a delight."

He thought anew, looking into her bright, happy face, that she could not be more than a year or two older than he. It was not a comfortable thought under the circumstances.

"I have never seen anything more breathtaking in my life," Sarah said when Nicholas took her hand and patted the back of it. "All the flowers! And the candles all alight in the chandeliers! Is this what a *ton* ballroom during the Season in London looks like?"

He smiled in some amusement. "There is never such a warm, festive atmosphere there as we have here tonight," he said.

He shook Robbie's hand and commended him on his archery skills. And he shook Andrew's hand and winked at him. The boy smiled back and indicated all the flowers, making circular motions from them to his nose as he did so, inhaling and half closing his eyes. *What a wonderful scent.*

Yes. Nicholas nodded.

Children over eight were allowed to attend the ball until just before the supper hour, when they would join the younger children in the nursery for a light banquet—if there was such a thing—of their own. But the young Cunninghams had already dashed off to join Gareth and Joy and a host of other friends they had made during the day.

Nicholas turned to Winifred. "You are looking delightful," he said, taking her hand and raising it to his lips. "Would you be willing to postpone our dance to the *second* waltz of the evening? It is the supper dance, though I promise not to use the time interrogating you over your credentials or discussing with you the dubious merits of refusing to engage in warfare, no matter what the provocation. I hope if you are not ravenously hungry you will step outside with me instead. It is a warm evening and will be perfect for a walk in the moonlight."

Had he gone too far, too fast? But dash it all, she was leaving with her family on Monday. He might never see her again.

She bit her lower lip.

"I do not believe I will be hungry," she said.

He smiled and let go of her hand to help his family greet the remaining guests. There would be very few lingerers. Country folk were generally not given to being fashionably late to social events.

Winifred would indeed have thought this one of the happiest days of her life had she not been constantly aware that on Monday—the day after tomorrow—she would be going home to Bath with her family, and all this would become a distant, bittersweet memory.

She tried desperately not to dwell on the future, even when it was as close as Monday, but to live for the moment and enjoy every one as it came. And there had been *so* much to enjoy, with the ball still to come. And her waltz with Colonel Ware. She had dared not read too much into his reserving the dance with her. They had become friends of a sort during the past couple of weeks. That was all. Both of them had come here half hoping—more than half in his case—to be betrothed to other people by today. But it had not happened for either of them, and it was perhaps understandable that they should turn to each other in a sort of friendship.

And thus she rationalized his interest in her today—and hers in him.

She had tried to convince herself all afternoon and again this evening that there was nothing more than friendship between them. There were too many valid reasons why they should not mean more to each other, not least of which was the age difference.

Mama had had a birthday just before they came here, her thirty-fifth. He was thirty-four. It was true that Mama was less than fourteen years older than she was. She had not given birth to Winifred, after all. But even so ... Well, Winifred was in the habit of looking upon her parents as being one whole generation up from her own.

Any relationship with Colonel Ware was impossible anyway, for all sorts of other reasons. Her realization of that fact had threatened to drag at her spirits all day. She had fought back by *remembering that day*, the happiest of her life. The day when Mama had asked her to go with her and Papa as their daughter when they married. The trouble was, though, that she always heard those words in her head in his voice—*remember that day*. She even tried to imagine what her life would be like now if there had not been that day. But it was impossible to do, and pointless anyway. For there had been that day and all the myriad blessings it had bestowed upon her. It really was not a terrible fate to be going back home on Monday to the life and surroundings that had always brought her happiness and a sense of purpose.

But now ...

Well, now he had shifted their waltz to coincide with the supper dance. But it was not so he would be able to sit and converse with her at supper. Instead, he had invited her to step outside with him to enjoy the cooler air of evening and a walk in the moonlight.

She felt sick with apprehension. And excitement. And forgot all the reasons why she ought to have said no. She very much feared she was in love with Colonel Nicholas Ware.

In the meantime, she chatted with villagers she had met today and with the family and guests from Ravenswood, including Mrs. and Miss Haviland, both of whom had looked more relaxed in the past couple of days, especially today, when Winifred would swear they had both been enjoying themselves. Miss Haviland had picked up an impressive court of followers. They would surely be clamoring and vying with one another for her hand when the dancing began.

All would be well, Winifred decided.

Finally, Eluned Rhys, as head of the committee in charge of the fete, stepped up onto the dais with the orchestra and waited for a hush to fall upon the crowd below. She welcomed them all, thanked the Earl and Countess of Stratton for making their ballroom available for the occasion, thanked the army of volunteers who had decorated the ballroom so lavishly and those who had provided the flowers in such abundance. She thanked those volunteers who even now were preparing to bring out the drinks and light refreshments to set on the tables. She especially thanked the Berrys, who had worked tirelessly to keep them all well fed throughout the day and would cater to the supper later. She was interrupted several times by bursts of warm applause. And she thanked everyone who had done anything to make this surely the best of all fetes within living memory.

There was an enthusiastic cheer.

And finally she announced the first set, and the dancing began.

Winifred danced the opening set of country dances with Bertrand, as she had done at Aunt Anna's ball, and the second with Owen, as she had also done then. She danced the first waltz with the vicar's son, one of Owen's friends, and saw that Mama was dancing it with Papa, the two of them looking thoroughly happy and absorbed in each other. Sarah was dancing with a tall, gangly young boy, all elbows and eager, uncoordinated movements. The Duke of Wilby danced with Pippa, Mr. Rutledge with Stephanie, Miss Haviland with Owen. Oh, and just outside the French windows, which had been opened wide to let in some cool air, Ben Ellis had raised his wife from her wheeled chair and was shuffling slowly with her in time to the music. She was moving awkwardly and laughing up at him, and he was gazing back at her, naked love in his eyes.

Oh!

Was any more romantic sight possible?

Winifred wanted to halt the forward progress of the ball at the same time as she wanted to hurry it along to the supper dance. It was fortunate, perhaps, that one's wishes had no effect upon the passage of time. Inevitably the second waltz was announced, and everyone chose their partners. Colonel Ware came to claim her hand.

He was so terribly handsome, she thought. Often, though she always scolded herself for it, she was intimidated by very handsome men, conscious of the fact that she had no beauty of her own to match theirs. But he had noticed her during the past two weeks anyway. He had bought her the silver daisy brooch this morning. *A humble, often overlooked, underrated flower that is nevertheless one of the prettiest and most enduring of all.* And he had said it must surely have been made just for her. He had asked her, quite unbidden, to waltz with him this evening. And he had wanted the supper dance so he could take her outside to walk in the moonlight.

She definitely, desperately wanted to halt time.

The music was lilting, the rhythm slow. She set her left hand on his shoulder as his right came about her waist and his other hand clasped hers. He was very large and very solid—foolish thoughts. He was wearing some sort of cologne, though nothing to assault her senses. She could not even identify what it was. But it emphasized his masculinity, as though it needed emphasizing. And she felt his body heat and the confident way he led her into the dance. She could not have taken a misstep or somehow got her feet beneath his if she had tried, she was convinced. It seemed to her as they danced that he was utterly trustworthy, not in any overbearing way, only . . .

Oh, she could not think of the words for which her mind reached. But she did not need words. This was the time to *feel*.

And she felt as though there was mere air beneath her feet. He twirled her about a corner of the ballroom, and all the myriad flowers and evening dresses and the light from the candles in the candelabra overhead and in the wall sconces swirled with them into a kaleidoscope of merging light and color. She felt the music in him and in her very bones. And never had the waltz been like this. She tipped back her head and smiled up at him. He was looking at her, but he was not smiling in return. There was an intense look in his eyes. His jaw was solid, his lips set firm, and she saw again the military officer who had ridden past her at the Horse Guards Parade that day of Trooping the Colour. At the same time, she saw Nicholas, and the two were all blended together to show her a complete and complex man who could not be defined by labels.

And she loved him.

No matter the impossibility of it all. She *loved* him.

The music drew to its inevitable end, and dancers and spectators began to make their way to the room next to the ballroom, which had been set up for supper. The noise of children at play beyond the French windows had stopped, Winifred realized. They must all have been taken to the nursery floor, lured there, no doubt, by the promise of their very own banquet.

"Will you need a shawl to wear outside?" the colonel asked.

"No." She shook her head. "If there is any coolness out there, I will welcome it against my bare arms."

"Shall we, then?" he asked, gesturing toward the terrace.

"Yes," she said. "Thank you."

CHAPTER TWENTY

General Haviland had contrived to have a word with Nicholas after tea, when most of the outside guests had disappeared homeward to snatch a bit of a rest before returning for the ball, and most of the family and household guests had gone indoors, some to their rooms, others to the drawing room to relax after what they all agreed had been a crackingly successful day.

The two of them had gone outside to stroll on the terrace.

"It is good to enjoy a bit of quiet time," the general had said. "We are honored to have been a part of all this, Ware. You have a gracious family."

They had not had any private conversation since their formal meeting in the library two days ago. Nicholas had braced himself for a blistering condemnation, but it had not happened. Rather, the general had proceeded to apologize for his daughter's refusal of Nicholas's very flattering offer.

"Her mother and I were dumbfounded when she told us," he had said. "It was the very last thing we expected. Grace has always been the most biddable of daughters. She seemed to agree wholeheartedly with her mother and me that marrying you would be to her advantage in every way. She seemed fond of you. She insists that she still is, in fact. If only she had *talked* to us. We would never dream of forcing her into something she did not want. She is all we have, Colonel. This has all been a great humiliation for us. I feel we have been invited here and treated royally under quite false pretenses."

"No, no, sir," Nicholas had said, acutely aware of the general's distress. "Did Grace not tell you that our decision was mutually and amicably agreed upon? Our conversation that day led us to the unexpected conclusion that while we genuinely like each other, and are and will remain friends, neither of us really desires the greater intimacy of marriage. Grace has looked happy today, as though, having faced her true feelings, she is ready to take up her life where she left it off after the terrible double blow of losing men she truly loved. Even Mrs. Haviland, if I may make so bold, has looked happy today. Perhaps it is seeing her daughter released from the numbness of almost a decade of mourning? Those years must have been very hard on both you and her."

"It is decent of you to understand," the general had said. "Yes, my ladies have found this day thoroughly enjoyable, with the ball still to come. And I have enjoyed their enjoyment. You have some interesting neighbors. And I cannot say enough in praise of your family. But they must all have been expecting an announcement of your betrothal. I do apologize again, Colonel, for any embarrassment I have caused you."

Nicholas had felt somewhat guilty, for he had surely nudged Grace toward refusing his proposal. She did not love him, of course. She had not really wanted to marry him. But she would have done so if he had not encouraged her to look inward to examine the state of her own heart and her dreams of the future. If she had remained firm in her decision to marry him, he would, of course, have honored the commitment.

What a reprieve he had been given, Nicholas thought now. Grace was not the only one who had woken up from a long period of... Of what? Of being almost frozen in place, unwilling to thaw because the pain might be too intense or life too bewildering? It had not been simple mourning with her, he guessed, but a terrible fear of one day being hurt beyond endurance. Better not to feel at all than risk that. And him? He had hardly been asleep or frozen for the past sixteen years. He had done a lot of living in that time, doing what he had always wanted to do, proud of what he had accomplished. But... Once upon a time he had dreamed of love with a woman who was warm and genuine no matter what she looked like or what her lineage. Perhaps he had not found her because he was afraid he would turn into his father. It sounded ridiculous. But certainly he had been afraid to love. And so, by the time he was thirty-four, he had lost the faith and almost settled for a respectable marriage with a beautiful, accomplished woman who would make an excellent wife.

... he had not found her.

Until now. When he had least been looking. Out of the blue. In the most unlikely candidate he could possibly have considered—if the choice had been left to his head instead of his heart.

And tonight, his marriage offer to Grace rejected, his peace made with General Haviland, Nicholas felt fully free to pursue his dream at last. Winifred Cunningham fulfilled everything he had ever hoped for. She had nothing for a pedigree. She had appeared in a basket outside an orphanage in Bath, aged about one month.

Nothing was either known or knowable about her origins. Understandably, that mattered to her despite her denials, but it did not affect his feelings about her by one iota. She was *not* a beauty. He could confirm that from the memory of his initial reaction to her at Trooping the Colour and the Netherby ball. Now she looked a vision of pure loveliness to him. He loved her open, eager face, with its perfect skin and broad forehead. He even loved the severe way she dressed her hair. He loved her slender figure, which he found very alluring. And she was *genuine*. There were no airs about Winifred, no artifice. If she thought a stranger cruel, judging solely on the set of his mouth during a military parade, she would say so to his face. Not content to describe him and his men as soldiers, she had quite bluntly called them killers—to his face. She loved her family, even or especially the difficult ones among her stepsiblings, not just with vague protestations of sentiment but with practical action. She would give up the pleasure of a picnic at the lake to allow her deaf brother to run endlessly down hills, pretending to be a bird.

Nicholas was not at all sure about the wisdom of what he was doing tonight. There were innumerable reasons he ought not to court Winifred or even consider marrying her. It was an impossibility, in fact. But how could he be sure of such an absolute? Perhaps a more appropriate word was *improbability*. But he did know that if he did not pursue her now, tonight, she would return home on Monday with her family and he was unlikely ever to see her again. Perhaps it would happen anyway, and if it did, well, so be it. But he knew he would never find another Winifred. He suspected he was the sort of man who loved once in his life and would never love in the same way again.

So here he was, leaving the ballroom with her while everyone else was heading toward the supper room, from which wafted the tantalizing aromas of the food the Berrys had prepared.

It was cool out on the terrace. But not at all dark. The sky was lit by myriad stars and a moon that was almost at the full. He was about to offer his arm, but he took her hand instead. It was slender and warm and small in his own. She did not immediately snatch it away. After an initial moment, she curled her fingers about his hand.

"Am I taking an unwelcome liberty?" he asked.

"By taking my hand?" she said. "No." She had turned her head to look at him. But not shyly, peering beneath lowered eyelids as many women would have done. Being Winifred, she looked him full in the face, her eyes wide.

"Perhaps you ought to be offended," he said.

"But why?" she asked.

He smiled. "Never mind," he said, lacing their fingers.

There was someone already up in the temple folly, a whole group of people by the sound of it, laughing and joking. They sounded like young people enjoying themselves too much to go indoors for supper just yet.

"There is a quite breathtaking view from up there in the moonlight," he said, nodding in that direction. "But I am not willing to share you with a group of revelers."

"And I am not willing to be shared," she said.

There was another reason too. The hill and temple during the ball at a fete brought back too many ugly memories from sixteen years ago. He led her past the hill and circled around it and back along the north wing of the house in the direction of the poplar alley.

"Will your parents worry about you?" he asked.

"No," she said. "Why would they? I am twenty-one years old, a full adult. They trust me to order my own life."

"Some parents never see their daughters as adults," he said. "They shelter them and rule them and never let them out of their sight until they are married to a man of whom they approve, and then *he* as like as not rules and shelters them."

"Ugh!" Winifred said inelegantly. "Then I am very thankful I have the parents I have. They raise us with a great deal of loving care and guidance, but they respect us as individuals, each special and each with special needs and personal dreams. Do you have dreams, Colonel, or have they all been fulfilled?"

"Because I am past thirty and cannot possibly still be a dreamer?" he said. "Until a couple of weeks ago my answer might well have been no. I lived by practical good sense. No longer, though."

"No practicality and no good sense left?" she said. "But are not those qualities essential to a man with your career?"

"Decidedly," he said. "But the career does not define the man."

"What has changed, then?" she asked.

"The answer ought to be *nothing*," he said. "I am thirty-four years old, Winifred."

"I know that," she said. "You just said so. At least, you told me you are past thirty, but you told me on a previous occasion how far past thirty you are."

"I was thirteen years old when you were born," he said. "About the age of that youth who was waltzing with your sister."

"Were you thin and uncoordinated and all elbows and self-consciousness and spots?" she said. "You must have been adorable."

Minx. He grinned to himself in the near darkness, though none of this was funny.

"Thirteen years is too wide an age gap," he said.

Instead of denying it, she fell silent as they walked on. "Yes, it is," she said at last, and despite himself it felt as though his heart had dropped inside him like a leaden weight. "I am—how was it you described me this morning? A *sweet young twenty-or-so*. You are an old man, as I told you then. But there is nothing we can do about our relative ages. I cannot suddenly pretend that I was ten years old when I was left in a basket on the orphanage steps. It creates rather a ridiculous image in the mind and would have made me *nineteen* when Mama and Papa adopted me."

They strolled onward.

"Did you perhaps take up your military commission when you were *eight*?" she asked.

He smiled rather bleakly into the darkness. "*Is* it a possibility, then?" he asked.

She did not pretend to misunderstand him. She shrugged. "What is the alternative?" she asked.

"Never seeing each other again after Monday?" he said, making a question of it.

She sighed. "Colonel Ware," she said, "I am a nobody. I have no pedigree whatsoever. Even if I pretend for a moment that Mama and Papa are my birth parents, that does not make a difference. Neither was born within a legal marriage. Papa was raised at the orphanage where I was found. Mama was the product of a bigamous marriage. You, on the other hand, are the very legitimate son of the late Earl of Stratton. You were raised *here*. You are a colonel in a prestigious cavalry regiment. I daresay all the other officers are sons of the nobility too. There is far more than a thirteen-year span separating us."

"Yes," he said. They had reached the summerhouse at the end of the alley. "Shall we go inside and sit awhile?"

"Yes," she said.

She sat on one of the comfortable sofas while he closed the door. After hesitating for a mere moment, he sat beside her. They were silent for a while as their eyes adjusted to the greater darkness cast by the trees on the alley and the silvered treetops and deep blue of the sky. In the distance there were the lights of lanterns in the stable block on the north side of the house.

"I asked you if you have dreams," she said. "You told me what answer you would have given a couple of weeks ago. What are your dreams now?"

"The same ones they were before I squashed them and adopted practicality as more appropriate to my age and status," he said. "In my career and day-to-day life, I have goals, and they have not changed. But beyond that, in my personal life, I dream of love and marriage and fatherhood. I dream of a home in the country, not too far from London and my work but far enough that my children can grow up with space and the beauties of nature surrounding them and my wife can be comfortable. But it is not just any kind of love of which I dream. There are all sorts of levels of attraction that can pass for love, but I dream of . . . Oh, of that one woman without whom I cannot live with any degree of happiness. That one woman who feels the same way about me. I have not expressed it well enough, though. How does one describe that kind of love? Language is quite inadequate to do it. But—"

"I know what you mean," she said.

He smiled and they sat quietly for a while, gazing along the alley and watching the silver tips of the poplar trees swaying in a breeze that had not been apparent while they walked.

"I dream of the sort of . . . oh, *nonsensical* love that does not recognize age and pedigree differences as being in any way relevant," he said. "As a young man I was afraid to search, afraid perhaps that I would find and then destroy the purity of the love with uncontrolled, promiscuous behavior. When I was in my thirties I settled for a sensible marriage with a friend whom I liked and with whom I could enjoy a comfortable sort of affection. A woman of the right age and pedigree. Now that I have been honorably released from that obligation, the dream has revived. With the power of a mighty storm."

He took her left hand in his and realized that she was a bit chilly—and perhaps a bit dazed? He glanced around for the lap blankets that were usually left here and got to his feet to fetch one. He wrapped it about her shoulders and kept his arm about her.

"For me?" she said, her voice high-pitched and breathless. "You feel that way *about me*? As though you had been struck by a mighty storm?"

Had he misread the signs? Was she not ready for this?

"I do," he said, and watched her close her eyes and bite her bottom lip.

"Oh, thank you," she said, snuggling into the blanket. He could feel her shivering.

"Would you like me to take you back to the ballroom?" he asked. He did not want her to feel trapped by her agreement to walk outside with him.

She turned her gaze upon him then, her face a mere few inches from his own.

"I have dreamed of love too," she said. "The love of which you speak. I did not expect ever to find it. I know I have nothing to recommend me to any man in whom I may be interested. Among other things, I am plain and lacking in femininity. But I have been unwilling to pretend to be what I am not. I lead a happy and useful life. I do not *need* marriage, as so many other women seem to do. I always feel so sorry for the poverty of their lives, which they cannot apparently live on their own account. Nonetheless, I would *like* to be married. But only if I loved, and if the man loved me. For a short while in London and even after we came here, I thought perhaps Owen . . . Well, I *liked* him exceedingly. I still do. And I know he likes me. We have a great deal in common. I thought we could work well together if there was a closer connection between us. I thought I could be happy, that *we* could be happy. But it was not the sort of love of which I had dreamed. It was more a *practical* love. Fortunately, I understood that in time to save both myself and Owen from making a dreadful mistake. He realized it too."

"But he did ask you to marry him?" he said.

"Oh, yes." She laughed softly. "In an impulsive burst of enthusiasm. His relief when I said no was palpable." She laughed again. "Oh, I *do* love him. But not in that way."

She looked at him again, and he looked back.

"*That* is the way I feel about you," she said, and bit her lip again.

They fell silent. From the direction of the house came the faint sound of music. The dancing had resumed.

"You are beautiful," he said. "And surely the most feminine woman I have ever known, for there is substance to your character, not just the sort of fluttering artifice that often passes for femininity. Remember that, Winifred, please. Always remember that you are beautiful."

"*Another* thing to remember?" she said, smiling at him a bit tremulously.

"You will not need to remember if I am there to remind you each day," he said. "And each night."

Her smile faded. Her eyes grew more luminous. But she did not lower her gaze from his.

He sighed. There was no point in trying to tell himself that at any moment now he would recover his senses, or that she would recover hers. Now was the time to risk speaking truth, whatever the outcome turned out to be.

"I love you," he said. And though his mind reached for more words, he knew there were no others. He had said it all.

"I love you too." Her hand came up, and she caressed his cheek with her fingertips. "Nicholas."

Ah. There was something about hearing one's name on the lips of the woman one loved.

He drew her closer and kissed her.

And ah, the sweetness of it. His memory of their first brief kiss on the island in the lake had been all caught up with guilt. This kiss was different. Guilt free. *Free.* Her lips were soft and eager, her breath warm against his cheek. And ah, the *rightness* of it.

Though it was not entirely unforbidden, was it?

He drew back his head, and she opened her eyes to gaze at him, her lips moist in the dim light of the moon and slightly parted.

"I ought to have had a word with your father before we stepped out of doors," he said.

"He will like it if you do it tomorrow," she said. "Though literally speaking, it is not necessary. I am of age. But perhaps this has been no more than a pleasant stroll outdoors to get away from the noise and stuffiness of the ballroom. A little flirtation with no commitment. Perhaps we ought to make our way back."

He stiffened. What the devil—? What had they been *talking* about?

"Is that what you want?" he asked.

She searched his face with anxious eyes. "Is it what *you* want?" she asked.

And he understood her sudden fright. The depths of her lack of belief in her own charms were unfathomable, it seemed. Despite her confidence in other areas of her life and her forthright way of speaking, she believed her chances of attracting a man to be slim to nil. She had panicked.

"You goose, Win," he said. "Has no one ever taught you that answering a question with a question is abominable? We could go on all night with *What do you want? No, what do you want?* What a bore that would be."

"But I do not know what you want," she said.

"What I want," he said, "is to go back to the house, though preferably not immediately, and stand in the middle of the ballroom floor between dances and announce, in my parade ground voice so no one can possibly miss it, that I love Winifred Cunningham and she loves me."

She made a squeaking sound, which might have been alarm but might also be suppressed laughter.

"Please do not," she said.

"Would you be embarrassed?" he asked her.

"Horribly," she said. "Nicholas!" She covered her mouth with one hand.

"You goose," he said again. "Did you really believe I had suddenly developed a case of cold feet by bumbling on about not having spoken with your father? Just after telling you I love you? Ah, Win. Will you marry me? Do you want me to go down on one knee even though I am an old man in his thirties and may never get up again?"

She lowered her hand, her eyes riveted to his face. "Oh, I do," she said. "Will you? But are you quite sure?"

He ignored the last question, went down on one knee before the couch, and possessed himself of her left hand.

"Win," he said, "will you do me the great honor of marrying me, even though we are an ill-assorted couple and any connection between us would seem to be an impossibility? Entirely because I love you with all my heart and wish to devote the rest of my life to making you happy?"

She tipped her head to one side and regarded him with a slight frown on her face. Being Winifred Cunningham, of course she could not be expected to give him the obvious answer.

"I do not know how to be a cavalry colonel's wife," she said. "I cannot be at all what your colleagues and friends will expect of your wife. Perhaps we ought to talk more about this before you regret it in the morning."

"Before *I* regret it," he said. "Will *you* regret it?"

"Only if you do," she said.

"Here we go again," he said. "*Will you regret it? Will you?* Can we just take a leap of faith here, Win? That is all life is, you know, for we can never predict the future. But I do know that whatever the future holds, I want you at my side. As my wife. I am kneeling on my bad leg, by the way. Any moment now it is going to be hopelessly cramped. *Will* you marry me?"

She drew her hand from his and cupped his face with both hands.

"You poor wounded thing," she said. "Yes, I will, Nicholas, though I am consumed with terror even as I say the words. But I do know that I cannot, I absolutely cannot, say goodbye to you on Monday, knowing that I will never see you again. My heart would break. I would endure that if you did not love me and had not offered for me, but I know that if I said no now, I would regret all my life that I was afraid to take the risk. I will love you always with everything that is me. I will live to make you happy. Despite all our incompatibilities, I will—"

"No," he said. "*We* will, Win. There would be nothing one-sided in our marriage commitment. I daresay all marriages face difficulties as two lives attempt to meld into one. We will do it together. We will each work to make the other happy and, in the process, make ourselves happy too."

He was well aware of the sentimentality of his words. But the thing was that he *meant* them with all his heart. He *loved* her. And, God help him, she loved him despite his age and the cruelty of his mouth—and his slightly lame leg.

They were smiling at each other then, his face in her hands, his hands braced on the edge of the sofa on either side of her. And she closed the gap between their mouths and kissed him, right on his cruel lips.

He surged to his feet, ignoring the twinge in his knee, swept her up into his arms, and seated himself with her cradled on his lap.

And he was conscious of feeling utterly at peace and happy, with the unlikeliest woman he could ever have dreamed of cuddled up against him, warm and relaxed beneath the lap robe he had rearranged about her, her head on his shoulder. And she was with the unlikeliest man—a soldier with a career and a history in battle that was unthinkable to her.

He kissed her again, parting her lips with his own and sliding his tongue into her mouth. Warm and sweet and inviting. And trusting.

Her arm was about his neck, the fingers of one hand threaded through his hair.

"Happy?" he murmured against her mouth.

"Oh, yes," she said. "Happy."

"And before you can ask," he said, "so am I."

"Mmm." She sighed. "Kiss me again, Nicholas."

"Yes, ma'am," he said.

CHAPTER TWENTY-ONE

If she was sleeping, Winifred thought, she really, really did not want to wake up.

She was not asleep, however, though she was sitting on his lap, warm and cozy beneath the small blanket, her head on his shoulder, her eyes closed. Her lips were tingling. They felt deliciously as though they might be swollen. She could feel him with every part of her, his solid, hard, man's body, his shoulder broad and firm beneath her cheek, his arm about her, holding her close, the other hand on her knee. She could feel his body heat and smell the faint musk of his cologne. She could hear his quiet breathing. She could taste him. His tongue had explored her mouth, slowly, almost lazily, until it had aroused aches and longings that had had her tightening her arm about his neck and moaning slightly with the feeling that a fire had been lit inside her. That was when he had ended the kiss somewhat abruptly and settled her head on his shoulder.

"We had better save the rest for our wedding night," he had said, his voice a bit breathless and not quite steady. "God, but I want you."

Her naïveté had been almost total. "Do you?" she had asked him, and she feared there had been some surprise in her voice.

"Win." He had groaned.

She had understood then. He wanted her. *Wanted*. And that was just what she had been feeling, what she still felt. She just had not understood or known the words. She *wanted*. She could not put into ordered thought quite what she wanted and *he* wanted, but she knew it was something sexual, a word that had always been quite foreign to her vocabulary.

She *wanted* him with all of herself. Every part of her. Every part of her body. *We had better save the rest for our wedding night.*

He was *Colonel Nicholas Ware*, she reminded herself in some wonder. He *loved* her. How could that possibly be? He wanted to marry her. He *wanted* her. He—

"Of all things," she said, sitting up and looking at him.

His head was resting against the soft, upholstered back of the sofa. He opened his eyes. In the dim light of the moon and stars beyond the summerhouse, he looked more than handsome. He looked languid and comfortable and . . . Oh, *what* was the word? Desirable? She was so inexperienced in all this. But she picked up her train of thought.

"Of all things, I have not wanted anything to do with the military life, even though I have always understood that military men are far more than just killers. They *are* killers, nevertheless. How many men have you killed, Nicholas?"

He had not moved, but his eyes were more alert.

"Me personally?" he asked her. "Or me as an officer who commands other men to kill?"

She huffed. "How many? Dozens? Hundreds? Thousands?"

"I hope not thousands," he said.

But he did not deny dozens—or even hundreds.

"War is brutal, Win," he said. "But often it is a brutal necessity."

"And how many lives have you saved?" she asked him. "You and your men."

"Thousands," he said without hesitation. "Now that you have had some time to reflect, are you finding that you cannot, as a matter of principle, marry a military man? Would you always, whatever the circumstances, see me as a killer?"

Two of her uncles—Uncle Gil, who was married to Aunt Abby, her mother's sister, and Uncle Harry, her mother's brother—had fought as officers in the wars. She loved them both dearly. They were not still in active service, however. Did that make a difference?

"I do not have the faintest idea how to be an officer's wife," she said. "Specifically, a *colonel's* wife."

"Can you be *my* wife?" he asked her. "Nicholas Ware's? Can you marry the man and not the colonel?"

"Can they be separated?" she asked him.

"Yes," he said.

She did not know how.

"I have never wanted to live in London," she said. "It would . . . It would kill my soul."

"I know," he said. "And I would not want my wife living there with me. Even less would I want our children to grow up there."

Oh, that was such a strange thought. *Children*. With *Nicholas*.

"I have always wanted children of my own," she said. "It has been a cause of considerable sadness to me whenever I think that I will probably never marry because I will never find someone who will love me for myself despite all the disqualifications."

"I love you sufficiently and then in an overflowing abundance," he said.

"You do like to exaggerate." She touched the fingertips of one hand to his cheek, and he caught her hand in his to turn it and kiss her palm.

"My ever prosaic Win, who will always keep my feet firmly on the ground," he said, folding her fingers one at a time over the place he had just kissed.

She sighed. "It is an impossibility," she said.

"Our marrying?" he said. "I plan to find a house in the country before my wedding, preferably just south of the Thames or perhaps in Richmond. Somewhere my wife can live in comfort and be happy, with a small park or at least a large garden where the children can play, possibly with neighborhood children, and grow up knowing an abundance of love and with an awareness of the beauties and marvels of nature. Perhaps with dogs and cats and a goat or two."

"And chickens?" she said.

"And definitely chickens," he said. "When she was very young, Pippa used to carry ours around as though they were house pets. They all had names."

She smiled at him.

"I may not be able to go home every night," he said. "There will be all sorts of business—military business for my other self to deal with—that will keep me late at the Horse Guards. But I will have my home and my wife and children to dream of when I get deeply immersed in work. My little bit of paradise, to which I will escape whenever I can. Is it, though, a one-sided, selfish vision?"

"No," she said. "For a husband and wife ought to feel free to live their separate lives, rich in satisfaction and meaning, so they can share more than just domestic matters and . . . oh, *romance* when they are together. I will surely have neighbors and find all sorts of things to keep me busy and useful."

"*Will?*" He raised his eyebrows. "You *will* have neighbors? Not *would*?"

She sighed again. "I love you so much," she said. "I want to be persuaded. But I am trying to be sensible."

"I am also thirteen years older than you," he said. "An old man. You must not forget that."

She laughed. "Now *that* does not matter to me, since we seem agreed that we can do nothing about it," she said. "And you are not *old*. How absurd."

"One item to cross off your impossible list?"

"Yes," she said.

"Win," he said, sitting up at last and lifting her to the seat of the sofa beside him. "I cannot change who I am or who I have been, and I would not if I could. You say you want to live a useful life. So do I. It is what I have always wanted. Protecting the land and the people who are precious to me has always seemed a worthy goal. And that land and those people do not have to be just the countryside about me and my family and neighbors. All of England and Wales and Scotland and Ireland are my land. I will not change even if I must lose in other areas of my life. But in that other area, my personal life, I have long looked for love and have found it at last. I will cherish that love and nurture it with everything that is my being if I am given the opportunity. My wife and my family, if I am so blessed as to have children, will be the be-all and end-all of my personal life. And frankly, I can see no great divide between the two lives I wish to live. They are not mutually exclusive. They complement each other."

She tipped her head sideways to lay her cheek against his shoulder again. The moon had dipped just behind the poplar trees on one side of the alley. The tops of the trees were moving in a slight breeze. Moonlight alternated with shade across her face as she gazed out.

"I do beg your pardon for having once called you cruel," she said.

She could not have been more wrong.

"Oh no, no," he said. "I do not believe you ever called *me* cruel. Only my mouth."

She laughed softly. "Then I apologize for that," she said. "I was wrong."

"*Will* you marry me?" he asked.

"Yes." She sighed.

"Thank you," he said. "Shall we return to the house before someone sends out a search party?"

The dancing must have resumed a while ago. Several times she had heard distant music. She got to her feet and folded the blanket, and he laughed.

"I suppose," he said, "I can never expect you to play the lady and wait to be assisted to your feet, can I? Or to leave housekeeping tasks to servants?"

"What nonsense," she said. "As though I cannot stand up unassisted. Or fold a blanket instead of letting it fall in a heap on the floor."

He held her hand and laced their fingers again as they set off in the direction of the house. The full force of what had happened in the last half hour or so hit her. They were *betrothed*. She was, after all, going to be married. To someone she loved with all her heart, someone who loved *her*. And he wanted children, just as she did. He wanted them to be free and happy and possibly a bit unruly, as her siblings were and as his had been. He wanted them to have pets in abundance. Even chickens.

"Win," he said. "Will you mind if we do not announce our betrothal tonight or even tomorrow? General Haviland and his wife and daughter will be here until Monday, and I would not want them to feel more uncomfortable than they already do. They came here expecting a different outcome, knowing that others, including my whole family, expected it too. They do not deserve what they might consider a public humiliation."

"What happened?" she asked.

"We agreed, Grace and I," he said, "that though we valued each other as friends, we do not love each other as two people planning to wed ought."

She somehow could not imagine Miss Haviland speaking of *love*. But perhaps that was uncharitable of her.

"She lost two fiancés within a few years of each other when she was very young," he said. "Both were officers who died in battle. She loved each of them in turn very dearly and has spent the intervening years mourning for them, whether it has been conscious or not. She has tried to eliminate deep sentiment from her life for fear of being cruelly hurt again. But I believe her experience here has helped her, and her ability to admit she did not want to marry me has somehow opened her to want to love again."

There. She *had* been uncharitable.

"She has been looking unusually happy today," she said. "I suppose you helped her see the truth."

"I hope so," he said. "I was obligated to her, you know, and would have married her if our conversation had gone differently. I had recently concluded that not having found love by the age of thirty-four, I never would find it and ought to settle for sober common sense instead."

"She is very beautiful," she said.

"Yes, she is," he said. "But not in the way you are beautiful, Win. The sight of her does not smite me to the heart."

"And the sight of me does?" she asked.

"Yes," he said.

"Then you must be half blind," she said.

He laughed. "I do love you," he said.

Nicholas let Winifred go alone into the ballroom and waited outside for a while. He strolled down to the southern corner of the house and breathed in the cool night air. There was no sign of life at the front here. No one was leaving yet, and no one had left the ballroom for a romantic stroll outside. Not in this direction anyway. Sounds of a sprightly country dance came from inside the ballroom.

He wondered if panic would strike, either tonight or tomorrow, when he must have a talk with Joel Cunningham, not to mention his own family. It did not seem to him that anyone suspected, though he could be wrong. What had seemed private and secret to him might be as plain as day to the people who knew him best. He just hoped none of the Havilands suspected.

He would *not* panic. He was as sure of his feelings for Winifred as he had ever been about anything. And despite the numerous and seemingly insurmountable obstacles, he did not doubt her love for him.

And yet, just a short while ago he had thought her plain and a bit drab and a whole lot naïve. And startlingly forthright. Unfeminine. *Real.* Attractive.

Yes, he had been attracted from the start. Even when she was forbidden to him in two ways—by his commitment to Grace and by Owen's possible commitment to her.

Now he was betrothed to her.

The country dance was coming to an end as he stepped into the doorway. The dancers were looking flushed and breathless. Couples drifted apart and either collapsed onto vacant chairs or looked about for their next partners. Bertrand had been dancing with Eluned, Owen with Ariel Wexford, his mother with Uncle Charles Ware, Grace with Clarence. Winifred stood with Andrew, his arm drawn through hers. He had been tapping his foot before the dance ended, Nicholas noticed. He must feel the rhythm and see it in the dance even though he could not hear it. He looked happy.

It occurred to Nicholas that he was going to be marrying a family, not just Winifred. It was no normal family, if there was such a thing. Was he going to mind? If, for example, she wanted to have one or more of her siblings stay with them for a prolonged visit? The silent Robbie and his dog? The deaf Andrew? The timid, clinging twins? The gigglers, Sam and Alice? The pretty Sarah? Who was left? Jacob—the *normal* Jacob. Was there such a thing as normality? He would *not* mind if any of them came to stay, he realized. Indeed, he would welcome the people who were so central to her life. And he would take her to visit *them* whenever he was able, if it was what she wanted. He suspected she would be homesick.

He would work hard to see that the house in which he would settle her became home to her very soon after their marriage. Somehow, he expected that she would work with him to achieve that goal. And perhaps by this time next year there would be a child on the way.

"Woolgathering, Nick?" Devlin asked, coming to join him. "The day has been a great success, has it not?"

"Perfection," Nicholas said. "There is nothing anywhere to match the Ravenswood/Boscombe summer fete."

"Not that we are biased in any way," Devlin said, grinning at him. "I just hope Gwyneth is not tiring herself out too much."

"To my knowledge she has always been indefatigable," Nicholas said.

"Except in the early months of a confinement," Devlin said.

Nicholas looked sharply at him. "Really?" he said.

"Really," Devlin said, gazing fondly at his wife, who had joined her parents on the sidelines and was smiling and fanning her face as they talked. "But will she listen when I tell her to slow down? I merely get accused of being a tyrant for my pains."

It was exactly sixteen years ago that they had discovered their passion for each other, and one day before a bitter, six-year separation. Gwyneth had been almost betrothed to a talented Welsh musician when Devlin came home from the wars, a hardened, embittered man. Sometimes miracles did happen, though.

"She still thinks she needs to give me a spare as well as the heir," Devlin said. "Heaven forbid that you remain my heir after Gareth. Not that she ever puts it that way, or even thinks it, I hasten to add."

Nicholas grinned at him. "Well, congratulations anyway," he said.

"We were hoping," Devlin said, "that you were going to be well on the way to being married yourself this week. Happily ever after and all that. It was just not to be, was it?"

"Friends, not lovers," Nicholas said. "Which is what I discovered with another woman a little over sixteen years ago, I seem to remember. Maybe I am fated to have a whole host of female friends but no lover."

"I doubt it," Devlin said. "Not when I see the way all the women here, especially the unmarried ones, have been looking at you all day. One of these days you are going to look back at one of them and fall in love. Good Lord, we sound like a couple of women. This is what being an expectant father—again—does to a man. It makes him hideously sentimental."

Nicholas laughed. Devlin did not suspect, then. Probably no one else did either.

"I had better go ask one of those women for the next dance," he said, "before they are all spoken for."

He could see that Owen was leading Winifred onto the floor.

Winifred was standing at the open window of her bedchamber later that night when her mother tapped on the door before opening it quietly and letting herself in. Winifred had been trying to cool her hot cheeks and quiet the teeming thoughts and emotions that tumbled around in her head and would surely make sleep all but impossible.

The ball had ended an hour ago, and all the outside guests had dispersed homeward. The family and houseguests had straggled off to bed a little more slowly. She had changed into her nightgown and brushed out her hair. But she had not lain down.

"I thought you might still be up," her mother said.

"Yes." Winifred smiled at her. "It has been a lovely day, has it not?"

"So," Mama said, coming to stand beside her at the window, though nothing was visible outside while the candles burned inside, "you and Colonel Nicholas Ware?"

"It was very hot when the waltz ended," Winifred said. "And neither of us was hungry. It was beautifully cool outside. And quiet."

"We thought it was Owen Ware when we came here," her mother said. "It never was?"

"Oh, Owen and I are firm friends," Winifred said. "We have a great deal in common. He is one of those people with whom I can talk endlessly without ever wondering how we are going to fill the silence."

"We thought that for Colonel Ware it was Miss Haviland," her mother said. "But there has been no announcement, and they have spent almost no time together today. So much for my matchmaking instincts and Papa's."

"He likes her," Winifred said. "He is fond of her. It turned out, however, that neither of them really wished to marry the other."

"And this he told you?" her mother said.

"Yes," Winifred said.

"He is not at all the sort of man I would have expected to capture your heart," Mama said.

Oh, and she had really thought when she returned to the ballroom that no one had noticed. *Of course* Mama had. Probably Papa too.

"Do you want to talk about it?" Mama asked. "I am guessing you will find it difficult to sleep left to your own company."

"He is the very last person with whom I would have expected to fall in love," Winifred said.

"But you have fallen?"

"Yes," Winifred said.

"Are you likely to have your heart broken?" Mama asked gently.

"Oh no." Winifred turned to look at her mother with raised eyebrows. "He loves me too, Mama. We are going to marry. He is going to talk to Papa tomorrow. He asked that we stay quiet about it tonight and tomorrow, though, out of deference for the feelings of the Havilands, who came here on the assumption that his betrothal to Miss Haviland would be announced during their visit.

And he did offer for her, because he felt obligated. She refused. And she has looked the happier for it today. I have not imagined that, have I?"

"I do not believe so," her mother said. "I have noticed a difference in her."

"Mama," Winifred said. "I am so happy I feel quite sick."

They both laughed, and her mother opened her arms to enclose her daughter within their comfort.

"It is all Papa and I have ever wanted for you," she said. "Ever since we fell in love with you at the orphanage school. That you be happy, that is, for what remained of your childhood and in whatever you chose to do when you grew up. It is all we want for all our children. One can shelter them only so long before most of them will choose to fly free. It is not a comfortable thing being a parent, Winifred. One wants the world for one's children but must allow them to choose the nature of that world for themselves. Shall we sit down on these chairs while you tell me how you came to fall in love with Colonel Nicholas Ware? I cannot pretend that I am not totally surprised. And puzzled."

Winifred sighed as they sat down.

"I think it began when he rode past us at the head of his cavalrymen at Trooping the Colour," she said. "Though I could see only the lower half of his face and was most struck by the firmness of his jaw and the cruelty of his mouth."

"Ah," Mama said. "A promising beginning to a romance."

"Yes," Winifred said, not hearing the irony in her mother's voice. "I believe it started to happen then. And the next time I saw him, at Aunt Anna's ball, I told him I had thought his mouth cruel, and he looked haughtily at me and bore me off at suppertime to sit opposite him at a private table while he interrogated me on my eligibility to marry his brother. And he was scornful when I told him, not quite accurately, that I was opposed to all warfare and could not approve of his way of life."

"Oh dear me," her mother said. "You tell such a delicious love story."

"Yes," Winifred said dreamily.

Nicholas was too restless to go to his room. He wandered back to the ballroom, where the Berrys and various other people were busy doing some essential cleanup jobs, though the bulk of the work would be done by a larger group of volunteers tomorrow.

"No, no," Jim Berry said, making shooing gestures with his hands when Nicholas offered his help. "We can manage, thank you, sir."

Nicholas guessed his offered help was seen as more of a hindrance. He stood in the doorway on the other side of the room, one shoulder propped against the frame.

"Dreaming, Nick?" Owen asked, coming up behind him and clapping a hand on his shoulder. "Afraid you will not sleep?"

"After such a busy day?" Nicholas said. "It would be strange if I could not."

"So," Owen said. "You and Winifred Cunningham?"

Ah. Someone had noticed, then.

"We went walking outside instead of going in for supper," he said. "Neither of us was hungry, and the air was cool."

"You are not dangling after her, are you, Nick?" Owen asked. "Toying with her feelings? She has a tender heart, I would have you know. My guess is she can be easily hurt."

Hell and damnation.

"You do care after all, then, do you?" Nicholas asked.

"Of course I care," Owen said, frowning indignantly at him. "And I will not have you using your famous charm on her, Nick, only to ignore her tomorrow and maybe break her heart."

"A poor opinion you have of me," Nicholas said. "When have I ever been a deliberate heartbreaker, Owen?"

"Probably more times than you realize," Owen said. "Leave her alone, Nick. Though it is probably too late now to save her from being hurt."

"It is not possible, you think, that I mean honorably by her?" Nicholas asked. "That I love her and intend to marry her?"

"Highly unlikely," Owen said. "I am devilish fond of her, Nick, but it is as plain as the nose on your face that she is not your type."

"My type being?" Nicholas asked. He was starting to feel annoyed.

"Well. Beautiful for starters," Owen said. "Voluptuous."

"To me she is the most beautiful woman in the world," Nicholas said.

"Eh?" his brother said inelegantly.

"And you had better not come out with any other implied insults," Nicholas said. "I may be tempted to plant you a facer. She is my lady, Owen."

His brother stared at him, openmouthed. "Well, the devil," he said.

"You missed your chance a few days ago," Nicholas said. "Now you may mind your own dashed business."

But his brother only grinned slowly at him and clapped him on the shoulder again.

"Well, the devil!" he said again.

CHAPTER TWENTY-TWO

The new portrait of the Dowager Countess of Stratton was hung after church late the following morning in the place that had been prepared for it next to the portrait of her eldest son and his wife and three children, which had been painted a year after Awen's birth.

Devlin had arranged for the placement while all his houseguests were still at Ravenswood. A number of them would be leaving on Monday. It was a magnificent piece, Nicholas thought, and its present setting showed it off to greater advantage than the dining room had during the family dinner on Friday evening. The family and the houseguests each drank a glass of champagne and toasted both his mother and Joel Cunningham, who looked faintly embarrassed. They all talked with enthusiasm about yesterday's fete, which all had enjoyed.

General Haviland explained that he and his wife and daughter felt greatly honored to have been invited, not just to the fete but to a couple of weeks of relaxation here, where they had been treated with warm hospitality.

"There are distinct advantages to being the commanding officer of a Ware of Ravenswood," he said to general laughter.

It was unlikely anyone was unaware of the betrothal that had been expected when the Havilands came here, but no one made reference to it. They had been wrong, and that was that.

"Nicholas has spoken highly of you and your family, General Haviland," Gwyneth said. "We wished to meet you, and what better opportunity could we have asked for than the summer of a village fete? He will have told you that we love to entertain houseguests."

There were murmurs of agreement while two footmen relieved them of their empty glasses, and they began to make their way downstairs for luncheon.

Nicholas held back.

"A word with you if I may, sir?" he said to Joel Cunningham, and the two of them waited until everyone else had left the gallery.

Nicholas wondered if any other man in history had had this particular talk twice in three days with two different fathers about two different daughters.

"I am afraid I acted rather precipitately last evening," he said. "I spoke to your daughter before first speaking to you. She assured me I did not need your permission since she is of age. However, I would like to have it if you feel you can give it. I wish to marry Winifred, sir. Entirely because I love her. I will spend the rest of my days putting her happiness before all else in my life."

Cunningham sighed.

"She is quite right," he said. "She is twenty-one and her own person. Neither Camille nor I will ever interfere in a choice she makes freely. We may *advise* her if she asks, but we will not interfere."

"*Have* you advised her?" Nicholas asked. "Since last evening, that is? I understand her mother visited her in her room after the ball."

"She has not asked," Cunningham said, looking him full in the face—rather reminiscent of Winifred herself. "Her mother is willing to accept her judgment. So am I. However, I do not have to feel untroubled about it. Your way of life is as different from hers as it could possibly be. I can understand the attraction of the match to her. You are, after all, a bit of a dazzler, Colonel Ware, and she has perhaps had her head turned, though she is usually rather levelheaded. I find it harder to understand the attraction of the match to you. I love Winifred dearly, and to me she is beautiful. But she is not beautiful in the way of the world, in the way of the *ton*. She is a woman without birth pedigree and without fortune apart from the dowry we have set aside for her. She is also years younger than you. You are in your thirties, I am guessing."

"Thirty-four," Nicholas said.

"You have just suffered a disappointment," Cunningham said. "You had your sights on an extremely lovely, charming lady, but she rejected you. At least, that is what I am assuming. How am I supposed to believe that my daughter is not just a temporary toy to you to fill in a gap, novel in the sense that she is the opposite of Miss Haviland in every imaginable way?"

Nicholas felt as though he had just taken a powerful punch to the chin.

"You are not being asked to believe, sir," he said, not quite truthfully. "Winifred believes me, and I am firmly convinced her feelings for me are not just dazzlement over my good looks—which

I do not deny. I have been plagued all my life with these looks and the apparent charm that go with them. The real me meanwhile is inside, desperately wishing to get out so other people will see something more substantial and more honorable. Winifred sees it, as I see the incredible beauty of the person she is. As for the age difference, it is unfortunate, but as she observed last evening, there is nothing we can do about it. Are we to give each other up because of thirteen years? Am I to lose the love of my life? Is she to lose the love of hers? Just on that account?"

He was aware that he was sounding rather foolish. And a bit argumentative. Winifred's father had every right to voice perfectly understandable doubts. He did, after all, love his daughter.

"I intend to purchase a cottage somewhere in the country close to London," Nicholas said. "Perhaps in a village, where Winifred may find friends and activities that are meaningful to her. A house with a fenced garden so children and pets may play safely."

"You intend to have children, then?" Cunningham asked.

"Oh, indeed, sir," Nicholas said. "I dearly want a family of my own. A family of *our* own. The declaration I made Winifred last evening was not as impulsive a thing as it must seem. Miss Haviland and I both realized after we came here that our friendship was really no more than that. We both agreed that we did not, after all, wish to marry. If she had not admitted that to me, I would have honored the commitment I had more or less made when I had my brother and sister-in-law invite her here with her parents."

"I must confess the lady was looking happy enough yesterday," Cunningham said.

"For almost two weeks I was obliged to fight a growing attachment to your daughter," Nicholas said. "I knew I loved her before I could admit as much to anyone else or even to myself. Yesterday I was free to tell her how I feel. She is a shrewd, intelligent woman, sir. She would spot insincerity from a mile distant—and say so."

Cunningham let out a short bark of laughter. "You are right about that," he said. "I am not going to forbid you to become affianced to Winifred, Ware. It would be pointless anyway. She is of age to make her own decisions. It has occurred to me that I am reacting as fathers of daughters have reacted all through the ages. With a form of jealousy toward the men they choose, I mean. With a refusal to believe that any other man could ever make them sufficiently happy. I wonder if I will be the same with Sarah and the others. It is not easy being a father. Not to girls and not to boys. Be warned."

"I will not let you down," Nicholas said.

"See that you do not," Cunningham said. "I would probably feel compelled to do something like coming at you with my fists, and that would be mildly suicidal."

They both laughed.

"I thought for a while it was going to be your younger brother," Cunningham said. "He seems a good sort, and they grew fond of each other very quickly when we were still in London. However, I daresay they are too much alike. It is not always a good thing. Camille and I have such a good marriage, I believe, because we are very different from each other. I am always away off in the clouds, and she always has her feet firmly planted on the ground. We are perfect halves to a well-rounded whole. Maybe you and Winifred are another such couple."

"I believe so," Nicholas said.

"We will be returning to Bath tomorrow," Cunningham said with a frown. "You intend to announce your betrothal today?"

"I would rather not, sir," Nicholas said. "It would seem

disrespectful to the Havilands even though the decision Grace and I made was mutual and amicable. They will be returning to London tomorrow. I was hoping you would postpone your leaving until Tuesday."

Cunningham looked at him and nodded slowly.

"I daresay it can be arranged," he said. "I had better go and have a word with Camille to put a stop to any wholesale packing that may be in progress. Moving an army of rowdy children and one dog about the country is no easy undertaking, Colonel Ware. Rather akin to moving a company of soldiers, I would think."

"That is what sergeants are for," Nicholas said with a grin as he took the hand that was being offered him. "Thank you."

Cunningham shook his hand.

They would be staying at Ravenswood until Wednesday.

It was Bethan Ware's birthday on Tuesday, and it seemed she had begged her mama to let the Cunninghams stay for her party out at the lake with a crowd of neighborhood children.

The Havilands left for home on Monday morning, sped on their way by a round of hugs and handshakes and well wishes from a gathering of family and guests out on the terrace.

That evening Sir Ifor and Lady Rhys and their son and daughter-in-law came for dinner. At the end of the meal the Earl of Stratton rose and clinked a spoon against a glass to draw everyone's attention.

"I have a happy announcement to make while champagne glasses are being distributed among you," he said. "My brother Nicholas has been fortunate enough to win the love of Winifred Cunningham, a lady who has burrowed her way into all our hearts,

I believe, during the last couple of weeks. I invite you to join Gwyneth and me in a toast to the happiness of the newly betrothed pair."

There was a swell of sound and the clinking of glasses. A few people were genuinely surprised, Winifred thought. Others smiled knowingly and indulgently. She did not believe that a single person at the table—except Nicholas himself—failed to hug her over the next several minutes while exclaiming with pleasure and offering congratulations and good wishes. Nicholas did not hug her because he was too occupied with being hugged himself. Papa was beaming at her, as were Mama and Sarah and even Robbie.

No one treated her as an impostor.

No one protested that she was not nearly gorgeous enough for Nicholas. Or not in any way worthy of him.

No one accused him of robbing the cradle.

Owen, whom both she and Nicholas had told before tonight, grinned at her and winked before he hugged her. "I am going to *love* having you as a sister-in-law, Winifred," he said.

"And a friend too, I hope," she said.

"Goes without saying," he said.

. . . a lady who has burrowed her way into all our hearts, the earl had said.

How she hugged those words to herself. It was what she had tried and tried to do and failed to do when she lived at the orphanage. Now, when she had not even been trying, she had apparently succeeded.

She was *not* an impostor.

She *was* Nicholas's equal.

So what if she was not *gorgeous*? She had never wanted to be. She had only ever wanted to be herself. And it was for that Nicholas loved her and the others had grown fond of her.

During that evening, she learned that the two families—the Wares and the Cunninghams—were really no different from each other in essentials. Family and familial love were more important to them than anything else in their lives.

Dinner was followed by an impromptu concert in the music room next to the drawing room. Sir Ifor played a pianoforte solo with every bit as much skill as he played the organ at the church. Stephanie sang a solo to his accompaniment. Eluned and Idris Rhys sang a duet, also to Sir Ifor's accompaniment, though Idris protested that the angel that distributed musical talent to every Welsh person at birth had inexplicably missed him. The Countess of Stratton and Nicholas, those childhood friends, sang a duet to Nicholas's accompaniment. Owen proclaimed a soliloquy from *Hamlet*, claiming that he had been tortured at school by the necessity of having to learn it by heart and had been unable to forget it ever since.

"I tell you," he said, "school can forever blight a fellow's life. Whoever would choose to have *Hamlet* rattling about in his head for a lifetime?"

Kitty and George Greenfield played a duet on the pianoforte. They were not very good, but what they lacked in skill and coordination, they made up for in merriment. Everyone ended up laughing and applauding with far more enthusiasm than the performance strictly deserved.

Winifred recited William Wordsworth's "I Wandered Lonely as a Cloud." It contained her favorite lines of poetry:

> When all at once I saw a crowd
> A host, of golden daffodils,
> Beside the lake, beneath the trees,
> Fluttering and dancing in the breeze.

The daffodil was her favorite flower, though perhaps it had recently been challenged by the daisy. Before starting, she touched her hand to the daisy brooch pinned to her dress.

What a lovely evening it had turned out to be. But... *there was only one more day before the long separation from Nicholas.*

Winifred and Nicholas did not go to the birthday party, which was primarily for children anyway. Instead, they went into the courtyard, where they spent the afternoon strolling in the paved cloisters and sitting in the rose arbor. They had tea brought out to them there.

They had been busy during the morning with both families, waving Bertrand Lamarr on his way home from the terrace and then the Taylors, Matthew's family, from the cottage and the smithy in the village. But the afternoon was for them alone.

Soon they would be apart for a while, for almost five months, in fact. But during that time there was a wedding to be planned and a house in the country to be searched for and purchased.

The wedding was to be at Bath Abbey just before Christmas. Nicholas suggested it. It was where the Cunninghams had married and where Winifred's life as their much-cherished daughter had begun. Her face lit up at the suggestion.

"Christmas has always been a very special time with my family," she said. "Will we be able to stay to celebrate with them?"

"It is why I suggested Christmastime," he said, setting one arm about her waist as they walked.

"Such a long way into the future," she said. "Have you heard of special licenses, Nicholas? I believe they can be procured in London. Perhaps—"

"You temptress, Win," Nicholas said, cutting her off. "A very firm *no* to that. You are almost irresistible, you know? Almost, but not quite. I want you to have a wedding you will always remember and one I will always remember. And weddings are, or ought to be, about families as well as just the bride and groom. They are about the love that binds two people together, but also the two people to their own families and each other's. I do not want just to marry you. I want to *wed* you. Is there a difference? To me there is, but—"

"Yes, there is," she said with an audible sigh. "And I want that too. I want to wed you in Bath Abbey. And I want everyone there. Will they all come? But they surely will. My family all love me, and yours loves you. Christmas it will be, then. But how am I to live between now and then?"

"As you usually do, by inhaling and then exhaling, one breath after another," he said. A trick he had learned during the wars. "One breath at a time and one day at a time. Five months does sound like forever, though, does it not? In the meantime, you must dress hunt, and I will house hunt."

"How trivial you make me sound," she said. "As though choosing a dress is the *only* thing I will need to do. I daresay I will be so rushed off my feet that I will have to beg you to postpone the wedding until Easter."

He laughed. "Please do not," he said.

They lapsed into silence for a few minutes while he contemplated almost five months without a sight of her.

"I will write every day," he told her.

"Is that possible?" she asked.

He raised his eyebrows.

"In my experience, men are not letter writers," she said. "I do not picture you as being one."

"What do you picture me *as*, then?" he asked her.

"I will write to you every day too," she said without answering the question.

He stopped to pull her into his arms. He touched his forehead to hers and kissed her—cruel lips to soft, slightly trembling lips. He smiled against them, amused by the image of himself as some sort of ruthless, dangerous rake.

She had not been totally distracted by the kiss.

"Almost five months to choose a *dress*?" she said, drawing back her head and frowning up at him. "And to write invitations? And help Mama with all the rest of the planning. *Five months*?"

"And to write to me," he said meekly.

Her eyes narrowed. "I will have my revenge for your saying no to a special license," she said. "In my letters I will describe each dress I so much as look at—or *think* of—in minute, excruciating detail."

He grinned at her. "I will look forward to it," he said. "But no description of the dress you finally choose, if you please, Win. That is supposed to be a wedding-day surprise for the groom."

"Oh, Nicholas," she said, suddenly sagging in his arms. "May we talk about something else? Something to take my mind off the fact that I will be in Bath tomorrow, and you will be in London before the end of the week?"

He kissed her again.

Then he took her hand, lacing their fingers as they strolled onward. And they talked—and talked and talked. He spoke of his years in Spain and Portugal. She wanted to know all the details despite her disapproval of warfare and the fact that a gentleman *never* spoke of such things to a lady. He told her of Devlin and Ben being there for a few years, though not in his regiment, but how comforting it was to see them occasionally. He told her of those long, bleak years for Devlin while he grappled with his estrangement from the rest of his family. And he told her about Ben, who was never a military man himself but who excused his presence in the Peninsula with Devlin by claiming to be his batman. He told her about Ben's unlikely relationship with a Cockney washerwoman and his insistence upon marrying her when he learned she was with child. He told her how they had named their daughter Joy, because that was what she was to them. And of what a joy she had been to him, a newborn niece in the middle of warfare. Life continuing.

She spoke about her childhood at the orphanage, of how she had tried so hard—and failed—to be perfect and therefore loved until the teacher who became her mama loved her anyway, though Winifred had done nothing particular to deserve it, and how her mother and father had lived up to their promise always to love her. She spoke of her grandmother and uncle and aunts on her mother's side, who had been disinherited when the discovery was made that their father, now dead, had married their mother bigamously, and of how the Westcott family had absolutely refused to let them go even though her grandmother had resumed her maiden name and gone to live with her brother in Dorsetshire for a while after taking her daughters to live with her mother in Bath. She warned him that he would never be able to work out all the intricacies of the Westcott family, and he was beginning to half believe her.

They sat among the roses while they had their tea, largely in silence and eating with diminished appetites.

"Such beauty," she said, gazing about. "And it will all disappear within the next month or so, the roses to wither and die, the fountain to be turned off for the winter."

"But everything will return with spring in the eternal changing of the seasons," he said.

"Something that can always be relied upon," she said. "And you will come back to me before spring."

"In the meantime, I will write to you every day," he said, reaching for her hand.

"I will hold you to that," she said.

"Even if it is just a word or two?" he asked.

She laughed.

CHAPTER TWENTY-THREE

His work kept Nicholas busy, for which fact he was thankful. Usually, he did not give much thought to the passage of time, but four and a half months was indeed a long time. He missed Winifred. He missed her cheerful demeanor, whether she was playing an energetic game with the children, or sitting patiently watching her deaf brother as he ran down slopes or chiseled away at a large stone for hours on end, or talking and laughing with Owen or Watley or Stephanie. He missed her plain, no-nonsense appearance, absent of all intent to lure or look different than she naturally was. He missed her conversation, whether serious or light and teasing, her very direct way of looking at him as she spoke. He missed her essential beauty, her . . . Oh, he missed *her*.

He did not neglect his social obligations. There were not many through the summer, of course. Most people who were fortunate enough to own country homes or were on friendly terms with those who did were happy enough to leave behind the closer confines of London, with its smoke and grime and smells.

He dined a few times with General and Mrs. Haviland. He had feared at first that it might be awkward, though he had told the general about his betrothal. But if they were annoyed with him, they did not show it. They greeted him as amiably as they always had. And he was spared the possible embarrassment of having to spend time with Grace, even though they had agreed that they would remain friends. She had gone to Gloucestershire almost immediately upon her return from Ravenswood to stay with a widowed aunt, who was only a few years older than she. She had not remained there long, however. The two women had embarked upon a walking tour of Wales.

"She is like a new person," Mrs. Haviland commented. "It is as if she had suddenly woken from a long sleep. I beg your pardon. Is that offensive to you under the circumstances, Colonel Ware?"

"On the contrary, ma'am," he said. "When it came time for us to decide whether to take the next logical step in our relationship and marry, we came to the surprising and quite mutual realization that it was not what we wanted. We were, and we remain, friends, but it would have been a mistake to try to make something else of it. I am delighted to hear of her transformation. I saw the beginnings of it, I believe, at Ravenswood itself, during the fete."

"It is good of you to say so," Mrs. Haviland said. "And of course, we are both delighted by your betrothal to Miss Cunningham. Grace will be happy too when she reads my letter. She actually predicted it when we were on the way home from Ravenswood. Will you convey our best wishes to Miss Cunningham?"

Nicholas did so in the letter he wrote the following day.

It had been a bit rash of him, he thought sometimes, to promise that he would write every day, when every day he must be confronted with a blank piece of stationery and little idea of how he was to fill it or at least make his mark upon it. However did Winifred manage to write at least one crowded page, often two, sometimes even three, every single day? Women were just better about such things than men, he concluded. They were brought up to it. While men went out for early morning rides and generally made themselves useless, women wrote letters.

He knew how she filled one paragraph each day, of course. She described a dress each time, sometimes in what he suspected was deliberately tedious detail, describing not only the color and the style but also the fabric and the size and manner of the stitches and the number of frills and flounces and ribbons and bows that adorned it. At other times—most times, in fact—he suspected there was no such dress as any of the fantastic monstrosities she described. They included everything from brilliant, bilious mustard in color to rich, see-in-the-dark puce—was there even such a color?—and everything from monstrous skirts or sleeves, or both, to skirts so narrow one had to shuffle along with mincing little steps and did not dare sit down. She was endlessly inventive.

He found himself looking forward to that paragraph each day and having a regular chuckle over it.

Sometimes he would give in to defeat. He would begin his own letter with bold handwriting and something like "My dearest love," followed by a long blank space and ending with something bold along the lines of "Your ever-adoring servant, Nicholas Ware." In tiny writing at the bottom, he might add "Nothing happened."

He did not tell her about the house hunt. He had decided he would not. His brain was addled enough as it was. It might well explode if exposed to her comments and opinions and suggestions and vetoes. After all, he told himself, if he already owned a house of his own, as he had thought of doing a number of times but had never got around to actually doing, she would expect to be taken there after their wedding, would she not?

He hired an agent to find a house for him and undertake all the tedious business of looking over likely prospects to see if they fulfilled the detailed list of essential criteria with which Nicholas had provided him. The man first recommended a house in Richmond, which backed onto the River Thames and came complete with a long, beautifully landscaped garden and a jetty for a boat. Nicholas went to see it and agreed it was gorgeous. Winifred would love it. But probably not to live in, he decided a bit reluctantly. The neighbors were exclusively upper-class people and frequently opened their homes to their peers for dinners and soirees and garden parties. Winifred would not be intimidated by them—her uncle and aunt were the Duke and Duchess of Netherby, after all, and her grandmother was a marchioness. But she would soon be bored by them. She would consider their lives frivolous. She would consider them shallow. Boring. She would never be able to have what she called a *real conversation* with any of them.

He rejected the Richmond house and settled instead for a small manor south of the river. The agent referred to it as a cottage despite the fact that it boasted twelve bedchambers upstairs and comfortable servants' quarters in the attic. Nicholas went to see it, expecting that he might find it rather too pretentious for his needs. But he knew instantly that it was *the one*. It was on the edge of a small village and within relatively easy reach of London. It was surrounded by a garden almost large enough to be called a park, a lovely expanse of lawns and trees and flower beds and sitting areas and kitchen gardens. The village boasted a church, a school, and an inn with sizable assembly rooms used for balls and community feasts and school concerts and rehearsals and performances by a drama group and a book club and a knitting club and an occasional debating chamber, the landlord explained when Nicholas bought a pint of ale and settled at the bar for a chat. A few other customers joined in, uninvited and unrebuked. There were people of all social classes in the village, and on the whole they mingled happily with one another and with neighbors, mostly farmers, from the surrounding countryside.

It was a friendly place to live, the landlord added, swiping at the counter with a wet cloth. There was no better in all England.

Except perhaps Boscombe, Nicholas thought. This place sounded rather similar.

He purchased the house and then hired a husband-and-wife team to decorate and furnish it for warmth and comfort more than for pure elegance. When they showed him some samplings of furniture and draperies and carpet and paint and wallpaper they hoped would suit him, he knew that they did indeed understand, almost as if they knew Winifred. He gave them carte blanche to proceed, hoping he would not live to regret it.

He ought, of course, to have consulted Winifred—on both the house and its furnishings. It would, in addition to anything else, have given him something to write about. But it would be too cumbersome and too frustrating to check every detail with her. And inviting her to London to see for herself was out of the question, though he longed to see her. The Netherbys, who would have welcomed her as a guest, were not in London. She would have had to stay at a hotel. And someone would have had to accompany her here—her mother or her father, who were busy people and had children at home in need of their care.

So he said nothing.

Every day he expected her to ask about the house search, but surprisingly she never did.

She had other things on her mind, of course. There were wedding preparations in progress in Bath, and he guessed that the women at least were fully occupied with all the busy details. He was surprised, however, when he learned that his mother was on the way there so she could more comfortably help Mrs. Cunningham with the plans. But it was just like Mama, he decided. Everything was going to have to be perfect for her second son's wedding, as it had been for Devlin's and Ben's. Pippa's had been a rushed affair, occasioned by the imminent death of Lucas's grandfather, who had wanted to see his grandson and heir married before he passed. That must have been a severe disappointment to Mama.

And so the months crawled by for Nicholas. If he had feared doubt would set in once he was back in the familiar surroundings of his bachelor rooms and his work in London, he was proved very wrong. He looked forward to everything that was being planned. And he looked forward to bringing his bride home afterward to their new house.

He could scarcely wait.

From the beginning of September, which Joel and Camille Cunningham had always declared to be the end of their family summer, the arts center that was also their home was busier than ever. Its reputation had spread, it seemed, and all sorts of music and drama and art and literature groups wanted to conduct a workshop or retreat there. It came of having a talented cook who produced three plentiful and excellent meals a day, Camille said. It came of being perfectly situated among quiet hills, overlooking Bath, with endless views in all directions, Joel claimed. Winifred thought it came from the atmosphere of the place, from the fact that the house was also a private home and peopled with congenial, welcoming hosts and a large, diverse family of children, who seemed obviously happy despite various handicaps. They were always willing to carry bags and instruments and easels and such, and always eager to watch the development of various art projects or listen to music or poetry readings or watch drama rehearsals without ever seeming intrusive or getting in anyone's way.

Winifred welcomed the busy life. Time seemed to go faster when there was a group staying there. And everything else somehow got done.

There were the wedding invitations to be sent out. She had the list Nicholas had given her of everyone on his side. She and her mother between them, with a few interjections from Sarah and Alice, compiled their own list. The combined lists were dauntingly long. Would all these people actually come? Would even half of them? Where would everyone *stay*?

There were several comfortable and prestigious hotels in Bath, her mother reminded her. There was the sizable house on the Royal Crescent, where her grandmother—Winifred's great-grandmama—had lived until her quiet passing in her sleep one night last winter. It now belonged to Winifred's grandmother and her great-uncle, the Reverend Michael Kingsley, whose church was in Dorset. A number of people would stay with the Cunninghams since there would be no group booked into the house at that time. Grandmama and Grandpapa, the Marquess of Dorchester, surely would stay there, Winifred thought, and probably Uncle Gil and Aunt Abby, her mother's sister, and Uncle Harry, her brother, and Aunt Lydia. And their children, of course.

Would everyone who did come for the wedding also stay for Christmas? They must all be invited to do so, Mama said, and then they would plan Christmas around those who said they would stay. But that was a separate issue, which they need not think about at present. It was enough to concentrate upon the wedding itself.

The wedding would definitely be at Bath Abbey two days before Christmas. The wedding breakfast would be in the famed Upper Assembly Rooms, setting of many formal assemblies held in Bath during what passed for a Season there, though sadly the city had fallen somewhat out of fashion in recent years. The rooms would be preferable to their own home as a venue for the reception, Mama said. They would be a bit squashed here, assuming that all or most of those who were invited actually came.

Winifred wrote every invitation herself, having refused her mother's help. Mama was already rushed off her feet with other things, but ever cheerful about it, it must be added.

There was a wedding dress for which to be fitted and a style and fabrics and accessories to choose. And since this dress was to be *special*—Mama put great emphasis upon the word—it must be professionally made. There was a dressmaker to be chosen.

Winifred gave in on the matter since it seemed important to Mama. However, she insisted upon a design that was starkly simple, a round-necked, high-waisted, slender-skirted, long- and slim-sleeved dress of white velvet. The dressmaker and Mama had the last laugh, however—though the former did not appear to have much of a sense of humor, being a bit too intent upon cultivating a French accent and exaggerated French hand gestures that did not seem quite authentic.

She followed Winifred's instructions to the letter, but the dress she produced succeeded somehow in making Winifred look rather stunning. Even she admitted it as she stared at herself, a bit goggle-eyed, in the full-length mirror. How was that possible with a dress that had no discernible shape and was to be worn by a woman with no discernible shape either? The dressmaker had somehow done it. Slim as it was, the dress moved about her when she moved and looked luxurious as the light caught various facets of the white velvet.

Winifred chose a white cloak with a wide hood, the whole lined with lambswool, to wear with the dress—it was going to be late December, after all, and the insides of churches were never really warm even in summer. She would wear Papa's gold chains and earbobs as her only accessories, she decided, with the gold slippers she had worn at Aunt Anna's ball in London. And her daisy brooch, of course.

An hour of each day was spent at the escritoire in her room, writing her daily letter to Nicholas and reading and rereading his letter of the previous day to her, even when it was no more than a few lines long—and *even when* there was nothing but blank space between the greeting and the closing. She had a good chuckle over that particular one. So did Robbie when she showed it to him. She did not usually share her letters with anyone, but she had learned to recognize the small absurd things that were likely to draw a rare smile and even a laugh from him. Robbie, she thought, was slowly, ever so slowly, healing from whatever hurt he had held inside himself since early childhood.

She never quite understood why Nicholas found it so difficult to find things to write about. His daily life was a busy one. She would have loved to read details of his work, especially as it related to horses and their training. She would have loved details of his social life beyond just a stark sentence or two. He was good with facts, but details eluded him when one was not present to coax and question them out of him. Were all men the same? One could never generalize about a solid half of the population of the country, of course, but she did believe there was a great deal of truth in her suspicion. How many men did she know who sat down almost daily to write letters? She knew plenty of women who did so. Her mother, for example, wrote regularly to Grandmama and her siblings, including Aunt Anna, among others. And they all wrote back—well, Aunt Lydia did on behalf of Uncle Harry. Papa did not write many letters, though he did write to Mama when a painting commission kept him from home for longer than a few days.

She would not grow cross with Nicholas, then, Winifred decided. He did at least keep his promise to write daily, and he always assured her that he loved her.

He made no mention whatsoever of a house search. And she would not ask him and seem to be pestering him. She was disappointed, however. She had expected that he would give the search priority over almost everything else during the months they were apart. She had expected him to describe properties and settings and neighborhoods and to ask her opinion. She had hoped, if he purchased a home, to be consulted on furnishings and draperies and decorations. She had wanted to be *involved*. But perhaps that was the whole point for him. Perhaps he had decided to wait until after they were married so they could look together and share opinions and choices.

It was an attractive idea in one way. But . . .

Well, what would they do right after their wedding? Would he take her to live with him in his bachelor rooms? Would it be allowed? She knew that some areas of London were reserved exclusively for gentlemen. So would he rent somewhere while they looked? For how long would she have to remain in London? And it would be during the winter, long before the spring Season brought the *ton* back to town in large numbers for the parliamentary session. There would be no Aunt Anna to visit or Great-Aunt Louise. Or Great-Aunt Matilda. No Bertrand or Estelle.

Oh, she *wished* Nicholas had done what he had said he would do. He did not have to do anything else in preparation for their wedding, after all. Surely he could have found some time to look for a house outside London but close to it to which to take her.

But she said nothing in her letters. She trusted that all would work out well in the end. She did, after all, trust his love for her. She never did doubt that, perhaps because she had stopped doubting herself. She was no raving beauty, and she had no lineage or fortune beyond the generous dowry Mama and Papa had set aside for her. But she was worthy of love and happiness, just like anyone else—even the love of an extraordinarily handsome and charming cavalry colonel and son and brother of an earl. He was fortunate indeed to have her. She always enjoyed a private smile at the thought and even a chuckle if she was alone. But she believed it. She was Winifred Cunningham, and she was proud of who she was.

So *there*, world. Take that!

Oh, the days and weeks and months rushed by and crawled by, and Christmas would surely *never* come.

In the meantime, there was always something at home to keep her both busy and interested, and replies to the invitations she had sent out began to arrive. Everyone seemed to be coming except Nicholas's grandparents, the elder Greenfields, who regretted they could not face the journey to Bath, especially in the dead of winter. They had been invited to spend Christmas with their neighbors, the Reginald Taylors, and their family. Estelle, Bertrand's sister, *was* coming, however, with her husband, Justin, Earl of Brandon, and their young son.

They must not worry about accommodation, the Earl of Stratton assured them in his reply. He would arrange for the Ware family to stay together at a hotel in Bath. Aunt Anna, writing on behalf of Uncle Avery, the Duke of Netherby, gave similar assurances about the Westcott family. They had stayed at the same hotel in Bath on a number of occasions and liked it. They would reserve rooms there for everyone.

Winifred's grandparents and aunts and uncles and cousins, including Estelle and Bertrand, would stay at the house. Great-Uncle Michael Kingsley and Aunt Mary would stay at the house on the Crescent, though they had made an interesting suggestion. If there was room at Camille and Joel's house to squeeze them in, they had written, they would vacate the house on the Crescent for the night of the wedding and a few days over Christmas for the convenience of the bride and groom.

Winifred blushed as she read it. She had wondered . . .

They would have a whole house to themselves.

If Christmas ever came, that was.

Sometimes she doubted it would.

CHAPTER TWENTY-FOUR

Christmas did indeed come.

Heavy clouds, blustery winds, and more than usually chill temperatures settled over Bath, and indeed much of southern England, during the second half of December, threatening heavy rains or even snow to disrupt holiday travel. Many a would-be traveler, eager to join his family for Christmas, kept an anxious eye upon the skies, wondering if the roads would become a quagmire before he could reach his destination or, worse, be buried under a few feet of snow.

The rare occurrence of a white Christmas was all very well if one could watch the magic of white fields and lawns and frost-laden tree branches from the warmth and safety of a dwelling hung with holly and ivy and a kissing bough and fragrant with the smells of mince pies and plum pudding and roasting goose and spiced wassail and other culinary delights. It was *not* all very well if one faced a lengthy journey or a Christmas spent unexpectedly at home without company or supplies or, horror of horrors, marooned at a country inn with other such unfortunates, all of them in a morose mood.

The clouds obligingly held their loads until December 22, when the last of the wedding guests arrived chilled but safe in Bath and settled at their various abodes or hotels. The early arrivals soon bundled up in warm cloaks and greatcoats, scarves and mufflers and muffs and boots, and sallied forth to explore the famous sites— the Roman baths with the Pump Room above them, the nearby Bath Abbey, the Pulteney Bridge, and for those who did not mind a bit of a walk, Sydney Gardens. Some climbed to the famed circular street, the Circus, with its stately Georgian architecture, and the horseshoe-shaped Royal Crescent, from which they had a panoramic view down over Bath, not to mention the full force of the December wind in their faces. Some of them, most notably the ladies, went shopping on Milsom Street and purchased Christmas gifts to add to those they had brought with them. Most of them drove up to the Cunningham home in the hills for a short courtesy visit. Camille and Joel, accompanied by the Marquess and Marchioness of Dorchester, drove down into Bath and called on the wedding guests, both Wares and Westcotts, at their hotels. Everything was set for the grand celebration of a wedding two days before Christmas.

"Provided it does not snow six feet and prevent Nick from getting here," Owen remarked cheerfully. "A wedding without the groom would be a bit of a flat affair."

His mother was too fearful of just such a disaster to appreciate his humor.

"Owen!" she chided, a hand over her heart, while Matthew set one arm about her shoulders and grinned at his stepson. "Do not even *think* such a thing."

"But I'll wager you will think of nothing else for the next day and a half, Mama—and the night between the two," Owen said, waggling his eyebrows.

"Enough, Owen," Stephanie said crossly. "If you must tease someone, let it be me. I have broad shoulders."

It did *not* snow six feet or even six inches, and Nicholas rode into the hotel stable yard exactly when he was expected, in the middle of the afternoon of his wedding eve. He had applied for and been granted a leave of two weeks despite the time off he had taken during the summer. He had not wanted to waste one moment of his time off by leaving his work before he had to.

He ought to have been exhausted by the long journey. But after hugging all his family members and answering all their questions and asking a few of his own, he hired a fresh mount and rode up into the hills, a setting he had imagined a thousand times. It lived up to all his expectations, though it must be even more impressive under a blue sky and warm sunshine. No matter. He had not come to admire a view or even a large house, perfectly situated for maximum access to the view.

Someone must have seen him coming. The front doors of the house crashed open as he approached, and a missile hurtled out of it and down the steps and across the gravel in what seemed like a suicidal attempt to have herself ground to pulp beneath the hooves of his horse.

"Nicholas!" Winifred cried, the very antithesis of dignified, disciplined, genteel ladyhood. "At last!"

He dismounted quickly and threw the reins to a groom who had trotted into sight from somewhere behind him.

"Win!"

He gathered her into his arms and felt again—at last—the

familiar slender lines of her body, taut with eagerness. He gazed into the bright, eager face she lifted to his and he thought, *Yes, just so she looked*. Sometimes it was annoyingly difficult to bring an absent face to one's mind, complete with animation and blinding inner beauty.

"Win," he said more softly, closing his arms more tightly about her as she twined her own about his neck, heedless of the exposed place where they stood. He wondered idly how many people were lined up at the windows inside, enjoying the show.

But to the devil with them if they chose to be shocked.

He kissed her.

"Ahhh." She sighed against his lips and moved her head back far enough that she could gaze into his face. "*That* is what you look like and *feel* like."

"Complete with cruel mouth?" he said.

"Oh yes," she said, sounding enraptured. "Complete with *that*. Grandmama warned me that you might not come all the way up here today and I must not be too disappointed. But I knew you would. You said so in your last letter. It was the *only* thing you said."

"Promise me that I will not have to write one more letter after tomorrow," he said.

"What?" she said. "Never?"

"Never," he said. "And even that will be too soon. How do you do it, Win? Your letters are always so long and so interesting, though I must confess to having found some of the descriptions of potential wedding gowns a bit of a yawn."

She laughed gleefully and linked her arm through his. "Come inside," she said. "It is *freezing* out here."

"Just for a short while," he said. "My family are all expecting me back at the hotel for dinner."

He patted her hand on his arm.

Winifred bounded out of bed the following morning and threw back the curtains from her window, half fearful of what she might see outside. Snow would not be the disaster it might have been before yesterday. Everyone who was expected had arrived. But driving down from the hills into Bath over snow-covered roads could be perilous, and drive down they must this morning—a whole cavalcade of carriages to convey everyone who was staying at the house.

"Oh," she said when she looked out. Clear blue sky with not a cloud in sight. Sunshine. Hoarfrost winking and dancing on the grass and turning the bare branches of the trees into a magical wonderland.

"Oh!" she exclaimed again at almost the exact moment there was a tap on her bedchamber door and her mother opened it quietly and peered in.

"Ah, you are up," she said. "And I can see you have looked out. What a wonderful omen, Winnie. This is the first time we have seen the sun in all of two weeks. Just look at the frost. Could anything be more awe-inspiring?"

She had crossed the room to set an arm about Winifred's shoulders.

"What a happy, sad day this is," she said. "Mainly overwhelmingly happy, of course. But sad too that after today this will no longer be your primary home. Tomorrow I will not be able to come in here like this to hug you and wish you a good morning. How we are going to miss you, Winnie. You are such a wonderful daughter. I would not be able to bear it were I not convinced that Nicholas can and will make you happy."

Winifred turned and hugged her mother close. "He will," she said, no doubt in her voice. "And I will make him happy. But I will miss you too, Mama. *All* of you. How wonderful you and Papa have been to me."

"How could we not be?" her mother said. "You are our daughter. And always will be. You will remember that?"

"I will not forget for a single moment," Winifred assured her.

"Come down now for some breakfast," her mother said. "Before we know it, it will be time to get dressed and leave for the abbey."

"I could not eat a single morsel," Winifred said.

"Then it will have to be *two* morsels," her mother said. "You do not want your stomach growling with hunger in the middle of the nuptial service, surely."

"Oh dear," Winifred said, and they both laughed—with tears in their eyes. "I will try."

This was her wedding day, Winifred thought. Her *wedding* day.

Nicholas wore full dress uniform to his wedding. He had not brought his valet with him, but his brother Ben had offered his services. He heaved the heavy scarlet coat snugly over Nicholas's shoulders and straightened the gold epaulets and draped the various gold chains just so. He rubbed a faint smudge off his highly polished black boots and made sure there were none on the brim of his shako, which would replace the bearskin he had worn at Trooping the Colour. Fortunately, that was worn only on ceremonial occasions. He straightened out the feathers and arranged the chains correctly over the crown.

"If she is not impressed *now*," Ben said, standing back for a final, critical look at his brother, "you are in trouble, Nick."

"She is likely to turn tail and run anyway," Nicholas said. "When she first saw me in my uniform she saw a killer with a cruel mouth, all that was visible of my face below my bearskin."

"Who told you that bouncer?" Ben asked. "Women love a man in uniform, as I seem to recall."

"Winifred is not *women*," Nicholas said. "She is one individual woman. *Very* individual."

Ben grinned. "Then why is she marrying you?" he asked.

"You may ask her yourself later," Nicholas said. "But not until after the wedding, if you please, Ben. It would be a bit of a humiliation if she abandoned me at the altar."

"Speaking of which—" Ben pulled a watch from his pocket. "It is almost time for you to think of going. I hope Owen is ready."

Owen was to be Nicholas's best man. But even as Ben spoke, there was a knock on the hotel room door, and it opened to reveal their youngest brother, looking half throttled inside an elaborately tied neckcloth. But he was not alone. And that was the trouble with spending the night of one's wedding eve at a hotel large enough to accommodate all one's family members, Nicholas thought over the next several minutes as his hand was wrung and his epaulets were slapped by the men and his whole person was hugged by the women.

"Oh goodness, Nick," Pippa said. "You seem twice as large in uniform."

"And twice as gorgeous," Stephanie said, grinning at him.

"Not possible, Steph," Gwyneth said, and they both laughed.

His mother sniffed back tears.

But it was indeed time for at least some of them to go. The disaster of arriving at the abbey after the bride was not to be contemplated.

REMEMBER THAT DAY

"You have the ring, Owen?" Devlin asked.

Owen patted a pocket. But even at such a solemn moment he could not resist playing the clown and whacking at himself wherever there might be a pocket, muttering a panicked "Now, where did I put it?"

Ben clipped his ear, Stephanie clucked her tongue and tossed a glance at the ceiling, and their mother shook her head and removed the hand she had clapped over her heart.

The family left first. They would occupy the seats on one side of the church together with Sir Ifor and Lady Rhys, Idris and Eluned, and the Havilands, who had been invited and had accepted. The extended Westcott family, of which the Cunninghams were one branch, would sit on the other side—vast numbers of them, Nicholas had been warned.

All the guests were in place when Nicholas arrived ten minutes early with his younger brother on a crisp winter morning brightened by the sun beaming down from a clear blue sky.

There was a murmur from the gathered congregation as they made their way along the nave to the seats that had been reserved for them before the altar. Their boot heels rang out on the stone floor. Nicholas felt awed and dwarfed by the size of the church, the dimness of its interior transformed by the light passing through the huge stained glass window behind the altar. If he had not fully understood the serious solemnity of the occasion before, there was no escaping it now.

This was his wedding day.

His wedding day.

Even as he thought it, he was aware of a renewed murmur and rustling from behind him, and he turned his head to see Mrs. Cunningham, on the arm of Robbie, take her seat across the aisle from his. She glanced over at him, raised her eyebrows as though in surprise, and smiled warmly.

There were other sounds coming from the back of the abbey, but they were soon drowned out by the majestic chords of the great organ.

Nicholas rose to his feet even as the clergyman, gorgeously clad in his clerical vestments, took his place in front of the altar rail and turned to face the congregation and motion for them all to rise.

And Nicholas watched his bride proceeding slowly toward him on her father's arm, small and slight and dazzling all in white velvet, a long spray of winter greenery—*Christmas* greenery—in her free hand. Her head was bare, her hair in its usual sleek style, with a knot high on the back of her head threaded with more of the greenery, in which there were tiny white flowers, he saw as she drew closer.

She looked nothing short of stunning.

Her eyes were on him, he saw as she came nearer, as his were upon her.

He was not smiling, he realized. Neither was she.

This was too solemn a moment. Too precious.

This was their wedding. No longer just their wedding *day*, but their wedding.

Winifred's thoughts were thrown back to that day in June when she saw Colonel Nicholas Ware for the first time. Her first impression had been a certain degree of fright and an unacknowledged attraction. How much had happened since then to transform him into a man, a *person* in her eyes, whom she could admire and like and trust and desire. And *love*.

Yes, he was a killer. And yes, he had killed. He was a military man, after all. He had fought in the Napoleonic Wars. But life was not as simple as it often seemed. He was also a defender of the helpless and downtrodden and innocent. He was a saver of lives. He also respected what made people different from one another. He went out of his way to understand and accommodate people many might see as handicapped when in fact they lived life according to their own reality. Andrew, who generally disregarded strangers, genuinely liked him.

Now, gorgeous and seemingly remote from her in his dress uniform, minus the bearskin helmet, he was about to become her husband. She had expected to feel nerves, even perhaps the last-minute desire to rush toward freedom before it was too late. But as Papa transferred her hand from his own to Nicholas's warm clasp, she had not been surer of anything in her life.

She *loved* him. She did not know what the future held. She did not even know where they would live or what she would do to occupy her days. Would it be in London of all places? But at this moment it did not matter. She *trusted* him. She was putting her happiness in his hands, and he would not let her down.

"Dearly beloved," the clergyman said.

And in all the splendor of Bath Abbey, where her parents had married twelve years ago and she had acquired a family of her own for the first time in her life, she gave herself to Nicholas Ware, as he gave himself to her. They became husband and wife, embarked upon their future together as their own family, supported by the love of the two larger families, the Wares on one side, the Westcotts on the other.

When the clergyman pronounced them man and wife, she smiled at last, and Nicholas smiled back. And oh, she almost wished she were not yet in love with him so she could fall all over again. She shook with silent laughter at the absurd thought and became aware of the collective sigh that came from the congregation around them.

Nicholas offered his arm and led her to the vestry, where for the last time she signed her name as Winifred Cunningham in the register. She was Winifred Ware henceforth, wife of Colonel the Honorable Nicholas Ware.

And surely the happiest woman in the world.

Nicholas took her hand in his and kissed the back of it.

"Beautiful, beautiful Win," he murmured.

"It is the white of my gown," she said. "It has dazzled you. I never wear white."

His eyes crinkled at the corners. Something she said had amused him. And goodness, he was *huge* in his uniform. Not to mention gorgeous. And if he meant to don that impressively adorned shako when they left the abbey, he was going to look larger still.

Sarah, who looked very pretty indeed in her dark green velvet bridesmaid's dress, came to hug her tight, and she was followed by Owen, who grinned and winked before hugging her and kissing her cheek.

"Be happy, Winifred," he said. "But you will be. You have a gift for happiness."

Did she? That certainly would not have been true of her nine-year-old self. But she had taken her immense good fortune at being chosen for love by Mama and Papa, and she had made happiness out of it.

She would continue to do so. And when she felt herself sink toward depression, as she inevitably would, rare though those occasions were, then she would recall what she had promised back in the summer.

Remember that day.

She set her hand on Nicholas's sleeve, and they left the vestry as the organ burst into a joyful anthem. They proceeded slowly along the aisle, smiling to left and right—at Mama and Papa and her siblings, at Grandmama and Grandpapa, Uncle Harry, Aunt Abby, Estelle and Bertrand, among others, on the one side; the Dowager Countess of Stratton, the earl and countess, the Duke and Duchess of Wilby, Mr. and Mrs. Ellis, Stephanie, Mrs. Haviland, and more on the other side. It was impossible to acknowledge or even see everyone. That would happen at the wedding breakfast in the Upper Assembly Rooms.

And after that . . .

Well, after the breakfast there would be no return home. Even now all her belongings were being taken to the house on the Royal Crescent where Great-Grandmama used to live, and presumably Nicholas's baggage was being taken there too from his hotel room. Tonight, and every night in the future, home would be wherever Nicholas was.

She was a married lady.

The bright sunshine of the outdoors was almost blinding as they approached the abbey doors and the paved churchyard, which included the famed Pump Room, beyond. Nicholas came to a sudden halt, and Winifred looked up at him.

"The devil!" he exclaimed. And then, completely contradicting himself, "Good Lord!"

And then Winifred could see for herself what had startled him into such irreverence. For outside the abbey doors, an honor guard awaited them: twelve cavalrymen in full dress uniform, astride twelve black horses, six on either side of the doorway, all absolutely still, as she had seen them once before on a parade ground awaiting the arrival of the king. On a word of command, they raised the lances they held to meet between the two lines in a sort of arch for bride and groom to walk through. General Haviland, also resplendent in dress uniform, stood at attention on the far side of them. He saluted as Nicholas settled his shako on his head and stepped through the abbey doors with his bride on his arm.

Beyond them all, a crowd had gathered to watch the spectacle or, in the case of the young relatives from both sides of the family who had left the church early, to pelt the newlyweds with flower petals they had acquired somewhere even though it was late December.

Nicholas saluted the general and Winifred smiled brightly at him after they had passed beneath the arch. Then Nicholas smiled at her, grasped her hand in a tight clasp, and hurried past the Pump Room, the flower pelters in hot pursuit, and on out to Stall Street, where his carriage awaited them. They were both laughing as he handed her inside, her white cloak and her hair now liberally dotted with colored petals. Winifred turned to wave as the carriage moved forward, accompanied by the predictable din of what sounded like a whole arsenal of pots and pans tied to the bottom of the carriage.

"Oh dear," Winifred said, turning her face to Nicholas beside her. But she could not hear her own voice.

He did not even try to answer her. He tossed his shako onto the opposite seat instead, set an arm about her shoulders and his free hand beneath her chin, and kissed her.

They did not hear the cheers of siblings and cousins and nieces and nephews.

The next few hours passed in a blur for Nicholas. He scarcely had time to look appreciatively at the Upper Rooms, about which he had heard so much, before the guests began arriving from the abbey. There was no receiving line. Everyone piled in, one after another. Every one of the men and boys shook his hand. Every one of the ladies and girls did the same, or hugged him or kissed his cheek—or all three. Some of the children wanted to talk to him.

"Did you see the *horses*, Uncle Nick?" Ben's Robert wanted to know.

Pippa's Emily wanted to show him her loose tooth.

The Cunningham twins gazed up at him, giggled when he winked, and dashed away, hand in hand. He was introduced to Winifred's grandmother and her husband, the Marquess of Dorchester; to her Aunt Abby and her husband, Gil Bennington; and to her Uncle Harry Westcott and Lydia, his wife. He had a previous acquaintance, though slight in some cases, with other relatives of his wife—the Duke and Duchess of Netherby and the dowager duchess; Lord and Lady Molenor, Mrs. Cunningham's aunt; Viscount Dirkson and his wife, the former Matilda Westcott, also Mrs. Cunningham's aunt; Alexander and Wren Westcott, the Earl and Countess of Riverdale; Lady Hodges, the earl's sister, and her husband. He had met the Reverend Michael Kingsley and his wife yesterday when he had called on them at the house on the Royal Crescent where he and Winifred would spend tonight. There were numerous children too. He committed to memory as many names and connections as he could. All these people, after all, were now his relatives too.

Winifred had an easier time of it since she had met his family at Ravenswood during the summer. She was engulfed in hugs whenever he glanced her way. Once she had two little ones in her arms, Ben's Belinda and Devlin's Awen. Gwyneth, Nicholas could see, was now noticeably increasing.

It was all a bit overwhelming. They eventually took their seats at long tables for the wedding breakfast, the two families mixed together according to the placements Winifred and her mother had planned. The children sat at a table of their own, the older ones interspersed with the younger. There was a great deal of animated conversation and laughter, and Nicholas was glad he had insisted upon a full wedding when Winifred had tempted him with the idea of acquiring a special license. Weddings were indeed for families, to bind them together, to remind them of the value of belonging—so absent from his wife's first nine years—and unconditional love.

They sat through speeches and toasts, and the cutting and distribution of the wedding cake, and three songs sung by the choir of children who had come with their teacher and conductor from the orphanage, where once upon a time Winifred, in a basket, had been set on the doorstep. The Duke and Duchess of Netherby, patrons of the orphanage—the duchess had grown up there and taught at the school there for a few years before the discovery of her real identity—had arranged for a grand banquet for all the children later, which they would attend, taking another wedding cake with them.

And finally, it was time to leave. Nicholas had dismissed his carriage when they arrived here and sent it back to the hotel where he had stayed last night. He would not need it again until early tomorrow afternoon. The Royal Crescent was just a short walk away, and some air and exercise would feel good. Winifred had agreed with him when he asked her before sending the carriage away.

He got to his feet, gave his hand to Winifred to draw her to hers, and acknowledged the near hush that had fallen all about them.

"Thank you," he said. "For coming here today and for making

this what will surely remain one of the most memorable days of our life together. We are going to leave you now, but I am sure you will all be welcome to remain here as long as you wish. We will see you all tomorrow."

He willed them—Owen especially—to withhold any ribald or risqué comments and to refrain from following them outside. Apart from a chorus of goodbyes and good wishes and both mothers coming to the door to hug them—and shed a few tears over them—before they left, he got his wish.

And so at last, he thought as they stepped outside into the brisk sunshine of a December afternoon, they were alone, just the two of them. Husband and wife beginning their married life together.

"Win," he said as he raised the loose hood of her cloak over her head and drew her hand through his arm. "Ah, Win."

"Nicholas." She laughed softly. "And sometimes that is all that needs to be said."

"Home," he said. "For what I predict will be a very early wedding night."

It was unclear whether it was the cold air or his words that whipped the rosy color into her cheeks and even the end of her nose. But there would be no false modesty with Winifred. She smiled boldly at him. "Oh, yes, please," she said.

And so it was. In the light of early dusk illuminating the window of the south-facing bedroom in the house on the Crescent, they made slow love in the large feather bed, warmed by the fire that crackled and flickered in the fireplace and, eventually, after passion had spent itself for a while at least, by the heavy down covers they had pushed aside earlier so they could see each other and move more freely in the intricate dance of intimacy.

"Win," he murmured. "My love."

"Mmm," she said, smiling, her eyes closed. "Can't hear you. I am asleep."

"That good, am I?" he said.

"Mmm," she said. "And me too."

No argument there, he thought as he drifted off.

EPILOGUE

Almost everyone stayed for Christmas. The house up on the hill above Bath was crowded and noisy and festive with Yule log and greenery and bows and bells and filled with the rich smells that only Christmas could offer. There was the church service on the night of Christmas Eve and bright stars to light their way down into Bath and back again. There was the exchange of gifts among individual families on Christmas morning, the distribution of gifts to the servants for whom this was the busiest time of year, carol singing, dancing in the drawing room to the accompaniment of the pianoforte, games both organized and disorganized with the many children, relaxation time before a merrily blazing fire for those who could find that rare commodity, a quiet corner. And bright, endless conversation.

But after Christmas it was time to return home, and most of them were glad. Family gatherings and festivities were wonderful things and provided memories that lasted a long while, sometimes a whole lifetime. But they were high peaks in lives that were lived mostly on the plains, where there was likely to be greater peace and stability and contentment.

One could not live one's life on the peaks, after all. They would become tedious and confining after a while.

Winifred and Nicholas were among the first to leave, early in the morning of the day after Christmas. They had a long way to go to London, though there had been no rain or snow over the holiday to slow them down, and none seemed to be in the offing.

It took a while for Winifred to turn her thoughts ahead. Leaving home had been far more heart-wrenching than she had anticipated. For of course she was not the only one involved. Mama and Papa had put a brave face on it and had smiled and hugged her. The children had been more long faced. Alice had cried, and the twins had followed suit. Jacob had looked glum and kicked the carpet, and Andrew had looked bewildered. Robbie had glowered and Nelson had nudged his hand and whined softly. Sam had told Nicholas he hated him because he had made Alice and the twins cry, and then would *not* say sorry even when urged to do so by his mother. Sarah's smile had wobbled at the edges.

Home would always be home, Mama and Papa had assured Winifred. But it never would be. Not really. Nothing would ever be the same again. Everything had changed, as everything always did. It was the nature of life.

Nicholas, beside her in the carriage, took her hand and laced their fingers, and gave her time to grieve before she turned her thoughts toward the new life that was ahead of her.

And oh, it was what she wanted more than anything else. For she both loved him and was *in* love with him, and never let anyone try to tell her there was no difference between the two. She was head over heels in love with him. Three nights of passion with him had exhausted her and filled her with energy and the yearning for more and more of his lovemaking. It was not *all* marriage was made of, of course. There was far, far more. But it was quite acceptable to crave it almost more than all else during these early days, the honeymoon phase of their life together.

She marveled over the wonder of knowing she gave him every bit as much pleasure and satisfaction as he gave her. *Her*, plain, ordinary Winifred Cunningham. No, correct that. Winifred *Ware*.

But where were they going? She still had not asked.

"Where are we going?" she asked now.

He turned his head to look down at her. "Home," he said. "Where else?"

"But where exactly *is* home?" she asked him.

"I thought you would never ask," he said.

"And I thought you would never tell," she said. "Is it London? Not your old rooms, surely. You promised to look for a house when you left Ravenswood, but you did not do so."

"How do you know that?" he asked.

She looked sharply at him. "Because you never *said*."

"Did I ever say I had *not* looked?" he asked her. "Or that I had *not* purchased? Or furnished and got it ready for you?"

She gazed at him and sank her teeth into her lower lip. "*Did you?*" she said. "*All* of those things?"

"Yes," he said.

"*All?*" Her voice had risen to a squeak.

"Yes," he said, and she punched the side of his arm.

He had chosen and purchased and furnished a house? And *got it ready* for her? He had done it all with her in mind, but with not a word to her?

Men! Really. *Men!*

"I suppose you want details," he said. "I am not much good with words, Win. Not to describe something visually anyway. What I see in my mind and what comes out of my mouth often bear little resemblance to each other. I will show you, though. I hope you will like it. I *know* you will. I know *you*."

Just like that? He knew her? He knew what sort of house and what sort of furnishings would please her? Could it be true? Curiously, she thought it might be.

She sat back in her seat and closed her eyes. And tipped her head sideways to lean against his shoulder.

"Tired?" he asked.

"Mmm," she said.

"You have not been sleeping well?" he asked. "Has something been keeping you awake?"

She smiled but did not answer.

When she woke up, they were not far from London. Except that, even when they arrived there, they did not stop but crossed a bridge over the River Thames and drove beside the water for a short while before turning south and finding themselves almost immediately in rural countryside and driving into a picturesque village, most of its houses and other buildings clustered about a green.

On the far edge of the village, just when she thought they were going to drive right on by, the carriage turned onto a short circular graveled driveway with what in summertime must be a colorful flower bed in its center. The house was sizable yet somehow gave the impression of being a cozy cottage. The roof was thatched, the walls whitewashed, the windows framed by green shutters. Ivy grew up one side wall. There were flower beds all along the front of the house, dormant now but surely ready to spring to life at the first sign that winter was over. To either side and at the back too, she guessed, there were lawns and flower beds and trees and bird feeders all awaiting the coming of spring.

"This is home?" She fell in love with it on sight.

"It is home," he said as the carriage rocked to a halt before the green front door, which opened to reveal a plump, comfortable-looking woman who must be the housekeeper. A man moved past her to open the carriage door and set down the steps while the coachman steadied the horses.

Nicholas vaulted out of the carriage and helped her alight. Despite his earlier confidence, he was looking a bit anxious now.

"It is gorgeous," she said, taking his hand and stepping down onto the gravel of her own driveway. "It is *gorgeous*, Nicholas."

He introduced her to the housekeeper, who had stepped outside to welcome them before turning with the man to the baggage coach, which was pulling in behind them.

Nicholas led Winifred toward the front door. But he stopped before they went inside and bent to sweep her up into his arms.

"Welcome home, Win, my love," he said as he stepped over the threshold with her.

Home.

It must be one of the loveliest words in the English language, she thought.

Do you love historical fiction?

Want the chance to hear news about your favourite authors (and the chance to win free books)?

Suzanne Allain
Mary Balogh
Lenora Bell
Charlotte Betts
Manda Collins
Joanna Courtney
Grace Burrowes
Evie Dunmore
Lynne Francis
Pamela Hart
Elizabeth Hoyt
Eloisa James
Lisa Kleypas
Jayne Ann Krentz
Sarah MacLean
Terri Nixon
Julia Quinn

Then visit the Piatkus website
www.yourswithlove.co.uk

And follow us on Facebook and Instagram
www.facebook.com/yourswithlovex | @yourswithlovex

PIATKUS